last resort

J.C. HANNIGAN

Editor: Catherine Muss

Cover Designer: Mignon Mykel (Oh So Novel)

*This book is dedicated to Granny Good Witch.
I love you, always and forever.
You created an entire legacy of love and laughter for us.
I am forever grateful for your magic light.*

CHAPTER ONE

Nellie

A PIECE of plastic had never been more intimidating. I stared at those two little pink lines, feeling the very trajectory of my life come to a screeching halt. The blood rushed to my head, and I felt faint. It was a good thing I was still sitting on the toilet. If I'd been standing, I likely would have keeled over.

"What does it say?"

The disembodied voice from the speaker of my phone roused me. I opened and closed my mouth, trying and failing to form words. It was as if my voice had been snatched by Ursula herself.

"Nellie?"

I squeaked. It was the only sound I could make. My free hand went to my mouth, covering it, as tears rushed to my eyes.

"Nellie!" my best friend, Sage, practically shouted.

"I'm—" I still couldn't say the words. "It's positive."

"Oh."

Whatever Sage had been expecting, it clearly wasn't this. Me neither.

After being diagnosed with endometriosis in my early twenties, this was a moment I never expected to happen. I'd been told by my gynecologist, endocrinologist, and family doctor that I'd have difficulty conceiving. I'd been warned that if I ever wanted to pursue a pregnancy, the likelihood of me needing fertility treatments was extremely high.

I'd never even had so much as a scare before. But I knew my body well, and I'd known something was up when my period was late. It was never late, much to my chagrin. Most women with endometriosis experience irregular periods, but not me. The damn thing was more predictable than Halley's comet. It came with vengeance every thirty days, and it often knocked me on my ass for a week straight. My flows were heavy and brutal, and when Aunt Flo hadn't come pounding on my door eleven days ago, I knew something was up.

I just didn't expect it to be this. I thought I was finally sliding into the irregular period camp of endometriosis.

"Okay, well, this is good...right? I mean, you always thought you weren't going to be able to have kids..."

"Good? How is this good? I am so not prepared for this! I work at a café, Sage. I have a roommate—who hates kids, as you know. Not that there's even space in this place for a kid." I was panicking. My voice was all screechy and high pitched, and the tears kept flowing no matter how much I wiped at my eyes with the back of my hand.

Sage knew my roommate, Angela, from when she used to live in Guelph and from her brief stay on my couch with her daughter, Daphne. Angela hadn't been thrilled with that situation, and despite me wanting to help my bestie in her time of need, I had to respect my roommate's wishes and cut Sage's stay short, forcing her to seek refuge at her mother's house.

"You have a job, though. Which is good for when you apply for maternity. As for the apartment situation, we could find you a new place."

"I can't afford a new place, Sage," I sighed, standing up on shaking limbs. I faced the mirror, taking in my splotchy face and the panicked flush. "Especially not on my own."

"Do you...do you know who the father is?"

Sage's question wasn't meant to sting, but it kind of did. Not that I blamed her. I wasn't exactly known for monogamous relationships.

I didn't do serious. I was afraid to trust, afraid to let myself care about people that would inevitably leave once they'd had their fill of me. The only exception to that had been Sage and her beautiful daughter, and I think I'd been able to let her in because of how desperately she'd needed me, too.

It was easier to keep things light and carefree, that way the disappointment couldn't reach me.

But Sage's question also stung because...well, I didn't know. "I've narrowed it down to a few contenders."

"Is one of them Noah, by chance?"

Sage's follow-up question made a swarm of butterflies take flight in my stomach. Or was that nausea?

One of the contenders was, indeed, Noah Wood, a friend of Sage's boyfriend from Hartwood Creek. I'd met him at the Witches' Ball. He'd dressed as The Witcher—my kryptonite. I know I went back to his place with him that night, but I couldn't for the life of me remember if we'd used a condom when we'd hooked up.

I didn't remember a lot about that night. Other than how amazing he felt, but for all I knew, that could have been the booze talking. I'd had a lot to drink that night, and so had he. The evening was a blur—a fun, magical blur, but a blur, none-theless.

"Maybe. I don't know for sure. Regardless, I'm obviously not in a relationship with any of the contenders. One of them waved every red flag known to mankind and couldn't even get me off, and the other one, well, I don't even know him."

A week or so after hooking up with Noah, I'd slept with a guy I'd been chatting with on Tinder for several months. After spending way too much time thinking about Noah Wood, I'd figured the best course of action would be to sleep with someone else, and prove to myself that the night we'd shared in Hartwood Creek was a night like any other.

The only thing I'd succeeded in proving was that even if I couldn't remember every single detail of the night I shared with Noah, I still knew I had a better experience than the night I'd shared with Tinder Guy. As soon as we hooked up—the one and only time—and red flags popped up like daisies. I'd ended up blocking him on Tinder.

Thankfully, I knew I'd definitely used a condom with Tinder Guy. But condoms weren't infallible.

"What if you moved here?"

"To Hartwood Creek? Why?!" I exclaimed. "I just told you, I don't even know if Noah is the father."

"Even if he isn't," Sage insisted. "I'm here, I could help you. It's cheaper to live here. You could easily find a job in town, and maybe Nix could give up the bachelor apartment and you could rent it. He's hardly ever there these days. It'd come fully furnished!"

"I..." I paused, blinking at myself in the mirror. I mean, it wasn't a terrible idea. It wasn't like I had family in Guelph, or a support system for that matter. For all intents and purposes, Sage was the closest thing to family I had. "I can't just uproot my entire life."

I didn't say the other thing I was thinking; that I didn't even know if this pregnancy would stick. I'd never been at the family planning stage of my life, but from what I'd read in my spare time about my condition, studies showed that endometriosis could increase the risk of miscarriage.

"But..." Sage said, and I could practically hear the wheels turning in her head.

"Just spill," I sighed heavily, knowing she was thinking a mile a minute.

"Are you honestly happy there? Working for Sal, living in that cramped basement apartment with Angry Angela?"

Sage's question posed a valid point. I wasn't happy here, and hadn't been for some time.

I used to like my life, back when I was young and hopeful. Freshly graduated from college after taking the Recreation Therapy program, I'd gotten a full-time position at the café I'd worked at throughout school, until something came up in my field.

Only, nothing ever did seem to come up in my field. Although Sal had hired me on as a barista, my job details and responsibilities seemed to grow daily, pushing me more into the management position—without the pay, I might add.

But rents were high, and apparently recreational therapists were a dime a dozen. I didn't have a snowball's chance in hell at affording my own apartment, so I was stuck with Angry Angela.

All of that would have been bearable if Sage was still around. We'd worked together at the café, and she'd included me in her little traditions with her daughter Daphne. For the first time, I'd felt like I had a true family. A sister, a niece. People who cared about me, and people who I cared about.

Sage had moved several hours away to the small town of Hartwood Creek after discovering her then-fiancé was cheating on her with his secretary. I didn't blame her, but I missed her and Daphne every day. Life seemed lonelier and greyer without them, like they'd taken some of the colour with them when they left.

"No, I'm not," I sighed again, pushing my hair out of my face. "But I really can't just uproot my life on a whim." Even to me, my argument sounded weak. I did most things on a whim. If I got an inclination for something, I flowed toward it eagerly. Case in point: going home with the handsome stranger I'd met at a costume ball.

"Why the heck not? I did." Sage giggled.

I smiled, although she couldn't see it. "Yeah, but you have family in Hartwood Creek."

"So do you," Sage said firmly, her tone brooking no argument. A sense of longing filled me, longing to be closer to the people I cared for most.

It's not that I didn't have family, it's just that my parents weren't the greatest. They'd had me later in life, and although they'd never neglected me in the financial sense, they had never planned on being parents, and their emotional support was severely lacking.

My parents provided for me, made sure that I attended the most prestigious school in the area, and always ensured I had money for the extracurricular activities I did. But they never emotionally connected with me. I'd often felt more like an expensive house plant than a daughter growing up.

Now, they spent most of the year down south in Florida, at their beautiful beach house on Miramar Beach, overlooking the white sand beaches of the gorgeous gulf. I couldn't blame them for skipping out on the cold Canadian climate for half the year. I just missed them, or the version of them I never really had.

They called me on occasion, sure, but they didn't actually want to hear about the trials and tribulations of my life. They were too involved in what was happening in theirs. Once I'd reached the tender age of eighteen, they had considered their "job" with me completed.

"Look, all I'm saying is that you have options, and I wouldn't hate it if you moved to Hartwood Creek. I'd love it a lot—so would Daphne. We miss you."

"I miss you both, too," I said, my eyes misting again as I thought back to how great it'd been to visit in October, to still be included in their Halloween tradition. Even if it looked majorly different from previous years.

I had to admit, Hartwood Creek put on a fantastic Halloween festival. I wouldn't be opposed to living there. In my heart of hearts, I knew I'd love it. The town was small, but had everything you could possibly need or want, and was only a half hour or forty-five-minute drive away from what it didn't have.

I worried about what Noah would say if I relocated to Hartwood Creek with a baby bump. I didn't even know if he was the father, but surely that wasn't a good look. Noah and I hadn't done much talking when we were hooking up after the Witches' Ball, but from what I'd gathered since then he was a playboy through and through.

And I was no saint, either. Heck, I couldn't even for sure say who the father of my unplanned baby was.

"There's plenty of time to decide what you're going to do. Book an appointment with your family doctor and think on things a little more. I'll run the idea past Nix, but I'm sure he would give up the bachelor pad in a heartbeat for you," Sage assured me.

A FEW DAYS LATER, I was waiting for Dr. Pinsent in the examination room. I'd already peed in a cup and had my blood-work taken by the nurse, now it was just a matter of talking to my family doctor about the results.

My stomach was a wreck of nerves and had been since I'd faced off with those two positive lines. I wasn't one to worry or live in fear, but I was in a constant state of worry and fear now.

The door to my examination room opened, and Dr. Pinsent stepped inside. I'd been seeing her since I was a small child. She knew my parents—a little too well, but I was confident that patient confidentiality laws would protect me for the time being, until I was ready to tell them myself. If there was anything to tell. It could be a false pregnancy. It could be a tubal pregnancy. Even if I was pregnant, I could still suffer a miscarriage. The thought turned my stomach, and I tried to breathe through that fear.

I hadn't even allowed myself to think about wanting kids, and yet now that I was faced with a positive pregnancy test, the mere thought of a miscarriage was enough to send me into panic mode.

"Good afternoon, Nellie," Dr. Pinsent smiled warmly at me, her brown eyes twinkling when they lifted from the reports to meet mine. "Looks like you're about seven weeks pregnant."

The air left my lungs on a whoosh, and I felt lightheaded. "Oh, wow. Okay."

"I'm sure this is a bit of a surprise, given your history of endometriosis." Dr. Pinsent said.

I swallowed, nodding slowly. "You could say that."

Dr. Pinsent moved her stool closer to my chair and sat down, facing me. "Would you like to discuss options?"

"No. I—I know it's unexpected, but I want to keep it, if my body lets me."

"Endometriosis does put you at a slightly elevated risk for

miscarriage, but you're young, and going off your last scans, your scarring is minimal. I would have to refer you to a high-risk obstetrician, who would follow you a little closer than a regular OB." Dr. Pinsent turned to her computer.

"Are there any high-risk obstetricians near Hartwood Creek?" The question spilled from my lips before I had time to think about it. "I'm thinking about moving there. It's closer to my support system."

Dr. Pinsent typed something into her computer, then glanced at me over her shoulder. "There's one in Springwood."

"Okay, that would be... That would be good," I nodded, knowing I sounded unsure.

"Is the father in Hartwood Creek?" Dr. Pinsent asked casually, going back to typing out the referral.

I blinked, wondering what I should say. I didn't want Dr. Pinsent to judge me for not knowing who the father was, but I didn't know for sure. "Something like that."

My evasive answer didn't seem to appease Dr. Pinsent, but I could tell she was too kind to probe.

"Did you need me to send a referral for a family doctor, too? I'm happy to continue seeing you until one becomes available, but Hartwood Creek is a bit of a trek if you relocate there."

"That would be good, I think," I nodded.

Dr. Pinsent finished typing and then spun around to face me. "Okay, we're all set there. You can pick up prenatal vitamins from the pharmacy, just make sure you're taking at least eight hundred milligrams per day of folate. The good news is that many women with endometriosis notice their symptoms get better during pregnancy, they benefit from the increased levels of progesterone."

"Well, hey, if I'd known that, I might have tried sooner to get knocked up," I joked, and Dr. Pinsent smiled, standing up.

"The referral for the high-risk OB shouldn't take more than a couple of weeks, but the wait for a new family doctor might be longer. If you have any questions or concerns, please don't hesitate to call and book an appointment with me," Dr. Pinsent said. "If necessary, we could do virtual appointments until we find you a family doctor closer to Hartwood Creek. Congratulations, Nellie."

CHAPTER TWO

Nellie

I WAS the kind of person that once I decided something, that was pretty much it. I was all in.

From the moment I asked Dr. Pinsent to send my referral to a high-risk obstetrician in Springwood, my resolve for my situation had only grown. I had a lot to figure out, but one thing was certain: I would be moving to Hartwood Creek.

It was a good thing, too, because when I got home from my appointment, Angry Angela was waiting for me in our shared living room. She practically flew at me the moment I opened the door.

"Why the hell is there a pregnancy test box in the bathroom trashcan?" she demanded, scowling at me with her arms crossed.

"Why are you looking in trashcans, Angela? That's strange," I shook my head, slipping out of my coat, and hanging it up on the coatrack by the door.

"Don't dodge the question, Nellie. Are you pregnant?"

I sighed, feeling a headache coming on. "Yes, Angela. I'm knocked up. I've got a bun in the oven. My eggo is preggo."

Angela's jaw slackened. "Oh my god. You know I can't stand kids! Why would you do this?!"

"It wasn't exactly planned," I frowned. "But I'm not sure why my life choices have any effect on you."

"Because! Either you bring a screaming, crying baby into this apartment, or I need to find a new roommate! Both options are terrible for me."

"I'm so sorry to have inconvenienced you with my life-altering news," I deadpanned. "But if it's any consolation, you'll be needing to do option number two. Obviously, this apartment is too small for a baby, and frankly—the environment isn't exactly nurturing."

Angela's scowl intensified, which I didn't know was even possible. "Great, just great. Do you have any idea how hard it's going to be to find a new roommate I can tolerate?"

"Angela, you barely tolerate me," I reminded her, rolling my eyes. "Either way, this is happening, so we're both going to have to deal with it. Me with growing a whole ass human, and you with finding a new roommate. I think you got the easier end of the deal."

She let out an aggravated huff and stomped off to her bedroom, slamming the door.

"That went well," I said to myself. Before I had time to reflect any more on Angela's reaction, my phone started ringing. I tugged it out of my purse, seeing Sage's name flashing on screen.

"How did it go?" she demanded.

"It's confirmed; I'm about seven weeks pregnant."

"Yay! I'm so happy for you, Nellie!" Sage exclaimed with far more excitement than I'd even managed to have for myself.

It was a good thing that I could count on her to be excited enough for the both of us, at least for a while. I had a feeling I'd be living in a perpetual state of worry and fear.

"I had her send my high-risk obstetrician referral to Springwood..." I paused, letting the words sit with her. The high-pitched squeal that followed had me moving my phone away from my ear.

"You're moving here?! You're moving here! Nix, Nellie's moving to Hartwood Creek!"

"I gathered that," I could hear Nix say with a chuckle.

"When are you moving?" Sage demanded, her excitement reaching unparalleled heights.

"I just told Angela, actually. I still need to tell Sal to kick rocks, and then I can leave whenever, I guess," I replied. Angela was technically the only renter on the lease, although I paid half the rent and the utilities. I could offer to pay the next month, but still leave. She wouldn't care what I did, so long as I didn't leave her hanging.

As for work...well. I should give Sal my two weeks' notice, because it was the right thing to do, but I was pretty fed up with him taking advantage of me.

I'd told him I was going to quit on numerous occasions, but he never took me seriously. Probably because I kept showing up at work the next day, but I digress. I could tell him something came up, a family emergency or something. He'd be irritated, but he'd have to deal with it. As far as I was concerned, Sal was no longer my issue.

My issue was the little clump of cells that would, with any stroke of luck, end up being a fully formed human in seven months' time.

It was kind of sad, when I thought about it, how quickly I could leave it all behind. I guess I hadn't put down roots here like I'd thought, at least not permanent ones.

In a way, that had been intentional. I was always hoping for something better to come along. A better job, a different place.

But I'd known for a while now that it wasn't going to happen for me, at least not in Guelph. It was time to seek out something better.

I'd been thinking a lot about Hartwood Creek since my little visit in the fall. I had fallen for the historic small town just as hard as Sage predicted I would. Everything about it was so whimsical and quaint, and the people were friendly and interesting.

It felt like where I was supposed to be. Not to mention, there was the psychic reading I'd had the night of the Witches' Ball rattling around in my brain. Though the rest of the night was a blur, that memory was perfectly clear, and had been replaying more frequently within the past week.

You'll find everything you've been looking for here. The medium's words resurfaced yet again, making me feel all the more confident about my decision.

"Okay, great! I'm so excited, Nellie. This is going to be an amazing thing for you, I can feel it in my bones," Sage said, jarring me from my thoughts.

"Having an inkling of your own, are you?" I chuckled. Sage used to make fun of what she affectionately referred to as my "inklings". I got a sense for people and situations, and nine times out of ten, I was right about them.

Like my inkling about her former fiancé, Warren. I'd had a feeling he wasn't the one for her. His aura had always seemed so...off, and so incompatible with hers. Warren's aura had been dark and negative, whereas Sage's aura was light and warm. But at the time, Sage hadn't paid any attention to my inklings. She just thought I didn't like him, and I didn't.

"I am," Sage said, her tone serious. "Don't you have one?"

I paused, considering her question. I hadn't really let

myself feel anything about the situation, other than worry and fear. But something was tugging me in that direction: to Hartwood Creek. I felt like maybe I really could find my happiness there, like the medium had said.

It wasn't just about Noah; he was scarcely a factor in this decision. It was something about the very town itself. I'd felt a shift in my energy the moment I set foot across the town border, and that sense of home had pulled at me even then.

Since returning to Guelph, I'd felt a restlessness I'd never experienced before. A deep settled unhappiness. Something in me had shifted, realigned, moving toward a new purpose, a discovered dream. A whisper in the wind, calling me north to Hartwood Creek.

"Yeah, I do. I think this is going to be the best thing for me. Even if things don't work out with, well, the baby situation."

"Don't say that; it'll work out," Sage assured me. "Ooh, I can't wait to throw you a baby shower!"

I laughed, feeling lighter than I had in weeks. "Let's not get too ahead of ourselves."

"Too late, I'm already on Pinterest!"

FOUR DAYS, and one carload. That's all it took for me to tie up loose ends and pack up my entire life in Guelph. Five days before Christmas I pulled up to the beautiful blue Victorian-style home in one of the older subdivisions in Hartwood Creek. With the freshly fallen snow, it looked like a Trisha Romance painting.

The detached garage with its pitched roof and intricately designed woodwork looked as pretty as the main house, with

Christmas lights and garland wrapped up the staircase leading to the apartment door.

Sage was waiting at the top of the small deck, waving at me with the biggest grin on her face, her blond hair blowing in the wind. Nix and his brother, Parker, were already trudging toward me.

Parker and Nix had the same Hutchinson brown hair and brown eyes, like melted dark chocolate. They were both muscular with broad shoulders, although Parker was a little taller.

"Hey, Nell," Nix said when I stepped out of the car. "It's good to see you," he gave me a brief but solid hug.

"It's good to see you too," I smiled. "Thanks for letting me take over your lease, and thanks for letting me move into your apartment, Parker."

"It's our pleasure. Saves us having to deal with the headache of finding someone new, and it was only a matter of time until Nix officially moved in with Sage and Daphne," Parker grinned.

"We'll move these boxes for you. We're under strict instructions to not let you lift a thing," Nix said.

My cheeks heated with embarrassment, and I wondered just how much of my situation Parker knew. I'd asked for Sage's discretion; I didn't want to tell anyone else until I was past the danger zone.

"Thanks, but I managed to pack everything in on my own."

"Well, here you have help. Get used to it," Nix cocked a brow at me and titled his chin in the direction of the garage apartment. "Go on up and get settled."

"Yes, Sir," I saluted him, then reached back into the car for my carry-on and my purse. I was exhausted from the long drive, but I'd had the foresight to pack everything I'd need quick access to. A pair of comfortable pajamas and my toiletries, an outfit for tomorrow, my phone charger, and the book I was reading were all tucked neatly in the carry on.

Someone had shoveled and salted the stairs in preparation. Already, I was being shown more care and consideration than the near decade I'd spent in Guelph. My stupid emotions were getting the better of me, and I wiped away tears before reaching the deck.

Sage immediately wrapped her arms around me in a hug, squeezing me tight. "I'm so glad you're here!" she squealed.

"Me too," I murmured into her shoulder, squeezing her back. I hadn't let myself focus on how much I missed my bestie—my soul sister. "Where's Daph?"

"She's in the house with Tabitha and the girls. They wanted to make you a little welcome home surprise." She released me, sending me a huge, welcoming grin.

"That's so darn sweet," I sniffled, the tears I'd been desperately trying to hold back spilling over. "I'm sorry, it's just the hormones, I think. And I'm exhausted," I added, catching Sage's concerned expression.

Sage reached for my hand and squeezed it.

"Coming up!" Nix called from the bottom of the stairs. Realizing we were still on the deck, Sage tugged me into the apartment.

Immediately, the warmth of the place enveloped me. The smell of fresh paint lingered behind cleaning products, and everything looked fresh and white.

"Did you paint?" I asked, my jaw dropping as I took in the space—the appliances were new and shiny, and the furniture certainly wasn't the old family room donations from Angela's parents.

"Yeah, it needed a fresh coat to brighten things up. The darker, more masculine colours made the space feel smaller."

I toed off my winter boots, leaving them on the shoe rack by the door.

"You really didn't have to do that, Sage. It's more than enough that you're letting me rent this space," I was fighting back tears again and I hadn't even seen the rest of the place. Nix and Parker set down the boxes they'd carried up by the door. From the looks of it, they'd managed to bring up all my worldly possessions in one go. "Thank you so much."

"Don't mention it, we're happy to have you here," Parker said. "I'm going head back inside and take over Bryson duty."

"I'll let you girls catch up," Nix grinned, pressing a tender kiss to Sage's cheek. "I know you've got a lot to talk about." He waggled his eyebrows at her while following his brother out the door, pulling it shut behind him.

Sage's cheeks heated at Nix's words, and she shook her head. "Come on, let's give you the grand tour!" she said, tugging me deeper into the apartment.

The apartment had a beautiful, airy, open floorplan. The kitchen was to the left, with cabinetry along the far wall and a double kitchen sink under the large window that overlooked Parker and Tabitha's house. There wasn't enough space for a table, but the long, narrow counter with bar stools provided a place to sit, and it broke up the space between the kitchen and living room.

A short hallway on the other side of the room led to the single bedroom and bathroom. The bathroom was spacious, with a huge tub I couldn't wait to soak in. The bedroom was bigger than my last one, with more than enough space to put a crib in.

Everything was painted a bright neutral colour, not quite white but not beige or Millennial grey, either. I could picture myself thriving here.

"It's..." I sniffled again, wiping the moisture from my cheeks. "This is all too much, Sage."

"No, it's perfect," Sage said sincerely. "You're going to be so happy here, I can feel it. This was the right move."

I knew at that moment she was right. Call it one of my inklings, but I suddenly knew everything was going to work out.

"I still can't believe it, any of it. I'm going to be a mom... that's so wild," I said in disbelief, the tears still flowing.

"You're going to be an amazing mom," Sage said.

"Hopefully," I murmured, thinking of my own mother as I ran my hand along the end of the made-up queen-size bed. I longed to flop onto it and sleep for a few days. I could smell the freshly laundered scent and it was making me feel even more tired. "Wait, is this mattress tainted?" I blurted, my intrusive thoughts getting the best of me.

"Define tainted?" Sage asked. Seeing my expression, she rolled her eyes in exasperation. "It's less than two years old, and it's super comfortable. It's never been without a mattress topper, but I threw the old one out and steam cleaned the heck out of it before putting a new mattress protector on. I'm pretty sure it's cleaner than your last mattress."

"Sorry, I don't mean to sound ungrateful. It'd be weird sleeping where you and Nix spent so much time boning."

"Don't be foolish, we did that on the couch," Sage assured me. "Which has also been steam cleaned," she added with a giggle.

"Thank you. I really do appreciate everything you've done for me," I told her, overwhelmed with gratitude.

"What are besties for?" Sage asked, grinning. "I'm so happy you're finally here! And just in time for Christmas!"

"Right, Christmas." It was one of my least favourite holidays, probably because aside from an e-transfer and a phone call, I didn't really hear from my parents.

"Christmas in Hartwood Creek is going to be different; you'll see. Oh, that reminds me! Auntie Em wanted me to make sure you know that you're invited to Christmas dinner. She expects you to be there for no later than four o'clock."

I tried to swallow past the lump in my throat. "Okay, I'll check my schedule and try to make it happen." I was kidding—my schedule was wide open, or at least it would be until I found a job.

"Mom! Mom, where are you?!" A familiar voice shouted from the door.

Sage and I went back to the main living area, finding Daphne and the twins carrying Tupperware containers full of baked goods. Tabitha was with them, and she was holding a casserole dish.

"Welcome to your new home!" she smiled, setting the casserole dish down on the bar counter. Tabitha had long dark hair and chunky bangs. Her bright cornflower-blue eyes were framed with thick dark lashes. "We made you dinner!"

"And dessert!" Daphne added, rushing toward me with her Tupperware container. Daphne was the spitting image of Sage, with her wispy blond hair and wide green eyes. She threw her arm around my waist, hugging me tight. I hugged her back, feeling more at home than I'd ever felt before. "We baked cookies galore!"

"Thank you so much, what a warm welcome," I was barely hanging on by a thread, and if everyone kept being so nice and sweet to me, it would only be a matter of time before I burst into tears again. I took the proffered Tupperware containers from Daphne and the twins. The twins looked just like their mother, with their dark hair and blue eyes, although they had the Hutchinson charm and smiled just like their father.

"I think Nellie is feeling pretty tired, so we're going to let her get settled now, okay girls?"

I could kiss Tabitha, and not just because the chicken parmesan casserole she'd brought in was making my mouth water and my stomach grumble.

Another squeeze from Daphne and they left, leaving me and Sage alone in the apartment again.

"Part of me wants to stay and help you get settled, but I know how exhausting the first trimester is." Sage patted my arm sympathetically. "I took the next two weeks off, mostly because of Christmas, but also so I could help get you settled."

"I'm sure I'll be fine, I am used to being on my own, you know."

"Yeah, I know. But you don't have to be on your own, not anymore," Sage told me.

Her words struck something inside me, and I bit the inside of my cheek to stop the onslaught of yet more tears. Pregnancy emotions were no joke.

"I'll be here tomorrow morning at ten o'clock with coffee and pastries."

"Sounds good," I managed, hugging Sage tightly, then she shoved her boots on and grabbed her coat.

"Do not unpack any of those boxes without me, do you hear me?" she ordered, pointing at me.

"I hear you. I'm going to stuff my face with this tantalizing meal Tabitha brought over, then probably crash." I promised.

CHAPTER THREE

Noah

"JEANNINE IS A NO-SHOW AGAIN." My younger brother, Easton, said after popping into the main office.

"You're kidding me," I grumbled, pushing back in the office chair with aggravation. I'd been covering for Jeannine for the past hour. She was supposed to start at eight o'clock. I figured she was delayed from the snowstorm we'd gotten the night before.

"Yup. Texted five minutes ago, let me know that a family emergency came up and she'll be out of town for a week or two."

"Fucking great. Just in time for Christmas."

Christmas was one of our busiest times of the year. Every single cottage and condo we had at Whimsical Woods Resort was booked steadily through the holidays and into the new year.

It was the worst time for Jeannine to up and decide to have

a family emergency. Normally, I would give someone the benefit of the doubt—family emergencies happened, after all. But Jeannine had used that excuse over Canada Day weekend, too. Plus, she was regularly late or screwing up reservations. It seemed like I was always fixing her mistakes or covering for her when she didn't show up.

"We'll have to call Damien in. If one of us is managing the office, that means we'll need more hands-on maintenance to get the snow cleared and the pathways salted." Damien would be pissed.

"You mean while you're managing the office," Easton smirked. "You know I don't do computer stuff."

Computer stuff was handling bookings and responding to emails. It really wasn't rocket science, but my younger brother had always refused to do any of the office work. He'd rather stay later handling maintenance issues than answer a phone call or input a reservation.

Mom used to handle the office before she and dad retired, but now it was on us to run the entire place. They were off enjoying their retirement after years of running Whimsical Woods Resort and raising us three boys.

"Yeah, yeah," I sighed, massaging my temples to ward off the stress headache I seemed to perpetually have these days. Easton ducked out while I picked up the office phone and dialed our oldest brother's phone number.

"Someone better be grievously injured, or something better be on fire," he growled into the receiver by way of greeting. He sounded slightly out of breath and irritated.

"It's nine o'clock, how are you already this pissed?"

"Because, dipshit. You're interrupting my favourite part of the day," Damien said. I could hear Charlotte say something in the background and the rustling of sheets.

"Damn, sorry brother. Didn't mean to interrupt your

morning nookie session, but we have a situation. Jeannine has flaked off again, and that leaves me stuck in the office and Easton to clear all the snow from the cottages, roads, and pathways. We need backup."

"What we need is to fire Jeannine and hire someone who actually shows up for shifts." Damien huffed.

"You're not wrong about that, and we will. One of the things I plan on doing today is putting up an ad for a new office administrator." I sighed, feeling every bit as frustrated as Damien sounded. I knew we couldn't go on this way. We needed someone reliable, someone capable of doing the job. Jeannine clearly wasn't that person.

"Good. Make sure you do that. I'll be there in an hour and a half," Damien said, hanging up.

I stood and stretched, then went to the staff kitchen to put on a pot of coffee. If I was going to deal with office work, I'd need all the caffeine I could get.

Being outside was my preference, too. The fresh air kept me invigorated and awake. Although, unlike Easton, I wouldn't refuse office work; it had to be done. I also managed the accounts and made sure all our employees were paid on time. If nobody was there to answer the phone, check emails and book reservations, and pay our employees—we wouldn't have a cottage resort.

Our current bookings were important, yes, but the future ones were just as important. They kept the lights on and the business running. My grandparents had started this cottage resort, and my parents had grown it to what it is today. I didn't want my brothers and I to be the reason we lost it all.

Coffee in hand, I returned to the office in time for the phone to ring. "Whimsical Woods Resort, Noah speaking. How can I help you?"

"Hi there, I'd like to book a reservation for a three-bedroom cottage over March Break," the woman's voice on the other end of the line said. I sat down and moved the mouse, waking up the computer.

"Let me see if we have any availability over March Break with our three-bedroom cottages," I told the woman. I clicked into our booking software program and checked. "Unfortunately, we don't have any three-bedrooms available, however we do have one two-bedroom cottage and a few four-bedroom cottages."

"Hmm. does Hartwood Creek still do the Maple Syrup Festival?"

"Sure does, every year! And we have plenty of activities planned all March Break long for families."

"Okay, I'll take a four-bedroom from the eleventh until the fifteenth." The woman said.

Five minutes later, the reservation was booked. Setting the phone receiver down, I picked up my coffee and took a much-needed sip, then opened the Word document that contained the pre-written job postings Charlotte had done up for us a year or so ago. The postings were mostly for summer positions and housekeeping positions, and there was the office administration listing from before we'd hired Jeannine.

I had to make a few adjustments to have it fit our needs now, but it was a great template to fall back on. Another half hour later, the posting was listed on the Hartwood Creek community page and the Ontario job listings website.

IT'D BEEN a long ass day. It was only five o'clock, and I already felt like crashing for the night. However, I had nothing to eat at home because I regularly put off grocery shopping.

I hated trying to figure out what to buy. I might be well into my thirties, but I'd never grasped the simplicity of meal planning. I could smoke meats and cook a mean steak on the grill, but that was the extent of my cooking abilities. If I couldn't barbeque it, microwave it, or toss it already-made into the oven, I avoided it.

So, instead of going home to crash on my couch and veg out, I went straight into town to do the dreaded task.

My family had lived in Hartwood Creek for generations. My great-great-great grandfather was one of the original founders of Hartwood Creek. He'd settled with his family on the large patch of land that was now the Whimsical Woods Resort. Back when the town first formed, it was an operational wood mill. A lot of the historic buildings were built with wood from Alexander Wood's mill.

It was a long running joke in our family that Wood wood could withstand generations of pressure and still stay sturdy and erect.

The charred ruins of the original Wood family homestead could be found on the trails in the middle of the forest just north of the farthest operational cottage. We included it in our Halloween Haunt walk, telling tourists that it was haunted. I didn't believe in ghosts, but the tourists ate up the story, especially because Alexander Wood had perished there when the family homestead burnt down.

The downtown area was less than a ten-minute drive when the roads were clear, a little longer when the plows hadn't been through. I drove a lifted truck with killer winter tires. Within thirteen minutes, I was pulling into a parking spot at the grocery store.

I grabbed a cart and started perusing aisles, nodding in greeting to all the familiar faces I passed as I tossed stuff in. I didn't want to have to come back for anything, so I loaded up on anything that caught my eye.

By the time I reached the junk food aisle my cart was almost full, and I was satisfied I'd have enough to eat for the next week or two.

There was a gorgeous woman in the junk food aisle, eyeing up bags of chips like she couldn't decide which ones to get. Long, rich chestnut brown hair tumbled down her back in waves. Something about her seemed familiar—something about her tugged at a memory just out of reach. Her delicate hand was reaching for a bag of Lays Dill Pickle chips.

"Can't go wrong with dill pickle chips," I said, and she startled, dropping the bag into her cart, her hazel eyes fixing on me.

Her pillowy lips opened in surprise. "Noah?"

"Do we know each other?" I asked, moving closer. The woman's pretty mouth pursed, and she narrowed those gorgeously familiar eyes at me. Fire sparked behind them, making the golden flecks of her irises stand out.

"Yes, unfortunately. Though you probably don't remember me. Just another name on your long list," she smarted, her hands gripping the bar of her cart tightly as she went to move around me.

Her voice. I heard it in my dreams. Had ever since the Witches' Ball. I reached out, grabbing the end of her grocery cart to stop her. Sage's gorgeous friend. The woman that had been starring in my wet dreams for weeks now.

"Hey now, no need for such hostility, Nellie. You were in full face makeup last time. I had a better chance of recognizing you naked than recognizing you without your epic makeup skills," I smirked, my eyes dropping down and taking in her covered body through her open winter jacket. I might not have recognized her fully dressed, but if I'd seen her naked again, I'd know every inch of her body.

"I guess you have a point," she allowed, still eyeing me like I was a decision she regretted.

God, I sure hoped I wasn't. I hadn't been able to get her out of my head since October, and I hadn't seen her natural beauty then either. Had I seen what she looked like without the expertly applied costume makeup, transforming her into a sexy feminine version of Dr. Jekyll and Mr. Hyde, I'd have been even more gone, but she'd slipped out early in the morning before I had a chance to truly soak her in—or appreciate her.

Nellie was breathtakingly stunning, the kind of beauty that rendered me speechless. It wasn't just her physical appearance, although she was a knockout, it was her aura. Her essence.

"Are you visiting Sage again?" I asked, my hand still on her cart.

"Something like that," she replied, looking at my hand pointedly. I removed it, grateful that she didn't immediately take off.

"Well, how long are you in town for? Maybe we could meet up for some drinks. Get reacquainted again before you leave."

"I'm not. Leaving, I mean. I just moved here," Nellie told me, her brow furrowing. "And I don't think drinks are a good idea."

I tried not to acknowledge the disappointment of her subtle rejection, and instead focused on the first part of what she said. "Hell, you moved to Hartwood Creek?! That's awesome! What brings you here?"

Nellie winced, like my question struck her. "Guess I needed a change of pace. Anyway, I need to go. See you around, Noah."

With that, she pushed her cart past me and walked like fire was nipping at her heels.

IT WAS FRIDAY NIGHT, and I was sitting at our regular booth at The Quarter Lounge with Parker and Nix Hutchinson, Auston Robertson, and Donavan Ashe. We were on our second pitcher of beer, catching up on all the random stuff that had happened.

Our regular get-togethers had slowly tapered off from weekly hangouts at the bar to biweekly, to almost once a month now that most of the guys had families and serious girlfriends. Donavon and I were the last two standing bachelors, and I was pretty sure he had a regular sneaky link that he'd been closed-mouth about.

"So, how's living with Sage officially?" Donavon asked Nix, pouring himself another beer. We'd been trying to get him to fess up on who the mysterious woman was he'd been spending a lot of time with lately, but Donavon wasn't biting—ergo the swift change of subject.

"It's amazing!" Nix grinned. He was so stupidly in love with Sage, I almost felt bad for him. And envious.

That was a new feeling, the envious bit. I hadn't much cared for monogamous relationships in the past. Give me a one-night stand or casual fling any time, but a serious girlfriend meant more effort than I had to give. Already, I was busy as hell with the resort and family demands. Adding another person to the list of things and people that relied and depended on me seemed like too much of a burden.

But then, October had happened. I'd spent one night with a girl dressed up as a sexy Dr. Jekyll and Mr. Hyde, and suddenly I found myself longing for more. Odd that a monster costume had affected me like that, but stranger things had happened in the town of Hartwood Creek.

Maybe it had more to do with the fact that Nellie had snuck out on me before I'd even woken up, and I'd never had the chance to get her number or ask her for a repeat. Usually, it was me sneaking out in the morning.

"As if he wasn't basically living with her before," Parker joked. Parker was probably one of my oldest best friends. I'd rented the apartment above his garage for a spell, while my cabin was being built. We'd always been tight, but I didn't get to see him as regularly as before, now that he was busy with his custom furniture and wood milling business, and raising a family with my cousin, Tabitha.

"I mean, you're not wrong. This makes it official. One step closer to forever, you know? It feels good," Nix said, a dreamy look in his eyes. "I plan on asking her to marry me once we finish building."

Nix was referring to the house he was building for them. He'd purchased the land years ago but had only recently broke ground. He'd drawn up blueprints and then amended them once things got serious with Sage, so that she could have some input on their forever home.

It made sense, and it was pretty romantic, but that was Nix. He'd always been thoughtful and romantic. I wasn't quite either of those things. Even my mother called me self-centred and unserious, and she wasn't wrong.

My attention span has always been short. The longest running commitment I had to date was to the resort, and that's because it was in my blood. I was serious about it in a way I'd never been serious about any woman.

For some unknown reason, Nellie's face flashed in my mind. I shook the thought of her away, unwilling to dwell on her. But before I could truly focus on something else, her name was coming up in conversation with the guys.

"Now that Nellie's moved into the bachelor apartment—" Parker was saying.

"Wait, Nellie as in Sage's friend Nellie?" I interrupted.

Parker and Nix shared a knowing look.

"The one and the same," Nix said carefully.

"I ran into her at the grocery store the other night," I said, trying to keep my voice casual. "She's looking good."

"I'm surprised you remembered who she was," Nix remarked. "You two were pretty drunk that night."

"Hard to forget a body like hers," I smirked, leaning back in the booth, and crossing my legs at the ankles. My encounter with Nellie had stuck with me, mostly because of how that gorgeous body had responded to me, and how I'd responded to it. It was one of the most explosive, toe-curling romps I've ever had.

Nix frowned, as if my nonchalant response disappointed him. "Yeah, well. Anyway, she's moved to Hartwood Creek. I know she's looking for work, so if anyone knows of anything through the grapevine..." he was directing his question more at the others, but I fixated on it.

"Tell her to shoot her resume to us. We need a new office administrator at the resort."

"You sure that's a good idea, Noah?" Parker asked, exchanging another look with Nix.

I narrowed my eyes in suspicion. "Why not? If she's got office skills, we could use her."

"Wouldn't it complicate things, seeing as you've already bedded her and moved on?" Nix added.

I got the sense they were teaming up on me, and they likely were. As Sage's best friend, Nix would feel protective of her, and Parker would back him. The Hutchinson family always had each others' backs.

"I can keep things professional," I scowled.

Besides, who said I'd moved on? Sure, I'd tried to, but I hadn't felt that pull of attraction, and I'd lost interest. I'd spent the last several weeks focusing on the resort and my family, not random conquests at the bar.

I hadn't let myself think too hard about why that was, though, and I wasn't about to admit that to the guys.

CHAPTER FOUR

Nellie

"I HEARD the resort is looking for a full-time office administrator."

My ears perked up at that piece of information as I strolled arm in arm with Sage along the downtown core of Hartwood Creek. It was the twenty-third of December, and I had one more day to find gifts for everyone on my list.

I'd put off shopping, first because I hadn't been feeling the greatest and it was all I could do to make it to work every day, then because I'd needed to process the earth-shattering revelation of impending motherhood and figure out my next steps. This last week, I'd been far too consumed with quitting my job and moving to worry about Christmas. But time was running out.

My shopping list was rather small. I had already gotten Sage a present months ago, and now I was on the hunt for a gift for Daphne and a host gift for Sage's aunt and uncle. It'd been kind of them to extend an invitation for me to join them for Christmas dinner, so I didn't want to turn up empty-handed.

I also wanted to buy a present for Parker and Tabitha, as a thank you for letting me live in their bachelor apartment without having to put down a deposit, as well gifts for their three kids, because buying gifts for kids was my favourite thing ever.

Sage still needed to get a couple of gifts, too, so we'd decided to spend the afternoon shopping. Nix was hanging out with Daphne, and we had plans to meet up later in the evening for dinner at The Hungry Hub and take a horsedrawn carriage ride through the snowy streets after. Nix insisted it was an experience we had to have for our first Christmas in Hartwood Creek.

I'd be having my first Christmas in Hartwood Creek the same time as Sage and Daphne. It felt like they'd lived here for years, even though they'd moved at the end of August. Still, it felt like a lifetime ago that Sage and Daphne had left Guelph —and me.

"Oh really?" I murmured, my eyes going to a mom-and-pop toy shop down the street that looked like a good candidate for the kids' gifts I needed to purchase.

"Yeah, Nix mentioned it this morning. You should send in your resume," Sage nudged me gently with her elbow.

"I've never really done office work before," I wrinkled my nose. My last several years of work experience had been at the café. I knew how to manage staff, run the café, and do up schedules, but that was the extent of my experience.

"I'm sure it's not that hard. You answer phone calls, book reservations, and I think do some light laundry. Linens and stuff."

"Where is this resort?"

"North of town. Whimsical Woods Resort," Sage said carefully.

"Wait…Whimsical Woods…as in Noah's family's resort?" I asked, whirling to stare at my friend.

"How'd you know his family owned it?"

"We did *some* talking that night," I replied, my cheeks heating at the dubious expression on her face. "Okay, maybe I stalked him a little after, but whatever. I'm not working for his family's resort, Sage. That's a bad idea."

"Or it's a fantastic idea," Sage arched her brow at me.

I glared at her, shaking my head. "I don't even know if he's the…*you know*." I whispered this last part, not wanting anyone on the street to overhear me, even though nobody was paying us any attention.

"It's not like you have to tell him anything about that," Sage waved away my concern with her free hand.

"I think he'd notice over time. It'd be so awkward having to work for him," I shook my head again. "It can't happen. It's not going to happen. The last thing I need is more…entanglement with him."

I thought about how he'd looked at me the other night when we'd run into each other in the grocery store—with hungry appreciation and unveiled longing.

Sure, he hadn't recognized me at first, but he was right. I'd been wearing a full face of special effects makeup the night we hooked up.

I tried to ignore the heat in my belly that his insinuation that he'd have no problem recognizing my naked body evoked, but I'd been fighting residuals of desire for the past two days. It irked me to no end. I didn't want to want Noah Wood, especially not now.

"But they need someone now, and you need to find a job

now so you can work enough hours for maternity leave," Sage pointed out as we drew closer to the toy shop.

She wasn't wrong, I really did need to find a new job as quickly as possible. "I'll think about it."

"Okay, good. That's all I'm asking. The resort is renowned for being one of the best local places to work at. High schoolers fight over the summer student positions, and they pay well. Better than Sal's café," Sage assured me.

I let out an exasperated huff of breath as I opened the door to the toy shop for us both. My jaw immediately dropped when I took in the shop. It was like a colourful toy eutopia.

The shop lacked the coldness of big box toy stores and instead reminded me of the toy store in A Christmas Story. There was a beautiful Christmas display near the window, with a metal toy train going in circles around what appeared to be a miniature wooden village display of Santa's workshop.

I'd been very humbug about Christmas before stepping inside, but after spending a few minutes amidst the warm twinkling lights and beautiful holiday displays, I was beginning to feel my Christmas spirit awakening.

I picked out toys for Daphne, and Tabitha and Parker's three kids with Sage's help while she did her last-minute shopping. When we checked out, the woman at the cash register asked if we wanted them gift-wrapped. We both said yes, me to save some time, and Sage because she knew Daphne would try and sneak a peek at her shopping bags.

Once the woman wrapped our gifts, she put them in reusable bags to make it easier to carry.

"How do you keep Daphne out of that place?" I asked as we neared the door, my eyes sweeping around for a final look. I was still in awe. They seemed to have everything: all the current popular toys, as well as an entire section of vintage toys.

I could spend hours here, happily combing through every single aisle.

"It's difficult," Sage admitted with a giggle. "I bring her once a month when she's saved up enough of her chore money to splurge on a new toy. Or whenever she gets invited to a birthday party, which happens a lot during the school year. School-aged children are always having birthday parties. You'll see."

"Right," I said, trying to ignore the wave of nausea that overcame me at the thought of school years and children's birthday parties.

In a year's time, I'd be celebrating my baby's first Christmas. Absently, my hand went to my still flat stomach through my open winter jacket, suddenly feeling emotional as well as nauseous.

Morning sickness hadn't exactly reared its ugly head yet, but I'd been doing enough reading on pregnancy to expect that to happen at any moment. I figured it'd happen in the early morning, not midafternoon in the aisle of a toy shop.

"Are you okay?" Sage asked, concerned.

"Yeah, just feeling a bit off," I admitted.

She looked through her purse, pulling out a candy. "Here, suck on this," she instructed, handing me the piece of candy.

"That's how I got into this predicament in the first place," I teased, my voice as wobbly as my current emotional state. Still, I unwrapped the candy and put it in my mouth. Ginger exploded on my tongue. "Urg, this is disgusting!" I looked around for somewhere to spit it out.

"Keep sucking on it. It's a ginger candy, it helps with nausea," Sage insisted.

"Has it been in your purse since Daphne?"

"No," she said, looking away and strategically avoiding my eyes.

"Why is it so disgusting?" it was all I could do to not spit it out. It required all my will power to keep the damn thing in my mouth.

"Do you still feel nauseous?" Sage asked, looking at me with a knowing smile.

I shook my head, admitting to myself and to her that the disgusting candy really had helped with the nausea.

"See, it works."

"Fine, it works," I grumbled. "Probably because it's so shockingly disgusting, it distracts you from the nausea."

She reached into her purse and pulled out another handful of the wrapped ginger candies. "Here, put these in your purse. You never know when you'll need another. They are little life savers."

"Why do you have a stockpile of them?" I asked, looking at my friend through narrowed eyes. They didn't seem like the kind of candy one enjoyed having. I couldn't picture popping these nasty little things in my mouth for enjoyment.

Sage opened her mouth, about to reply, then the bell over the door rang, alerting us to more shoppers coming into the toy shop. Three old ladies strolled in, talking seriously amongst themselves. "Uh oh, incoming: it's the Hartley triplets," Sage whispered.

The three women spotted us and immediately made a beeline over. All three of the Hartley sisters had a striking resemblance to each other, and it was obvious that they were related, although they weren't identical. Each of them seemed to have their own unique style. I'd met them briefly during my visit, when I'd accompanied the entire crew to their local café, Tout de Sweets, for the Halloween costume contest. They'd been dressed up as the Sanderson sisters from Hocus Pocus.

"Sage Whitaker! It's so good to see you again!" the lady

with short, dyed red hair exclaimed, her large eyes sparkling with mirth.

"It's good to see you ladies, too. You remember my friend, Nellie Banks? She was here for Halloween."

"Ah, yes, you had the remarkable Dr. Jekyll and Mr. Hyde costume, didn't you?" the sister with long white hair braided over her shoulder asked, smiling at me knowingly.

"Yes, that was me," I admitted.

"We just loved your makeup!" the third sister exclaimed. She wore a fashionable hat over her short snow-white hair. "So creative!"

"Thank you," I was surprised they remembered me, although I shouldn't have been. Sage had filled me in on the Hartley triplets. They practically ran Hartwood Creek and knew everything about everyone.

"We hear Nix officially moved out of the apartment," the one with dyed red hair remarked, fixing her all-knowing smile on Sage. "That's wonderful, dear. Are wedding bells in the future?"

"I'm not sure about that, Betty," Sage chuckled awkwardly. "We're taking it one step at a time and enjoying the journey."

"Ah yes, such a beautiful way to look at it," the sister with longer hair sighed dreamily. "Take your time and enjoy yourselves."

"That's the plan, Dorothy," Sage smiled.

"It is the twenty-first century; I suppose there's not so much pressure in today's society for women to marry before living with a man." Betty said thoughtfully.

"Good thing, too. I was ever so tired of the rigid expectations placed upon women. Notice it was never the men who had to carry those expectations? I'm loving the new-age freedom women have," Dorothy added with a twinkle in her eye.

"Although we do love a good wedding," the sister wearing the hat remarked. "And a baby shower."

"Alice!" both Betty and Dorothy scolded. Alice smiled happily, sending a knowing look my way.

"Are you visiting for the holidays, dear?" Alice asked me, although I could tell by her question that she already knew the answer.

"Actually, I just moved here."

The sisters didn't seem surprised at all by my answer.

"Yup, Nellie's Hartwood Creek's newest resident," Sage chimed in, tossing her arm around my shoulders. "I convinced her to move closer. She's taken over renting the bachelor apartment above Parker and Tabitha's garage."

"Well, isn't that lovely! Welcome to Hartwood Creek, Nellie. I'm sure you'll be very happy here."

"Thank you. I think so, too," I replied.

"Well, we better get back to shopping! We've got to meet Daphne and Nix soon for dinner." Sage smiled.

"We won't keep you then, dearies. We have a lot of shopping to do ourselves. Have a Merry Christmas!"

"Merry Christmas!" Sage and I said at the same time. The Hartley triplets made their way deeper into the toy shop, and we walked outside.

"Okay, was it me, or did they act like they know something?" I asked once we were on the street, a door and brick walls away from the Hartley triplets.

"Oh, they undoubtedly do. They have an uncanny ability of knowing everything, even before people know it themselves..." Sage glanced over her shoulder to make sure they weren't behind us listening in. She linked arms with me, guiding me away from the toy shop. "They call themselves the Messengers."

"The Messengers?" I repeated, bemused. "That sounds

somewhat ominous."

"Yup. Remember how I told you they like to meddle with townfolks' lives, and have a tendency of trying to trick couples into drinking the infamous love elixir?"

"Oh my gosh, I remember that now. You were so panicked after your first date with Nix!"

I'd laughed at the time, but after speaking to the Hartley sisters, and seeing their knowing gazes, I was a touch uncomfortable. A shiver rolled through me, not an unpleasant one, but an intuitive one. It told me that they knew something about me. Probably a lot of somethings.

"Yeah, so. Make sure you're checking the ingredients on things and avoid drinking anything they offer you. Also, try not to order the In The Name of Love Latte from Tout de Sweets if you can help it. That's the most common way to ingest the love elixir. It's said to possess magical powers that make the couples who drink it fall undeniably in love."

"This town needs to have its own guide for newcomers," I muttered, shaking my head. I'd never before lived in such a quirky town full of such lore, but I couldn't deny it: I loved it. The whole idea was unfathomable, but bewitching.

"They have one, actually!" Sage said, guiding me toward the book shop.

Beyond the Pages was located beside the Tout de Sweets café. It had beautiful, exposed brick walls lined with thick mahogany shelves and a black iron spiral staircase leading to the upper level, which, according to Sage, was where the local author signings and other bookstore events were held.

Several table displays were arranged in the middle of the store, with popular books and new releases. Sage brought me over to the local section and picked up a book called *The Complete History of Hartwood Creek*.

"It has maps, family trees, and a section dedicated to the

history of the love elixir Morgana Hartley created. It's said that In The Name of Love Latte is derived from the original elixir."

"That's wild," I shook my head, looking at the cover of the book. It appeared to be a painting of the original town from the eighteen hundreds.

"Consider it a welcome to Hartwood Creek gift," Sage said.

Noah

AFTER WORK ON SATURDAY, Easton and I went into town to meet the rest of the family at the park. It was an annual tradition we started the night before Christmas Eve, when Damien's twin girls, Aria and Ronan, were a few years old. After their mother abandoned them, we wanted to make their first Christmas without her as magical as possible.

Now, Damien had his fiancé, Charlotte, and the girls had a wonderful stepmother, but the family all got together anyway to ride the horsedrawn carriages and have hot chocolate from Tout de Sweets while taking in the Christmas lights. Much like Halloween, Hartwood Creek went all out for Christmas. Every store front and streetlamp was decorated with lights and garland, and so was the gazebo in the park.

Hartwood Creek often looked like the set of a Hallmark movie this time of year, and normally, I loved it. Christmas was one of my favourite times of the year.

But I wasn't feeling it this year. I was beyond stressed with the Jeannine situation. She'd officially given her two weeks' notice this morning, coinciding with her impromptu two weeks off for the supposed family emergency. Suffice to say, she wouldn't be back, and she'd left us in a lurch.

Things were crazy busy at the resort, and the whole family had to rally together to get through it. Aria and Ronan were on Christmas break, and Mom and Dad had to watch them so Charlotte could help with the Kids Club events we hosted every winter break. I was stuck in the office taking reservations, answering phone calls, and dealing with guest issues, while the maintenance jobs fell on Damien's and Easton's shoulders.

"Uncle Noah! Uncle Easton!" my nieces shouted when they caught sight of me and Easton lumbering over. They ran out of the gazebo in the centre of the park, flying toward us. Mom, Dad, Damien, and Charlotte watched as the girls launched themselves into our arms. I spun Ronan around while Easton pretended to toss Aria in the snowbank.

"Why so late?" Damien grumbled, always the grouch.

"One of the faucets in the bathroom at the Sunrise cottage burst, so we had to do a quick plumbing job," I answered, setting Ronan down.

"Did you fix it, or do we need to call a plumber?" Damien's scowl increased. I knew he was taking on that stress.

"We'll probably want to call a plumber, just to make sure," I replied.

"Better to deal with it now than have a bigger, messier, more expensive situation on our hands later," Dad said, clamping a hand on Damien's shoulder.

"Can we go for the carriage ride now?" Aria demanded, interrupting the terse conversation.

"Sure thing, sweetpea," Damien said, his voice softening in a way it only ever did for his girls and Charlotte. Everyone else got the grumpy version of Damien. I didn't mind, it was his nature, and besides, those girls deserved the softest version of him.

Our group started walking toward the edge of the park, where the carriages were.

There was a bit of a lineup, but that was common. People swarmed to Hartwood Creek the entire month of December to look at the beautiful light displays, shop the historic downtown core, and experience horsedrawn carriage rides from Stonewood Farm.

Stonewood Farm had been operating for two generations. My great-great aunt started it with her husband, Oliver Stone, in the nineteen thirties. They were a well-established equestrian facility with an indoor arena, sand ring, grass ring, obstacle course, and trails.

The farm was located northwest of Whimsical Woods Resort, and they provided and ran the horsedrawn carriage rides at the resort over the winter holidays and March Break. They also offered discounted packages for resort guests for trail rides and beginner horseback riding lessons.

"Hey, Tabs. Fancy seeing you here," I joked, spotting our cousin Tabitha ahead of us in the line with her kids. The baby boy she was holding whirled around to look at me when he heard my voice, giving me a big toothy grin. "Where's Parker?"

"He's getting hot chocolate for the girls," Tabitha answered, tilting her head in the direction of her twins. Tabitha's girls were standing in front of her with another little girl, Nix's girlfriend's daughter. When the three of them caught sight of Aria and Ronan, they went to go play in the snow together.

"Are Sage and Nix here too somewhere?" I asked, looking around as discreetly as I could for Nellie. If Sage was here, Nellie probably would be too.

"Yeah, they're here. Nix, Sage, and Nellie went with Parker to the café."

I nodded.

"Is Uncle Bob driving tonight?" Damien asked from behind me.

Our aunt and uncle, Tabitha's parents, still ran Stonewood Farm, along with the help of her siblings. Tabitha used to work there too, before she and Parker got married and had a family. Now she focused on raising her kids, although she'd occasionally help at the farm and for events.

"Nah, Rob forced him to take the night off, so he's driving one of them. Lucy's driving the other one. It was looking like we were going to have to bring in the third and interrupt Dad's night off, but it's slowed down a bit and people don't seem to mind the wait." Tabitha explained, referring to her brother, Robert, and her sister, Lucinda.

There were probably about fifteen people ahead of my cousin, which meant we'd be standing for a bit. My mom asked Tabitha how her mom was doing, and Tabitha happily filled her in.

Easton had spotted some friends, so he'd gone over to chat with them while Damien and Charlotte watched as the girls played in the snow. Damien had his arms wrapped around Charlotte from behind, and he was whispering something to her. It seemed like they were lost in their own little world.

I kind of half-listened to Tabitha and my mom chatting while I kept looking around for any sign of Nellie. I don't know why I wanted to see her so badly again, but I did. After telling Nix about the job posting for an office administrator last night, I'd hoped all day long I'd end up with Nellie's resume in my email inbox, but no such luck. I don't even know if he told her, but I wanted to ask her myself.

It would put Nellie at close quarters with me, but it would

also selfishly help me out. I was already damn tired of office work. We still had the rest of the holidays to get through, and the new year. If I didn't find someone soon, I'd go stir crazy. I dedicated a day every week to payroll in my office, and the rest of the time, I wanted to be outside managing the resort, not stuck in the front office playing receptionist.

Parker and Nix strolled back to join Tabitha; their hands full of to-go cups of hot chocolate from Tout de Sweets. A little way behind them walked Sage and Nellie. My heart seemed to jump in my chest, pumping a little faster as I took her in.

Her dark hair was tucked beneath a warm, red toque. Her black winter jacket was zipped up to her chin, and she had mitts and a scarf wrapped around her neck that matched the toque she was wearing. She didn't notice me at first, not until Parker saw me.

"Noah! S'up, man?" He greeted me. His twins ran up to him, and he passed them their hot chocolates, taking Bryson from Tabitha and passing her the last cup.

Nellie's eyes shot to me the moment she heard my name, then back to Sage. She had a guarded expression on her face. Sage lifted a shoulder, sending her an apologetic look, as if she was saying, *I didn't know he'd be here.*

Was Nellie that pissed at running into me again? What had I done to entice such a negative reaction from her? Had I misremembered our night together? In my memories, we'd both been extremely satisfied, and the chemistry had been downright explosive. But Nellie couldn't seem to get away fast enough the next morning, and she'd bailed on the group breakfast. My ego had taken a bit of a hit, and I spent weeks worrying that I'd creeped her out or that the whole thing wasn't as enjoyable for her as it had been for me.

"Not much, just doing the old Christmas Eve-Eve tradition with the fam jam," I replied, gesturing to my brother's twins. At least one person every other generation had multiple births. Usually twins, but there'd been a few triplets scattered throughout the family tree.

The long running joke was that the love elixir made the Wood and Hartley lines very fruitful.

"Cool, cool. Good night for it," Parker said.

And it was, the weather wasn't too cold, and snow was falling sporadically but gently, making conditions perfect for a carriage ride along the beautifully lit streets of Hartwood Creek.

Some more idle chit-chat later, and the carriages returned. Passengers got off, and the next wave of people went; a group of eight climbing into Lucy's carriage, and a group of six climbing into Rob's carriage.

We all shuffled forward to the start of the line. I moved around the group, coming to stand beside Nellie. "Hey, I wondered if I could talk to you for a minute?" I said to her, ignoring the curious glances of everyone else.

Tabitha was staring at me with an intrigued, almost giddy expression on her face, while Parker seemed mildly curious. Sage looked hopeful, but also like she'd come at me if I said one wrong thing, and Nix had a cautious look about him, like he didn't trust me as far as he could throw me.

Nellie looked guarded. "You're talking now, aren't you?"

"Yes, you are." I said, loving her sass. "Heard you were in the market for a job. Did Nix or Sage get a chance to tell you that we're hiring at the resort?"

"Sage might have mentioned something," Nellie said carefully.

I noticed she wasn't meeting my eyes. She was looking anywhere but directly at me. "Is it something you'd be interested in?"

"I haven't given it much thought," she replied, shrugging her shoulders.

"Well, think about it. We could really use you," I don't know why I was pushing it—hell, Nellie might not even have the credentials for the job. But I somehow knew in my heart it was a good fit: she'd be the perfect addition.

Nellie sighed. "I don't have much experience with office work. I have café experience. I can run a schedule like nobody's business and I'm excellent at event planning, but other than that..."

"We can train you in all that other stuff," I pushed away her concerns with a wave of my hand. "The program we use for booking reservations is straight-forward, it practically does everything for you. And if you're excellent at event planning, you're already an asset to us. We do a lot of events for the guests at the resort. The rest of it is answering emails and phone calls."

Nellie worried her bottom lip, deliberating. She glanced at Sage, and Sage nodded, her eyes wide and eyebrows lifted as if she was trying to convey the message: *say yes*.

"I could give it a try, I guess." Nellie replied, finally meeting my eyes.

An electricity seemed to pass between us when our gazes linked. It surged through my veins and charged my heart with its energy.

"When is the expected start date?"

"Well, ideally we need someone to start as soon as possible, since it's our busiest time of the year. But I know you just got to town and are getting settled, so really, whenever works for you."

I could feel Damien's eyes narrowing on me, and knew I'd face some intrusive questions later about how come I was practically hiring her on the spot, and why I was so nonchalant about when I wanted her to start. I'd been griping about having to run the front office for several days now, and he knew that I'd wanted to find someone as soon as possible to take over.

"I could come in on Boxing Day to check it out and drop off a resume. Other than Christmas Day, I don't have anything going on."

"No big New Year's plans?" I asked, prying a little.

"Not really," Nellie's expression seemed even more guarded, and she seemed to look back at Sage for a rescue.

"We'll probably ring in the new year at Tabitha and Parker's," Sage volunteered. "What are you up to for New Year's?"

Nellie shot her a displeased look.

"No plans as of yet," I said, shoving my hands in my coat pocket to warm them up. "Probably sit around at home."

"You're welcome to join us, Noah," Parker said. "We'll have all the kids, so it's going to be a chill, kid-friendly night."

"Sounds great, I could use a chill night." While I had none of my own, I didn't mind hanging out with kids.

Nellie didn't look ecstatic about the invitation, but before she had a chance to complain, the carriages returned. I made sure to give her space, letting her climb up into Lucy's carriage with Parker, Tabitha, Nix, Sage, and the kids, while I climbed into Rob's carriage with my family.

"What was that?" Damien demanded, shooting me a perplexed look. "You practically hired her on the spot."

"Well, we need someone as soon as possible. She needs a job. Seemed right."

My mom sent me a knowing smile. "Sometimes, you get a feeling about someone, don't you, dear?" she nudged Dad's arm gently. He hadn't been paying a lick of attention to my conversation with Nellie, but he still nodded in agreement.

"Absolutely, your mother's right. When you know, you know."

"If it doesn't work out, Noah can hire someone else," Charlotte interjected, patting Damien's hand as if to reassure him.

Damien drew in a breath, still not convinced I was thinking with my brain. To be fair, I wasn't.

The problem was, I didn't know what appendage I'd been thinking with.

CHAPTER SIX

Nellie

I AWOKE EARLY on Christmas morning to a quiet apartment. It was disconcerting, the silence. I hadn't realized how used to random noises I was until I moved. It was much quieter in the bachelor apartment over Parker and Tabitha's garage than it had been in the basement apartment I'd lived in for so many years.

I lingered in bed for a little while, doomscrolling on my phone while I slowly woke up. I didn't have anywhere to be until later, so I was in no rush to leave the warmth and comfort of my bed.

Usually, I'd guzzle back a couple black teas while I went about getting ready for my day, but since learning about the pregnancy, I'd cut caffeine out. The first week after I'd found out, I had read far too many articles online about pregnancy and endometritis, and I was terrified to do anything to increase my risks of complications. They were already high enough.

It was why I didn't want to be around Noah. Being around him made me think about the possibility of this not working out, and that scared me. I was doing my best to do everything I was supposed to, while not thinking about the pregnancy too much. I was eating all the right food, taking prenatal vitamins, drinking plenty of water, and not over-exerting myself.

I knew worrying wasn't going to help, so I'd done my best to put the whole situation out of my mind and focus on other things; things that I could control, like unpacking and making this place more of a home.

But part of focusing on what I could control also meant finding a new job, and now that I was unpacked, that was the next thing on my to-do list. No matter what the future had in store for me, I'd need a new job to pay my bills and get the hours I'd need for maternity leave.

Again, I thought about Noah's offer to work at his family's resort. If I removed the whole complication of our past and my current situation, I had to admit, it sounded like a pretty good opportunity. It might be office work, but there was always the possibility for other jobs at the resort.

Last night, I'd researched the Whimsical Woods Resort and noticed that in addition to cottage rentals, they ran programs for guests. They needed help in the main office now, but perhaps down the road, they'd be open to me helping run some of the programs—or maybe even creating my own.

My phone started vibrating in my hand, alerting me to the fact that my parents were calling me for their annual Christmas chat. "Hello?" I answered.

"Merry Christmas, Ellen!" my mother said, using my full given name. No matter how many times I'd begged growing up, my parents refused to call me anything but Ellen. "Are you still in bed? You sound half asleep still."

"I'm up, actually!" I replied. "I haven't used my voice yet today. Merry Christmas."

"Oh, good. You don't want to waste the day in bed!" Mom lectured, and I exhaled slowly.

"I won't be. I've got plans later, so I'm about to do a little baking."

"What plans do you have? With a boyfriend, perhaps?" Mom asked, forever inquiring about my relationship status. It bothered her that I never spoke about any serious relationships. She thought I'd have my whole life figured out by now, and maybe be married with a kid or two. After all, she'd been married at my age, even if her and Dad hadn't had me until much later. She'd also had her career.

"No, actually. I'll be joining Sage at her aunt and uncle's house for Christmas dinner. I, uh, moved to Hartwood Creek last week."

"Really?" Mom sounded surprised. "Why on earth would you do that?"

"I liked the town when I visited, and figured it was time for a change of scenery."

"Did you have a job lined up?" Dad asked, ever the pragmatic one. I rolled my eyes, thankful they couldn't see the action.

"Not yet, but I—"

"Foolish to have moved without having a job lined up," my dad interrupted. I could practically hear him frowning. "Does a small town even have employment opportunities for a recreational therapist? You didn't have luck in Guelph."

Dad's comment stung, but he wasn't wrong.

"Do you need money, Ellen? We were planning on sending you a wire transfer as your Christmas gift, but we can send more if you need." Mom added, going straight to assuming the worst.

"It's okay, Mom. I have a lot saved up, and I have an interview tomorrow that looks very promising."

I was only telling her this to appease her, but naturally, Dad wanted to know more. "Where abouts? Not another coffee shop, I hope."

My barista job hadn't been much for them to brag about.

"No, it's for a job as the receptionist at a cottage resort here in town. They offer recreational programs for guests too," I said, hoping that was enough details to satisfy Dad's curiosity and Mom's assumptions. It was.

"Excellent. Good luck, Ellen. Let us know how it goes! Oh, and tell Sage and her family we said hi and Merry Christmas," Mom said.

"I will. It'll be nice to not spend it alone," the comment fell from my lips before I could call it back, and I felt momentarily guilty about it. I tried not to hold things against my parents, especially because I knew they loved me, in their own way.

I don't even think the dig registered, though. My mom went on to talk about their plans for the day, and I let my thoughts drift.

When I was born, Mom was forty-two and Dad was forty-five. They'd been married for twenty years before they had me. I was the only thing in their entire life that was unplanned and unexpected.

My parents were so accustomed to their life as it was, that they never really adjusted to having a child around. Our relationship had gotten better the older I got, because I'd learned what to expect from them and what they expected from me in turn.

They were both in their seventies now. I saw them roughly once a year when they returned for a few weeks in the summer. They'd rent the same fancy cottage up north, owned by their politician friends, and invite me up for a couple of nights.

"The weather is perfect," Mom cooed, bringing me back to the present conversation. "You should really try to come out and visit again, you could use a beach vacation."

"She should focus on finding a new job, Beatrice," my dad grumbled. Yup, he was definitely not impressed with me for my brash decision to move without first securing a job. It was predictable, and shouldn't have hurt as much as it did, but no matter how old I got, my parents' disappointment was difficult to handle.

I sighed. "Dad's right, it's not a good time for me to travel right now," I said. Despite the heaviness I felt, I was thankful for the excuse. I wouldn't be going on any kind of vacation any time soon.

Heck, I had no clue how to even tell them about my biggest predicament. Forget not having a job; I was knocked up.

Inhaling slowly again, I centred myself; I didn't have to worry about that yet. The time would come when I'd have to fess up and admit a night of reckless decisions led to a baby, but that moment wasn't today.

"Well, your mother and I were about to go have breakfast." Dad said, signaling that the call should end.

"Have a Merry Christmas, Ellen. We'll talk soon," Mom added.

"Merry Christmas, Mom and Dad. Talk to you later," I said right before they disconnected.

I sighed. I'd tried once to show them how to FaceTime. I'd even bought them an iPad and set it up for them, wanting so desperately to at least see their faces every once in a while, but they couldn't understand the concept, and had refused to learn.

Sometimes Mom would send pictures over email. I supposed that was better than going a full year without seeing their faces, but it still hurt.

AT FOUR O'CLOCK on the dot, I was walking up the front steps of the elegant white house that Sage's aunt and uncle resided in, holding the gingerbread bundt cake I'd spent the day making and the gifts I'd purchased.

Ed and Emelia's house was only a few blocks away from Parker and Tabitha's place, nestled on a beautiful lot surrounded by tall pines and birch trees. A fresh cover of snow blanketed the yard and rooftop, making it look like the ideal Hallmark movie set.

I rang the bell, and it wasn't long before the door was swinging inward to reveal Sage. She threw her arms around me, hugging me and wishing me a Merry Christmas, and taking some of the bags off me.

Sage led the way into the beautiful house, pausing in the living room to set my bags of gifts under the tree and introduce me.

I'd met Ed and Emelia during my brief visit over Halloween, but I hadn't met any of Sage's cousins or their partners. I greeted Joseph, Livia's fiancé, and Patrick, Madeline's husband, as well as nix and Ed, then Sage put her hand on my elbow and led me down the hall toward the back of the house.

We passed an elegant dining room, the table set and ready for people to gather around. Everything looked so warm and cozy, and Christmassy.

We stepped into the gourmet kitchen, finding Sage's cousins and aunt busy prepping for dinner. The kitchen was stunning. Heck, the entire house was stunning, like it should be featured in a holiday décor magazine. Even the white sand-coloured cabinets were decorated with garland and bows.

Sage's aunt stopped stirring the pot of gravy, turning away

from the five-burner gas stove, and greeting me with a bright smile. "Nellie! It's so good to see you again. Merry Christmas, love!"

"Merry Christmas, Mrs. Alcott."

"Oh, please! Call me Auntie Em," Emelia insisted, waving away my formalities with her hand.

"Okay..." I said, trying to push down the welling emotions that her maternal warmth coaxed out of me. I wasn't used to it, and it made me feel homesick for something I'd never really had to begin with. "Well, thank you for letting me crash your holiday dinner. I brought gingerbread bundt cake," I added, setting the cake down on the granite countertop.

"You are always welcome here, Nellie. And thank you so much, it looks and smells delicious!"

Before I could respond, Emelia was wrapping her arms around me in a hug. For a moment, I didn't know what to do with my arms.

My mother wasn't a hugger, neither was my father. Emelia, however, was a hugger, and she had the strange ability to make me feel comfortable. I found myself hugging her back.

"We are so glad you moved to Hartwood Creek, Nellie. How are you liking it so far?" Em asked, pulling back to study me.

"I'm loving it. My apartment is so quiet, it's a nice change of pace from the hustle and bustle of the city. Plus, the town is so charming in the winter, with the snow blanketing everything. It's like the set for a Hallmark movie."

"Actually, it's been used as the filming location for a few of those," one of Sage's cousins said from the other side of the counter. She had dark hair and a smile as welcoming as her mother's.

"That's Cate, she works in film and has directed a few of those movies," Sage explained.

"That's so neat!" I exclaimed. "I always thought working in film would be a fun career."

"It really is, I love it," Cate replied.

"Our resident celebrity," one of her sister's said, putting her arms around Cate in a hug.

"Oh, stop, Livia," Cate huffed, rolling her eyes. Another Alcott sister leaned against the opposite counter, her hand massaging her protruding belly.

"You're too humble, Cate. Brag a little," she said, her hand still on her stomach. All three women looked like their mother, with their dark hair, bone structure, and sparkling light eyes. Madeline's hair was in a trendy bob while Livia and Cate wore their hair longer. Livia's hair was curly, like Emelia's, while Cate's hair was straight like Ed's and Madeline's.

"What are we bragging about?!" A tall blond said, entering the room with a dazzling smile and an air of chaos. She had the same bone structure as the other women in the room, so I pegged her as the last Alcott sister.

"Jo-Anna, you're finally here!" Madeline grinned as the blond, Jo-Anna, hugged Cate, then crossed over to hug her and greet the belly.

"Yes, your favourite auntie is here, and I brought all kinds of gifts for my new little niece," Jo-Anna cooed, rubbing her hands on Madeline's belly. "Ooh! She kicked!"

"She's been doing that a lot lately," Madeline chuckled.

My throat felt a little tight with the sisterly display of love and affection. Sage wordlessly put her arm around my shoulders, smiling at her cousins while giving me a comforting squeeze.

Sage could relate. Her mother wasn't very maternal, either. We'd bonded over that fact, relating to each other on a deeper level. In Sage, I found the family connection I'd been missing with my own parents.

But Sage had gotten to grow up visiting the Alcott's, so she'd had more exposure to this familial affection. Not to mention, Nix's family was very involved. I swallowed, wondering about that pesky little thing called the future.

"Who wants wine?" Livia asked, holding up two bottles of wine, one white and one red.

"Oh, me. You know I need to drink away the traffic," Jo-Anna chuckled as Livia set to pouring glasses.

"None for me, thanks. I'm off drinking for a bit." I said quickly when Livia went to offer me a glass.

"It's good to do a detox every now and then. I'll join you in not drinking," Sage added.

"You're both braver than me. I cannot face the holidays without a cup of good cheer, if you know what I mean," Jo-Anna said, lifting her wine glass up and taking a generous sip.

"Jo-Anna! Are you insinuating you need to drink to be around your family?" Auntie Em asked, sounding more than a little hurt.

"Of course not, Mom," Jo-Anna answered, putting her glass down and wrapping her arms around her mother. "But it helps!"

Auntie Em smacked Jo-Anna with the dishtowel she was holding.

"What! I'm just saying, it's not always the easiest being around lovey-dovey couples on the holidays," Jo-Anna pouted.

"Hey, I'm single," Cate pointed out, accepting a top up from Livia.

"Yeah, but you're also a fancy film director," Jo-Anna rolled her eyes. "It's not the same as holding a deadend up that's going nowhere." She seemed to look at Sage and me for reinforcement.

"You're not wrong there," I sighed.

"You're both single by choice," Sage pointed out with a

laugh. "Jo-Anna, because she's the pickiest human being I've ever met, and Nellie because—" Sage hesitated, her cheeks colouring.

"No, go on. I want to hear this. Why is Nellie single?" Jo-Anna demanded, her eyes sparkling with mirth.

"I'm picky, too," I replied quickly.

"Sure, we'll call it pickiness," Sage rolled her eyes with a smirk. "You're guarded."

"I am not!" I sent her an affronted look.

"It's not a dig, Nell," Sage assured me. "Lots of people are guarded. Jo-Anna's guarded too; she hides it behind pickiness."

"This is true," Jo-Anna confirmed with a nod. "And I'm not ashamed, either. I'm holding out for that one-of-a-kind love, the kind that Mom and Dad have."

"Aww," Auntie Em put her hand over her heart, noticeably surprised and softened by Jo-Anna's comment.

"Anyway, enough about that," Livia waved her hand, as if warding off the heavy direction the conversation had gone in.

AS I SAT with the Alcott's around their formal dining room table later that evening, I allowed myself to settle into the auras around me. With Em and Ed's girls home for the holidays, the atmosphere was joyous and welcoming. Conversation flowed easily while everyone shared about their lives and the things they were thankful for, or discussed shared memories while talking over each other.

The laughter was so frequent, I couldn't help but smile, even if it made me a little homesick for something I'd never experienced before.

My parents didn't have relatives outside of a few distant

cousins, so holiday dinners were never spent around a huge table with extended family when I was a kid. The house wasn't full of joy as people exchanged gifts and jabs.

On Christmas morning, I would quietly open my perfectly wrapped presents while my parents watched from the couch, sipping their coffees and basking in the knowledge that they'd gotten me everything on my wish list. I would thank them after each gift, and after I'd finished opening them all, I'd give them quick hugs that I always wished lasted longer than a second, and they'd wish me a Merry Christmas then go back to bed for a couple hours while the turkey cooked. I'd play with my new gifts, alone in the living room, secretly wishing I'd gotten the one thing I'd only ever asked Santa for: a sibling, so I wouldn't feel so alone all the time.

"Just think, this time next year we'll have another new addition at our table," Em declared after feeling the baby kick in Madeline's stomach during dessert.

"I can't wait, there needs to be more kids," Daphne piped up from beside Sage. Everyone chuckled, and Nix ruffled her hair. "It's boring being the only kid."

My heart went out at that statement: didn't I know it well. Daphne knew it, too. Before moving to Hartwood Creek and gaining cousins through Nix's side, she'd been the only child. Sage had made a lot of effort hosting slumber parties with Daphne's old school friends, but I knew it wasn't easy for her, that she'd struggled being the younger mom in the group.

I made a promise to myself: that my baby would never know that kind of loneliness I'd grown up with. Even if I didn't have a close bond with family through blood, I'd made my bonds with family by choice strong enough that my baby would never know the difference.

CHAPTER SEVEN

Noah

MY FINGERS RAPPED on the Formica countertop as I waited for the coffee to finish percolating in the coffeemaker. I'd put on a fresh pot, anticipating Nellie's arrival. I'd already had several cups, but that wouldn't stop me from having another.

I'd barely slept the night before. After returning home from Christmas dinner at my parents' house, I'd been unable to think about anything else but seeing Nellie today, and about how badly I wanted her to take the job.

I'd already decided I'd be offering it to her, regardless of her experience. My gut told me it was the right thing to do, and not because it would put her at a closer proximity to me.

Damien and Charlotte had overseen hiring Jeannine, and clearly, that hadn't been the right move. I was sure that had I been there during the hiring process, I would have known she wasn't a good fit for the resort.

My gut feelings about people were pretty accurate, and my gut feeling upon meeting Jeannine hadn't been a good one. Ignoring the fact that she was always hitting on one of us—and it really didn't matter which one of us—she made frequent mistakes, and I didn't like her tone with the more difficult guests. She was also notoriously bad at the laundry portion of the job.

We had a lot of cottages, which meant we had a lot of laundry to switch over, even on a day-to-day basis. House-keeping did what they could to stay on top of things, but a lot of the laundry fell on whomever was in the office.

I took a deep breath, reminding myself that my days of worrying about what Jeannine was or wasn't doing were over. The next person we hired would be competent, I was sure of it.

The bell above the office door chimed, alerting me to the arrival of who I hoped was Nellie, and not Easton poking his nosey head in.

I left the staff room kitchen to see Nellie standing in the doorway and holding a folder in her hands. My breath caught as I observed her taking in her surroundings. She'd styled her hair in loose curls. She'd kept her makeup minimal and seemed to be dressed to impress in office-appropriate dress pants and a blouse.

"Morning, Nellie. Hope you had a good Christmas?" I said once I'd found my voice.

"Hey, yeah. It was good. Hope you did, too," Nellie replied.

"I did," I scratched the back of my neck, needing to do something with my hands to control the sudden urge to touch her. "Well, let's get to it, shall we?"

I led the way into the dining room. It was where staff ate their lunch, and where we hosted our staff holiday parties and appreciation days. We also rented it out to guests if they needed a bigger spot for family functions while in town. It was decorated for Christmas, with a large tree in the corner near the stone fireplace. Stockings hung from the mantle, which was decorated with a heavy garland.

"Make yourself comfortable, I'll be right back," I gestured to the table that I'd set up for our interview. The employee binder was there, along with the pamphlets I'd printed off about our resort. I went into the staff kitchen to grab the pot of coffee and the tray with creamer, sugar, and two mugs.

"Oh, you didn't have to do that," Nellie said with surprise when I carried it in and set it down.

"Trust me, after yesterday's festivities, I need it," I laughed it off, pulling my chair out and sitting down. I poured myself a coffee, keeping it black but adding a couple scoops of sugar. I went to pour her some, but she shook her head.

"Er, no thank you. I don't drink coffee," she said, and I nodded in understanding.

"So, let's get to it, shall we?" I said, lifting my mug and taking a sip.

"Shouldn't someone else do the interview process? Given, things?" Nellie frowned, a little crease between her eyebrows appearing.

I knew she was insinuating that the night we spent together would somehow influence my decision in hiring her. Maybe she was right, but she was also wrong. If my gut told me it wasn't the right fit, I'd listen to it.

The problem was my gut was already screaming at me that this was the best fit.

"I can remain professional," I assured her, lifting a brow as if to ask her if she could. Her frown vanished, a determined look sparking in her eyes as she lifted her chin.

"Right then," Nellie nodded, then drew in a breath and opening the folder in front of her. She pulled out a stapled printout of her cover letter, resume, and references, holding it out to me. "Although I don't have any official experience in office administration, I have extensive experience with making schedules and all but running the café I used to work at. I also graduated top of the Recreation Therapy program I took in college."

Both my brows lifted this time, impressed. I looked down at her resume, eyes scanning as I quickly read her cover letter and flipped it over to her work history. She'd spent over eight years at her last job, so she was a loyal employee. That was a huge bonus.

"The office administration part of this job is the main focus, but it's fairly easy to get a grasp on. We use a user-friendly booking system for reservations, and the computers do most of the work there. Other than answering and returning calls and emails and dealing with guests when they come into the main office, you'd be responsible for staying on top of laundry, washing the linens and towels, and folding them, putting them away for the housekeepers. You'll also be asked to do light cleaning around the main building. The bathrooms, staff room, dining room, etc. You'll also be expected to help decorate for the holidays and put away decorations after."

"Seems easy enough," Nellie nodded.

I slid the pamphlets over to her. "Whimsical Woods Resorts is one of the best places to work locally. This resort has been in my family for generations, and we take care of our employees. When you work for us, you are part of our extended family."

An undecipherable look passed in her eyes as Nellie looked down at the pamphlet, but it was gone before I could figure out what it meant.

"How much do you pay?"

"Nineteen twenty-three per hour to start, with a raise after the probation ends," I answered. I knew it was above average.

"And, um, how long is your probation period?" Nellie asked.

"Three months. Partway through that time, we'll have a meeting and discuss how things are going."

Nellie nodded. "And what's the policy about time off? If I need to go to a doctor's appointment or something?"

Something about her question had my intuition prickling, but I kept my expression neutral. "If you need a day off for a doctor's appointment—or something—give me enough notice to make sure we have the front office covered. You get six unpaid sick days, and we accommodate legitimate medical absences."

Nellie pursed her lips and nodded, looking back down at the pamphlet.

"Are you looking for full-time or part-time?" I asked.

"I'm looking for a full-time position," Nellie answered, glancing back up at me.

"Good, we are looking for full-time help," I sat back in my chair and lifted my coffee, taking a sip of it. "When can you start?"

"As soon as possible," she replied.

"How about today?" my lips kicked up in a half smile.

Nellie frowned again, that little crease reappearing, making me want to lean forward and massage it away. I didn't. "Don't you need to contact my references?"

"We're desperately in need of a new office administrator, the faster we can get you to start, the better. I'm a pretty good judge of character, and I know Nix is, too. I'm confident your references will check out."

"Well, how do you know I want the job?" Nellie challenged, tilting her head.

"You're here, aren't you? Unless you just wanted an excuse to see me again..."

"Hardly," Nellie scoffed. "I'm not sure this is a good idea," she gestured between us.

"Ah, I see. Well, if you'd have too much trouble keeping your hands off me, I understand."

"I didn't say that," Nellie's frown deepened. "I don't know if I can work in an environment with you with our past. It's awkward, isn't it?"

"Aside from teaching you the ropes, you won't see much of me. My usual job description involves me being outside, doing maintenance. Or locked in my private office, doing payroll." I leaned back, considering her. "Besides, I don't think our dynamic feels awkward at all. Do you feel awkward, or uncomfortable?"

"No, but..."

"Then it's settled. We'll keep things professional between us. I know you need the job, and you know I need the help. It's a win/win."

Nellie's gaze held mine. "Alright, Noah Wood. If you're offering, I'll accept the job."

"Oh, I'm offering alright," I said. "Let's do a tour, then you can come back here and fill out the employee paperwork."

NELLIE

NOAH'S INSINUATION that I couldn't keep my hands off him made me want to prove him wrong, and I found myself accepting the job offer before I could really think things through. Not that there was much to think through: I needed this job, I needed to replace my income and start banking hours for maternity leave.

I was too much of a chicken shit to mention my predicament to Noah. I didn't want him to know, and I didn't want my situation to either be the reason he gave me the job, or the reason I didn't get the job. I knew I couldn't hide it from him forever, but that was a problem for another day.

After the tour finished, Noah led me back into the dining room and left me alone to fill out the paperwork he'd need to process my hiring. Once I was done, it was almost time for lunch. My stomach grumbled, and I was starting to feel nauseous. I hadn't expected to be there all day, and I was starving. Apparently, if I didn't snack regularly, my morning sickness revved up.

I was rooting through my purse for the dreaded ginger candies when the scent of cheese and pepperoni reached me. Looking up, I caught Noah walking into the room with a couple of pizza boxes.

"I had Easton go pick up some pizza," Noah said, setting the pizza boxes down on the table. "I realize you probably weren't expecting to spend the day here."

"Oh, thank you. That's...kind of you." It was hard to be irritable about pizza, and since I hadn't expected to be hired on the spot or start working immediately—I hadn't exactly packed a lunch of my own.

"Like I said, we look out for our employees," Noah winked, the action sending a strange sensation to my belly. He was undeniably attractive, it was why I'd fallen so eagerly into his bed all those weeks ago. But in addition to his handsome looks, he was charismatic and considerate. A dangerous combination if I ever saw one.

It's why I'd hesitated at first about accepting the job. Noah was dangerous in a way I couldn't even articulate to myself. But despite that danger, he didn't make me feel uncomfortable. If anything, I felt relaxed around him, like I was where I was supposed to be. That was also a dangerous feeling to have, especially given the secret I was keeping from him.

I drew in a breath and smiled. "Well, thank you again. I've finished the paperwork," I told him, collecting it in a neat little pile and handing it to him.

"Perfect. Forgot to mention you get a half hour unpaid for lunch, starting at eleven thirty. Everyone eats around the same time usually, in here. So, the rest will be along shortly."

"Okay," I nodded, trying to stifle a yawn. Noah caught me, and gave me a small smile, opening the pizza boxes and pushing them closer to me. One pie was a meat lovers dream, while the other was a basic cheese and pepperoni.

"If you want to call it a day after eating, you're welcome to. I fully understand that you weren't planning on starting today."

"I didn't have anything else to do," I shrugged, helping myself to a cheesy slice of pepperoni pizza. "Might as well get paid for my time. Wait, I am getting paid, right?"

"Yup. Your first official workday started the moment we shook on it. I'll show you how to fill out the time sheets after lunch, then we'll get started on teaching you how the booking system works and how to put together guest packets for check-ins."

"That sounds good." I didn't have any plans for the after-noon, and the pizza would fuel me for a couple hours more.

I didn't want to go home yet, I knew I'd end up thinking about what a stupid choice it was for me to accept this job. What was done was done, and I'd rather focus on learning what was expected of me, than sitting around beating myself up for saying yes.

"Great." Noah sounded relieved. I got the sense that he was

eager to pass off the office duties to me as soon as possible. He'd mentioned his usual jobs were maintenance and payroll.

Noah set my paperwork aside and pulled out a seat, sitting down across from me. Before I had time to worry about eating lunch alone with him, the bell to the main office chimed and two people walked into the dining room.

I recognized them as Noah's brothers, both from their family resemblance to Noah, and from the other night at the park.

"Nellie, meet my brothers. That scowling, scary looking fellow is Damien, although don't let his gruff exterior fool you, he's a softie at heart. The one grinning like an idiot is my younger brother, Easton. And yes, he's an idiot."

"Hey, newbie," the younger brother said, his grin widening as he helped himself to a slice of pizza. "Welcome to the ranks. I'm not an idiot, and I'm also not at all surprised Noah hired you on the spot."

"Easton, knock it off." The older brother said, his scowl deepening. I got the not-so-subtle impression that Damien wasn't thrilled with my presence, but I shook it off when he gave me a forced smile as he grabbed a slice.

"Noah's been whining for days about having to cover the office," Easton chuckled. "I'm impressed with how quickly he managed to find someone to fill the role."

"It just worked out like that," Noah interjected, giving me a soft smile. "We're lucky that Nellie was available to start so soon."

Damien grunted, going over to one of the other tables to sit while Easton took the chair beside Noah. Easton opened his mouth, about to say something, when the bell chimed again and two older women walked in.

"Nellie, this is Rhonda and Denise, our head housekeepers. Rhonda and Denise, this is Nellie, our new receptionist."

The women both smiled in greeting. "Hello," the one on the right said. I wasn't sure which one, but never-the-less, I smiled in greeting.

"Nice to meet you all," I told them.

"There's plenty of pizza left, ladies. Help yourselves," Noah said.

CHAPTER EIGHT

Noah

THREE HOURS LATER, I watched from the window in the office as Nellie's car pulled out of the small parking lot by the main building.

I'd spent the afternoon teaching her how to use our booking software. She was a quick learner, and she picked up on it faster than Jeannine had. She just had to work on her confidence when answering the phone. All and all, I was impressed with her—and not just because she'd left a lasting impression on me weeks ago. It felt right, having her around, and that settled the restlessness that had taken hold of me since the night we'd spent together.

Hiring her had been more of an on-the-spot decision than Damien would have liked. As expected, I heard all about his reservations when I'd gone out to ask Easton to go pick up the pizza from Pizza Picasso. He would have rather the two of us had sat down and gone over her resume, called her references, then offered the job to her.

He felt like my hiring her on the spot was a desperate move, and maybe it was. Maybe I was desperate to have her around, and desperate to get out of the office. All those things could be true at once, and they were.

I had seen the hesitation on Nellie's face when it came to accepting the job. I wouldn't jeopardize things by acting on my residual feelings from the night we spent together, especially not now. Maybe down the road we could revisit that night, if she ever gave any indication that was what she wanted.

The back door beeped, signaling someone was entering through the laundry room. A few moments later, Damien appeared in the office.

"I'm leaving now. Pathways have all been shoveled and Easton's finishing up putting sand down."

"Alright, sounds good." I nodded.

"How'd it go with the new girl?" he asked, lifting his chin toward the front desk.

"It went well, considering it was her first day and all."

"It shouldn't have been," Damien grumbled.

"Are you still pissed that I made an executive decision?" I challenged.

"Kind of, yeah. What if she's a thief? Or a terrible employee?"

"I doubt she would have kept her previous job for eight years if that were the case, Damien." I rolled my eyes at his dramatics. "She only left that job because she moved to Hartwood Creek."

"Yeah, well. Maybe she had a prior record that her former employer was okay with, but that wouldn't fly on a family resort," Damien was grasping at straws, and he knew it.

"Well, good thing she's on probation, right?" I pointed out.

Damien didn't look any more appeased by that reminder. I sighed. "I'm still planning on calling her references, but relax. She's capable, and I have a good feeling about this."

"Your 'good feeling' better not be in your pants," Damien grumped, shaking his head as the door to the laundry room swung open behind him.

"Oh, are we talking about good feelings in pants?" Easton chimed in, a devious look on his face. "Not exactly workplace appropriate conversation material, brothers."

"I thought you were leaving?" I asked Damien, irritated.

"I am," Damien said, heading back out through the laundry room. We often parked in the back lot, to keep spaces free for guests out front.

"He's in a mood," Easton said, watching our older brother storm off and slam the door behind him.

"When is he not?" I retorted, roughly pulling out the chair and sitting down. We answered phones until five during the week. Easton leaned against the front counter, a bemused smile on his face.

"So, the new girl is pretty hot. Is that what's got Damien pissed? He thinks you hired her because she's good looking?"

"He thinks I rushed into hiring her without doing my due diligence of checking references, but she's a friend of Sage's and has Nix's approval. I'm not worried about the references."

"Yeah, fair enough. Rumour has it, though, that she's a former hookup of yours."

"What rumour?" I scowled, pissed off that my private life was even up for discussion. Normally, I didn't give a shit what people said about me or my former encounters with women.

"Hey now, I'm not going to reveal my sources. I'm just saying. Maybe Damien has a tiny reason to be worried you hired her for an alternative purpose," Easton replied, making a pinching motion with his finger.

"Oh yeah? Do you think that too?"

"Personally, I told Damien you'd be hard pressed to find a local woman around our age that you hadn't slept with."

"Fuck off," I growled, chucking my water bottle at him. Easton caught it with ease and laughed.

"You both need to lighten up," Easton chuckled, tossing the water bottle back. I caught it and frowned. "Anyway, I'm off. Got a hot date tonight."

"Surprised you can find someone to date that I supposedly haven't slept with," I grumbled.

"It's definitely not easy, I had to go to Springwood," Easton teased with a smirk, and darted back into the laundry room before I could whip the water bottle at him again.

Easton's comment got to me more than it should have, and it wasn't like he was wrong. I kept things easy and casual, always. I didn't do commitment. So why was his flippant remark settling like lead in the pit of my stomach?

NELLIE

"I KNEW you'd get the job!" Sage said, the excitement evident on her face. She'd been at Tabitha and Parker's when I got home, picking Daphne up from a play date with the twins, and had all but bombarded me in the driveway when I pulled up.

"Yeah, it's great. Except for the whole..." I gestured to my midsection.

"We'll figure that out later," Sage waved my concerns away with her hand. "The important thing is that you have a job! You're employed! We should celebrate."

"I'm going to eat something and crash. I'm tired."

"The first trimester is an energy suck," Sage nodded sympathetically. "How about this Friday we go out for dinner?"

"Sounds good," I nodded, fighting off another yawn. "Tell Daphne I said hi."

"I will," Sage gave me a quick hug.

We parted ways, with me going up the stairs to my apartment while Sage walked back up to Tabitha's to collect Daphne. Normally, I'd have tried to spend some time with Sage and her daughter, but I was so exhausted.

I opened the door, walking inside to my new place, and couldn't even feel a sense of pride over what I'd accomplished in the span of a few short weeks. I was too tired. All I wanted to do was go to bed, but it wasn't even five yet. I knew I needed to force myself to eat something and try to stay up until at least seven.

Em had sent me home with a lot of Christmas dinner leftovers, so I didn't have to cook anything. I heated up a plate of turkey, potatoes, stuffing, and carrots, then sat down on the sofa in my living room.

I ate dinner while I mindlessly watched reruns of Friends, barely paying attention. It was both my comfort show, and the show I put on for the background noise. My thoughts kept drifting back to the unexpected day I'd had.

Being around Noah had been...nice. I didn't know how else to describe it. I hated that I felt so comfortable around him, even when I was keeping such a huge secret. I knew I was going to have to have a conversation with him sooner rather than later, but I worried about what that would mean for me job wise.

If I could make it through the probation period, he couldn't fire me over it. Not that I thought he was the kind of person to do that, fire an employee for being pregnant, but he might not be thrilled about potentially being the father.

I didn't know for sure, and I didn't want to blow up Noah's life, or my own for that matter, on a hunch. Even if he was the father, I wasn't expecting him to step up and be a parent. Noah had consented to a night of fun, not a lifetime of raising a kid.

It was me that wanted this baby, even if I hadn't expected to have it.

THE NEXT MORNING, I arrived fifteen minutes before my shift at eight. I had packed myself a lunch and snacks for the day. I'd also brought my large water bottle to keep me hydrated, and several bags of decaffeinated tea.

I was expecting to see Noah waiting for me in the front office, but to my disappointment, he wasn't there. Instead, a woman with strawberry blond hair tied back in a ponytail was manning the desk.

"Good morning, you must be Nellie! I'm Charlotte," she said, standing up when I walked into the office. "I'll be helping train you this morning."

"Okay, great," I said, pushing away the disappointed feeling and putting on a smile.

"Did Noah show you where you could put your stuff yesterday? I know it's been a kind of whirlwind twenty-four hours for you," Charlotte chuckled.

"Yeah, he did," I replied. "I've never been hired on the spot before. Feels good for the ego."

"I bet it does," Charlotte's laugh was light and airy, and her smile was friendly. "I'll let you get settled. You've still got some time before you're officially on the clock."

I nodded my thanks, disappearing long enough to put my

lunch in the refrigerator and hang my coat up on the row of coat hooks in the laundry room.

There was a bulletin board beside the back door with timesheets for employees. A new one had been added, with my name printed in barely legible scrawl. Yesterday's hours were already filled out, so I wrote the time I arrived today on the sheet then joined Charlotte back in the office.

She smiled as I walked over and pulled out the computer chair beside her. The receptionist's desk was essentially a long counter that spanned almost the entire length of the front office, dividing the small shop area from the workspace. A half-wall built to match the front paneling of the desk blocked off the laundry room door.

There were two computers and two phones on the main desk. On the far wall, behind the receptionist desk, was a built-in shelving unit with filing cabinets galore. One of the cupboards housed all the keys to the cottages, condos and outbuildings.

The main office's small shop didn't sell much, just merchandise like sweaters and T-shirts, water bottles and hats, all with the Whimsical Woods Resort logo on it.

"So, Noah said he gave you a crash course in the booking system yesterday, and showed you how to ready guest packets for check-ins?" Charlotte asked.

"Yes," I nodded. Noah had given me a bit of a run down yesterday of how things worked, but I was far from confident about managing it on my own. I hoped the training period lasted a little longer than a day.

"Okay, great. I guess we'll kick things off by showing you how to check voicemails," Charlotte smiled.

"Sounds easy enough," I said once she'd walked me through how to check voicemail messages.

"It is. A lot of people call after hours with booking

inquiries, so we ask that you stay on top of answering voice-mails and emails. Inquiries lead to bookings, and we want those," Charlotte said. "The first thing you do each morning should be to check voicemail messages and write down who you need to call back."

Charlotte put me to work, allowing me to take down the messages on the notepad by my phone.

"Great! Now we're going to start calling those people back," Charlotte smiled once I'd finished. "We also get a lot of inquiries throughout the day, so it's important to stay on top of things. I'll handle the first one, then you can try."

"Alright," I nodded, trying not to let my nervousness show. It was new-job-jitters. It'd been such a long time since I'd had to learn a new job. I was confident that I could do it, but it'd take some getting used to. It was a totally different vibe than being a barista at a café.

CHAPTER NINE

Nellie

"DON'T STRESS! I know it's not easy learning a new job, but you're doing great!" Charlotte assured me an hour later, after I'd screwed up the summer rates on a phone call.

"I guess I have a hard time with getting things wrong," I sighed. I could run the café with my eyes closed, but this was a whole different kettle of fish.

"It's only your second day, and there's a lot to memorize. We have different rates, depending on the season." Charlotte gestured to the stack of binders beside me on the desk. "These binders will be your lifeline for the next little bit. Full disclosure, I rely on them sometimes, and I've been here for a few years."

"Okay, that makes me feel a little better."

"Did you want a coffee? I'm going to go make a fresh pot," Charlotte said, standing up and stretching a little.

"Oh, I'm okay. I might make a tea in a bit," I answered.

"Ah, a tea drinker. You'll fit right in with Mama Wood. She loves her specialty teas! She probably still has a stash of good ones in the kitchen cupboard. I'll put the kettle on, too, for you."

"Thank you!"

"No problem, you keep reading those binders, and I'll be right back."

Charlotte left the office, leaving me alone for a couple minutes. I took a deep, cleansing breath, reminding myself that Rome wasn't built in a day. A lot of aspects of this job were easy, it was remembering all the small things.

Before I could start reading, the dryer chimed, signalling that the cycle was complete. I stood up and made my way into the laundry room, ready to switch the load and start folding.

The back door beeped as someone opened it. I looked over, my heart fluttering when Noah stepped inside. He was dressed warmly in a winter jacket, his long hair pulled back and tucked beneath a black hat that had the resort logo on it. He blinked away the snowflakes on his lashes, almost seeming to freeze when he saw me.

Dimples on his cheeks appeared when he smiled, his eyes lighting up. "Hey. How's it going?"

"Pretty good," I replied, although it seemed I'd suddenly forgotten how to fold a fitted sheet.

"Here, let me help you with that," Noah chuckled, moving over to assist me.

If he weren't technically my boss, I'd snap at him that I could figure it out myself, but he was my boss, so I let him help me. Our fingers brushed against each other as we folded the sheet together, a current sparking between us—likely from the static of the sheet, but Noah swallowed hard, as if affected.

"How's your day going so far?" he asked, his blue eyes lifting to meet mine. "Charlotte teaching you the ropes?"

"Yeah, she's great. It's going well. Lots of stuff to learn, but I like a challenge."

"Good, there's lots of challenges around here for you," Noah said, his voice deeper than usual.

Before I could respond, Charlotte walked into the laundry room, probably looking for me.

"Oh, hey Noah! I put a pot of coffee on, should be ready in a couple of minutes." Charlotte said.

"Great, we'll need it."

"Kids Club not going well?" Charlotte asked, her voice sympathetic.

"Oh, that's fine. Those high school students we brought in are a lot of help," Noah answered. "It's cold and snowing, and the family in the Pine View cottage is keeping Damien on his toes."

"The Miltons? Uh oh. What's going on? We haven't heard any complaints from them yet today."

"That's because they keep pulling Damien away from shoveling. They couldn't figure out the coffeemaker, then they complained about the toaster not toasting properly. Not sure why they'd go to the grumpiest of us with their issues, Damien hardly has the customer service skills to manage their complaints. But he's trying."

Charlotte smiled, her eyes softening. "Well, I can go check on things if you'd like to help Nellie manage the front for a bit."

"Yeah, I could do that," Noah said, his gaze coming back to me.

The butterflies in my stomach fluttered—or was that morning sickness?

Charlotte put on her coat and outdoor boots and headed out the back door.

"So, the Miltons sound like they have a bit of a reputation?" I asked, continuing to fold the last of the sheets.

"They do," Noah said, tugging his hat off and shoving it in his coat pocket and hanging it up on the coat rack. "They come every winter break, and their favourite pastime is to complain about anything and everything they can. We've got a few repeat customers like that."

"They keep coming back, though, so they must like it," I said, placing the last folded sheet with its match. Once they were neatly piled, I carried the sheets over to the shelving unit to store them by size.

"I think some people don't know how to enjoy themselves, even when they are enjoying themselves." Noah snuck a smile at me.

"Some people enjoy complaining," I said. "We had several customers like that at the café. They were always complaining about something, but they'd come back the next day all the same."

The phone rang in the front office, interrupting our conversation, and we went back into the office so I could answer it. "Do you want me to answer it on speaker phone? That's what Charlotte's been having me do."

"Sure, have at 'er."

It was even more intimidating with Noah standing right over my shoulder, coaching me. I swallowed, answering the call. "Whimsical Woods Resort, Nellie speaking. How can I help you?"

"Nellie, you say? You must be new!" the woman said. She sounded like the friendly grandmotherly type, the cadence and kindness of her voice instantly putting me at ease. I was new at office work, but even in the café, you could always tell if a customer was going to be difficult by their tone.

"I am, it's technically my first day answering the phone," I admitted, smiling.

"Well, I'll go easy on you! It's Georgia Moran calling. I'd

like to pay for our summer stay, please. We always stay for a week in August, in the Lakeview Cottage."

"Can I put you on hold to check the availability for the Lakeview Cottage in August?" I asked, looking at Noah for approval. He nodded, his smile putting me at ease and making me feel like I wasn't completely screwing things up.

"You sure can, Nellie," Georgia Moran said. I pressed the hold button and opened the booking software.

"Georgia Moran and her family come out every year and have for about twenty years now," Noah explained as I clicked over to bookings for the month of August. "They prefer to stay in the Lakeview Cottage, and each year before they leave, they pay a deposit to book it for the following year."

Noah leaned closer to the screen and pointed where Georgia Moran's information was already listed in pink. His rugged scent of mint, pine, and outdoors invaded my senses, making my mouth water. That was one thing I remembered about our shared night together, how good he smelled—and the taste of him.

"Okay, so. I go back on the line and tell her she's booked for the week of August eighteenth?" My brain felt muddled from his proximity, and I tried not to swoon when his minty breath fanned across my cheek.

"And doublecheck her credit card information," Noah nodded, straightening with an encouraging smile.

I did as he requested, somehow managing to pay enough attention to get through the call without any mishaps. Noah moved to sit at the other computer, watching me while I wrapped up the call with Georgia Moran.

"Good job," he praised me, and my thoughts instantly went back to that night, when he praised me for...other reasons. Noah hesitated and seemed to wince, as if realizing the innuendo behind what he'd said.

"Thanks," I said, feeling my cheeks heating. I let my hair fall in front of my face to mask my reaction while I fumbled for my water bottle, suddenly parched. It was almost like by catching a whiff of him, I'd awakened memories of our night together. Which was inconvenient, especially considering he was now my boss as well as potentially the father of my unborn baby.

The web was getting even more tangled, and I didn't know if I could do this. It was only my second official day on the job, and I was already having a visceral reaction to Noah.

A bell chimed from the laundry room, and a few moments later, Charlotte was stepping back into the office, her cheeks rosy from the cold.

"How'd it go with the Miltons?" Noah asked her.

"As expected, everything works perfectly fine. They don't like to do things for themselves. I told them to call the office and speak to me if they had any more concerns, because our mainte-nance guys need to focus on keeping the roads and paths cleared and sanded."

"And how's Damien holding up?" Noah questioned, a smirk appearing on those kissable lips. Just lips, I corrected myself mentally. I couldn't afford to think about Noah's lips as kissable, even though I knew that they absolutely were.

"Much better now," she assured him with a wink before going to the kitchen.

"Charlotte is engaged to Damien, and she's pretty much the only one that can bring a smile to his grumpy face," Noah informed me.

"Does the whole family work at the resort?" I asked, feeling a tug in my chest.

It really shouldn't have been a surprise that Noah's family worked at the family resort, but I guess my main concern had been about how complicated it'd be working with Noah. I didn't even factor in his family's presence. What would they think of my predicament? Sure, they might be a family-first kind of business that normally wouldn't bat a lash at a knocked-up employee, but given the murky circumstances with Noah, this was an even bigger recipe for disaster.

"Pretty much, yes. My parents are retired, but they still help on occasion. Mostly they watch the twins so Damien and Charlotte can work, though."

"Oh right, Damien has twins, too," a sick sensation welled up, and I took another sip of water, hoping to wash away the nausea. "Do, uh. Twins run in your family?"

"On and off," Noah chuckled with a shrug. "Tends to skip a couple generations. My great grandma was the twin sister of Tabitha's great grandma. There were no twins until Damien and Tabitha both had theirs."

I swallowed hard, battling the wave of nausea. Tabitha had twins, Damien had twins—what was the likelihood that I'd end up with twins, if Noah really was the father?

"You okay, Nell? You're looking pale." Noah said, concerned.

"Oh, yeah, I'm fine. Probably need a snack or something, low blood sugar," I stood up abruptly and made my escape into the kitchen. Charlotte was in there, fixing herself a cup of coffee.

"Hey, the kettle's boiled if you'd like a tea," Charlotte said.

"Thanks." The decaffeinated green tea bags I'd brought would probably help with the nausea, but so would some distance from Noah.

I opened the refrigerator and grabbed my lunch bag, found the granola bar I'd stashed inside for a morning snack and took a bite while I grabbed a mug from the cupboard.

"Everything okay?" Charlotte asked as she leaned against the counter and sipped at her coffee.

"Yup, I need a snack and a tea," I replied. Charlotte nodded like she didn't quite believe me. The phone rang again, but before I could scurry off to answer it, Charlotte shook her head.

"I can get this one, you get your tea ready," she went back to the office with her mug, leaving me alone in the kitchen. I took a few deep breaths, trying to centre myself and will away the nausea as I poured the boiled water into my mug.

I left the tea bag in and finished chewing on the granola bar while it steeped. Once I had that bit of food in me, the nausea eased up. I used a spoon to fish the tea bag out and squeezed it on the side of the sink, dropping it into the compost bin beneath the counter.

When I returned to the office, Noah was gone.

CHAPTER TEN

Noah

AFTER NELLIE WENT pale and all but ran off, the spell between us broke as suddenly as it was cast, and I came to my senses. They'd been more than a little out of whack since I leaned over her to help her with Georgia Moran's call.

That was a mistake. I shouldn't have gotten that close, shouldn't have let the strawberry scent of her hair draw me in. I shouldn't have been paying such close attention to the way her breath caught at my nearness. I shouldn't have been wondering if she'd been thinking about our night together, too.

I definitely shouldn't have put my arm so close to her to needlessly point out the reservation on the booking software. Nellie had eyes; she could find it herself.

But I hadn't been in control of myself. I'd had to force myself to step away and sit down, giving us the space we needed.

I suited up and went outside, needing the fresh air to snap me back into reality.

It was cold and snowing lightly. The perfect weather for ice fishing, ice skating, and tobogganing.

Walking aimlessly toward the frozen lake shore, I hoped the cold air would jolt me back to my senses. I needed to get my head on straight, but Nellie's presence skewed my sensibilities. I had no choice in my body's reaction to her. It'd been that way ever since the first night I met her.

The night of the Witches' Ball, I'd noticed Nellie the second I arrived. She was in the middle of the dance floor with Sage and our other friends, her back to me—her body moving in perfect time to the music. The short skirt of her costume put all her incredible assets on display, her well-toned glutes and her killer legs that left me panting. Half the dress was made to look like a doctor's jacket with green spills on it, while the other half was a brown suit dress style, strategically torn.

When she turned, her ample breasts stole my attention. I wanted to bury my face in them, which was a roguish thought to have but my physical attraction to her had been like a strike of lightning.

I caught a glimpse of the half of her face not obscured by the purposely grotesque Jekyll makeup and contact lens, and it was evident that beneath the special effects makeup, she was hot. Then she caught me checking her out and flashed me a smile, and I was hooked without reservation. I felt the overwhelming need to get to know her.

She looked like my kind of fun, and as the night progressed she proved that she was. The moment my hands went to her waist when we started dancing, I felt the thing between us brewing. By the end of the night, our desire for each other was boiling over.

We took shot after shot, letting the liquor drive us closer

and closer together, until we were all but entwined on the dance floor, until I was whispering in her ear that she should come home with me. And then she did.

That night had left more of a mark on me than I ever could have imagined.

The cold bite of winter wind did nothing to douse the flames of the memory. My desire for Nellie still lived beneath my skin, and it took her returning for me to acknowledge it.

But I couldn't just act on that desire the way I had that first night. Nellie had been very much into it. There had been no walls erected around her for me to climb over, no boundaries in place.

Even with those walls—those boundaries—I knew that if Nellie gave even the slightest indication that she was interested in a repeat, I'd happily get on my knees for her.

NELLIE

SAGE TEXTED ME AFTER WORK, asking if I wanted to meet her at The Hungry Hub for dinner. I managed to score a parking spot out front. When I entered the bustling diner, I spotted Sage sitting in a booth near the back.

She waved at me, and I made my way over, past tables full of patrons. The delicious smell of food wafted over, and my mouth started to water in anticipation. My appetite was out of control. I was always hungry, and if I wasn't, I was nauseated. It was one extreme or the other.

"No Daphne?" I asked as I removed my jacket and hung it up on the hook on the wall that divided the booths.

"She's having a sleepover with Riley."

"Oh fun!" I sat down across from her. Sage was looking at me with a huge, knowing smile. "What?" I asked.

"Just wondering how today went," Sage said innocently. She picked up her glass of iced tea and took a sip, waiting.

The server appeared before I could answer, so I made her wait a few minutes longer while I gave her my drink order. "Could I get a Sprite, please?"

"Absolutely!" the waitress, who's name tag read "Emily", said. "I'll be right back with your drink and to take your order."

I opened the menu in front of me, perusing it while Sage tapped her foot with impatience. "What are you getting?" I asked her without looking up from the menu. I was trying to buy myself some time before the inquisition.

"The cheeseburger. It's to die for and I've been craving it all week. The home fries are also good."

"Hmm, alright. I'll take your word for it," I closed the menu and sat back, lifting my eyes to look at her. She arched a brow at me, her impatience clear as day. "It was fine. Sort of."

"Sort of?" she leaned forward, but before I could start filling her in, Emily was back with my Sprite.

"Have you ladies figured out what you'd like to order yet?" she asked, setting the cold glass down in front of me.

"We'll both have cheeseburgers and home fries. Extra pickles and onion on mine," Sage answered.

"Oooh, extra pickles on mine too, but hold the onion," I made a face. At Sage's questioning look when Emily left, I explained. "Onion is one of those foods that isn't sitting well with me. Even the idea of onions makes me feel sick."

Sage nodded with understanding, then leaned forward. "So, spill it. What do you mean it's 'sort of' fine?"

"I don't know," I sighed, not really wanting to get into it all in the middle of a diner on a Friday evening. I didn't know anybody around me, but they probably knew Noah, or the

Wood family. "I really didn't think this through. I mean, his entire family works there, so I'm not just keeping a secret from him, I'm keeping a secret from them all. What if they hate me for it?"

"They're not going to hate you for it," Sage rolled her eyes at my dramatics. "The Woods are easy going, family-oriented people. They'll understand your...situation."

"Sure, but that's providing he's not the, *you know*," I looked around, checking to see if anyone was listening in, but the patrons around us all seemed pretty involved in their own meals and conversations.

"Whether he is or isn't the father, they won't fire you for being pregnant, Nellie. First of all, it's illegal to fire someone for being pregnant in Canada. And if you really wanted to know for sure, why not tell Noah and ask if he'd get a paternity test?"

I chewed on my bottom lip thoughtfully. "I'm not sure I want to know."

Sage studied me for a moment, considering. "Why not?"

"Because, then I'd have to let him be a part of everything." I shifted uncomfortably in my seat, suddenly feeling like I wanted to crawl out of my skin.

"And that makes you feel...vulnerable? Scared?" Sage was trying to understand, but good luck to her, I didn't even understand it.

"I guess? I don't know," I shrugged. "I always got the impression Noah was a player who didn't want to settle down. Me strolling into town and saddling him with a kid is the opposite of his preferred bachelor life."

"There's a chance he's the father, and I think you need to give him the opportunity to be there if he wants to. You can't make that choice for him," Sage replied.

"I know, but..."

"You work for him now, Nell. You aren't going to be able to hide this forever, and he's going to have questions."

I frowned, not liking what she said, even if it was the truth. At some point, Noah was going to notice my growing belly. Surely, he'd put two and two together and suspect.

"I'll tell him...eventually," I managed to say. "I want to wait until I'm absolutely certain it's going to stick."

My inkling told me it would, that in one year's time, I would be the mother to an actual human being, but my fears told me to not get my hopes up. It was early, and so much could go wrong.

It was better to not get my hopes up too much, at least not until I was well into my second trimester.

Noah

I AVOIDED Nellie as much as I possibly could for the next two days, seeing her only when I stopped back in to scarf down some food at lunch and fuel up on coffee.

I kept my distance, letting Charlotte take over on training while I busied myself with the mountain of maintenance tasks outside, or the pile of paperwork in my office downstairs.

To appease Damien I called her references, and I wasn't surprised at all to hear her former boss Sal thought she'd been an asset to the team and was missing her something fierce. However, I was surprised when Sal asked after Nellie's "family emergency" that drove her to up and leave Guelph on such short notice.

I couldn't avoid her anymore though; we needed to discuss her hours going forward. It was the holidays, and I'd needed the office help to get through our peak season, but we typically didn't work New Year's Day. Unless a guest had an issue that needed to be dealt with immediately, the office was closed.

When I walked into the office around lunch on Sunday, Nellie was there checking out one of our weekend guests. Charlotte was sitting in the far computer chair, letting Nellie handle the guests by herself, but there if she needed to help.

I debated on leaving, but something kept me rooted in place. Maybe it was seeing Nellie fitting into the fold like she belonged there, like she'd always been there.

Jacob and Marcia Wallace were gushing about how wonderful their stay had been. Marcia was looking at Jacob with stars in her eyes, and Jacob looked at her as if she hung the moon. The Wallace's had gotten married at our resort twenty-five years ago, and they came back every year to celebrate their anniversary.

They always got our couples package, which included a weekend rate at one of our one-bedroom cottages with a Jacuzzi tub and a romantic gift basket with specialty cheese and crackers, meats, a couple bottles of a chocolate stout from the local brewery, and a bottle of wine from the local winery.

"We'll have to hope the brewery has more of that stout in stock before we head back to the city," Jacob said, putting his arm around Marcia and tugging her closer.

"And the Amour Au Chocolat was delicious. Is that new?" Marcia added.

Nellie looked a little confused, so Charlotte stepped in. "Yes, the Amour Au Chocolat is newer, made by a local winery on the outskirts of town."

"I love how you support local businesses," Marcia gushed.

"We love spreading the love." Charlotte winked.

We had arrangements with the owners of Elderberry Amour Winery and Klaus Bauer, the owner of the brewery to include their product in our couples package. Klaus had been supplying The Choco Temptation stout for a few years now, but the Amour Au Chocolat from Elderberry Amour Winery was a recent addition.

Both the stout and the wine included Hazel Hartley's Spanish chocolate, one of the rumoured ingredients in the infamous Tout de Sweets love latte. The Love Latte was infamous in town for getting couples to "fall in love" with each other. It was a latte variation of the original Hartley love elixir spell that had been handed down from generation to generation.

My ancestor's older brother, Alexander Wood, consumed it when Morgana Hartley slipped him a pastry with the elixir baked into it.

The Wood's were related to the Hartley's through Alexander and Morgana's marriage, which meant my family was related to the mischievous Hartley triplets. Alice, Dorothy, and Betty were technically distant cousins through marriage. My brothers and I had grown up hearing all sorts of lore about that side of the family, so we knew to stay away from any whispers of the love elixir and made sure we were aware of anything sold in town that contained it.

I'd always veered far from anything containing the love elixir, so I'd never tasted Amour Au Chocolat or the Choco Temptation myself, although I've been known to trick the occasional friend into drinking it.

Like Nix, when he was trying to set up the perfect first date with Sage. I'd recommended Choco Temptation with a straight face. Nix had been all but in love with Sage since we were all gangly teens, and I'd wanted to help him out a little, and see how well the Choco Temptation worked on couples who hadn't yet proclaimed their love for one another.

I had no doubt the Choco Temptation helped push things along for Nix and Sage, solidifying their inevitable fall. I had zero regrets playing matchmaker there, but I'd let the Hartley triplets take the credit for that one.

"We're happy to hear you enjoyed yourselves," Nellie said, printing out copies of their receipt. "Would you like to book next year's trip now?"

"Why not! We know we'll be coming back," Marcia giggled.

Nellie smiled and set to booking their next reservation for the same cottage a year from now. Jacob and Marcia paid the deposit, took their receipt, and all but skipped off together.

Happy guests were what I loved to see, but more than that: I loved to see Nellie in action. She was a natural and looking at her, I couldn't help but feel she fit in perfectly here. That should scare me, but it didn't, it balanced me.

"Mind if we have a chat before lunch, Nellie? I want to go over your hours for next week."

"Yeah, sure," Nellie looked a little nervous, but she smiled at me and made tentative eye contact, something we'd both been avoiding the last few days. I felt a jolt, like there was a live wire connecting us and surging with energy every time her gaze connected with mine.

"Normally, we wouldn't have asked you to work weekends, but I wanted you to get a few consecutive days in a row for training, and your work week is interrupted next week due to New Year's Day. So, you'll be off Tuesday and Wednesday, and back at work Thursday and Friday. After that, your typical work week will be Monday to Friday, 8 a.m. until 3 p.m. with a half hour for lunch. Sound good?"

"Yes, that sounds great," she nodded.

"Speaking of lunchtime! I'm starving," Charlotte said, standing up and stretching. "Watching other people work makes me hungry, and Nellie's been doing everything!"

"I haven't been doing everything," Nellie said as she stood, smoothing away imaginary wrinkles on her black dress pants. The action caused my gaze to follow the path of her hands along her upper thighs, and I had to force myself to look away. Charlotte caught me and smirked. I narrowed my eyes at her.

The three of us made our way into the kitchen to grab our lunches, then to the dining room to sit down. Nellie and Charlotte sat beside each other, and I sat down across from them. The pull to be near Nellie was difficult to ignore when she was right there. But I'd promised her we'd keep things professional between us, and I didn't want her to regret taking this job. I had to keep telling myself she was here for the job, not me.

A few minutes later, Damien joined us. Easton was off today, and so were Rhonda and Denise.

Damien strolled over to Charlotte and pressed a kiss to her lips and sitting down across from her beside me.

"I texted your mom, the girls are having so much fun tobogganing with your dad." Charlotte told him, holding up her phone so he could see the picture Mom must have texted her.

"If you guys want to head out after lunch, you can. We have two more checkouts to deal with."

I was sure after watching Nellie with the Wallaces that she had checkouts covered, and if she didn't, I'd be nearby to help.

Damien's brow furrowed, and he sent me a distrustful look. I cocked a brow back at him, challenging. Did he think I was going to spread Nellie out on the desk and have my way with her? I mean, the idea of having my way with her again was enticing. If I wasn't careful, I'd get myself worked up over the thought alone, but I wouldn't do that when I'd promised not only my brothers I'd keep it professional, but Nellie too.

It bothered me that he thought I'd treat Nellie with anything less than the respect she deserved. I wasn't used to feeling so bad about my previous reputation, or wishing I could change the narrative on it, but I found myself wishing I could do that.

Maybe my reputation had everything to do with Nellie's reluctance toward me. The thought coiled around me like a dark shadow.

"What do you think, Nellie?" Charlotte asked our new employee, tilting her head.

"It's up to you, I'm okay either way," Nellie replied. She was careful not to look at me while she took a small bite of her pasta salad. I didn't like that she avoided gazing at me; I wanted her eyes on me all the time.

"Hmm. Well, I do think you can handle those checkouts without me hovering over you. Besides, Noah's right, Damien. It is quiet today, and we're not supposed to get more snow until tomorrow."

"Alright, sounds good."

Damien and Charlotte left after they finished eating, and I tried to ignore the quiet tension that bloomed the moment Nellie and I were alone. I played it off, smiling and doing what I could to put her at ease.

We made it through the rest of the day without incident. The pull between us was a constant companion, and I didn't know if it was due to my realizations or Nellie's avoidance, but it sat heavily between us.

Finally, the workday was over. I felt like I was suffocating on all the things I knew I couldn't address. Nellie wasn't ready to hear it, and I didn't want to push her or make her feel uncomfortable.

Nellie gathered her things while I locked up the back door, then we left through the front office, and I locked that too. I almost started walking her to her car, then realized that wasn't a very boss-like thing to do.

"Well, have a good night." I said, awkwardness sweeping

over me as she paused, her gaze gliding to me. My hands itched to reach out and touch her, but I kept them at my side, sliding them into my coat pockets.

"You, too. See you later, Noah," she smiled tentatively as she opened her door and climbed in.

I tried not to watch as she drove off.

CHAPTER ELEVEN

Nellie

BEFORE I KNEW IT, it was my unofficial weekend, and New Year's Eve morning. I woke up around ten to a text from Sage, asking if I wanted to come by Tabitha's and help set up for the New Year's party.

Parker and Nix had taken the kids tobogganing to get them out of the house for a few hours so Tabitha and Sage could get everything ready. I'd been invited to join them, so I got up, ate some breakfast, then had a quick shower and dressed in my most comfortable pair of sweats. I'd get dressed and worry about my makeup closer to the party.

Tugging a baggy old college sweater over my head, I grabbed my phone and walked over to the house.

I rang the doorbell and waited a couple minutes until it swung open. Tabitha smiled at me; her dark hair piled in a messy bun. She led the way through the beautiful home, leading me to the open-concept kitchen and dining room at the back of the house.

Sage was sitting at the island, a cup of coffee in front of her. She was dressed similarly in comfortable clothes.

"What did you need my help with?" I asked, glancing around the immaculate kitchen. It seemed like everything was already good to go. The place sparkled from top to bottom. Christmas decorations were still up, along with a banner in the dining room that said, *Happy New Year!*

"Oh, we didn't really need help," Tabitha giggled.

"Technically, the guys didn't have to take the kids out of the house at all. We thought it'd be nice to get a little break for a couple of hours." Sage said.

"The holidays are long with all three of them home," Tabitha added. "Without them underfoot, we had the entire main floor cleaned in under an hour. We're having a coffee break, then we're going to focus on the playroom. Can I get you a coffee?"

"Nellie's a tea drinker," Sage interjected before I had a chance to reply.

"Oh, no worries! I've got green tea and English Breakfast."

"English Breakfast sounds good," I answered, pulling out the stool beside Sage. I'd been trying to limit my caffeine intake, but the odd cup of caffeinated tea wouldn't hurt.

While Tabitha put on the kettle, I took in my surroundings and studiously ignored Sage—who was trying to catch my eye. The kitchen was beautiful—with green-painted cabinets and marble countertops. Big windows overlooked the backyard, framed by casework that extended to the countertop. "I love your house, it's beautiful," I told her.

"Thank you! We've had a lot of fun renovating it," Tabitha smiled at me over her shoulder. "Did you want something to eat? We've got fresh croissants Nix and Sage brought from Tout de Sweets."

"I'm addicted to the cheddar croissants," Sage admitted, sliding the box toward me.

"Fine, twist my arm why don't you," I joked, taking one. Even though I'd had some toast earlier, I was feeling a little hungry again.

Sage smiled, her eyes bright and excited. The kettle finished boiling, and Tabitha poured the hot water into a cup, placing it in front of me and leaning against the counter. "So, I have something I wanted to tell you both." Sage announced once I'd started chewing the delicious croissant.

"Oh?" Tabitha asked, feigning surprise. "And what's that?"

"I'm pregnant."

"I knew it!" Tabitha screeched.

Sage's announcement caught me by surprise, and I swallowed the bite of croissant I'd taken a little too quickly. I wasn't full-on choking on it, but it got caught in my throat enough to make me have a bit of a coughing fit.

Concerned, Sage patted my back while Tabitha grabbed a glass of water, passing it to me so I could wash it down. Once I'd finally caught my breath, I whirled on her. "You're pregnant, too? How far along?"

"About eight weeks," Sage said sheepishly. The same as me. My jaw dropped, astonished, all I could do was stare while Tabitha raced around the counter and gave Sage a congratulatory hug. "Pretty sure we conceived the night of the Witches' Ball. Things got a little heated afterward, and we weren't as careful as we usually are."

"Why didn't you tell me?" I demanded.

"You had so much going on already," Sage replied, taking my hand. "I was going to tell you at dinner the other day, but then the Hartley triplets came in and, well." She shrugged.

I nodded, remembering. They'd arrived after Emily brought our meals to us, and we stopped talking about anything we didn't want them to overhear. Which meant the topic of pregnancy—both of ours, apparently—was off the table.

"Wait, too? Who else is pregnant?" Tabitha asked.

"I am," I said, still in shock.

"*You're* pregnant, too?! Oh my gosh! This is amazing!" Tabitha gave me a hug. "How far along are you?"

"Apparently, we might have both conceived on the same night," I answered.

"Isn't that the night you went home with my cousin?" Tabitha tilted her head, studying me. "Oh my god, is Noah the father?! Does he know?"

My stomach twisted with anxiety. I hadn't meant to spill the beans on my situation, but I'd been so thrown off by Sage's, it hadn't even registered that I'd blurted it out.

"I don't know for sure if he is, but no, he doesn't know I'm pregnant. And I'd like to keep it that way. For a bit, anyway. I'm still trying to wrap my head around it."

"Understandable," Tabitha nodded, pulling out the third stool and sitting down. "Woah. This is a lot of information to take in, ladies."

"Yeah, it is," Sage giggled. "I've been dying to tell you both, but I was trying to wait until the twelve-week mark. I managed to avoid drinking at Christmas, but I knew tonight was going to be difficult. I figured I'd tell you both now, and Nellie and I could drink the alcohol-free champagne Nix picked up for the kids. He grabbed us a few extra bottles."

"Oh, that's good." I eased up a little. I'd been worrying about that, especially if Noah showed up like he'd mentioned. The last time we partied together, I tossed back shots like it was my full-time job and ended up going home with him. Surely he'd get suspicious if I didn't drink this time.

"Dammit, that's right. I thought we were all going to get drunk tonight," Tabitha pouted a little.

"You won't be drinking alone! Lilah, Ophelia, Annalise, and Isla are all still coming, right? And the guys will all be drinking."

"I know, it's fine, I was kidding. I'm not concerned about that at all. I'm actually really happy for you—for the both of you," Tabitha said, putting her arms around both of us. "There's nothing like being pregnant with your bestie, and having a baby close in age to your bestie. Then your babies can be besties, too!"

"I know, I've been so excited about that," Sage admitted, catching my eye. Hers were watering a little.

I was still stunned, but a good, happy stunned. "Well, congratulations. Guess this explains why you had all those nasty ginger candies in your purse." I chuckled, wiping a tear from my own eye.

I'd already been looking to Sage for guidance, what with her having been through this once with Daphne. Now that I knew we would be going through the same things at the same time, I felt less alone—and, dare I say, more excited.

"Sure does," she giggled. "I'm surprised you didn't guess it sooner."

"Yeah, I'm sorry for being so self-involved."

"Oh stop, you've been preoccupied with your own news, and with moving here and starting a new job. You've got so much going on!"

"Nix knows, right?"

"Yeah, he's the only one so far. Other than him, nobody knows about Nellie, and nobody knows about me."

"So, this is in the vault. Got it," Tabitha nodded, mimicking closing her lips with a zipper.

"At least for a few more weeks, and until we can figure out for sure if Noah's the bio dad." Sage glanced at me.

"How do you plan on figuring that out?" Tabitha asked, turning her head to look at me.

I shrugged. "I guess by a paternity DNA test when the baby's born?"

"First she has to tell Noah she's pregnant, and that he might be the father," Sage interjected unhelpfully.

"Well, why don't you tell him? I think you can do DNA tests while you're pregnant."

"For starters, I don't want to freak him out before I absolutely have to," I replied, as a sudden wave of nausea hit me. I couldn't tell if it was morning sickness, or situational sickness. Either way, I tried to swallow the bile. "It's still early, and like Sage, I want to get into my second trimester before I cause a massive upheaval."

"Nell took a job as the receptionist for the resort, and she's worried about rocking the boat too early." Sage offered, rubbing my back as if she could feel how nauseated the whole situation made me.

"Well, who wouldn't be worried! They just hired me and I'm bringing so much drama to the table," I groaned, putting my head down against the cool countertop. It helped a little, but I still felt sick.

Tabitha murmured with understanding. "I can understand waiting a few more weeks. But don't be afraid to tell him. I know my cousin would want to be a part of this, and I can promise you; you won't lose your job over it. My aunt would never allow them to fire an expectant mother."

I nodded meekly.

"And now that Tabitha knows our secrets, she'll be able to help cover for us tonight!" Sage gently nudged my arm with her elbow.

"We start by removing the non-alcoholic labels from the champagne bottles." Tabitha said, nodding with determination.

SEVERAL HOURS LATER, I was standing in Parker and Tabitha's kitchen again. This time, I was dressed up in my favourite red wine-coloured ribbed knit mini dress, black nylons, and knee-high boots. The dress had a square neckline and long bell sleeves, and it was very form-hugging, but also stretchy.

I'd curled my hair and went for a more glam look with my makeup and included a bold lip in my favourite cream lip stain in Cherry Moon. I knew I looked good, but more importantly, I felt good for the first time in a while.

Parker and Tabitha's extensive list of guests started to arrive around nine o'clock. There were a lot of unfamiliar faces, but Tabitha and Sage took the time to introduce me to each one of them.

Tabitha's friends arrived first: Annalise Hastings, Ophelia Loucks, and Isla Bennett. I'd met them briefly at the Witches' Ball, but that night was a bit of a blur for a lot of us, so Tabitha happily reintroduced everyone.

Ophelia arrived with all the fixings for sangrias. At the Witches' Ball, she'd dressed as a shield maiden, which had really suited her long, curly red hair, porcelain complexion, freckles, and hazel eyes. She made herself at home and started making sangrias, talking about her job as a destination wedding consultant.

Annalise had walked in with her. I remembered her from her name. She worked at her family's bed and breakfast, the

Hastings Inn—which had hosted the infamous Witches' Ball that had changed the trajectory of my life.

Isla was a freelance graphic designer who worked from home. She brought her husband and their two kids, ages four and two. Her kids immediately joined the others in the play-room, where the kids were having their own little shindig.

Once the first batch of sangrias were made, Ophelia tried to coax me to try some, but Nix came to the rescue with glasses of non-alcoholic champagne for Sage and me. I told her maybe later, but hoped she'd forget as the night went on.

The other Hutchinson brothers, Preston and Paxton, showed up with their arms full of champagne, and treats for the kids. Sage and I were tucked away from prying ears, and I couldn't help but lean toward her.

"So, are you terrified there's more than one bun in the oven, what with all the dang twins in this town?" I whispered, lifting my non-alcoholic champagne glass in hello to Preston and Paxton.

"A little, but I think it'd be kind of fun to have twins," Sage whispered back.

"Speak for yourself," I shivered with fear at the idea. Sage could find it fun all she wanted. She had the extra hands. I'd be on my own and completely new to everything, so the idea of having two babies depending on me terrified me even more than one baby.

Parker's friends came soon after. Kaleb and his wife, Donovan Ashe, Auston Robertson and his girlfriend Lilah Willard with her daughter Riley.

Finally, Noah arrived.

I hated the way my breath caught when he walked in the room. I hated the way my heart stuttered when his eyes imme-diately found me. I hated the way I reacted to that smile—that devious smile.

I also hated how good he looked. Dressed in a black leather jacket, a dark blue Henley, and dark wash jeans. He'd even gotten a haircut for the occasion, his usually long locks cut short on the sides and longer on top, styled to look effortlessly tousled.

I loved his longer hair, but this haircut had me longing to run my hands through it and see if I could tousle it more.

"Woah, you cut your hair!" Parker said, doing a double take when Noah walked over.

"Yeah, I, uh, figured it was time for a change," Noah said, and something about that statement charged something within me.

I lifted my glass of non-alcoholic champagne to my lips, just to give myself something to do.

CHAPTER TWELVE

Noah

MAYBE SHOWING up to a New Year's party after getting a haircut for the first time in well over a decade was a bad call. I'd been thinking about getting a haircut for a while, but something prompted me to go downtown yesterday.

I ended up popping in to Get Buzzed to pick up some of their salon special shampoo and conditioner—I refused to use anything else—and there was a cancellation. I figured it was a sign and decided to let Booker Smith chop it off.

However, I wasn't anticipating everyone else's reaction. Parker's in particular.

"Man, you haven't cut your hair since your last serious relationship!" Parker said, loud enough for Nellie to hear and look over with an unreadable expression on her face.

"It's just hair, dude," I was trying not to show how irritating Parker's remarks were. I hadn't even clued in about the timeline, but he was right: I hadn't cut it since my last serious relationship—in high school.

Tabitha seemed to sense my frustration, and like the angel she was, she floated in to distract him.

"Noah! I'm glad you're here," she said, slipping her arms around Parker's waist. "Are Damien, Charlotte, and the kids coming? I mentioned it to them, and they said they might. I know Easton's probably at The Quarter Lounge looking for his next conquest."

"They were going to, but the girls came down with a cold, so I think they're going to stay in now," I replied.

"That's too bad, I hope they feel better!" Tabitha said.

FOR THE FIRST FEW HOURS, Nellie tried to keep her distance from me. Any time I got too close, she'd find somewhere else to scoot off to, or get absorbed into someone else's conversation. I was trying to play it cool, so I let her play her avoidance game.

But I'd seen her reaction when I walked in. I'd seen the way her eyes had heated as she looked at me. I'd seen the interest reflecting in her irises, and the way she immediately tried to stomp it down.

I knew I was playing a dangerous game myself. She was, after all, an employee. But I wasn't planning on luring her to a dark corner to have my way with her. I wanted to talk to her, see if she felt the spark that flickered between us, or if it was all in my head.

Finally, at a quarter to midnight, I ended up beside Nellie. The table was full of snacks and other delicious spreads, and she was loading a plate with some desserts while talking to Auston's girlfriend, Lilah.

I was feeling hungry, too, so I'd gone over to get a plate while talking to Donovan about some home renovation project he had gone on. I tried my best to listen, but I was distracted merely by her presence, and trying to play it cool and unaffected.

Nellie and I both reached for the same cannoli at the same time. Our fingers touched, and a small shock at the contact had Nellie pulling her hand away like it'd electrocuted her. "Sorry," she said quickly.

"No worries, it's all yours," I nodded at the pastry.

Nellie's eyes narrowed, dropping down to my lips until she forced her gaze away.

"How chivalrous of you," she said, fighting a smile.

"I am a gentleman," I said. I'd won an almost-smile from Nellie, and it made me feel like I could walk on water. I could hear Donovan chuckling beside me, and I discreetly elbowed him to shut him up. In my peripheral, I watched him shake his head and walk off, leaving me to it.

"Uh-huh," Nellie replied, seemingly biting her tongue on a further retort. She knew exactly how ungentlemanly I could be. Judging by the pinkish hue on her cheeks, she was thinking exactly that.

Auston came up behind Lilah, putting his arms around her and whispering in her ear. "Come dance with me."

Lilah let out a giggle, setting her plate down to follow Auston out to the living room. Tabitha and Parker had pushed their furniture back enough to make space for a little dance floor.

The big screen in the living room was tuned in to CBC so we could all watch the countdown in various capital cities across Canada, but the volume was muted, and music was playing loud enough to hear and dance too, but low enough that conversations could still happen.

Nellie watched Lilah and Auston dance with a small smile on her face.

I inclined my body toward her. "Are you having a good time?"

"Oh yeah, the party is great," Nellie answered, looking around at the room full of people and revelry.

"T-minus ten minutes!" Tabitha called out as she made her way around the room with a tray, offering glasses of champagne to everyone for the countdown. Nix carried another tray, and he stopped by long enough to press a kiss to Sage, then headed back out of the living room to get the stragglers in other rooms.

Sage slipped over to where we were still standing by the food table, two glasses of champagne in her hand. She offered one to Nellie.

"Where's mine?" I joked, but before she could reply, Tabitha was thrusting a glass at me from her tray and whirling off. "Wow, fast service around here. Almost makes The Quarter Lounge look slow."

Sage and Nellie exchanged a loaded look with each other. Sage tilted her head, and Nellie shook hers, taking a small sip of her champagne. I felt like they were having a whole conversation without a word, and that conversation was about me. I couldn't tell if that was a good thing or not.

"Can you guys speak out loud, you're making me feel insecure."

"You? Insecure?" Sage laughed. "I didn't think I'd see the day."

"I'm flattered you think I'm so self-assured that telepathy wouldn't make me uneasy."

Nellie snorted, her smile lighting me up inside. "I'm sure you'll be okay," she patted my arm gently. "Besides, who's to say we were even talking about you?"

"Oh, now that hurts my ego."

"It could use a little deflating," Nellie said cheekily, and Sage nodded in agreement. "It's abnormally large."

"Oh, you remembered?" I teased back with a smirk.

Sage was taking a sip of her champagne and ended up spitting a little out when she saw Nellie's vexed frown.

"Three minutes!" Tabitha called out over the din.

"It's impossible to forget how big your ego is, it takes up all the oxygen in the room," Nellie retorted, rolling her eyes.

I chuckled as Nix made his way back through the crowd, his focus on making it to Sage. It didn't matter that Nellie was teasing me, so long as I had her attention.

"It's nice to know I left you breathless," I murmured into her ear.

Sage was watching the two of us with a delighted glint in her eyes, although she was trying to look irritated on behalf of her friend—whose skin I was definitely getting under, judging by Nellie's annoyed expression.

"One minute!" Tabitha shouted again, and someone, probably Parker, turned the music down so the countdown could be heard on TV. Everyone chimed in, the entire room counting down with the timer on the TV.

"Five, four, three, two, one: HAPPY NEW YEAR!" everyone shouted, and the room erupted in cheers as couples came together to share their first kiss of the new year.

Everywhere I looked, couples were kissing and embracing. Nellie froze beside me, as if she didn't know where to look either. We ended up looking at each other.

That simmering connection between us zapped and

sizzled, and I swallowed hard. I wanted to kiss her more than I wanted to take my next breath, but she'd shown little interest in me romantically.

Nellie bit her lip, and my eyes tracked the movement. "Happy New Year, Boss."

Her calling me Boss rocked me with the reminder that I couldn't blur these lines.

"Happy New Year, Nellie," I said gently. "I hope all your dreams come true this year, and more."

Her eyes misted, and she smiled. "Thank you, Noah. The same to you," she said, then set down her glass and wove around the couples.

NELLIE

I HAD to get out of there. I grabbed my coat and slipped out the front door, intent on getting back to the security and safety of my apartment.

Not only was I tired—really tired—but with all those kissing couples, I was feeling dangerously close to asking Noah to be my first kiss of the new year, so I wouldn't start the year off as lonely as I'd been the year before.

But that was a dangerous, foolish idea. Especially given the fact that he was my new boss.

Setting aside the mess of him being my boss entirely, the whole baby situation made everything beyond complicated. What if he wasn't the father? I couldn't decide which was worse, the idea that he might be, or the idea that he might not be.

If he was the father, we'd be tied together forever through

co-parenting another human, and that would influence how he saw me.

But all I could think about while I'd stood beside him, with couples all around us counting down the seconds into the new year, was how I didn't feel so lonely with him beside me.

When we'd made eye contact, I felt that undeniable pull that I spent so much time fighting and ignoring. For a second, I'd wanted to stop fighting it and fall into that feeling. I'd wanted his lips on mine, his kiss stealing the breath from my lungs. I'd wanted to see if this thing between us was real, or imagined. I had almost allowed myself to forget everything going on.

Knowing how much I'd enjoyed kissing him before had my mind muddled and my heart aching to connect with him.

I let out a huff of aggravation, walking along the pathway that led to the garage and my apartment. I told myself I could not catch feelings for Noah Wood, not right now, maybe not ever.

It didn't matter how compatible we were in bed, or how my body had bloomed under his expert touch. It didn't matter that I dreamt of that touch, of that feeling, so vividly, I'd wake up aching for him. It didn't matter that the way he looked at me fanned the flames of something that had been burning since the moment we first made eye contact at the Witches' Ball.

I didn't do long term relationships for a reason, and I couldn't try now—not when my focus needed to be on myself and my future.

Thankfully, I made it up to my apartment without anyone noticing I was gone. I locked the door behind me and peeled off my knee-high boots, doing my best to ignore the tight tugging sensation in my heart.

I left the lights off, making my way through the dark apartment to my bedroom, where I changed into a pair of comfortable pajamas and texted Sage and Tabitha, letting them know I was tired and was back home so they wouldn't worry.

Then I crawled beneath my heavy, comfortable comforter and let the tears flow.

CHAPTER THIRTEEN

Noah

AFTER NELLIE LEFT, I wanted so desperately to follow her, to find out what had put that devastating look in her eyes. But I held back, locked in place by her calling me Boss.

I couldn't help but mentally kick myself for hiring her and blurring those lines. But at the same time, I knew that hiring her had been the right move, and that decision had been bigger than the both of us.

I felt this tug toward her, and I wanted to explore it. Boss or no, promises to my brothers or no. I couldn't ignore that tug, that feeling that this was it—she was it. Every second I spent in her company affirmed that feeling, that our souls were somehow connected. Entwined.

I wondered if she felt it too, and if she was fighting it because I was her boss, or if there was something more going on, something I was missing.

But I felt like I couldn't talk to anybody about it. I'd

promised my brothers I hadn't hired her to get her in my bed again, and everyone else thought I was a playboy who had an aversion to serious relationships. That had been true, before Nellie, before that night we'd spent together after the Witches' Ball. One night with her rewired my brain.

Something had awoken in me that night, and at first, I hadn't noticed—or I hadn't let myself notice. I didn't realize until I saw her again that she'd been the last woman I'd had in my bed, and the only one I wanted in there now. Something about her clicked with me.

I knew that was all so heavy, so sudden, for what it was supposed to have been: a casual night between two strangers. But I got the sense that she was so much more than a one-night stand, and I didn't know what to do with that information now that I'd acknowledged it.

The sounds of the party felt muddled, as if I was underwater. I set my untouched glass of champagne down and tried to discreetly leave. Tabitha caught me trying to slip into my jacket.

"Leaving so soon?" she asked, looking disappointed.

"Yeah, I have to be at the resort early," I replied. It was an excuse, and we both knew it. Tabitha tilted her head, looking at me.

Out of all my cousins—and I had a lot of them—Tabitha and I were probably the closest. We were the same age, but beyond that she'd ended up married to my best friend. I'd spent a few years living in their apartment over the garage while my cabin was built.

I knew without Tabitha saying a thing that she sensed something was off with me, like she knew without me saying a thing that something was off.

"I saw you and Nellie talking," she said. "Looked like you guys were getting along."

"I thought we were," I shrugged, looking away from her penetrating blue eyes as I slipped into my boots.

"Give her time. She probably needs to feel more settled here."

Tabitha's advice made sense, but I bristled anyway.

"Don't get any ideas, Tabs. It's not like that," I told her.

Tabitha could be just as bad as the Hartley triplets with her meddling in my love life. She'd tried to fix me up with so many women over the years, I'd lost count. She'd stopped after she realized the most they'd get from me was a casual hookup.

"Oh, I think it's like that," Tabitha smiled. "But I promise, I won't interfere. Whatever's going to happen, will happen."

"Sure, cuz. Well, I'm going to head out. Thanks for the invite, the party was great."

Tabitha hugged me before I could open the door. "Happy New Year, Noah. I have a feeling this year is going to be unforgettable for you."

"And I have a feeling you've had a little too much champagne," I retorted, patting her on the head and releasing her. I turned around and opened the door. "Tell Parker I said bye."

With that, I was on my way out. My gaze went to the apartment above the garage. A part of me wanted to go knock on her door, ask her why she'd run like fire licked at her boots, but I reminded myself that wasn't a good idea. There were no lights on, giving no sign that Nellie was even still awake, or wanting company for that matter.

MY HEAD WAS POUNDING, and it wasn't from a hangover. I hadn't had much to drink the night before, and I'd been in bed by one thirty, but I ended up tossing and turning for hours. I might have finally fallen asleep around six or seven, but when my alarm went off at nine, I felt like I'd been run over by a transport.

I had to go to the resort. I didn't have a choice. We'd gotten more snow again sometime after two o'clock in the morning, and the pathways needed to be cleared for guests. The office was closed, but guest safety was a priority, and Easton wouldn't be functional enough to do it.

With Damien and Charlotte home with both girls sick, that left me. Thankfully, it had stopped snowing, so it only took me a couple of hours to clear and sand the pathways. I'd cleared the parking lot by the front office and the road leading to the resort on my way in.

Once I was finished, I made sure none of the guests staying needed anything and then I headed back to my place.

My quiet, empty place.

I couldn't help but think about Parker and Tabitha's house, how full of life it was, even when it wasn't jammed packed with guests for a party. With three kids, there were always toys laying around, or some sign of kids and family life. It was warm and inviting, and chaotic in a way that made me homesick.

My cabin was sixteen hundred fifty-nine square feet, with three bedrooms and two bathrooms and a cozy loft. It was a blend of modern comfort and classic charm, the windows in the vaulted great room offering me a panorama view of the woods surrounding my little slice of property.

The great room had a woodstove that heated the entire cabin. The primary bedroom also had a vaulted ceiling, and so did the dining room and kitchen area. There was a walk-in closet and an ensuite, and a sliding door that opened onto the back deck from the primary bedroom and a sliding door on the opposite side, in the dining room.

At the front of the house, I had two guestrooms for

company that had yet to see a single guest outside of one of my brothers. The kitchen wasn't massive, but it wasn't small either, it had plenty of storage and counter space. The dining room was separated by an island and had an open concept floorplan with the great room.

Off the dining room and kitchen was a small hallway that led to the front door, the front closet, and the second full bathroom.

Everything was masculine and minimalistic, almost completely devoid of a woman's touch—or personality, for that matter. The only photographs in frames had been gifted to me by my mother, and the only art hanging were paintings of the resort and lake my grandmother had done.

It was beautiful and rustic, and I was proud of it, but right now it was somewhere for me to sleep and eat when I wasn't at work or out. Compared to my cousin's house, and to my older brother's place, it felt sterile, like an updated version of one of our cottages.

I didn't even have a pet. I'd always loved dogs, but I hadn't wanted the responsibility of another living creature. It'd mean I couldn't come and go as I pleased, not that I'd been doing much coming and going since October.

But I was too tired to think about why things had changed. The physical labour of clearing snow had me peeling off my outer layers and heading straight back to bed. I crashed before my head hit the pillow, falling into a heavy, dreamless sleep.

NELLIE

. . .

TEN DAYS HAD PASSED since Tabitha and Parker's New Year's party, since I'd all but run out on Noah after he genuinely wished that all my dreams would come true. I'd worked Thursday and Friday with had the weekend off, which I'd spent catching up on laundry, resting, and reading. Then I was back to work on Monday, and it had been a strange week.

I was on my own a lot in the office, seeing the other employees for only brief periods throughout the day, at lunch or when the housekeepers brought in loads of laundry.

I saw Noah plenty, but he seemed to be keeping his distance from me, too. His smiles were more reserved. I didn't need much help when it came to managing the front office or staying on top of laundry. Any questions I did have, Noah answered with a polite indifference.

I hated it.

I preferred the way he was before, the flirty smiles, the long glances. But it was my fault. I'd drawn the line in the sand by ignoring his flirtatious comments and jokes, by never showing him that I felt something more. I'd made it clear I wasn't interested in even talking to him outside of work, not with how I'd taken off mid-conversation at New Year's.

It appeared Noah agreed that crossing that line wasn't in either of our best interests.

I tried to tell myself that was fine—that was the way it should be, the way it needed to be. It didn't stop the ache in my chest when he was around, but so distant. Still, I put a smile on my face and carried on, throwing myself into doing the best job that I could, especially since I'd need them to accommodate my appointments.

Today, I'd cut out early to make it to Springwood for a 3 p.m. appointment with my new obstetrician. Dr. Kramer was a high-risk OB and wanted to see me every week to ensure that everything was going smoothly. So far, it was looking good, but she warned me that it didn't mean I wouldn't encounter issues down the road. I was still at risk for miscarriage, and I'd be at risk for preterm birth, too.

She'd confirmed that my due date was July nineteenth. I'd be having a summer baby—right smack dab in the middle of peak-season at the resort.

I left the appointment feeling panicked. Noah had told me my regular schedule would be Monday to Friday. I don't know how he would feel about me needing to take an afternoon off every week. I could get a doctor's note, but it'd clue him in on why I needed to go to those appointments. Which meant I needed to tell him sooner rather than later, and that terrified me.

Not to mention, I'd be out for peak-season, and I knew that wouldn't align with what the resort needed from its full-time receptionist.

When I pulled into my designated parking spot at Tabitha and Parker's after my appointment, Tabitha was getting the kids out of the van from school pickup. She had Daphne with her, who immediately ran over to give me a hug.

"Hi, Auntie Nell!" she exclaimed, nuzzling into me.

"Hey buddy, how was your day?" I asked, feeling lighter than I had since my appointment.

One of the best parts about moving to Hartwood Creek and being near my bestie again was moments like this; getting to see Daphne as much as I had before, if not more. Tabitha watched her every day after school while Sage worked at the hardware store.

"It was good! We had a spelling test and I aced it!" Daphne replied, giving me a wide grin that showcased her missing tooth.

"That's awesome! Way to go," I ruffled her hair and looked up to see Tabitha walking towards us, carrying Bryson in her arms. He looked grumpy as all get out, all bundled up in a blanket with his hat on over his ears.

"Feel like coming in for a tea?" Tabitha asked, smiling at me warmly.

"Oh yes! Come inside, we can put on a fashion show for you!" Daphne pleaded, grabbing my hand and tugging.

I didn't have anything pressing to do, and sitting alone in my apartment with my thoughts sounded like a bad time anyway. Tabitha was sweet, and she went out of her way to talk to me each time she saw me.

"Sounds like fun," I said, following Tabitha while Daphne continued holding my hand. The twins had already run ahead and had unlocked the front door, leaving Tabitha's keys in the lock and the door wide open.

They'd taken off their winter boots and snow gear in a whirl of chaos, leaving their coats and snowpants in a pile by the stairs.

"We're working on that," Tabitha chuckled, retrieving her keys, and waiting for me and Daphne to step inside, closing the door behind us.

Daphne removed her coat and boots, hanging her coat up and setting her boots on the rack, then she started pulling her snowpants off.

"Come on, Daphne! Let's get ready for the fashion show!" one of the twins yelled from the top of the stairs.

"Brielle, Bella, before you do that, come put your boots and snow stuff away, please." Tabitha instructed as she freed Bryson from his cozy blanket and warm hat.

"Ugh, fine!"

The girls stomped down the stairs and did as they were told, hanging their coats and snowpants on the hooks by the door and setting their boots on the shoe rack. By that point,

Daphne had finally gotten her snowpants off and hung them up, then the three of them raced back upstairs.

The chaos was a little preview of what was to come, and I loved it.

I followed Tabitha into the kitchen, where she set to filling the kettle and put it on the stove to heat, still holding Bryson on her hip.

"What kind of tea can I interest you in? I have English breakfast, green tea, and I restocked the herbal blend I discovered while pregnant with Bryson. It's a blend of fennel, linden, and cinnamon, and it doesn't have caffeine. It's tasty and it helped relieve some of those pesky early trimester symptoms."

"Oh, I'll try that one," I said. I'd always loved herbal teas, but I was relying heavily on them now.

Tabitha grabbed down two mugs and set them down on the island, then she grabbed the sugar bowl and tea from the cupboard.

"Can I help?"

"I've got it! You relax. I've become an expert at doing everything one-handed. You will too," Tabitha chuckled, pressing a kiss to Bryson's forehead. He giggled and squealed, grabbing at her face and returning the kiss with a drooly one of his own.

I smiled tightly, hoping that was true. Dr. Kramer's cautions still bouncing around in my head.

"Everything okay?" Tabitha caught the strain in my smile, and concern lined her expression.

"Oh, yeah. It's fine, I guess. I had my first OB appointment today. Everything's going well, for now, but the OB wants to see me every week because I'm considered high risk."

"Why are you considered high risk?"

"I have endometriosis," I explained with a shrug. "It puts me at a higher risk of miscarriage or preterm birth."

"I'm so sorry." Tabitha put her hand over mine.

"It's why I didn't want everybody knowing until I'm out of the woods for miscarriage." I sighed.

"That makes total sense." Tabitha nodded, her eyes soft and understanding.

"But I'm going to have to tell Noah soon. I can't expect him to let me take an afternoon off every week without explaining why."

"He'll understand," she assured me.

I sent her a doubtful look, a million worst-case scenarios running through my head.

"It might take him a minute to come to terms with the news that he might be the father, but he'll understand you need the time off and happily give it to you." She said with a wry smile.

"I hope so," my stomach still twisted with nerves. Although Sage and Tabitha both assured me I wouldn't lose my job over being pregnant, I was still in the probationary period. They technically didn't need to give a reason to let me go, they could say it wasn't working out.

Bryson started whining and wiggling, pointing to the floor. Tabitha pressed another kiss to his head and set him down, letting him crawl over to the cabinets. He pulled a drawer open, revealing a collection of Tupperware, and started pulling containers out one by one. Tabitha didn't seem to mind in the slightest.

"Sage should be here any minute," she told me, setting the kettle on a different burner on the stove and grabbing another mug down and moved towards the Keurig. "I figured I'd brew her one too. I'm going to stick to coffee, since that one kept me up all night." She jerked her head in Bryson's direction, who was still happily pulling every single Tupperware out of the drawer.

"Teething?" I asked, taking a guess from his pink cheeks and the amount of drool dripping down his little chin.

"Yup, he's getting some molars. I'll be glad when all his teeth are in! He's much more dramatic about it than the girls were. You'd think two babies teething would be more of a nightmare, but they were easy about it. Bryson, however, likes to make his discomfort known."

"Poor guy," I felt for him, and myself. There were so many facets to parenting that I hadn't even considered yet. A baby keeping me up all night teething was another one of them, but I decided to worry about that in the future. For now, my focus was on how to get those afternoons off and telling Noah about my pregnancy.

"As for my cousin," Tabitha said, grabbing the creamer from the refrigerator. "You're probably making up worst-case scenarios in your head, and I can pretty much guarantee that none of them will come to pass. Noah's great, really. You couldn't have chosen a better sperm donor."

"Potential sperm donor," I reminded her.

"Either way. He's very family oriented. I don't know if you've seen him with his nieces, but he spoils those little girls. My kids all love him, too. Just because he hasn't found the right one yet to settle down with, it doesn't mean he's destined for a life of bachelorhood."

"I don't doubt that he's incredible with kids," I sighed. "I'm worried my current situation will be too much—for us both."

"I promise he'll understand and accommodate your OB appointments. You can always offer to make up the time you'd be missing, maybe offer to come in on the weekend."

"Good call." Bartering time off could work in my favour, especially if I dangled a Saturday morning sleep in for Noah. Not that he seemed to be the type that slept in. He was always at the resort before I arrived and stayed after I left. From what I'd gathered, he was there more and longer than either of his brothers.

"He works hard, and he should take more time off. It's difficult when your family runs it, though." Tabitha remarked as she put the creamer back in the refrigerator. She sounded as if she was speaking from experience. "My family owns Stonewood Farm; there's really no such thing as days off. I'm the only one of my siblings with kids, so I've taken a bit of a step back, but even I go in sometimes to help when they're overwhelmed."

"Oh yeah, I remember Noah telling me that when he was explaining the winter and March Break programs. I guess you guys outsource your horsedrawn carriage rides to the resort?"

"Yup," Tabitha smiled.

The front door opened and closed, and Sage called out. "Sorry for running late! I hope I didn't miss the fashion show!"

"We're still getting ready!" Daphne yelled back from somewhere upstairs.

"Excellent," Sage said as she came into the kitchen. She didn't seem surprised at all to see me sitting at the island. "Hello, hello! Oh boy, what a day. Seemed like everyone in town came into the hardware store."

"Everyone must be starting their New Year's projects," Tabitha said, fixing her coffee. "I made a tea for you, it's that herbal blend I was telling you about."

"Perfect! You are an angel," Sage sank down in the stool beside me and turned to face me. "How'd it go today?"

"It went. Everything looks good, but Dr. Kramer wants me to come in every week."

Sage put a comforting hand on my arm. "That means you'll get to hear the baby's heartbeat more frequently than the average expectant mother," she winked. "How's your pain been?" she added, referring to my endometriosis. She'd offered to come with me to my appointments, but Sage had her own life, and I hadn't wanted to lean too heavily on her. It was something I felt I needed to do myself.

"Not as bad as usual," I replied. With the absence of my monthly, my pelvic pain wasn't as severe as it usually was during my period. I still experienced some discomfort and pain, but it was manageable with the occasional Tylenol and a heat pack.

"That's good. By my calculations, we're officially at the twelve-week mark. When are you going to tell Noah?"

"I have no clue," I replied. My stomach twisted a little at her words. I knew I had to tell him soon, and I would. But I was scared, and it wasn't only the fear of losing my new job holding me back.

"He seemed pretty bummed out when you took off at New Year's," Sage said, taking a sip of her tea.

"He really was," Tabitha confirmed with a smirk. "He left not long after you did."

"Really?" I asked, surprised to hear that.

"Why did you run off? And don't feed me that 'I was tired' bull. I've never seen you move that fast."

"He, uh…" I started, staring intently at my mug. "We almost kissed. I think, anyway. But I called him Boss, and then he told me he wished all my dreams would come true. And I panicked."

"Him wishing your dreams would come true made you panic?" Tabitha asked.

I swallowed hard. "Yeah, because my dreams involve having a baby that might be his. And he looked like he wanted to kiss me."

"He probably did want to kiss you. He wants you; we all saw the way he was looking at you," Sage chuckled.

"He's just a flirt, that's all." I frowned.

"You're right, he is a big flirt, but I noticed he was into you that night in the park. New Year's Eve solidified it. I haven't seen him pay this much attention to anyone since...well, since his high school girlfriend. His first—and last, I might add— serious relationship." Tabitha said.

"What happened?" I asked Tabitha, unable to help myself. I was curious.

"Like most high school relationships, it ended," Tabitha shrugged. "She moved away for college and dumped him. He decided he'd rather play the field than let himself be vulnerable to that kind of heartbreak again."

"Kind of like you, Nell," Sage said, gently prodding me with her elbow. "They really are a match made in heaven."

"You're both getting way ahead of yourselves." I rolled my eyes.

"I know my cousin, and I can tell he's very interested in you." Tabitha smiled gently.

CHAPTER FOURTEEN

Noah

KEEPING my distance from Nellie was a lot more challenging than I anticipated. Of course, I wasn't expecting it to be easy by any means. With her being an employee of ours, I knew I'd see her at lunch and several times throughout the day. But I wasn't counting on how much I gravitated to her, and how hard I'd have to fight myself to keep that distance.

Nellie had picked up on all the roles and tasks of her job with an ease that didn't surprise me, but did disappoint me a little. It was like I'd been secretly hoping she'd struggle, and I'd have to be near her to help. But after the first few weeks, she didn't need much guidance at all.

It was for the best, though. It was challenging being close to her. Every time I smelled her shampoo, rational thought seemed to vacate the premises, and I was inundated with inappropriate urges to reach out and touch her.

I was trying so hard to remain professional and not think

about how badly I'd wanted to kiss her at the New Year's party three weeks ago, when she called me boss and all but ran out on me.

After that night, I made sure to avoid her as much as possible without coming across as rude. I pushed my lunch until later, citing all the maintenance work as my reason for it. Damien and Easton could see right through that, but I didn't care. It was more for my sake. I could feel my resolve weakening.

At the end of the day on Tuesday, my resolve was gone, and I found myself walking into the main office to give her a paycheck.

Cheques were dated biweekly on Wednesdays, and while most of our employees opted for direct deposit, I still hadn't received Nellie's banking information.

I could have left her paycheque in an envelope and pinned it to her timesheet, like I did with pay stubs for everyone else, but I couldn't resist the pull of seeing her again, especially after spending the last day doing payroll in my office downstairs.

Plus...I was getting tired of keeping my distance.

"Oh, there you are! I was afraid I was going to have to come hunt you down before I left." She let out a nervous laugh.

"Everything okay?" I asked, pausing by the counter.

"Yeah, everything's fine," she took a breath, as if bracing herself. Her brown eyes skirting away from me, then she quickly pulled them back. "I have a follow-up appointment on Friday, and I was wondering if I could head out early that day. I could come in Saturday morning to make up for it."

"Of course, you can. There's no need to come in on the Saturday," I said, studying the subtle cues of her discomfort and anxiety. I wondered if these appointments had anything to do with the family emergency her old boss had asked about. "In the future, if you have to schedule any more appointments,

Fridays are usually our busiest day for weekend check-ins, so the beginning of the week would be better."

"Okay, that's totally fair," Nellie nodded, biting her lower lip. "I'll make sure anything I schedule from here on out won't be on a Friday."

I smiled softly at her, hoping to ease her discomfort. "Here's your paycheque." I said, passing her the envelope. "Don't forget to grab me a void cheque from the bank, so we can get you set up with direct deposit."

"Right, thanks," she took it, our fingertips briefly touching until she pulled her hand back.

I could leave. I'd done what I set out to do. But I found myself lingering, wanting to bask in her company a little longer.

"Any exciting plans this weekend?" I asked, leaning on the counter, and shooting her a flirtatious smile.

"Not really. I need to get caught up on laundry and do some grocery shopping." She shrugged, her expression anticipative. "I might do a girls' night with Sage."

"Sounds like my weekend. Aside from brews with the boys Friday night, I'll be doing all the mundane errands I've put off the last few months."

"Fun, fun," Nellie said.

"Maybe I'll see you at the grocery store again," I teased, referring to the last time we ran into each other there when she was new in town, and I had foolishly not recognized her.

"Yeah, maybe. It is a small town," she smirked.

Before I could think of a witty retort, the phone rang, and Nellie set to answering it and booking another reservation for April.

I left her to it, not wanting to distract her further.

FRIDAY NIGHT at The Quarter Lounge, I sat at a table with Parker, Nix, Auston, Donovan, and Kaleb, one of Nix's employees that occasionally joined us. I was nursing a beer, listening to Kaleb recount some hilarious mishap that happened on the jobsite with one of their new employees, and doing my best to not think about Nellie and what she was—or wasn't—doing.

Earlier that afternoon, she'd avoided eye contact with me when I came in to take over the phones so she could leave. She'd thanked me, but there was something concerning about the way she drew into herself. I couldn't help but wonder what sort of appointment she had, and why it'd brought about such tension in her.

If the guys noticed my unusual silence, they didn't call attention to it, and for that I was grateful. But that peace only lasted until Nix, Kaleb, Donovan, and Auston went to lay claim to one of the pool tables when it became available.

Parker cornered me the moment we stood to join them. "You've barely said a thing all night. What's going on, Noah?" he demanded.

"Nothing," I said, trying to brush it aside.

"Don't bullshit me, you've been weird ever since the party. What's up? Are you that pissed I commented on your hair? Cause I'm sorry. Tabitha gave me shit for that. I didn't realize it was such a sore spot for you."

"I couldn't give a fuck about that," I scowled at him. He sent me a pointed look, and I knew my reaction wasn't helping. I sighed. "I'm tired. It's been a busy few weeks at the resort." And it had been. Between the winter storms we'd had, and the fact that we were booked solid all throughout winter break, I'd been spending a lot of time at the resort.

We would be seeing a bit of a decline over the next few weeks as we transitioned into the off-season, and if the weather cooperated, maybe I could dial it back a bit and take a rest, but I really had been tied up there.

I'd been busy before—every peak-season, for that matter, and I hadn't really let myself feel the exhaustion of that. As much as I didn't want to admit it, I knew that a lot of my current exhaustion came from avoiding a certain brown-eyed beauty that had been steadily occupying my thoughts since her return to Hartwood Creek, and my life.

"Okay, well. You know you can talk to me, right man?" Parker asked, putting a heavy hand on my shoulder.

I willed myself not to shake off his touch. "I know, and I appreciate it. But there's nothing to say." I assured him.

"If you say so," Parker said, looking at me as if he didn't quite buy it. "But, I mean, if this was about a certain new tenant of mine..."

"It's not," I all but growled, my eyes narrowing.

"Tabitha seems to think so," Parker raised his hands in a don't-shoot-the-messenger way. "I'm just saying, if it was about a certain new tenant, you could talk to me about that. You could also come 'round a little more. I miss having beers in the garage."

"It's a little harder to do now that I'm not living above your garage," I pointed out dryly. Parker looked a little defeated. "But yeah, I'll try to come around more," I added, feeling a little guilty.

I used to see my friends more than one night every couple of weeks, but when my parents decided to retire a couple years ago, my responsibilities at the resort increased and I pulled back a little. It wasn't intentional, it was a lack of work and life balance. I still showed up to our guys' nights at The Quarter Lounge, but I didn't drop by randomly when I was in town. Usually because I didn't make it to town often.

It'd been different when I lived above Parker's garage. We'd had plenty of beers in his garage, and late night hangs in his backyard by the fire pit. With my cabin so close to the resort, there wasn't much of an excuse for me to be in town unless I was grocery shopping or running errands.

"We miss you," Parker said, trying to shrug it off. "Besides, if you did come around more, you'd see Nellie."

I sighed. Parker knew me better than even my brothers knew me. "Yeah, well. That situation is complicated. She works for me, and she doesn't seem interested in pursuing anything other than a working relationship, and maybe a reluctant friendship."

"I don't know about that," Parker said, taking a sip of his beer. His eyes sparkled like he knew something.

"You guys playing, or what?" Nix called out from the pool table before I could ask Parker to elaborate. The game was set up and they were waiting for us to join.

My friend grinned, like he knew he was leaving me with a thousand unanswered questions, and clapped my shoulder and taking off, leaving me to reflect on his tone and expression.

NELLIE

OUR GIRLS' night in had begun around six with pizza from Pizza Picasso. Then when Nix left, Daphne, Sage and I painted our nails and put on facial masks. Daphne chattered about all the exciting things happening in her world. The little girl talked until her eyes got heavy, then Sage helped her wash off the face goop and tucked her into bed.

We had an impressive spread out for snacking, even though

we'd consumed an entire cheese pizza already. Our usual wine had been replaced with sparkling water, which we drank out of wine glasses—because, well, why not?

"So, have you thought anymore about how you're going to tell Noah?" Sage asked over the movie that we weren't paying attention to. It was mostly on for background noise.

"Not really," I replied. I'd been ruminating about it for weeks now, knowing that I needed to come clean about my situation, but dreading it at the same time.

My inkling told me Noah was it; he was the father, but I also had to acknowledge that could be wishful thinking.

Maybe I wanted Noah to be the father, because of our mutual attraction and proximity to each other. Not that our mutual attraction would make co-parenting a child together easier, but at least his proximity would help. Plus, I knew he'd be a decent father, even if nothing more happened between us.

I barely knew the other prospect, and what I did know about him wasn't exactly positive. He'd left a bad taste in my mouth, and I wouldn't be reaching out him to let him know about the possibility, even if I had a way of contacting him. I didn't know his last name, and I'd blocked and deleted his number after our unsatisfying encounter, when he'd shown way too many red flags.

If Noah wasn't the father, I'd be doing it one hundred percent alone, and I was oddly fine with that. I was more nervous about the prospect that my inkling was right, because it meant I'd have to find a way to share this part of my life with him for eighteen-plus years without allowing the mess of my emotions and feelings get in the way.

It would be better if my inkling was wrong, but that was the thing about my inklings: they were hardly ever wrong.

"Are you still worried you'll lose your job over this?" Sage asked, looking sympathetic.

"Yeah, I am. No matter what, I'm going to be giving birth during the summer. That's peak season for the resort, Sage. They need a full-time receptionist, especially during the summer. And what if I can't work full-time in the coming months? What if I end up on bedrest?" I asked, voicing my deepest concern.

Dr. Kramer had told me that with the elevated risk of preterm birth, I may end up on bedrest to ensure that didn't happen. I hadn't even allowed myself to think about that possibility. It was too scary.

Sage could sense my growing anxiety over that, and she shifted so she could take my hands in hers. "That's not going to happen. But if it did, if you ended up on bedrest, I promise you, we'd figure it out. You're not alone in this."

My eyes welled with unshed tears, my heart squeezing. "I appreciate you so much," I told her, trying to blink them away. Her eyes misted, too.

"You're the sister I never got to have growing up, and I'm so glad I found you," she squeezed my hand. "This next chapter of your life—of both our lives—is going to be so magical and amazing."

Sage's words unleashed the floodgates.

"I know, but seriously, can we change the subject before I start ugly crying?" I laughed, wiping away my tears with my free hand.

"Is it even a girls' night without ugly crying?" Sage asked, blinking away her own tears with a self-deprecating smile.

"It's a slippery slope with the way my hormones have been lately. I'm afraid I won't stop once I start."

"Mine, too." Sage said, releasing my hand to grab a chip from the bowl on her coffee table.

Sage and Nix hadn't told Daphne yet about the baby. Sage said she wanted to make it special for her, and that Nix's idea was to tell her by bringing her to the house he was building and letting her help design the baby's room.

However they told her, I knew Daphne would be over the moon about having a sibling.

"I still can't believe we're pregnant at the same time," I admitted, shaking my head and smiling.

"I know, it's great, isn't it? Last time I was pregnant, all my friends were in their college partying era. It was kind of isolating. This time, we'll be shopping for maternity clothes and baby things together." Sage's eyes lit up. "Oh my gosh, we could have a double baby shower!"

"Oh, yeah," I tried not to let the sadness I felt suddenly creep into my tone. I was excited, but Sage's mention of a baby shower made me think of my mother, who traditionally would be expected to help throw said baby shower.

"I know you're thinking about your mom," Sage sent me a sympathetic look. "I promise you, no matter what her reaction is, things are going to be okay."

Out of everyone, Sage would understand exactly what I was feeling. She'd been through it once before with her own mother when she was pregnant with Daphne. But this time around, she had her aunt, her uncle, and her cousins—plus Nix's incredible family. I had met his parents at Halloween, and they seemed great. I could tell that they were happily involved in their children's, and grandchildren's, lives.

I was happy Sage had all those folks in her corner, though, and I didn't want the slight twinge of jealousy I felt over not having that to bring my friend down. She deserved their support and their excitement.

"You're right," I smiled. "And a double baby shower would be great."

"It really would be," Sage said dreamily. "I didn't have one last time, with Daphne. My mom wasn't excited, and like I said, all my friends were in their college party era. Nobody was thinking about baby showers."

"Well, this time will be different," I assured her. "Speaking of your mom, have you told her yet?"

"She'll be the last to know," Sage shrugged a delicate shoulder. "I'm still not exactly over her telling Warren where I was."

A few months ago, Sage's mother had told her ex-fiancé where to find her, and he showed up at a school fundraiser she was volunteering at to "talk to her". Nix had handled that situation like a hero in a romance book, backed by his brothers, and Warren got the hint that Sage was over him for good.

I'd never liked Warren and was glad to see Sage cut him out of her life. Especially because it left room for Nix, and I adored him. He was good to her in all the ways she deserved. I'd never seen my friend so happy and fulfilled.

"Yeah, I haven't told my parents yet, either. Not sure when I'm going to."

There was so much about my life that my parents didn't know, because they didn't ask. I didn't volunteer the information because it always seemed like they were calling me out of duty, not because they genuinely wanted to hear how I was doing.

CHAPTER FIFTEEN

Noah

TALKING to Parker the other night had made me realize I'd been too much of a hermit lately, avoiding going into town and throwing myself into working at the resort.

Sure, I may dislike the task of grocery shopping, but it got me into town, and I forgot how much I used to look forward to my trips into town. I forgot how much I loved how friendly the residents were in Hartwood Creek, I couldn't walk into a store without recognizing someone and stopping to catch up. I forgot how much I loved how everyone in the community took care of each other.

If something bad happened to someone, everyone in the community would rally and help them however they could. When the Stewart's house burned down a few years ago before Christmas, everyone pulled together to make sure that the three young Stewart kids still had a magical Christmas.

Grant Hillman, a real estate mogul with several rental

properties he mostly kept open for the summer tourism session, allowed the Stewart's to stay in one of his houses until their house could be rebuilt. He didn't charge them rent, he only asked that they covered utilities while they were there.

Nix Hutchinson and Dan Truman, two contractors with competing businesses, offered their services free of charge to help with the rebuild, and ended up setting aside their differences and working together on the job. The Hutchinson Lumber Yard and the local hardware store donated supplies.

A local roofing company, Shingle Shenanigans, owned and run by Easton's friends, Torin Davis and Lucas Black, donated supplies and labour to complete the roof. Expenses for the roof had been covered by their monetized social media accounts, which only propelled their popularity online and helped them further grow their roofing company. They now had two crews and did a lot of work all over the place.

When Alma Durand, who lived in one of the apartments above the hardware store, got cancer six years ago, the town rallied together to make meal trains to stock her refrigerator and freezer. People in town took turns driving her to her radiation appointments in Springwood.

Those were a few examples of the people of Hartwood Creek taking care of each other.

On the regular day to day, townspeople shopped local and paid it forward in small but significant ways. Sure, it could be a little stifling at times, what with everyone seeming to know everyone else's business, but I still wouldn't trade it for the indifference of big city life. The community's involvement with each other kept us all afloat and thriving.

My nieces were celebrating their birthday tomorrow, so I'd decided to stop off at the toy store before grocery shopping. I'd gotten them several gifts for Christmas, but being a December baby myself, I knew how disappointing it could be to have a birthday around the holidays. I always made sure to spoil them extra on their birthday.

I perused the shelves for something that they'd like, and that Damien would hate. It was my calling as an uncle to make sure whatever gift I got my nieces was either super loud, or incredibly messy. The magic potion kit kept drawing my eye. I knew Damien would despise it, and that alone made it a worthy contender.

Another contender was the mini karaoke machine. It came with a portable Bluetooth speaker, and two wireless microphones. It was also pink, which the girls would love.

"Noah Wood, is that you?" an all-too familiar voice cooed. I turned my head, not at all surprised to see the Hartley sisters staring at me with their scheming smiles.

The Hartley sisters were triplets, but aside from sharing a family resemblance and a love for pantsuits, they all had a different style. Betty dyed her hair red and kept it short. Dorothy had let her hair go white without a fight and kept it long and usually braided over her shoulder. Alice had also let the white stay but kept her hair short like Betty's.

They all dressed to complement one another perfectly, and they'd been doing so their entire lives.

"Oh, it is! I told you, Betty! Booker said he got a haircut," Dorothy interjected, gently knocking Betty's arm.

"We love it, Noah! It's about time you chopped that mop off. It's nice to see your handsome face." Alice grinned.

"Any reason in particular for this sudden change?" Betty inquired, a knowing glint in her eyes.

"Just wanted a change, ladies. Don't read into it too much," I answered, knowing that they would. That was the Hartley triplets—always reading into everything. They were Hartwood Creek's most notorious busybodies, always scheming and gossiping. They weren't malicious about it, they genuinely cared about everyone in town, but they didn't often concern themselves with boundaries.

"Well, regardless of your reasoning," Betty said, exchanging a knowing look with Dorothy and Alice, "your haircut looks lovely, dear."

"Thank you."

"We also heard you hired Sage's friend, Nellie, was it, to work at the resort? That was kind of you."

"We needed to hire a new receptionist, and she needed a job. Nothing kind about it, really." I shrugged, on guard. I knew what they were insinuating. They weren't exactly being subtle about it.

"Regardless, what a wonderful opportunity for you both," Alice said. "I love a good workplace romance."

Betty elbowed Alice, as if she was warning her to watch her mouth.

"Who said anything about a romance?" I narrowed my eyes at all three of them.

"A little birdie told us you and Miss. Banks hit it off at the Witches' Ball," Dorothy explained, her tone somehow both conspiratorial and grandmotherly.

Great. The Hartley triplets knew Nellie came home with me after the Halloween party.

I snapped my fingers. "That's who that was!" I was kidding, obviously, but I really didn't want to encourage their antics.

Betty's lips twitched, like she was repressing a smirk. The three of them exchanged a look that said a thousand things without any of them uttering a word. I knew they didn't buy my nonchalant brush off, but they thankfully picked up on the hint that it wasn't up for discussion either way.

"We won't keep you. We were on our way to lunch. Say hi to the family!" Dorothy said, and as suddenly as they appeared, the Hartley triplets went. A whirlwind of bangles and pantsuits and knowing smiles.

Shaking my head, I resumed the task at hand, trying to put aside their comments.

The Hartley sisters' interest in me wasn't new, by any means. They were oddly fascinated by any of the single folks in town, and always trying to play matchmaker. Their mission was to ensure that every single person in Hartwood Creek found true, everlasting love. The number of relationships they'd interfered with was so vast, I would even go as far to say that every relationship in town had seen some variation of their meddling.

But they seemed doubly interested in the romantic happenings of my brothers and me. Probably because they were distantly related to us.

Out of our branch of the Wood family tree, the Hartley sisters had meddled with my parents' relationship early on, and with Damien and Charlotte's relationship, and I knew they had their sights on Easton and me.

I'd better watch my step.

AFTER BIRTHDAY SHOPPING for my nieces and deciding on both the magic potion kit and the karaoke machine, I found myself doing the dreaded grocery shop.

I pushed my cart around, leisurely grabbing items of interest off the shelves. I'd come in with a list but barely glanced at it, sticking to my usual shopping habits and tossing whatever looked appealing in the cart.

I found her in the chip aisle again, stocking up on dill pickle chips.

"We have to stop meeting like this," I said when I caught sight of her dark hair.

Nellie didn't even seem surprised. "Ha," she said, tossing me an unamused glance over her shoulder. She looked tired, and a little sad.

"How's your weekend been so far?" I couldn't help but move toward her, wanting to be closer.

"It's been good," she replied. Her expression was more open than it'd been in a while. She seemed like she wanted to talk to me. "How's yours been?"

"Pretty good. Ran into the Hartley triplets."

"Huh, I did too. They seem to be everywhere all the time."

"It's how they keep a finger on the pulse of this town," I said, earning a small smile from her. "Did they say anything to you?"

Nellie's cheeks heated. "Not really."

I could spot the lie in how she shifted her gaze back to the shelves of chips, as if she was considering adding another few bags to her cart, although she didn't make a move to grab any more.

For some reason, her cageyness made me want to be upfront about my interaction with the Hartley triplets.

"Ah. Well," I pretended to look at the chips lining the shelves. "They mentioned you to me," I added casually. I could see Nellie's head whip toward me from the corner of my eye.

"What did they say?"

I looked back at her, trying to keep my expression neutral.

"Nothing much, just that they'd heard you were working for the resort now." I answered. "I found it a little strange that they were talking about you. Are you sure they didn't say anything to you about me?"

"Oh, well." her cheeks went a darker shade of pink. "I

mentioned it when they cornered me outside the drugstore. They asked if I'd found a job yet, so…"

"They'd find out whether you told them or not," I chuckled. "They seem to think there's a romantic possibility between the two of us."

I tried to say this part casually and not watch too closely for her reaction, but I was tuned in to her every breath.

"Oh?" Nellie said again, her brow furrowing.

"Yeah, they mentioned the Witches' Ball and how we, well, hung out after." Hung out was a euphemism, and we both knew it, but I couldn't help but wonder if it'd been awkward to point it out.

"They know about that?"

I pretended to check that the coast was clear and stepped closer to her. "They know everything that happens in town. They probably have spies watching us now." I said, keeping my voice low, as if I was worried people would overhear me.

"Why, though?" Nellie looked utterly perplexed.

"I'm sure Sage has mentioned their love of playing matchmakers?" I asked, and Nellie nodded in confirmation. "Well, it seems they're obsessed with the idea of getting us together, and they'll probably start meddling now. I'd be super cautious of drinking or eating any freebies you get from the café, or even other shops in town. Nowhere is safe once the Hartley triplets get a love match potential in their heads."

Nellie scowled. "A love match? Are you serious?"

"Yup. And there's only one way to get them off our backs."

"How?"

"We go out on a date," the idea spilled from my lips before I could really think it through, but once I'd said it…I didn't regret it. I'd wanted to ask her out on a date since that first time we ran into each other at the grocery store. Being in the same aisle as we were that night somehow felt kismet.

Nellie's expression was so far from amused, it would have been laughable if it didn't sting so much. I found that I wanted her to say yes to a date to me, and not because of the Hartley triplets.

"What? It's true. They won't let up until they see us try. If it doesn't work out and there's no chemistry between us, they'll drop it."

"Sounds like you're fishing for a date, Noah Wood," Nellie called me out, but she took a step closer to me.

"So, what if I am?"

"You're my boss. That's weird."

"Technically, I'm one of your bosses. My brothers are as much your bosses as I am."

"Still. Isn't it against company policy or something?" she looked wary, but there was something beneath the wariness. Hope. Intrigue.

My lips twitched. "We don't actually have any policies against co-workers dating, oddly enough. It's a family run resort and has been for generations, so a lot of the employees are related or married already." I pointed out. Charlotte had never worked for us prior to getting with Damien.

Nellie's frown increased, and she tossed her hands up in exasperation and letting them fall to her sides. "Again, it's weird. This whole thing is weird."

"Maybe. But it's also our only hope to get the Hartley triplets off our back. I'm used to their antics, but you? You are fresh meat. If not me, they'll pick another unassuming single male in town and start trying to fix you up with him."

It was true, and I found I loathed that idea entirely. If anyone was going to take Nellie on a date, it was going to be me.

Nellie didn't seem to like that idea either. The colour

drained from her face, and she bit her lip, considering my proposition.

I meant every word of it: now that the Hartley triplets had their sights set on us, they would focus their efforts on doing everything in their power to get us together.

But I didn't point out the fact that if they caught a whiff of the chemistry between us, their efforts would only increase tenfold—and there was no denying the chemistry between us. Although Nellie was trying her best to deny and ignore it, and I was doing my best to laugh it off and not think about it, it was there, and we both knew it was there.

The night we'd spent together had opened the floodgates for that intense wave of chemistry, and even Nellie sneaking out the next morning and me failing to recognize her in person the next time I saw her again couldn't lessen that fact.

Because the truth was, I had recognized her. At least on a subconscious level. It's why I'd immediately hit on her, despite not clueing in at first that it even was her. But even before that moment, I hadn't so much as looked in another woman's direction, not since she fled my bed in the wee hours of the morning.

"Fine."

Nellie's one-worded reply caught me by surprise. I'd expected her to fight me a little harder.

"Fine?" I repeated, my eyes widening.

"Let's do it. One date, to throw them off us. We'll tell them it didn't work out. That there's no chemistry or whatever." Nellie bit her lip, as if she was already regretting this decision and looking for an excuse to back out.

I swallowed the lump in my throat, nodding even though I hated the idea of it not working out between us more than I cared to voice. "Okay, yeah. Let's do it. Are you free tonight?"

"Seems a little eager," Nellie arched her brow, and I smirked.

"Maybe I don't care about appearing too eager," I shrugged. "I'm busy tonight."

"Got a date already?"

"Yes, with Sam and Dean. I have a very important date with season twelve of Supernatural," Nellie replied, her lips quirking. "How about this upcoming Saturday?"

"Works for me," I nodded, trying not to grin like an idiot.

CHAPTER SIXTEEN

Nellie

STUPID, stupid, stupid! I scolded myself when I got back to the apartment with my groceries. What in the hell was I thinking? Saying yes to Noah's ridiculous idea to go on a date?

Especially when I knew it was all bullshit. Going on a date and saying there was no chemistry between us wasn't going to magically throw the Hartley sisters off our trail. If anything, they'd see right through our antics to the chemistry that so clearly existed between us.

The very chemistry I was trying my hardest to ignore, because I knew—I knew—that once I told Noah I was pregnant, everything between us would change.

And yet...I'd been unable to resist his charm, his crooked smile, and his affable attitude about the whole situation. It was almost like he thought the whole matchmaking business was a silly little joke.

At first, I'd said yes to test him. To see if he'd retract those words, but when he didn't, when he proceeded to pick a date, I'd found myself growing excited and hopeful.

For one blessed minute, I'd forgotten about the circumstances between us, circumstances that Noah had no idea about, and let myself imagine the date going well. The possibility of a kiss at the door, of more dates in the future.

For one singular moment, I'd allowed myself to imagine what it'd be like to fall for Noah. Then reality set in, and the fear that came with it.

But it was too late. The date was set. Noah said he'd pick me up at seven Saturday night, and to leave the planning to him.

I put away my groceries, still trying to think of a way out of the situation I'd gotten myself into.

My phone rang, and I pulled it out of my coat pocket. It was Sage, video calling me. "Hey, Sage," I said, setting my phone down on the counter and propping it up against the fruit bowl.

"I heard a rumour," Sage's eyes were sparkling with excitement, and I froze, the bag of sugar I'd been about to put away in the cupboard suspended in the air.

"What rumour?"

"That you and Noah were spotted at the grocery store, making plans for a date," Sage relayed.

"How fast does news spread in this town?!" I scowled, shoving the sugar bag in the cupboard. "I literally just got home."

"It spreads fast, very fast," Sage said sympathetically, though she couldn't hide her excitement. "So, it's true then?"

"Kind of." I sighed, bringing my hand to my forehead to massage my temple. I could feel the beginning of a headache coming on.

"How do you 'kind of' plan a date?" Sage's lips quirked. "Either you planned a date, or you didn't. No 'kind of' about it."

"We're going to go on a *fake* date to get the Hartley triplets off our backs. Apparently, they've got their sights set on us as a love match, and if we don't get ahead of it, they'll start meddling." I accentuated the fake part of the date, so she'd know.

Sage snorted. "And you think that going on a 'fake date' will help with that?" she asked, using air quotes.

"I don't know, maybe? It was Noah's idea."

"Of course, it was," Sage said. "But I'm pretty sure you already know that's not going to work. If anything, it'll encourage them more. Especially because you and Noah have some serious chemistry going on. If you weren't pregnant already, the looks alone he was giving you at the New Year's party would have done it."

I felt a little sick at that. I mean, I knew we had chemistry, and I knew Noah knew it. But was it that easily detectable to outsiders, or was Sage seeing it because she knew our history?

Sage could see me internally freaking out. She moved her phone closer to her face, like she could get closer to me. "It's not a bad thing, Nell. I think this is a good thing. Fake date pretense or not, it'll give you the opportunity to talk to him, and you do need to talk to him."

"Yeah, that's true." Sage had a point, as reluctant as I was to admit it. Noah had been understanding about my request for taking another Friday afternoon off, but he'd also sort of reprimanded me. I could easily switch my appointments with Dr. Kramer to Mondays, but he was still going to wonder why I needed time off so frequently.

Plus, I'd started showing. It wasn't detectable to anyone but me, but that would change in no time at all. I needed to put my big girl panties on and tell him already.

"This is a good thing," Sage repeated. "And, I mean, if your intention was to have word get back to the Hartley triplets about you two pursuing a romantic relationship, you are kind of ahead of the game now. If I heard the news, they probably did, too."

"I guess so," I sighed, wondering if that was a good thing. Maybe we'd put even more pressure on ourselves.

THE WEEK PASSED IN A BLUR. I was busy at work booking reservations and staying on top of the daily tasks required of me. On Friday morning, I put together all the check-in packets for that weekend's guests entirely by myself, the additional task serving well to distract me from tomorrow night's plans.

Despite Fridays being check-in days for many guests, I had limited contact with them. Most folks arrived after I'd left for the day.

There were two wooden boxes mounted to the wall beside the door labeled check-ins and check-outs. The check-in box was slightly bigger, the lid opening to reveal the packets with each guest's name on it. The check-out box was smaller and locked, with a slot for the keys to drop in.

All payments were processed the day guests were set to arrive, so there was no need for them to wait around until the office was open to pay for their stay.

With all the check-in packets ready to go by noon, I put them in the check-in box then returned to the office and keeping myself busy while I waited for someone to come in and relieve me so I could go to my appointment in Springwood. I was simultaneously hoping and dreading that someone would be Noah.

I hadn't seen much of him this week because he'd been busy helping with some plumbing issues one of the cottages was having. The only time I caught a glimpse of him was at lunch briefly, and despite the winks and flirty smiles he sent me across the table, he'd kept his distance.

I expected his brothers to call us out, to demand to know why we thought it'd be appropriate for us to go on a date, but neither Damien nor Easton said a thing about it. It was as if they didn't know—and maybe they didn't. I wasn't about to bring it up, even if I'd entertained the idea briefly as a way to get out of the date in a moment of insecurity and panic.

The bell in the back chimed, and I waited with bated breath until the door to the laundry room swung open, revealing Charlotte.

"Hope it's going better in here than it is in the Sprucewood Cottage," she winced, shaking her head.

"Yeah, it's been quiet. Booked a few more reservations and I have all the check-in packets ready to go out front. I take it the plumbing issue isn't going so well?"

"You could say that," Charlotte sighed. "The guys are still trying, but I'm going to make an executive decision and call a plumber. They might be handy, but they aren't that handy, and I'm worried about the hardwood floors if they keep trying it their way."

"Ommf, yeah." I opened the web browser, about to type in local plumbers.

"I'll call James, he's our usual plumber."

"Right," I wrinkled my nose at myself. I should have guessed they already had contacts.

"Noah tells me you're off to Springwood for an appointment?" Charlotte asked, picking up the phone and dialing a number straight from memory.

"Yeah, I should head out soon if I'm going to make it in time," I replied, hoping Charlotte wouldn't ask any further questions, like what my appointment was for. I didn't want to have to lie to anybody, but I wanted to tell Noah first.

"Okay, no problem. Thanks for getting all the check-in packets ready," Charlotte smiled warmly, sitting down in the desk chair, and turning her attention to the phone. "Hi, James? Yeah, it's Charlotte. We've got a bit of a situation here, can you come out?"

I grabbed my coat and outdoor boots, dressing and putting away my indoor work shoes on the shoe stand. Then I made my way to the kitchen to grab my lunch bag and headed out.

The drive to Springwood passed quickly with the help of my extensive playlist. Waiting for Dr. Kramer, however, felt like a slow and torturous process.

The OB was running a few patients behind, so I didn't get seen until forty-five minutes after my appointment. Dr. Kramer came in, looking a little frazzled. "Sorry about that, Nellie. We had a delivery last night, and it set me back."

"No worries," I assured her. I figured that was typical for an OB. They did deliver babies, after all.

"How have you been feeling?"

"Pretty good," I answered. "A little nervous about everything we talked about last time, but otherwise, I'm okay."

"A little nervousness is to be expected," Dr. Kramer smiled kindly. "You're growing a human, after all. But your progesterone levels look good, your blood pressure is on par with where it should be."

"That's good to hear," I murmured, relieved.

"Sure is! I want you to watch for the following symptoms:

facial swelling, headaches, trouble seeing or changes in vision, and pain below the ribs. Those are all signs of preeclampsia, which as we discussed last week, you are at an elevated risk for."

"I have been having some headaches, but I'm probably not drinking enough water, and stressing too much," I said.

Dr. Kramer nodded sympathetically. "Keep an eye on those headaches, and try to up your water intake. It's always good to be hydrated, especially while pregnant."

"I can do that. When is my next ultrasound?" I asked.

"Your next ultrasound will be scheduled for the twenty-one-week mark, so six weeks from now," Dr. Kramer answered. "If you want to find out the gender, we can do so during that scan."

"Okay," I nodded again.

Dr. Kramer gave me a quick examination, and then I was free to go.

Noah

MY BODY WAS ACHING from hours of laying on my side in frozen mud, trying fruitlessly to fix the pipes under the Sprucewood cottage with Damien and Easton. Most of the cottages didn't have basements, just a small crawl space.

Easton and I were secretly relieved when Charlotte called James. Damien wouldn't allow us to admit defeat, at least not until he had no choice in the matter.

When James took over, he was able to spot the problem that had evaded us all day in five minutes. Unfortunately, fixing it was going to take a little longer. He'd have to squeeze us into his already busy schedule, and order the proper piping to replace the old stuff that was all but rotting away.

"Truth is, all of the cottages could use new pipes," Easton grumbled. He was as filthy as I was. We were debriefing in the laundry room, waiting for Charlotte to lock up the front before we all called it a day and went home to shower.

"We'll cross that bridge when we get to it," Damien scowled. "We've already had to move the Joneses, and we'll have to reschedule anyone who booked the Sprucewood cottage for the next two weeks at least."

"We could always open up the Rustic," I suggested.

"It's smaller, and we'll have to comp the price difference. But fine, whatever, do that then. Wait until after we open it up tomorrow and make sure it's good to go. With our luck, the heat won't work or something," Damien's scowl deepened.

The door to the laundry room swung open, and Charlotte entered. Damien's scowl immediately vanished.

"Alright, we're all locked up for the night," she said. "Was James able to figure it out?"

"He'll need to come back," my older brother explained, his tone much gentler with his fiancée. "We've got to replace all the pipes in the Sprucewood."

"That's to be expected," Charlotte sighed. "Unfortunately, a lot of the cottages need their pipes replaced."

Damien didn't get irritated at her for the remark, even though he'd seemed close to throwing a punch at Easton for making the same comment. Easton grinned, noting the difference, too. They took off, leaving me and Easton to make sure the back door was locked up.

"So..." Easton said when it was the two of us, his eyes sparkling with entertainment. "I heard something interesting the other day."

"Oh yeah?" I had a feeling I knew what he was referring to.

"You asked Nellie out on a date, huh?" my younger brother shook his head, like he couldn't believe how stupid I was.

"Yeah, I did. What of it?"

"Messing around with employees," Easton whistled. "Never thought I'd see the day."

I usually made sure to avoid entanglements with employees. So far, it hadn't been a problem, but most of our employees were either related to us, or older than us by a couple of decades. Minus Jeannine, who'd tried her best to get with each one of us—even Damien, who'd been in a happy relationship.

"Technically, I messed around with her before she was an employee," I pointed out.

"Damien's still not going to like it. He already thinks you hired her because you have a crush on her."

"I do have a crush on her, but that's not why I hired her, and you know it. She's good at her job. She seems to fit in great with everyone."

"Oh, yeah, I'm not saying anything contrary there. She's leagues better than Jeannine. But you know Damien's going to have a burr in his ass about it."

"He has a burr in his ass about most things, so I don't really care," I shrugged.

"When are you going to tell him? You've been lucky so far that he—and Charlotte, for that matter—haven't heard the gossip."

"Whenever it comes up, I guess," I said, reaching my truck.

"Well, I hope you know what you're doing. If this date doesn't work out, then you've created an uncomfortable situation for an employee of ours. What if she decides to quit?"

I opened the door to my truck and climbed in. "Or, what if the date works out and she's here long-term, like Charlotte?" I said, closing my door in his face.

Easton's eyes widened, like he hadn't realized how serious

my feelings were for Nellie. Heck, I didn't even realize it until I found myself saying it out loud.

I didn't wait around for him to say anything else. Peeling out of the parking lot, I went home to shower the mud and cold off my skin.

CHAPTER SEVENTEEN

Nellie

NOAH PULLED up at seven on the dot to pick me up. I watched as he walked up the steps to my apartment, carrying a bouquet of flowers. I forced myself to wait until he knocked to open the door for him.

"Good evening. You look ravishing," Noah said, a smile gracing his kissable lips as he seemed to drink me in.

"You clean up well yourself," I replied, taking him in, too.

He was dressed up in a tailored blazer, a dress shirt, and a pair of navy chinos. He'd taken the time to style his hair similarly to how he'd styled it the night of the New Year's party.

I'd never seen him look so suave before, and every version of Noah was appealing. The Witcher version, the drunken-still-asleep one, the casual winterwear one, the work clothes, the some-what-dressed up for New Year's Eve one. Noah could pull off every look, it seemed.

At least I'd dressed up for the occasion, whatever it was.

The long burgundy lantern sleeve sheath knit dress accentuated my curves and hid the slight belly I'd started to develop. I'd paired it with my knee-high boots and a black, fold-over collar dress jacket.

I'd curled my hair loosely to fall in voluminous waves down my back. My makeup wasn't overly dramatic, but I'd played up my eyes and coated my lips in a sheer gloss.

Noah's easy smile made my heart skip a beat in its chest, and so did the beautiful flowers he'd brought me: snowdrops and white roses, nestled in lush greenery to offset them.

"These are for you, my gorgeous date," Noah said, holding out the flowers to me.

"Thank you," I took them from him, swallowing back the emotion rising in my throat as I carried them into the kitchen, setting them down on the counter, thankful that they'd come in their own clear vase.

I didn't have a vase. I'd never had a date bring me flowers before, so I'd never needed one.

Not that I'd really dated before. Casually hooked up, yes—but the expectations for flowers and fine dining weren't exactly a prerequisite for casual hookups. This was something different for me, and I felt like I was on completely unstable ground.

But this wasn't a real date, or at least it wasn't supposed to be. So why did it feel like it was?

"I booked us a reservation at seven thirty at The Harvest Table," Noah was saying from the doorway, his voice getting more and more muddled, as if I was sinking underwater.

I was fiddling with the flowers in their vase, my back to him, desperately trying to collect myself before I turned to face him or respond. But my emotions and my panic were getting the best of me. My breaths were choppy, like I couldn't pull in air calmly, and my eyes were watering.

I couldn't sit through a dinner with him looking at me the way he did and not have the truth explode from me.

It'd been hard enough to get through the week without blurting it out. The heaviness was suffocating me. I felt light-headed and dizzy. I swayed, gripping the counter to catch myself. Noah was suddenly at my side.

"What's wrong? Are you okay?" he asked, his voice full of concern and his hand steady and warm on my side.

"I can't do this," I whispered, my voice croaking. I hadn't realized I was crying until Noah cupped my face and tentatively brushed away the tears on my cheek with his thumb.

"Is the idea of going on a date with me that repulsive?" Noah's voice was teasing, but I could tell he was concerned and trying to make light of things.

"No, it's not you, it's..." I stopped myself, taking a deep breath. Rip it off like a Band-Aid, I thought, closing my eyes again. "I can't go on this date, at least not until I tell you something."

"Okay..." Noah said carefully, letting his hands fall away.

I couldn't tell him with him so close. I stepped away from him.

"I'm pregnant." The words came out on a whoosh.

Noah stared at me for several beats, like he was processing what I'd said. "You're pregnant?" he repeated, sounding uncertain and confused.

"Yes. I am," I said, feeling relief that I was no longer holding this secret in. "I'm going to be fifteen weeks as of tomorrow."

"Fifteen weeks?" Noah asked, and I could tell he was mentally counting backwards. "Isn't that, wouldn't that mean you—"

"Yeah, I conceived around Halloween," I clarified.

"So I'm—"

"I don't know for sure," I interrupted. "There was also one other...possibility."

At that, Noah's eyes darkened. "Who's the other possibility?" he asked, his voice low, like the idea I'd been with another man made him envious.

"Nobody," I answered. "I mean, I don't know his last name and I'm not in contact with him."

Noah nodded, his jaw working as if he was trying to chew this information.

"You must think I'm terrible." I covered my face with my hands, feeling ashamed.

He gently pulled my hands away from my face, peering at me with a perplexed look on his face. "Why would I think that?"

"Because I don't even know for certain who my unborn baby's father is." My lips trembled, and I tried to blink away more tears. I didn't usually feel shame for my sexual liberation, but I felt shame for not knowing who the father of my unborn baby was.

Noah crouched a little, making sure we were perfectly level so he could look intently into my eyes.

"I don't think that, not at all," he assured me. His voice was even, steady. "I'm the last person that would judge you for that, okay? We'll figure it out."

"I'm not expecting anything from you, I just...I can't go on this date without you knowing. And if you want to cancel, I understand completely. It was stupid to set this up without talking to you first, and I—"

"Oh, we're going on the date," he said decisively, his gaze resolute. "Unless you don't want to?"

"No, that's not it. I'm a mess right now," my shoulders dropped, and so did my gaze. I stared at his fancy dress shoes, feeling emotionally depleted.

Noah gripped my chin gently, tipping my face up to look at him. His expression was soft. "You're not a mess, Nell. And even if you are, you're the most beautiful mess I've ever seen."

I couldn't help but snort. "That's some line, Noah."

"Thanks, I thought of it myself," he said, his smile blinding. I couldn't help but give him a tentative smile back. "I'd still like to take you out on this date if you're up for it. Seems like we've got a lot to discuss, and I bet you're hungry."

"Why, because I'm pregnant?"

"No, because it's dinner time and we're supposed to go out, so I doubt you've eaten," Noah responded. He paused for a moment, thinking. "And maybe also because you're pregnant."

I laughed despite myself, relieved that he was taking it so easily. Aside from his initial irritation that he wasn't the only potential father, I mean.

"You're sure you still want to go out with me?"

"Even more now. Get your coat, let's go," Noah instructed.

I grabbed my dress jacket off the coat rack.

<h1 style="text-align:center">CHAPTER EIGHTEEN</h1>

Noah

AS THE WAITRESS, Gabrielle, led us over to a private table, I let out a breath of relief. Ever since Nellie dropped the news, my head had been buzzing with a thousand thoughts. I'd always taken extra caution to use protection every single encounter I had, but...

I couldn't for the life of me remember if I had with Nellie. From the first time I laid eyes on her, I'd been consumed. I'd written it off at the time as being really drunk, but after seeing her again, after hiring her and having her become a part of my daily life, I knew that wasn't entirely true.

I mean, I'd still been drunk enough to not remember if I'd grabbed a condom, but I realized my hyperfocus on her wasn't purely alcohol-driven. Something about her soul called to mine. I'd been so wrapped up in the moment, so utterly captivated.

"Here you are," Gabrielle smiled, laying out our menus on the beautifully set table for two. There were fancy glasses full of lemon ice water and a low centerpiece of winter greenery with a touch of gold.

Gabrielle had gone to school with my older brother, Damien. They used to date back in high school, so she knew our family well. The breakup had been amicable, and she was seeing someone from Springwood, last I heard.

I'd originally chosen this venue not only because it was the most romantic place in town to dine, but because I knew Gabrielle would spread word that she'd seen me and Nellie together. The gossip would eventually get back to the Hartley sisters, thus ensuring our little plan to throw the Hartley sisters off our backs worked out.

Only now, our little plan was shot to shit. I mean, I'd not been serious to begin with about fake dating. I'd actually wanted this to be a real date as soon as she agreed to it—but now? Now, I didn't know what to think.

One word kept echoing in my mind: Mine.

I felt like I was moving robotically as I pulled Nellie's chair out for her. She sat, giving me a hesitant smile, like she knew I was still grappling with what she'd told me. I pulled out my own chair, sitting down heavily.

I'd handled it well enough initially, more concerned with how upset she was and wanting to make sure she understood I didn't judge her. Not for a single minute.

Was I miffed that she'd been with someone else? Maybe a little, but again that had more to do with the greediness I felt toward her and less to do with her choices. I knew I was no saint. I had a track record a mile long, and it was a damn miracle I hadn't had a scare like this before.

I'd been careful, my older brother's experience with father-hood reminding me to take that shit seriously. Raising kids as a single parent wasn't easy. I'd watched how isolating it was for Damien, not having a teammate, a partner to help with the responsibilities and concerns. The girls' birth mother had never been interested in parenting, so everything had always fallen on Damien, until Charlotte. In her, he found an equal partner, someone willing to help him carry the load of parenthood.

I'd never given much thought to kids myself, always telling myself that if I found the right person, maybe. But every time I thought back to that night I shared with Nellie, I couldn't remember reaching for the box in my nightstand. I remembered heated, desperate kisses and touches, smudging her makeup around her mouth a little. Even still, she'd been a vision, those eyes captivating me—hooking me like ecstasy.

"Can I get you some of our house wine to start?" Gabrielle asked, jarring me from my thoughts. She looked between me and Nellie expectantly.

I floundered. My plan had been to order a bottle of wine to split between the two of us, but Nellie wouldn't be drinking, and I should really refrain in solidarity or something...shouldn't I?

"Is the winter lemonade good?" Nellie said after scanning the drink menu options.

"Oh, yes," Gabrielle nodded her head, her brown eyes widening. "It's made with blood oranges and cranberries. It's got a bit of a punch-y taste to it. The cranberries give it a zing and the blood oranges add a sweet tanginess."

"I'll try that, please," Nellie said. "Non-alcoholic, if that's possible?"

"Sure is," Gabrielle nodded, turning to look at me. "What about you, Noah? Whisky and Coke?"

I'd been there a time or two before, usually for staff holiday parties in The Loft, but I guess my drink of choice was known among our circles.

I glanced at Nellie, and she nodded, as if urging me to order whatever I wanted. Truthfully, I could use a drink. Maybe it would quiet the buzzing in my head. "Sure, yeah. That sounds great."

"Great, I'll be right back with your drinks," Gabrielle said, heading off to the drink station.

Nellie bit her lip, watching Gabrielle go. "Maybe this wasn't such a good idea."

"Are you kidding, it's a great idea," I leaned back in my chair and shot a flirtatious grin at her, trying to pull myself out of my existential crisis. I could spiral later, right now I had a beautiful woman in front of me whose life was irrevocably changed.

"Well, it doesn't really seem like a good place to, you know, talk." She glanced around at the other tables. They were spaced out enough that it gave the illusion of privacy, but I suppose she still felt exposed.

"We could talk about that later, if that'd make you more comfortable." My suggestion made Nellie's face fall. "I mean, there's not much more to say right now about it, right? You are, and you're not sure if I am," I added, summarizing things as vaguely as I could while trying to wrap my head around it at the same time.

"Yeah, I guess you're right about that." Nellie picked up her glass of lemon water, taking a tiny sip. "Maybe I should have waited to say something, this feels so awkward."

"It only feels awkward because you're making it awkward," I joked.

She shot me an unimpressed look.

"Seriously, if you focus on how awkward you think it is, you're only going to make it awkward. I don't feel awkward. Shell-shocked, maybe, but not awkward."

Nellie's lips twitched with a repressed smile at my honesty. "Well, what did you want to talk about?"

"I don't know, let's get to the heavy stuff. What are your

hopes and dreams for the future? I mean, clearly motherhood is happening. But what about the other stuff?"

"What do you mean?" Nellie's brow furrowed, and I leaned forward.

"I mean, do you want to get married?"

"Jesus, Noah, you're terrible at dating," Gabrielle interjected, appearing suddenly at my elbow with our drinks.

"Ah, yes. A critique of my dating skills, just what I ordered," I shot back.

Nellie snorted, trying to hide her smile behind her hand.

"Sorry, I know you're out of practice, but save the heavier questions for after the appetizers, maybe?" Gabrielle winked at Nellie, as if they were in cahoots.

Gabrielle had a point. We hadn't even looked at the menu. "Fine, we'll start with a breadbasket."

Nellie waited until Gabrielle left again, then looked back at me. "She's right, you know. Bringing up marriage on a first date is kind of intense."

"Right off the top this night started intense," the words slipped out before I could really think about how they might make her feel. I caught a hint of hurt in Nellie's expression before she schooled her features, and it made me feel like absolute shit. The last thing I wanted to do was hurt her.

"To answer your question, I don't know. Maybe if I found the right person, sure. But I'm not looking for a marriage commitment, I don't even have the headspace to date right now. I'm trying to get through the next five months."

"I guess this explains why you need time off for appointments."

"Yeah, but I can talk to my doctor about moving my appointment day to Mondays, so I don't leave you hanging on Fridays."

"Don't worry about that. Whenever you need to go, go. I'll handle the office," I assured her.

Gabrielle brought the breadbasket and fresh butter, setting them on the table between us. "Are you ready to order yet?"

"Sorry, Gabs. Haven't even looked at the menu yet," I said. "Can we get a minute?"

"Sure thing, I'll be back in a few minutes." Gabrielle went to check on other patrons, and I kept my mouth shut long enough for Nellie to have a look at the menu.

"Everything sounds so good, I have no idea what to order," she said.

"It's all incredible, but I'm probably going to go with prime New York strip loin," I told her.

"That does sound good," Nellie bit her bottom lip, and I could tell she was looking at the prices.

"Get whatever you want, Nell," I told her, lifting a brow. I fully expected to pay for our evening, and I didn't want her worrying about how expensive anything was.

Gabrielle chose that moment to reappear at our table. "Are you ready to order yet?" she asked.

I lifted my chin at Nellie, urging her to go first. "I guess I'll have the prime New York Strip loin."

"How would you like your steak done?"

"Medium rare, please. Could I get mashed potatoes and asparagus, too?" Nellie asked, her eyes darting to me to make sure it was okay.

"I'll have mine done rare and a baked potato instead of mashed," I told Gabrielle when she looked at me. She nodded, taking our menus, and headed back to the kitchen.

I grabbed a slice of the fresh bread, coating it in butter and offering it to Nellie. She took it, giving me a small thankful smile, taking a bite of the bread and closing her eyes as if savouring the taste. "Mmm, this bread is delicious!"

"Sure is. They bake it fresh every day." I buttered a slice for myself. Nellie swallowed and took a sip of her lemonade, her eyes taking in the details of the restaurant.

I had a thousand questions I wanted to ask her, but I got the impression Nellie didn't want to risk anyone overhearing us.

"So, how are you liking Hartwood Creek?" I asked, trying to find neutral ground.

"It's been a bit of an adjustment. Sage tried to warn me, but even with her warnings, the reality of small-town life is taking some getting used to," Nellie replied, fighting a smile. "Did you know Sage called me the moment I got home from the grocery store last week to say that someone overheard us making plans to go on a date?"

"Doesn't surprise me. I told you there were eyes and ears everywhere," I chuckled, grabbing another slice of bread and pushing the basket toward Nellie.

"Yeah, well. It's freaky. But kind of sweet, I guess? I don't know how I feel about it, yet. I'm not used to anybody knowing my business, let alone everyone." Nellie shook her head, frowning.

"The longer you live here, the more you get used to it. But you'll find the focus of interest shifts quickly," I said, shrugging my shoulders.

"So, eventually I'll be yesterday's news?"

"Something like that." My lips twitched. I didn't think she'd ever be yesterday's news.

"At least until word gets out about my predicament," Nellie said darkly, sighing.

"You're not the first unwed single parent in town," I said low enough that nobody could overhear me. "And I could help with that."

"I told you, Noah. I'm not looking for a marriage proposal." She rolled her eyes dramatically.

"I'm not proposing—yet, anyway," I said, lifting my glass to take a sip. I set my glass down, leaning forward as I kept my eyes on hers. "But I'm interested in you, Nell. I'm really, really interested in you, and I have been for a while. If you're up for it, I'd like to give us a try."

"Noah..." Nellie sounded conflicted. "I don't even know if—"

"I don't care about that, Nell," I interrupted. "I mean, I care, but not in the way you think. It doesn't matter to me if I am, or if I'm not. I'm interested in you and all that comes with you."

She swallowed, her eyes glistening, and nodded. "I don't even know how to be in a relationship, Noah. I haven't been in one since high school."

"Fitting, neither have I," I smirked. "We can figure it out together."

"I—"

"Think about it, Nellie. As much as you want to act like we don't have chemistry, I feel it, and I know you do, too."

"That's not the issue, Noah," Nellie sighed. "You know what the issue is."

"Trust me when I say, either way I'm in. I know that's not what you were looking for when you told me, I know you were telling me because you felt I should know, and I'm thankful for that. But I'm in, Nellie. I want this, all of it." I told her, looking pointedly at where her stomach would be, although I couldn't see it through the table.

And I meant it. Nothing about Nellie's situation changed how I felt about her. If anything, it made those feelings stronger.

NELLIE

.   .   .

MY MOUTH OPENED AND CLOSED, my brain whirling for something to say—anything at all, but I was speechless.

The last thing I expected from this date was a relationship proposition before the main course arrived at our table. Especially after dropping the bombshell of my pregnancy before we'd even made it out the door, but Noah surprised me.

I was spared having to respond by Gabrielle appearing with our dinner. She set both plates down with a flourish in front of us and exchanged some words with Noah that I couldn't focus on. I couldn't hear past the roaring in my ears. How he could remain so calm when it felt like my entire world was spinning off its axis was beyond me.

She was gone a moment later, leaving us to eat, only I was frozen, all of my reservations and fears buzzing around in my brain like angry bees.

"Breathe, Nell. Like I said, I'm not proposing. But I think we owe it to each other to see what's here."

"You're not just doing this because of the Hartley triplets' interest in us?"

"I don't do things unless I want to." Noah grinned mischievously. "But I admit, I might have used their interest in us as leverage to get you to actually say yes to a date."

"Really?"

"Yup, but I was hoping my undeniable charm would seal the deal and you'd want to see me for real."

I snickered, shaking my head at his ridiculous confidence and ease, but grateful for it. "I don't know. There are so many complications. I work for you, and I'm also maybe—"

"Knocked up by me?" Noah interjected with a disparaging grin. "Well, that's the point of dating someone, to figure it out. Either way, you're still going to keep working for the resort."

"No matter what happens?" I asked, frowning. I hated that I needed the assurance.

"No matter what happens," Noah nodded seriously. "Until you leave on your own accord. Maybe for a job with better benefits."

"So, I'm not going to lose my job for needing time off to go to doctors appointments, or for being due in the middle of peak season?"

"Of course not." It was Noah's turn to frown, as if my question offended him deeply. "When are you due?"

"July nineteenth," I answered.

He nodded. "Okay, that's fine. We've got plenty of time to figure that out. And we will figure it out, Nell. I don't want you worrying about anything."

His earnest expression had me believing him. Noah's words were a comforting blanket over me, spreading warmth through my system and helping me relax for the first time in weeks.

The rest of dinner passed by comfortably, the both of us settling into the ease of each other's company. Noah kept the conversation light but interesting, asking me about my hobbies and my life back in Guelph, and regaling me with stories about some of the trouble he and his brothers had gotten into over the years.

I smiled a lot, enjoying the stories, even if they prodded at the bruised part of my heart—the long, ignored hurt of my parents' indifference. It wasn't Noah's fault that he'd been brought up in a loving family, and I'd been brought up by duty and obligation.

I hadn't heard from my parents since Christmas, although that wasn't uncommon. Part of me was grateful that they were too involved in their own lives to check in because it meant that I didn't have to dodge telling them about the pregnancy, but it still hurt.

After dinner, Noah walked me up the stairs to my door. We paused on the little deck, turning to face each other. He had an expectant, determined look on his face.

"I had an incredible time with you tonight, Nellie," he told me, stepping closer and cupping my face in his hand.

"I had a good time, too," I admitted, tracking his every movement.

"I'd like to take you out on another date."

He swallowed, and I watched as his Adam's apple bobbed. I fought the urge to press my lips to it.

"Okay," I murmured as he moved in closer, his breath cascading over my lips. I was thankful we'd both sucked on mints on the drive home. But as soon as Noah kissed me, all worries about bad breath flew from my head.

It was a slow, tender kiss that I felt all the way to my toes. He took his time kissing me, following the subtle cues I didn't even realize I was giving him. I parted my lips, allowing him entrance, and he deepened the kiss. My fingers gripped the lapels of his dress jacket, as if that would anchor me against the free falling sensation taking over.

It was a stark contrast to our hurried, drunken kisses the night we shared together, but somehow it was just as hot.

I felt the passion liquifying between us with each supple pass of his tongue against mine. At one point, I let out a quiet moan, unable to stop myself. I could feel Noah's smile against my mouth.

When he finally ended the kiss, my body was aching for more.

Noah pulled back enough to look at me, his eyes reflecting the same molten passion I felt. "Good night, Nellie. Sleep well." His voice was low and affected, stroking the flames of my own wanton need.

"Good night," I whispered. Noah waited until I unlocked

my door and stepped inside, then he headed back down the stairs to his truck. I watched from the window as he drove away, my finger pressed to my lips that still buzzed from our kiss.

I'd wanted desperately to invite him in, but I also wanted to take things slow this time. Make sure it was something we both really wanted—especially him. He'd just found out about the pregnancy, and I knew he needed to process that before we went any further.

Then I called Sage to fill her in on what happened, and have her help me work through all my feelings and reservations.

True to her role as my best friend, Sage celebrated the news that I was, sort of, officially dating Noah Wood, then she lectured me on how I shouldn't let my previous lackluster relationships and familial trauma stop me from something that had amazing potential.

A necessary reminder, as we both knew I tended to self-sabotage.

CHAPTER NINETEEN

Noah

I THOUGHT about Nellie for the rest of the weekend. Under normal circumstances, I would probably try to play it cool, but circumstances weren't normal. Nellie was pregnant, possibly with my child, and I had a lot of thinking to do.

I'd meant what I said, about how it didn't matter to me one way or another because I was interested in her, first and foremost, and I had been since I woke up to find her gone from my bed after the night we spent together.

I wanted Nellie, and it didn't matter to me that she was possibly pregnant with someone else's child. It didn't matter to me if the baby was biologically mine or not, I wanted everything with Nellie.

But because she was pregnant, that meant that I had to show her I was serious about her, and that meant a good morning text Sunday morning, and a good evening text Sunday evening, too—to let her know I was thinking about her.

She was consuming my every thought.

So was the fact that I'd have to come clean to Damien sooner rather than later. Keeping things casual between us was no longer an option. Not that it ever really was, with the Hartley sisters' interest in us.

I got my chance early Monday morning, a half hour before Nellie was scheduled to start. Damien walked in after clearing the parking lot, when I was in the kitchen brewing a pot of coffee. I hadn't slept well the last two nights, my mind too busy to truly shut off.

"The Rustic is officially up and functional, so you'll be able to move all those bookings for the Sprucewood," Damien said when he joined me in the kitchen. He grabbed a mug down from the cupboard and poured himself some coffee.

"Great, we'll do that today," I replied, leaning against the counter. Damien nodded and went to leave again. "Mind if we chat for a minute?"

"About what?" Damien scowled at me, taking a sip of his coffee.

"I wanted to let you know that I took Nellie on a date Saturday night, and we've decided to start seeing each other."

"Okay."

I kind of expected my brother to throw a fit, but Damien didn't seem surprised in the slightest.

"Okay?" I repeated, confused.

"How did you want me to respond? By telling you it's a stupid fucking idea to date employees? I'm pretty sure you already know that, but you're doing it anyway." He shook his head, taking another sip of coffee.

"You're right. Normally, I wouldn't have asked her out. But we have a connection, and we've had it since before she started working for us."

Damien let out a *hmpf* and continued staring at me, like he knew I wasn't finished with what I had to say.

Part of me wanted to blurt out the news that she was pregnant, and I might be the father. Mainly because Damien had experience as a father, and I could barely wrap my head around the idea of becoming one.

But I didn't think Nellie was ready for that news to make the rounds yet, and I wasn't either. I needed more time to come to terms with it myself, and I needed to figure out how she really felt about me.

The kiss we'd parted with suggested she was as interested in me as I was her, but this pregnancy thing added a whole other layer to it. Serious relationships were already outside my wheelhouse, but serious relationships and pregnancy? That was so far out of my wheelhouse, it was practically in another dimension.

"Hope it works out for you both, I guess," Damien finally said, his voice gruff. "And not just for the sake of the resort, but because I haven't seen you interested in seriously dating a woman in a long time." He finished his coffee, setting the mug in the sink.

"Thanks, I think," I frowned, not sure if I should be offended by that or not.

With a dip of his chin, Damien headed back outside—likely making himself scarce so I wouldn't try to pull him in for anymore brotherly chats.

Shaking my head, I topped up my coffee and went back to the office, deciding to get a start on calling guests who'd booked the Sprucewood.

Technically, that was a task Nellie could do, but I found myself wanting to lessen her workload, and it also gave me the excuse to be near her.

She walked in when I was on the phone, sending me a shy smile in greeting, then she headed to the kitchen to put her lunch in the refrigerator.

"We're sorry about any inconvenience this has caused you. We'll be comping the price," I said, my eyes tracking Nellie's movements as she walked into the office, unzipping her coat as she headed to the backroom to hang it up and swap out her winter boots.

The door swung shut behind her, and I continued my conversation with the guest. They were the second booking we had for Sprucewood, and they'd taken the news rather hard.

"Isn't the Rustic on the far side of the resort? We prefer to be closer to the main office," the guest, Mrs. Whitcomb, was saying. I tried to give her my full attention, but I could hear Nellie in the backroom, switching the laundry over.

I shook my head to refocus, opening the reservation software to see what else I could offer Mrs. Whitcomb.

"We do have one availability in the main building, Woodview A. It's a two-bedroom unit located on the top floor of our main building. The primary bedroom includes a queen-size bed and a whirlpool tub in the ensuite bathroom. The second bedroom includes a double bed and a twin bed. There's a full kitchen with a dishwasher, a deck with a BBQ, and incredible views of Hartwood Lake. There's also a woodburning fireplace and TV in the combination living room and dining room."

"Hmm, that could work," Mrs. Whitcomb said thought-fully. "Will we be comped for that as well?"

"Our Woodview units are actually more than the Sprucewood per night, but we could honour the Sprucewood prices for your weekend for the disruption to your plans."

"Okay, I suppose that would work."

Nellie walked in while I was finishing making the changes to Mrs. Whitcomb's reservation. Once I confirmed she was okay with the changes, I told Mrs. Whitcomb we'd see her over the weekend and ended the call.

Swiveling in my chair, I turned to face Nellie. "Morning." My gaze roamed, taking in the cute way she'd styled her hair in a thick twist over her shoulder, and the form-fitting black dress pants and flowy blouse. Walking past me to the other computer and pulling out the chair.

"Good morning," she replied, her cheeks a little flushed.

"How was the rest of your weekend?"

"Peaceful," she answered, shooting me a glance. "I mostly napped and read."

"What are you reading?"

"*The Complete History of Hartwood Creek*," her blush deepened when she caught my wide smile. "Sage got it for me as a welcome to town gift, but it's pretty interesting. Your family is mentioned a lot."

"I bet they are," I chuckled. I hadn't read that particular book, but it didn't surprise me.

"What did you get up to?" Nellie asked, changing the subject.

"Mostly sat around. I had a lot to think about," I answered, noticing when she tensed.

"Oh?" she didn't look at me. She kept her focus on the computer in front of her, waking it up and typing in the password.

"Yup. I thought about how delicious you tasted, and how I wish I would have stayed a little longer."

Nellie turned to look at me. "You can't talk like that, we're at work."

"So? Nobody's around," I pointed out.

She bit her lip, deliberating. "Well, I wish you'd stayed a little longer, too. But it was probably for the best."

"Why? It's not like you have to worry about getting pregnant," I teased. She scowled at me. "What? Too soon? I'm just saying."

"Not helpful, Noah," she giggled, despite herself, and rolled her eyes. "Ugh, I should have known you wouldn't take this seriously."

"Au contraire," I scooted closer to her in my chair. "I've never been more serious about anything."

"That's not exactly saying much," she pointed out, smirking. "You're notoriously unserious."

I grabbed the arm to her chair, tugging her closer to me. "I'm looking forward to proving you wrong." I smirked as I leaned forward and capturing her lips in a kiss that wasn't exactly office friendly.

Not that any kisses were really office friendly, but this one? Yeah. Probably shouldn't have done it, but I couldn't help myself. I needed to taste her.

Nellie had let out a squeak before our lips met, but once we started kissing, she all but melted into it.

"Noah," she chastised, pulling back and looking around, as if making sure we were still alone. "We really shouldn't do that here."

"You're right, I'm sorry. I needed to kiss you again, and I couldn't wait for our next date."

"We haven't set a next date," she replied dryly.

"Exactly. How am I supposed to wait for that, when I have no idea how long it will be?"

Nellie's eyes narrowed. "You're impossible."

"I wouldn't say I'm impossible," I replied, lifting a brow. "But while we're on the topic, when can I take you out again?"

"I'm free this weekend." Nellie shrugged, fighting a smile as she clicked on the reservation software.

. . .

NELLIE

IT WAS STRANGE, going to work the Monday after my date with Noah, after he declared his intentions and asked me out officially. Especially when he acted like a boyfriend when I arrived, all flirty smiles and stolen kisses.

I tried to put a stop to that. We were at work, after all—but Noah wasn't concerned. I, however, felt like everyone else at work had opinions already, and that made me feel claustrophobic.

At lunchtime, Easton kept smirking knowingly at me, which was almost as disconcerting as Damien's refusal to look in my direction. Damien was always grumpy, and it frequently seemed like he was mad about something. I had no reason to believe I was the cause of his irritation, but his refusal to even grunt a hello at me made me feel like I was the cause.

Especially because he was ignoring Noah, too. He sat at the usual table he and Charlotte usually occupied, eating his lunch in stony silence across from Easton, who'd sat there probably to annoy him more than anything.

Rhonda and Denise didn't seem to treat me any differently. They kept to themselves at their own table toward the back of the dining room. Neither of them spared any conspiratorial glances in my and Noah's direction.

Noah sat with me, as he usually did, save for that short period of time when I think he was attempting to avoid me. He kept a respectable distance, keeping to his side of the table as he talked about mundane things. Mostly what we could all expect from the next two weeks while we waited for the plumbing issues in the Sprucewood cottage to be dealt with.

Rhonda and Denise didn't seem too excited about having to

add The Rustic into their rotations, even though they'd be removing the Sprucewood for the time being. The Rustic was far enough away that they'd have to reorganize their cleaning schedules.

Apparently, it was a bit of a hike from the main office. The Rustic was one of the more private cottages on the northern side of the property. Noah said they normally kept it shut down during the winter seasons, opening it up only during the summer.

I half-listened to the conversations happening around me, distracted by the way Noah kept stealing glances and smiling at me. The feel of his lips earlier that morning hadn't done anything to douse the fire he started Saturday night, when he'd kissed me at the door.

I felt wound up and I didn't like it. I knew myself well enough to know that when I got into a certain state of provocation, so to speak, I could make some poor decisions.

Noah's kisses and touches had activated that part of me that I thought was dormant. I'd honestly thought my libido had fled the building upon seeing those two pink lines on the pregnancy test—and it had, for a spell.

Until Noah awakened it.

I needed to talk to Sage, and STAT. But first, I had to get through the workday. And it dragged on and on.

When Noah stepped out to go deal with maintenance jobs or whatever else he handled during the day, two hours after lunchtime all but froze.

It was eerily quiet in the office. No pressing tasks to occupy my mind and make time pass quicker. I was caught up in laundry, so I found myself sitting at the desk, waiting for the phone to ring or a pressing email to come in that required my attention.

Noah's absence and a lull in phone calls made it so I had no choice but to overthink everything. Mainly Noah's lips on mine. Unable to handle the silence and lack of distraction, I picked up my cell and texted Sage.

ME: Help. I suddenly feel like I've been hit by the horny bus. I blame Noah, and his stupid kisses and smiles.

Sage: Hahaha! Well, that doesn't surprise me...welcome to the second trimester.

Me: What do you mean?

Sage: Your libido is *the highest* during the second trimester, because nausea decreases, and energy levels increase. Lucky Noah. Nix is loving this stage, so far...

Me: TMI, Sage.

Sage: Sorry, not sorry.

Me: I can't sleep with him.

Sage: Why not?

Me: It's too soon. We just said we'd give things a go...I don't want to complicate it with sex.

Sage: It's already complicated, my friend.

Me: Ugh, don't remind me.

Sage: All I'm saying is, you'll feel *much better* when you jump his bones.

Me: You're not helpful at all. ☹

Sage: Hehe, sorry. Wanna meet at Tabitha's after work for tea and chats?

Me: I guess so.

Sage: See you then!

. . .

THE OFFICE PHONE RANG, putting an end to the lull. I put my cell down and picked it up.

"Hello, Whimsical Woods Resort, Nellie speaking. How can I help you?"

CHAPTER TWENTY

Nellie

WE WERE SITTING around Tabitha's kitchen island later that evening, after Sage made me fill Tabitha in on everything that had transpired so far between me and Noah.

Tabitha practically swooned when I told her word for word —at Sage's request—what Noah had said when he found out I was pregnant.

"The fact that he doesn't even know for sure if he's the father, and he's all in!" she squealed, practically jumping up and down. "I'm so excited for you both, especially for Noah! I feel like the whole town's been waiting forever for him to settle down with a nice girl."

"Okay, hold your horses. Who said anything about settling down? We just started dating!" I could feel the familiar panic that a monogamous relationship usually inspired in me rising. Or maybe that was pregnancy related panic, it was difficult to tell.

"I know, but I feel like you guys are endgame," Tabitha waved my protest away with her hand, as if batting a pesky fly away from her. "I felt it at the Witches' Ball, and again at the New Year's party."

"Tabitha's highly intuitive." Sage nodded confidently.

"It's that Hartley blood," Tabitha giggled. "It's diluted, but I can sense out love-matches."

"Well, so am I!" I protested with a point. "Intuitive, I mean. I get inklings about things."

"Yeah, but your fear of committed relationships and intimacy tends to block your inklings from working on you in that department," Sage said.

"I have no problem with intimacy, clearly." I gestured to my belly. "Otherwise, I wouldn't be in this predicament."

"Okay, that part you're okay with. At least until feelings get involved." She gave me a pointed look.

"Is it too early in our friendship to ask why you have a fear of committed relationships and feelings?" Tabitha asked, leaning against her counter, and looking at me expectantly with wide, honest blue eyes quite like Noah's. One of the few familial resemblances they seemed to share.

"Ugh, I hate getting into it but basically? My parents aren't the greatest, and the one relationship I had sucked, and now I run scared because I'm used to being on my own." I shrugged, summarizing it as much as I could without getting too into it.

"Ah, I see," Tabitha nodded, pursing her lips thoughtfully. "Well, Noah's got a touch of commitment-phobia too, although he doesn't really have an excuse. I mean really, who hasn't been burned by their high school love?" She rolled her eyes dramatically.

"Oh, so we're two commitment-phobic people trying to make a go of it. Great. This isn't a recipe for disaster or anything."

Tabitha smiled kindly at me. "I think you'll both be coming from a place of understanding, which is never a bad thing."

"She's right," Sage interjected. "The important thing to remember is to communicate. You feel scared? Tell him. You feel like running for the hills? Tell him."

"I'm sure he'll love hearing every other second that I'm having misgivings; it'll really boost his confidence."

Tabitha smirked. "His ego could use a little deflating, I'm sure it'll be good for him."

"When is your next date?" Sage asked.

"This weekend." I rolled my shoulders, trying to work out the kinks in them. My body was a little achy today, especially after spending most of the day in a near-constant state of tension.

"What are you guys going to do?" Sage asked.

"No clue, I don't have the energy to plan dates. My idea of a perfect date would be staying in and wearing sweatpants, but I don't think we're there yet. We're still trying to impress each other."

Sage snorted with laughter, then covered her mouth in embarrassment. "Ugh, did your sinuses get all screwed up while pregnant? Or is that a me thing? It happened with Daphne, too."

"Ah, the classic pregnancy rhinitis." Tabitha nodded. "I had it with the twins, but not with Bryson."

As if she summoned them, the twins raced into the kitchen, with Daphne trailing behind them.

"Can we get a snack? We're super hungry," Brielle said, peering up at her mother with hopeful eyes.

"Okay, but you've already had cookies, so you can have fruit or veggies. What's it going to be, girls?" Tabitha asked, opening the refrigerator and looking over her shoulder. The three girls exchanged a look with one another, as if deliberating.

"Fruit," Brielle answered for everyone, and Daphne and Bella nodded in agreement. Tabitha's lips twitched as she pulled out a Tupperware full of fruit and set it on the counter and grabbed three plates.

"You can eat your snack in the living room, but please bring the plates back when you're done," she said, putting a mixture of honey dew, cantaloupe, watermelon, and berries on each plate.

"Okay!" the girls said in unison, grabbing their plates and heading back to the living room.

Tabitha turned to face us again. "I think you guys should go to Juan in a Million. They have the best chimichangas and enchiladas, and they were featured in an episode of Food Fanatics!"

"I second that suggestion," Sage nodded enthusiastically. "The food is delicious, and it's more casual than The Harvest."

"We'll see. Don't get me wrong, it sounds delicious, but I think we need to go somewhere a little more private. We need to talk."

"I thought you were having issues not jumping his bones at work. Are you sure you want to go somewhere more private with him?"

"I'd like to think I have some restraint," I frowned, but Sage raised a valid point. "We do need to talk, though, and the last thing I need is for the entire town to catch wind of things."

"Yeah, that's true," Sage wrinkled her nose, thinking. "Too bad it's freezing out. There's a lot to do in Hartwood Creek when it's warm out. Picnics by the lake, hikes in the woods."

"You can do stuff in the winter, too," Tabitha argued. "Ice skating, tobogganing—"

"Things she probably shouldn't do while pregnant," Sage pointed out.

"Right, not really that safe. Hmm. What about a romantic

horsedrawn carriage ride? Noah has a connection he could use," Tabitha winked.

"Guys, I'm sure he's thought of something already. And if not, it doesn't have to be so grand. We could grab something to eat and go for a walk or a drive. The important thing is we need to talk about how all this is going to work."

Noah

THE REST of the week passed by in a bit of a blur. James started working on the plumbing in the Sprucewood cottage, and he told me tonight that he should be able to wrap things up with it sooner than anticipated.

On Friday night, I was expected at my parents' house for dinner, so Nellie and I planned our date for Saturday. She didn't seem overly enthusiastic about the prospect of going out again, and kept insisting the date was to talk more about 'the situation'. Regardless of her trepidation, I was going to make it a good one.

But first, I had to get through a family dinner. I was fully anticipating an interrogation, of sorts. There was no way that word of Nellie and I dating hadn't reached my parents yet, especially not with Charlotte knowing.

Damien must have told her Monday night, because she came to work on Tuesday with a smug smile and quizzed me for twenty minutes, until Nellie pulled up. Blessedly, she'd left Nellie alone, but the secret smiles she shot my way every time I interacted with Nellie said it all.

I showed up at my parents' house a little after six thirty. They lived in the same house we grew up in, a beautiful, four-bedroom log cabin north of the resort. My brothers and I maintained the unassumed road that led to their cabin as part of resort management, though Dad was able to keep their property itself maintained.

The cabin was built in the early eighties, using wood milled from the extensive property my dad had inherited from his parents. The resort itself was at the beginning of the property, lining Hartwood Lake and going north into the woods.

Hartwood Creek flowed from behind my parents' house, sweeping around the back and travelling through the woods, connecting my property and Damien's, as well as the property that had belonged to our grandparents and been passed down to Easton. The creek went all the way to the northeast side of town.

Easton was already there, and so was Damien, Charlotte, and the girls. I'd been the last to arrive because I'd gotten held up at the resort answering a guest's questions.

"What took you so long? We almost started eating without you," Easton said when I finally walked in and took off my coat.

"City folks," I sighed, shaking my head. Everyone at the table let out a murmur of sympathy.

"Was that the couple in the Whispering Pines cottage? Yeah, called it soon as I saw their electric vehicle pull in." Easton chuckled.

"And yet, you left me to deal with it."

"You're the best at dealing with disgruntled guests," Easton pointed out. "Damien scares the shit out of them, and I have a hard time not laughing in their faces."

"That's true," Charlotte agreed. "I've had to come to the rescue a few times when Easton's dealing with a guest. They don't take too kindly to being laughed at."

"Exactly." Easton pointed at Charlotte with a smirk. "I can't help it that my face reveals my thoughts. Damien's the same, only his face reveals his want to murder anyone who talks to him. So, it falls on you, brother dearest, to handle the difficult guests."

"How is the new girl at handling guests?" Mom asked, setting a serving bowl of salad down at the table. She'd made an obscene amount of spaghetti and meatballs for dinner, along with a large Caesar salad and homemade garlic bread. Spaghetti and meatballs were the girls' favourite meal, and Mom often cooked for their palates.

"Yeah, Noah, how's the new girl at handling *guests*?" Easton smirked, ignoring Damien when he turned to scowl at him in warning. He tilted his head towards his daughters as he scooped some pasta onto their plates.

"From what I've seen, she can handle her own," Charlotte interjected, coming to my rescue with a sympathetic smile. "She's picked up on the job quickly, I don't even have to check on her anymore."

"Definitely an improvement from Jeannine," Damien shocked me by putting in his two cents' worth. "At least she shows up when scheduled."

"Yeah, that's definitely a perk." It made me feel relieved that my brothers and Charlotte all seemed happy with Nellie as an employee.

"But that's not the only perk, right, Noah?" Easton was still goading me, and I sighed. If I didn't come clean soon, Easton would probably blurt it out for me.

"What's that supposed to mean?" Mom asked, picking up on the back-and-forth tension.

"We're kind of seeing each other," I admitted, taking the bowl of spaghetti off my father to serve myself. "It's a fairly new development, but we like each other."

"Oh."

I could tell my mom was at a loss for words. I knew she was probably thinking about how I hadn't had a serious relationship in years, and it was no secret that she wanted me to date seriously again. I don't think she expected me to start dating our new employee.

Mom would love more grandchildren, a fact that she often told us. Damien's girls were getting older, and I knew she missed the baby stage. But more than anything, she worried about her two remaining bachelor sons, wondering if we'd ever find love and settle down.

It didn't escape me that if I had it my way, both her wishes would come true; I'd be settling down and she'd get a new baby grandchild to love. I knew it wouldn't matter to her either, whether or not the baby was biologically mine.

"Are you sure it's wise? To date an employee?" she asked as she pulled out her chair at the head of the table nearest the kitchen. Her tone was cautious and delicate.

"I don't know," I admitted, grabbing a piece of garlic bread and swirling it around in the sauce. "I've never dated an employee before, so this is entirely new to me."

"I'm glad to see you're interested in dating again, but be careful. We might be a family-owned resort, but there are still power dynamics in place you need to consider. Your relationship could create an unfair advantage or disadvantage. It could also cause tension between other employees."

"You're basically the unofficial human resources manager, Mom," Easton pointed out with a smirk. "Can't you draw up some kind of paperwork?"

"I mean, we could probably find a template online," Charlotte said, thoughtfully. "A written agreement, for if things turn south for you both."

"I don't think that's necessary." The little food I'd eaten already was sitting heavily in my stomach.

Nellie was already apprehensive about the boss-employee dynamic, and she'd been worried about losing her job over the pregnancy. I didn't think my family would consider it an unfair advantage to keep her employed regardless, but would the rest of our staff feel the same? Or would they feel like I was showing favouritism?

Mom tilted her head, studying me for several beats and nodding. "Well, from here on out, make sure Damien handles any employee issues she may have. Time off requests, that sort of thing."

Damien's jaw clenched, but he nodded in agreement. I nodded too, realizing we'd have to fill him in sooner rather than later about the pregnancy situation so that he could accommodate Nellie's appointments without being a total prick to her. I'd have to talk to her about it tomorrow, which could put a damper on the whole date.

Inwardly sighing, I continued eating while the conversation moved from my dating life to the girls' extra-curricular activities. Both Aria and Ronan played hockey for the Hartwood Creek U7 team and had several tournaments lined up. Our family tried to be there as much as possible to cheer them on.

CHAPTER TWENTY-ONE

Noah

AT TWELVE THIRTY I picked Nellie up for our date. I had texted her after getting home from my parents' house and asked if she'd wanted to start our date earlier, so we could have lunch and explore some shops downtown, and she'd seemed into the idea.

She was dressed casually in a pair of thick leggings and a long, cable knit sweater. Her winter coat was unzipped, and her hair was straight. She wore her red toque and matching scarf.

"You look warm and cozy," I smiled when she stepped outside, tugging the door to her apartment shut behind her. She turned to face me, giving me a hesitant smile.

"Thanks, I didn't know what we were doing..."

"What do you want to do?" I asked. I hadn't booked a reservation this time. I figured there were enough places to eat downtown that didn't require a reservation.

"I don't know. Let's start with getting lunch, then we can figure it out? Tabitha and Sage were talking a lot about Juan In A Million, and I've been craving that ever since."

"Juan in a Million it is." I loved pretty much everything on their menu, plus service was quick. We walked down the stairs and out to my truck, my hand on the small of Nellie's back.

I opened the door for her, and she used the holy-shit handle to pull herself up and in. I grinned; there was nothing more attractive than a girl that knew how to climb into a lifted truck without assistance, even if I'd been hoping to offer a little assistance in the form of my hand on her ass.

There'd be plenty of time for that, I reminded myself, thinking about when she'd be further along. Her rounded belly would make it harder to climb up for sure. Then I started thinking about how I should probably invest in a more family friendly vehicle, but I forced myself to stop getting ahead of the situation.

Sure, I had long-term plans to keep Nellie and the baby in my life, but I didn't need to go trade in my truck. That would probably freak her out more than me telling her we had to draw up some official paperwork of our relationship, just in case, and tell Damien about her situation, since he would now be overseeing any day off requests.

My smile slipped a little as I walked around the front of my truck, but Nellie didn't seem to notice.

Resolving to put those thoughts aside at least until later, I drove downtown, finding parking in one of the downtown lots. We had a bit of a walk to Juan In A Million, but it wasn't too far.

Grabbing a hold of Nellie's hand, I lead the way through the walkway between two buildings. A mural had been painted along the side of the one building, which housed the art gallery.

The mural depicted a historic Hartwood Creek with witchy vibes, encompassing the folklore of the town.

"The downtown core is so cute," Nellie remarked with a smile, taking it all in. "It reminds me of Guelph, a little."

"How so?"

"It's got the historic vibes, but it's cozier," she lifted her shoulder in a shrug, the movement lifting our hands.

"I guess that's true, but I'll have to take your word for it. I've never actually been to Guelph."

"Really? Where's the furthest you've been?"

"Probably Ottawa, for a hockey game," I answered. "Haven't had much of an excuse to travel."

"Did you go to college?" Nellie asked, looking at me.

"Yeah, I took Business and Management at Springwood College, and I have a degree in accounting."

"I guess I figured you didn't have any formal training, since it seemed like you've always had a guaranteed job in the industry," Nellie said, going for a teasing tone.

"I did have a guaranteed job," I nodded, not denying it. "It was important to my grandparents that the resort stayed in our family, but they made sure we understood that we needed to know what we were doing ahead of inheriting. If we hadn't shown that we were determined and responsible, I don't think it would have passed down to us. Grandpa used to say that we were responsible for continuing the legacy in an honourable way, since we provide jobs to the locals. All of us—Damien, myself, and Easton—had to go to college. Damien took Hotel and Resort Management, and Easton has a diploma in Tourism."

"That makes sense," Nellie nodded. "It must be nice, to have inherited such a legacy."

"Sure, it is. But it's not all fun and games. We have a lot to live up to. My grandparents were a cornerstone around here, giving back whenever and wherever they could to help Hart-wood Creek to continue to grow while retaining its small-town charm."

"Are they..." Nellie stopped herself, as if reconsidering asking that question.

"They passed away about five years ago, almost one after the other," I replied. I still missed them both, but I was thankful they'd lived until their late eighties and had gotten to meet Aria and Rowan before they passed away. I was also relieved that neither one had to live long without the other, since my grand-parents had always been so in love and had done everything together.

"I'm sorry," Nellie sent me a sympathetic look, and I squeezed her hand in response.

Death was hard, especially when you loved someone, no matter how old that someone was.

"I'll miss my grandparents for the rest of my life, but I'll always cherish the memories I have with them. I was blessed to get so many years with them."

"You are lucky," Nellie said softly, glancing at me. "I never knew my grandparents."

"No?"

"Nope. I have no childhood memories of them coming over for Christmases, or to birthday parties. My parents were older when they had me, and their parents had already passed away."

"I'm sorry to hear that." My heart ached for Nellie.

We reached the doors to Juan In A Million, and I held it open for Nellie to walk in. The delicious scent of Mexican and Spanish cuisine wafted over to us, immediately making my mouth water.

Juan In A Million was decorated to embrace Mexican culture, with bright, vibrant colours and bold murals.

There was a glowing sign that read *feed me tacos and tell*

me I'm pretty, and the focal point of the establishment was a beautiful floral dahlia mural of Frida Kahlo painted onto the far wall.

"Woah," Nellie said, taking in the restaurant with wide eyes. "This place is amazing!"

"Wait until you try the food," I whispered in her ear as the hostess approached us.

"Hello! Welcome to Juan In A Million!" the hostess, Lucia Lopez, said with a big, welcoming grin.

She led us to a booth near the front windows and took our drink order as we slipped out of our coats and sat down on the bright yellow booth seats.

"It smells amazing in here," Nellie practically moaned, picking up the menu. She flipped it open, her eyes scanning the options. "I don't know what I want, it all sounds so good."

"I'm going to go with an order of beef chimichangas," I told her. "I'll share, if you want to order something else to try."

"Chicken enchiladas?" Nellie asked, looking up at me hopefully.

"Sure. They give you massive portions, so we'll be able to split everything and still probably have leftovers," I chuckled.

Lucia chose that moment to reappear with our two ice teas. "Have you decided what you'd like to get?" she asked.

"Sure have, Lucia. We'll take a plate of beef chimichangas, and the pretty lady will have chicken enchiladas. Extra sour cream, guacamole, and salsa, please."

"Coming right up," Lucia said, finishing taking down our order and heading to the kitchen.

"The mural is so beautiful," Nellie said, taking in the beautiful artwork on the walls.

"Freyja Durand painted it. She owns the art gallery in town and has done a lot of the murals around Hartwood Creek. She painted the one in the alley, too."

"That's so cool!" Nellie's face lit up with excitement. "Is it open today?"

"I'm sure it is, she usually offers classes on Saturday mornings and evenings. We could go check it out if you'd like."

"That would be great. I love art."

"Are you an artist?" I asked, thinking about the elaborate makeup she'd done for her Halloween costume.

"I wouldn't say that."

"Could have fooled me, your costume makeup was incredible. So incredible, I had a hard time recognizing you without it." I smirked.

"I mean, I'm decent with face painting, special effects, and makeup, but I don't draw or paint or anything. I just...like art, I guess. Guelph had a lot of art galleries near where I used to live, and sometimes I'd go to shows to do something. They always had wine and cheese, and I could pretend to be cultured for an evening." Nellie's lips twitched, fighting a smile.

"Well, we'll check it out."

NELLIE

AFTER LUNCH, we put our leftovers in Noah's truck and walked around downtown. Noah gave a more guided tour than the one I'd gotten from Sage. She'd mostly shown me her favourite stores, but Noah gave me a thorough history lesson on the businesses and the people of Hartwood Creek.

Our first stop was the art gallery since it was closest to where we parked.

Before we went inside, Noah filled me in on the history of it. It was apparently opened by Mrs. Durand in the nineties, who happened to be Sage's neighbour in the apartments above the hardware store. I hadn't met her yet, but Sage had shared a few funny anecdotes with me. Her grandniece, Freyja, ran it now that Mrs. Durand had retired.

It was open, and Freyja was busy cleaning up from her morning art class with kids, and preparing for a paint night class. She came from the backroom when the door chimed, drying her hands on her smock.

"Can I help you? Oh! Hi Noah."

Freyja's face lit up at the sight of Noah. He gave her a returning smile and put his arm around me.

"Freyja, I'd like you to meet Nellie. She wanted to come check out the gallery after she found out you did the murals in Juan In A Million. Nellie, this is Freyja. We went to high school together."

"And middle school, and public school." Freyja laughed.

I smiled at Freyja. "It's nice to meet you. Noah's right, I was admiring the murals. You're very talented."

"Thank you!" Freyja flushed at the compliment and held out her hand to shake mine. "It's so nice to finally meet you, Nellie. I've heard a lot about you."

"Oh really?" I glanced at Noah, sending him a questioning look.

"It's the Hartley triplets," Freyja explained, lowering her voice as if she expected them to overhear her. "They came in the other day and couldn't stop talking about the pretty newcomer that captured Noah's attention."

"Ah, right," I shifted awkwardly on my feet.

"Nellie's still not used to their level of community involvement," Noah explained with a laugh.

Freyja sent me a sympathetic smile. "I can understand that. They mean no harm, they're like..." She paused for a moment. "They are like overly-involved grandmothers. To everyone."

"Yeah." I laughed awkwardly, thinking back to earlier,

when I'd felt a little sorry for myself for not having grandparents. Seems like I might have surrogate grandmothers after all, and I wasn't sure if I'd get used to their interest in me.

"Anyway, would you like a bit of a tour? It's a little messy in the back right now. I'm cleaning up after a morning art class with kids," Freyja offered with a smile.

"Sure, I'd love a tour!"

"Excellent!" Freyja clapped her hands together, then began the tour.

She told me that her aunt Alma had opened the gallery in the early nineties, and that it used to be a gallery strictly for artists to sell their work. She hired her sister, Freyja's grandmother, as the art curator and to manage and oversee things so she didn't have to.

When Freyja took over, she expanded in the back and created an area where she could host classes. She showed us the back, where she hosted the art classes. She did paint nights, pottery courses, mixed media courses, painting, and sketchbook courses. She had classes geared to kids and to adults. She had her liquor license, so she could serve wine at the adult paint nights and gallery shows she hosted.

I made a mental note to drag Sage along to one of her adult paint nights. It sounded like a lot of fun, even if we couldn't drink the wine.

"Local artists still sell their work through the gallery, and every couple of months, I host art shows to feature their work." Freyja explained as we walked back into the front gallery. "I team up with my friend, Jolie Loucks. She makes the best charcuterie boards! Our next art show is on the last Saturday of the month."

"We'll be there," Noah said, sending me a flirty little smile that made the butterflies in my belly swirl and dance.

"Great!" Freyja grinned.

"How is Mrs. Durand doing?" Noah asked, and they launched into a conversation about Freyja's aunt.

While they talked, I wandered over to one of the walls in the gallery, my gaze pulled to a painting there. It was a landscape of a babbling creek and an old worn bridge in a heavily wooded area. There was something about it that called to me, and if I had the funds, I'd have bought it on the spot to hang in my apartment.

Unfortunately, I didn't have the funds, so I could only stand and admire it for a couple of minutes, embracing the peaceful feeling that washed over me while I looked at it.

"Are you ready to head out?" Noah asked, coming up behind me.

"Yeah, sure." I nodded, pulling my gaze away from the painting. "Where to next?"

"I say you check out Enchanted Echoes," Freyja suggested. "No tour of Hartwood Creek is complete without seeing the original Hartley homestead."

"She's right, it is a staple." Noah said. "We'll see you later, Freyja. Thanks for the tour."

"Any time! Hopefully, we'll see you at the art show!" Freyja called out as we made our way out of the gallery.

"Is Enchanted Echoes that crystal store?" I asked, feeling a pull toward it.

"It sure is. It's run by Delia Hartley. She's Dorothy's granddaughter."

"So, another cousin of yours?" I rolled my eyes.

"A distant one." Noah smirked.

"Gosh, no wonder you had a hard time dating. You're related to practically everyone in town."

"Not everyone, but yeah. Quite a few of them, either through the Wood family line or the Hartley line." Noah chuckled.

I'd been meaning to check out Enchanted Echoes out ever since I'd moved to town, but I hadn't gotten around to it. I hadn't wanted to go alone, but I hadn't wanted to drag Sage, either. She didn't exactly believe in the metaphysical.

I, on the other hand, wasn't completely opposed to the idea. After all, Delia's reading on the night of Witches' Ball set things in motion for me, and I wondered if she'd have any other insights to share about the path my life had taken.

The original Hartley homestead was located on the far northeast side of town. Noah explained it was the last building before the trails lead to the Whimsical Woods Resorts.

"The road to get to Hartwood Creek is on the west side of town, but you can get there by foot using the trails. It's how Morgana Hartley visited Alexander Wood," Noah explained.

My skin pebbled with goosebumps as I glanced toward the pathway leading toward the trails.

I'd read about Morgana Hartley and Alexander Wood in the book Sage had bought for me. There had been a few old sepia photographs of a couple from long ago, and their triplet daughters.

The original homestead was over three hundred years old, and it looked like it. The stairs had recently been rebuilt, and they'd added a wheelchair ramp for accessibility, but the house itself looked like it'd been scooped up from the seventeen hundreds and dropped on a snowy street in Hartwood Creek. It was timeless.

The stone and log cabin had the original wooden door that had seen better days but still looked solid. It creaked when Noah opened it, and he held it for me as I stepped inside.

The floors were all original hardwood. Thick, worn pine slats that creaked beneath my feet as I walked into the shop. There were tables and displays brimming with all sorts of different kinds of crystals in the centre of the room. On the right side of the large room were old built-in bookshelves full of books and other various items.

To the left of the expansive space, there was a large stone hearth with an old, cast-iron pot that looked suspiciously like a cauldron hanging on the ancient trammel hook over the fire, which kept the room comfortably warm despite the windchill outside.

The sight of the fire surprised me, especially with the age of the cabin. The fire seemed to be heating whatever was in the cauldron. It smelt of cinnamon, orange, and cloves.

There was a counter at the back of the room with a vintage cash register. On the wall behind the counter was another shelf with hundreds, if not thousands, of various vials. To the right of the counter was a doorway covered with a wooden bead curtain.

"Good afternoon!" an airy, recognizable voice called out from the backroom. The wooden beads made an almost musical sound as they knocked together when Delia Hartley parted them and stepped into the storefront. "Ah, Noah. I see you've brought our new friend with you. Nellie, isn't it? I remember you from the Witches' Ball. I trust you had a good night?"

Delia smiled knowingly. She was gorgeous with her long, wavy dark auburn hair and vivid green eyes framed by thick lashes. During the Witches' Ball, she'd dressed up as a fortune teller, although her outfit today was quite similar.

"Yeah, it was a good night," I said.

Delia's lips twitched with amusement, her eyes moving to Noah briefly, then flitting back to me. "And how are you finding Hartwood Creek?"

"It's very welcoming," I answered.

Delia's smile widened at my answer, and she inclined her head. "Well, we are very glad to have you as an official resident," she said. "I have a gift for you."

"You do?" I frowned, watching as Delia went behind the counter and grabbed something. It was a small brown paper bag with purple tissue paper peeking out the top.

"I do, it's a welcome gift," Delia smiled. "I've been waiting for you to come by so I could give it to you."

"Wow, that's really nice of you, Delia," Noah said, putting his hand on the small of my back.

She smiled. "I hope the items within bring you comfort and ease, Nellie. Please don't hesitate to visit if you need anything at all. I offer energy healing, spiritual mentoring, and group healing classes, as well as all the lovely items you see in my store." Delia chuckled, waving her hand around the room.

"Okay, yeah, that sounds great. Thank you," I said, holding the gift bag closer to my body. I felt like I needed to buy something, so I perused the shelves and ended up selecting two jars of all-natural body butter that Delia told me she made herself.

"It's great for stretch marks," Delia said, her knowing eyes sweeping down for the briefest of moments, a secret smile playing on her pillowy lips. It should have made me feel uneasy, but there was something about Delia's aura. It was nurturing and mystical, and I felt at home in her presence. Like I'd known her forever, even though I really hadn't. This was only my second time speaking to her.

I told myself I was being silly, anyway. There was no way Delia knew about my little secret yet. The word hadn't spread. Only four people knew about it, and those four people were sworn to secrecy. Tabitha hadn't even told Parker yet, and although Parker knew that Sage was pregnant, he had no idea I was, too.

I tried to pay for my purchases, but Noah beat me to it. "It's my treat," he murmured.

"I'll be seeing you soon, Nellie," Delia said, smiling her secretive, all-knowing smile.

We said our goodbyes and left Enchanted Echoes, then started walking back to the heart of downtown. "Feel like checking out the bookstore, or are you tired?" Noah asked. I really wanted to find somewhere to open my gift from Delia, but something told me to wait until I was alone.

"Sure," I replied, shrugging my shoulders. I'd already been in the bookstore a couple times, with Sage and on my own, but I firmly believed there was no such thing as visiting a bookstore too much.

The bookstore owner was an older gentleman with greying hair and square glasses and a little round belly. He dressed impeccably, in dress pants with suspenders and button up shirts, and sometimes wore a newspaper hat.

The first time I'd gone into the bookstore with Sage, he'd been there. The second time when I'd been on my own picking up a new romance book to fill the lonely hours at night, his wife had been behind the counter, too. She'd struck up an entertaining conversation about her favourite romance books of the year—many of which I'd added to my to-be-read list.

I hadn't realized until moving to Hartwood Creek how much I longed for that sense of community, that sense of belonging.

While we browsed, Noah playfully whispered that he wasn't related to the Loves, but that they'd moved to Hartwood Creek almost thirty years ago to purchase Beyond The Pages and raise their daughter.

After he gave me the 411 on the Loves, Noah went to check out the display table of new release thrillers and mysteries. He picked up one, flipping it open to read the synopsis. I couldn't help but pull my phone out and take a picture of him. I was not so ashamed to admit that I followed the Hot Dudes Reading account on Instagram, and Noah with a book was great fodder.

"Are you a reader?" I asked him, watching as he picked up another book to check it out.

"I haven't had much time to read lately, but yeah, I enjoy i.," Noah's cheeks flushed, almost as if he was embarrassed to answer. But his answer made him even more attractive to me.

"The playboy bachelor likes to read, too." I gave him an appraising look, which did nothing to douse the horny flames that had been licking up my body since the night of our very first date. If anything, it only made my libido increase like a hormonal teenager at a boy band concert.

I found it incredibly attractive when men read, ergo why I followed that account. Heck, a guy reading instantly went up in ten points on the attractive scale, no matter what level he started at. But Noah reading? It did something to me on a primal level.

CHAPTER TWENTY-TWO

Noah

THE WAY NELLIE was checking me out made the blood rush down south. I shut the book after trying to read the synopsis twice and not registering a damn thing about it. I could practically taste her arousal in the air, and it was distracting.

"I'm no longer a playboy, or a bachelor. I have a girlfriend, now. I asked her out and she said yes." I smiled, reminding her of my intentions.

Nellie's lips twitched with amusement, and she rolled her eyes. "Are you going to get the book?"

"Sure. Did anything catch your eye?" I asked.

"Yes," Nellie answered, her gaze slowly taking me in again, her tongue darting out to slowly lick her bottom lip. "A few things, actually."

I had a feeling she wasn't referring to the book she held in her hand.

I used the book I was holding to shield my growing arousal

and cleared my throat. "After you," I said, gesturing with my chin toward the cash register.

Nellie cast a knowing glance downward as she walked to the cash register. She put the book she was holding down on the counter, smiling at Corin Love.

"Did you find everything you needed today?" Corin asked us both, scanning the books we set on the counter. Nellie had chosen a romance book, while I'd grabbed one of the random new releases. I had no clue what the damn book was about, but that didn't matter.

"Sure did, thank you," she answered, pulling out her debit card before I could wrestle my wallet out of my coat pocket. "My treat," she insisted when I went to stop her.

"Thanks," I let her have this, knowing I'd irritated her by covering lunch and her purchases at Enchanted Echoes.

"If you're interested, Noah, the author of this book, Atticus Connelly, is doing a signing here next Tuesday night," Corin informed me, slipping a pamphlet into my book. "He's from Springwood. His family lived in Hartwood Creek, back in the day."

Nellie's face lit up. "That's so cool!"

Corin seemed delighted by Nellie's enthusiasm. "I think so, too. We love hosting local authors at our bookstore, and I've been trying to get Atticus Connelly to do one for a while now. He's a recluse, from what I understand. Doesn't do the whole social media thing and doesn't often do appearances, either. I had to pull some strings."

"We'll try to make it out," I replied, putting my hand on the small of Nellie's back while Corin put our new books into a reusable tote with the bookstore's name on it. I took the tote, sliding the body butter jars and the little gift bag from Delia in it and pulling the straps over my shoulder. "Thanks again, Corin."

"Thank you! Have a great day," Corin said, his eyes twinkling.

"There are a lot of local events happening in this town," Nellie said, as we stepped back out onto the street. It wasn't as busy as it was in the summer with all the tourists, but the downtown core of Hartwood Creek still saw a lot of traffic on the weekends. "I'm a little surprised. I mean, I knew they did a lot of cool events around Halloween and Christmas, but it seems like there's always something going on."

I took her hand as we walked. "Yeah, there really is. It's a small town, but it's never lacking in things to do. And everyone tries to support each other by attending the various events, so you'll probably see a lot of townies at the signing and the art show."

"That's so nice," Nellie said, her voice heavy with emotion. She blinked a few times, her eyes misting with emotion. "I can't get over how closeknit this town is. Like, everyone is so supportive and involved."

"It's a great place to raise a family, for sure," I said, casting a look in Nellie's direction when I heard her sniffle. She was wiping a few tears away with her free hand, and she drew in a shaky breath.

"God, I'm an emotional mess today. I'm sorry," Nellie apologized, her voice a little wobbly.

"Don't apologize, it's okay," I dropped her hand so I could pull her closer to my side, bending so I could plant a kiss on her cheek. "Real men don't fear emotions. Real men take their women out for hot chocolate when they're feeling emotional."

"Do they now?"

The smile was back on Nellie's face, and that was all I'd aimed for.

"Sure do, let's stop in at Tout de Sweets before we head to

the truck." I gestured to the café beside the bookstore, and Nellie nodded.

"I could go for a hot chocolate, especially if it comes with a shot of caramel and whipping cream."

"It will," I promised her.

It was busy inside the café. Tout de Sweets was a popular spot in town any day or time of the week. We made our way to the front counter, waiting in line for our turn.

Nellie had stepped out of my embrace when we entered the café, but I didn't take it personally. I knew she wasn't comfortable with the attention we'd been garnering, and there were more people in the café than there had been on the street.

"Hey, Noah! Good to see you. How's the fam?" Evelyn, another distant cousin and the manager of Tout de Sweets asked. Evelyn's facial structure was similar to Delia's, although where Delia had auburn hair with reddish undertones, Evelyn had dark hair and tawny eyes.

"Everyone's good, Evelyn," Noah answered. "How's things around here?"

"Busy as always," Evelyn answered with a laugh. "Ma and the aunties are holding court in their usual spot."

"Ah," I glanced over my shoulder, spotting the Hartley triplets in their favourite spot near the gas fireplace. It did appear as if they were holding court. The sight of it made me shake my head with amusement.

Nellie didn't look so entertained, though. She sent me an anxious look and tried to position herself so that I was blocking her from view if the Hartley triplets should look this way.

Betty was Evelyn's mom, and she—along with Dorothy and Alice—still owned Tout de Sweets, although only in name. They left the day-to-day management to Evelyn, and allowed her to make any decisions regarding the menu.

"What can I get you two?" Evelyn asked, pulling my attention back to her.

"Two hot chocolates, both with a shot of caramel, whip cream, and some chocolate shavings on top, please." I noticed Nellie eyeing up the desserts in the display case. "Oh, and maybe an assortment of baked goods."

"Coming right up," Evelyn said with a smile, as Jayden, the other full-time employee, set to making our hot chocolates. "What kind of baked goods do you want?"

"Pick out whatever you want," I told Nellie.

She worried her lip for a moment, considering all her options, finally deciding on a couple brownies, butter tarts, and cinnamon roll bites.

I paid for our drinks and goodies before we moved over to the side to wait for Jayden to make our drinks. "Do you want to sit inside for a bit, or head to the truck?" I asked, leaving it up to Nellie.

"If you don't mind, maybe we could go back to the truck? I mean, we still have some stuff to discuss, and I'd rather not get pulled into the Hartley triplets' orbit until we've clarified things a little more."

"Sounds good." I nodded in agreement. It wasn't easy sneaking out without capturing their attention, but the Saturday afternoon rush made it possible, although we'd both probably get an earful next time we ran into the Hartley sisters. It was only a matter of time before whispers got back to them that we'd been in the café and hadn't stopped to say hi.

We sipped at our hot chocolates as we walked back to my truck. The silence between us wasn't strained or uncomfortable, but I could tell Nellie was in her head about things. I wanted to ask her what was on her mind, but I knew I needed to wait until we were alone for that.

I unlocked my truck and opened the passenger door,

reaching inside to place the box of baked goods and my hot chocolate in and taking Nellie's from her and holding it so she could climb inside.

We sat in the cab for a few minutes, continuing to sip our hot chocolates as we waited for it to warm up.

"Did you have fun with me today?"

"Of course I did." Nellie seemed surprised by my question. "Did you have fun with me?"

"Obviously. I always have fun with you. It's kind of why I asked you to be my girlfriend."

"Well, that's good, I guess. It's good to have fun with the person you're dating." She said, her tone not giving away much.

"You don't seem so enthusiastic about the labels," I pointed out.

Nellie glanced at me, her eyes guarded. "It's not that. Okay, well, maybe it's a little that. I'm not used to labels and serious relationships, and I'm hormonal and horny and it's all a recipe for disaster."

"Sounds like a recipe for a good time for me. Especially that horny part."

Nellie shot me an unamused look. "I just...I'm worried, Noah. I like you, I do. I feel like we have a connection, I guess. But it's all so confusing with me being pregnant. Like, do we have a connection, or is that pregnancy hormones? Are we good for each other, or are you feeling responsible for my," she paused, her nose wrinkling, "*situation?*"

"I mean, I hope I'm responsible, but even if I'm not, I told you, Nell. I'm all in here. And I don't care how long it takes you to realize it." I gently cupped her chin, looking into her eyes. "I'm all in." I emphasized, holding her gaze.

Nellie drew in a deep breath to centre herself. "I don't know. I think I'd feel better if we maybe did the DNA test?

Then you'll know for sure, and if you're not, and if you change your mind about being here for me, I'll understand."

It was my turn to take a deep breath. "Nellie, I promise you that I will do whatever you want to feel more comfortable and secure. If you want me to take a DNA test, I will. But I mean it when I say it doesn't matter to me."

"I think it matters to me," Nellie whispered, looking at me with watery eyes. The golden flecks in her irises seemed brighter.

I swallowed hard. "Okay, that's fine. We'll get the DNA test. But I'm telling you, it won't change anything."

"How can you say that? You don't even know me." Tears were now sliding down Nellie's cheek, and I wiped them away with my thumb.

"I may not know every detail about you yet, but I know I want to be with you. I know I've felt this way since that night we spent together. Sure, maybe I didn't recognize it for what it was until you came back to town, but I know what I feel, Nell. I haven't been with anyone since that night with you."

She watched me while I spoke, realization dawning in her eyes, and before she could open her mouth to question my intentions again, I silenced her with a kiss. She tasted like hot chocolate and caramel, and she melted against my mouth like whipped cream on a hot drink.

Like the greedy bastard I was, I deepened the kiss, hungering for the taste of her. Nellie matched me, meeting each stroke of my tongue with her own. She consumed me as much as I consumed her; her hand going up to wrap around my coat sleeve, like she had to hold herself steady.

Breathless, I pulled back a little, taking in her heated cheeks and the dreamy look in her eyes. "Believe me yet?"

She smiled, shaking her head as she licked her lips, like she was trying to taste the kiss again. "I'm going to reserve judgment for a bit."

"So long as you promise to stop questioning everything and let it happen," I challenged, casually adjusting myself. That kiss had gotten me all worked up.

"I thought you didn't do relationships, so how come you're falling so easily into this?" I could hear a hint of insecurity in Nellie's voice, but she was working to mask it with a teasing smile.

"I'm a guy that knows what I want, that's all," I shrugged, putting the truck in drive and pulling out of the parking spot.

CHAPTER TWENTY-THREE

Nellie

WE DROVE TO HARTLEY PARK, which had beautiful panoramic views of the frozen Hartwood Lake. Noah kept the truck idling, the heat on to keep us both warm while we ate some of the baked goods and sipped our hot chocolates from Tout de Sweets and talked about the concerts we'd been to. We discovered we'd both gone to The Tragically Hip's final concert in Kingston.

We both agreed, it was like being a part of a little slice of Canadian history.

When we'd finished commemorating the Hip's incredible last concert and our hot chocolates were empty, Noah drove me home. By the time he pulled into the driveway, it was almost four o'clock. I was stuffed from lunch and all the snacking, and knew I'd probably end up having a light dinner and going to bed early.

Noah walked me up to my door. He insisted on carrying

my portion of leftovers from Juan In A Million, the tote from Beyond The Pages, and the box with the rest of the baked goods that we hadn't gotten to.

I unlocked my apartment and invited him in for a minute. He stepped inside, toeing off his boots, then he carried everything over to the island while I took off my coat and hung it up on the coat rack.

"It looks so different in here."

"Since Nix lived here? They apparently painted it."

"I used to live here, too," Noah told me, looking at me with his mischievous grin. "Before Nix. Back when I was building my cabin."

"Oh, I didn't know that!"

"Yeah, it wasn't for long. About eight months? I can't remember. It looks really good though." Noah said, his gaze taking in my space. I hadn't done much to make it my own yet. Angela hadn't exactly let me decorate our apartment, so I didn't have much to work with.

"It's getting there." I tucked a strand of hair behind my ear. For some reason, my thoughts went back to that painting of the creek at the gallery.

"I don't want to end our date on a stressful note, but I do need to talk to you about something work related," he said, those kissable lips frowning a little.

"Oh?" I was feeling slightly better after our chat earlier, but at the mention of work, I tensed up again.

"It'd probably be best if Damien handled your day off requests, and other employment needs. I don't want the other employees thinking I'm playing favourites just because we're dating."

"That seems fair."

"So, that means we're going to have to fill him in on what's going on with you. I know I've already approved your request for Friday afternoon, so don't worry about that, but going forward..."

"Yeah, of course." I nodded. I didn't like the idea of telling Damien, but everyone was going to find out eventually.

"And I was thinking, if you were okay with it, that I could come with you to the next appointment." Noah looked at me hopefully. When he saw the bewildered look on my face, he rushed to explain. "I mean, so we could do the DNA test."

I blinked, not expecting that at all. "Uh, if you want to, I guess?"

"I do. Want to, I mean." Noah smiled at me, like I'd given him a gift by saying yes. The way his blue eyes lit up had the butterflies swirling around in my stomach.

"Okay," I whispered.

Noah stepped closer, his eyes soft. He put his hand on the side of my hip, drawing me to him, and lowered his mouth to mine. The kiss was chaste, but tender—so tender it almost made me want to weep.

He touched me and kissed me with such reverence, and he gazed at me with such fealty. I'd never felt so seen and so exposed. It turned me on, calmed me, and terrified me in the same breath.

Noah didn't overstay his welcome. And as much as I could tell he wanted to, he didn't deepen the kiss. I was thankful for that because my restraint was thinning.

"I should go," he murmured, his gaze dropping to my swollen lips and lifting again. "I'll see you Monday, okay?"

"Sure, yeah." I nodded, sounding just as frazzled from our kiss as I felt.

A large part of me wanted to invite him to hang out longer, but I knew if I did that, we'd end up in bed together again. I was trying to take things slow, trying to protect my heart until we could find out for sure if Noah was the father of my baby.

His words kept replaying in my head, but that didn't change the fact that I needed to find out for sure before I allowed him to fully commit himself to me. Sure, he might think he wants this—me, a baby that might not be his—but his opinion on the matter could change if he found out he wasn't the father.

So, it was better to end the date now, before it could go any further. He closed the door behind him, and I listened to his heavy steps on the stairs. A few moments later, I heard his truck start. Only then did I peek out the window and watch him drive away.

Besides, if I'd invited him to stay, I wouldn't have been able to open the gift Delia gave me.

I grabbed the gift bag and brought it to the living room, setting it down on the coffee table. I proceeded to stare at it for several minutes, working myself up to opening it.

"You're being ridiculous," I told myself after twenty minutes had passed. Shaking my head, I reached for the gift bag and set it on my lap. I pulled out the tissue paper and peered inside. There were several things inside the gift bag, so I started pulling them out one by one and setting them on the table.

There was a bag of loose tea called Mother's Intuition, and two small white cardboard boxes.

Inside the first box was a crystal no bigger than the palm of my hand. The crystal was the colour of blood and fire. It looked like it was glowing, and when I picked it up in my hand and held it, it was cool to the touch. There was a small cardstock note underneath it, with the name of the crystal and a description.

The Carnelian crystal is a highly energetic healing crystal that glows like a flame. It can keep you grounded and make you feel invincible, giving you the courage and strength to transition into motherhood. It works at any stage of your motherhood journey.

Carnelian has been known to strengthen and help the organs heal, to boost your stamina, and connect to your sacral chakra and stir up your inner fire. It can be used from conception right through birth, and for those who need a hand healing from childbirth. It is for those who are struggling with the idea of strength and grants you stamina, both mentally and physically.

Inside the second box was a moon-shaped crystal pendant. The crystal was soft shades of purple and pink and it was a little smaller in size. It, too, came with a cardstock description.

Lepidolite is a natural tranquilizer and a soother for souls that feel pulled in a thousand directions. Whether stressed about conception or looking for a mood-lifter, Lepidolite keeps mothers-to-be in harmonious joy so that they are better equipped to welcome the transformation at hand.

Beneath the boxes was a handwritten note from Delia. Her penmanship was neat and feminine.

Dearest Nellie,

I have thought a lot about you since our reading on the night of the Witches' Ball, when the cards showed me your future so brightly. I foresaw that it was only a matter of time before you found yourself back in Hartwood Creek, and not just for a visit.

I know you are apprehensive about the days—and months— ahead of you, but I've been dreaming a lot about you, and I know everything is going to work out for the three of you.

These crystals and this tea will help you on your journey to motherhood. The tea is safe to take while pregnant; I assure you. It is a brew my ancestors passed down containing ginger, citrus peel, lemon balm, and rosehips.

If you ever need anything at all, please don't hesitate to come see me.

Much Love,

Delia

P.S. Welcome home.

After reading Delia's letter, I sat back on the sofa and stared at the crystals. I'd anticipated that she would have given me something, well, witchy, given she was the owner of Enchanted Echoes and a descendant of Morgana Hartley. I hadn't expected her to know about my pregnancy, however, and be so aware of my fears and apprehension.

I suppose it made sense, though. After all, she'd read my cards during the night of the Witches' Ball and told me I'd meet the love of my life and change the course of both our lives forever.

My phone rang, rousing me from my thoughts. It was Sage.

"So, how was it?" she asked, her tone all giddy.

"It was good," I answered distractedly, my gaze going back to the gifts Delia had given me.

"Just good! Come on, spill the deets! Where'd you go? What'd you do?" Sage's pestering pulled me back.

"We went to Juan In A Million for lunch, and it was amazing," I answered, knowing if I didn't start talking, she'd end up driving over to pull it out of me in person. "Then we walked around town and stopped at a few stores."

"Ooh, which ones?" Sage was fully invested in this. I heard her chewing something.

"Are you eating popcorn?"

"Maybe," Sage answered, her mouth full. "I'm hungry. Anyway, keep going. What stores did you go to?"

"The Art Cave, which was really great. Freyja is a sweetheart. We should do a paint night there."

"I'm down!" Sage exclaimed, her tone clearer now that she'd chewed and swallowed the popcorn.

"Then we checked out Enchanting Echoes."

"Oooh, I haven't braved that store yet," Sage said. I could

practically hear her shiver through the phone. "Apparently, she sells a lot of ingredients of the love elixir, and even has a book on how to incorporate the love elixir into various baked goods and drinks."

"Yeah, it was pretty neat. She sells a lot of crystals and some natural body butters. I got us both a jar. She said it helps with stretch marks."

"She said that? Like, to your face?"

"Yeah, and she gave me a gift, like, a 'Welcome to Hartwood Creek' gift. And in it, she gave me some crystals and included tea called Mother's Intuition and wrote a little note saying the tea was safe to take while pregnant."

"HOW DOES SHE KNOW!?" Sage practically shouted.

"I don't know! I mean, she seems like she knows things. Plus, she read my cards at the Witches' Ball." I shrugged, even though she couldn't see me.

"That's freaky," Sage sounded creeped out. "Sometimes, this town wigs me out a little."

"With the whole witchy thing?"

"Yeah. And the love elixir, and so on."

"I think it's cool," I replied. "I mean, you ended up drinking the elixir and are the happiest you've ever been, right?"

"Yeah, but I don't like to credit my happiness with Nix to some weird love potion thing. That's insane," Sage huffed. "Although..."

"What?"

"We should do a test! You and Noah should drink the love elixir, like, willingly. And see if that helps."

"How's that supposed to help?" I asked, bewildered.

"Well, for starters, it's supposed to only work on soulmates. It gives them a push to let go of their fears and give in. You could use that push."

"Hey!" I exclaimed, my brow furrowing. I was irritated by the call-out, But, Sage wasn't wrong.

"What! I'm not wrong, am I?" Sage giggled. "And I know you're dying to prove to me that all this weird, witchy, meta-physical stuff is real."

"I couldn't care less if you don't believe in it," I corrected. "I think it'd be strange to see all the evidence in a town like this and still deny it's a possibility."

"Eh, call me a denier until you and Noah take the love elixir."

"Well, I guess you'll be a denier forever. I'm not asking him to take some love potion with me. Then I'll be even more confused and conflicted over whether he really wants to be with me because he wants to, or if he feels forced to settle with me because I'm pregnant and he's under a love spell."

"Not this again." Sage sighed deeply.

"I told him I wanted him to take a DNA test," I said. "I feel like if he knew for sure, he could make a decision based on that fact, you know?"

"I guess that makes sense. What did he say?"

"He said it didn't matter, that he was all in either way, but that if taking the DNA test was something I needed, he'd do it," I replied. Sage let out a dreamy sigh. "He said he wanted to come to my next appointment."

"That's so sweet!" she said, her voice wobbling with emotion. If I knew her like I thought I knew her, Sage was likely wiping away a tear or two.

"It feels like things are moving so fast," I said, my voice barely above a whisper.

"Maybe they are, but when you think about it, nine months goes by quickly. Heck, three months already have gone by. You only have six months before the baby arrives, and don't you want to figure out your relationship situation before then?"

"I don't know. Maybe?" I glanced back down at Delia's letter. Re-reading her words soothed my anxieties a little. Her easy confidence had hope flaming in my chest. Maybe I could trust my feelings when it came to Noah.

I know, everything is going to work out for the three of you.

CHAPTER TWENTY-FOUR

Noah

"I HEARD you soft-launched your relationship this weekend," Easton said while we worked at clearing the freshly fallen snow from the main office parking lot Monday morning.

"Oh, yeah?"

"Yeah, it was all anybody could talk about at The Quarter Lounge Saturday night! How Noah Wood and the new girl spent the entire day together, walking around downtown holding hands and checking out shops."

"Okay." I shrugged, not really caring. One way or another, the town was going to talk about one of its unofficial long-term bachelors changing his relationship status.

"Word on the street is that the Hartley triplets are taking credit for this match."

"Of course, they are." I huffed, rolling my eyes. "Even though they technically did nothing. Neither Nellie nor I have consumed any variation of the love elixir."

"Well, they're saying that they 'put the bug of pursuing her' in your ear." Easton smirked. He found the whole situation hilarious.

"You know, I wouldn't be so smug about this if I were you."

"Why not?"

"Because, once I'm off the market their focus is going to be solely on you," I reminded him. The pompous grin on his face slipped, as if he truly hadn't considered that fact.

"Whatever, they can try." My brother puffed out his chest, acting impervious.

"Trust me, they will," I murmured, shaking my head. I turned the snowblower on again to finish up the parking lot. Nellie was supposed to arrive for work within the next half hour, and I wanted the parking lot cleared and sand tossed down before she set foot on it.

I'd always been serious when it came to keeping the parking lots, roads, and paths at the resort clear of snow and sanded for the guests, but there was an even heavier importance on it now, with Nellie's condition.

Not that pregnancy was a condition. I mean, technically it was, I guess. Either way, I wanted to make sure there were no obstacles for her, and that she didn't slip and fall.

Which reminded me, we'd have to call a meeting with Damien today to inform him of Nellie's pregnancy and her need to take time off every week for her OB appointments.

Damien was off clearing snow, too. He was using the ATV that we'd attached a snow plow to. It pulled a small trailer full of sand for him to toss down, and a shovel for him to clear the porches and walkways to the cottages. He likely wouldn't be finished for another couple of hours.

After ensuring the snow was cleared and sand was tossed down out front, I had Easton take the snow blower to the back lot, and went inside to make a pot of coffee while I attended to a few office things.

A content creator and social media influencer named Misha Demsky had reached out last week to see about collaborating. She specialized in local destination and locally owned businesses and brands. After I'd investigated and determined that she had a legitimate and large following on Instagram, I'd decided to respond with a few different available time slots for a complimentary stay in exchange for her content creation services.

Misha had a lot of viral Reels on Instagram about other local destinations she'd stayed at, and she had an eloquent way of showcasing them that appealed to me. Being featured on her Instagram of over forty-five thousand followers would only boost interest in our resort, and she offered to provide materials for us to use for our social media marketing, too.

I was clicking *send* on the follow-up email to Misha when the front door to the office chimed, alerting me to Nellie's arrival.

I stood up, making my way into the kitchen and catching her as she was opening the refrigerator door to put her lunch inside.

I leaned against the doorway, crossing my arms and smiling, waiting until she'd closed it and straightened.

"Morning, gorgeous," I said, startling her.

She jumped, putting her hand over her heart. "Noah, I didn't hear you," she said, her voice a little breathless. "Good morning."

I crossed over to kiss her, unable to help myself. It was a chaste kiss, slow and tender despite my growing hunger for this woman. As I kissed her softly, I unzipped her jacket for her, putting my hands on her hips and pulled her a little closer to me, deepening the kiss as I did so.

A distant chime of the back door sounded, alerting me that someone else had come in through the laundry room. I reluctantly pulled away, stepping over to the cupboard with the mugs.

Nellie had a few seconds to regain her composure, which my kiss seemed to have shaken. I sent her a wink and poured myself a cup of coffee. "Want me to boil the kettle?"

"I have a tea already," Nellie said, grabbing her travel mug from where she'd set it down on the counter by the refrigerator. She also had a large bottle of ice water with lemon slices.

Damien came into the kitchen, his eyes narrowing at me when he saw me alone with Nellie.

"Morning, brother dearest," I said cheerfully, grabbing another mug down and pouring a cup of coffee for him. I passed it to Damien, earning a scowl, who grunted in response as he reached for the mug.

Nellie smiled shyly and grabbed her water bottle, then scurried out of the kitchen like she couldn't wait to get away from Damien. Not that I blamed her. My brother could be intimidating if you weren't used to his scowls and sullen silences.

"At some point today, we need to have a sit down with Nellie and discuss some important matters," I told Damien, keeping my voice low so that Nellie wouldn't overhear me.

"I'd say." Damien grumbled, lifting a brow. He took a deep sip of his coffee.

"Don't be a dick," I warned, pointing at him.

"That's kind of his MO," Easton chimed in, catching my warning and nothing else. He rinsed out his travel mug and filled it back up, sending a taunting smirk to our older brother.

"Don't you have work to do? Because if you don't, I can assign you something," Damien huffed, his aggravation evident.

"I've got plenty to do, thanks. I'm taking a quick coffee

break to refuel. Is that not allowed? Or are coffee breaks only allotted to the big bosses and their bed warmers?"

"Watch it," Damien warned, his eyes narrowing.

"Just a joke, bro." Easton replied. "Don't worry, I'm getting back to work." He left the kitchen with his travel mug of coffee.

Most of the time, Easton was the laidback jokester who didn't seem to take things seriously. But occasionally, he said something that made me think he cared more than he let on that he didn't have a bigger role at the resort like me and Damien.

At the time, he hadn't wanted it. With Damien's Hotel and Resort Management diploma and my diploma in Business Management and degree in accounting, he hadn't felt the drive to follow suit since we had it covered.

Easton still had gone to college, but he took the Tourism program because it sounded fun, and he could spend a semester in Cancun. He ended up working at a resort in Cancun for a couple of years, until my parents decided to retire officially.

He handled a lot of the outside maintenance, and he was the driving force behind a lot of our outdoor recreational programs.

He'd been pushing for us to do a tree-top trekking obstacle course for a while now, but Damien and I hadn't felt it would be worth the investment and risk. To construct it would cost us almost fifty-thousand dollars, and our insurance would go up.

Damien sighed heavily, placing his now-empty mug in the dishwasher and headed back out, presumably to check on the Sprucewood situation. James was there again, working on the plumbing, and while it was off the roster for guests, Damien had taken it upon himself to do some thorough maintenance on the cottage.

Once both my brothers were gone, I went into the front

office to find Nellie returning calls that had come in over the weekend. I let her do her thing, sitting down at the computer beside her.

I opened the resort email, checking and responding to any inquiries that had come in over the weekend. Some people—far too many—went to any lengths to avoid phone conversations. I did my best to respond to the ones that didn't leave a phone number, urging them to call to book a cottage.

"You know, a lot of places use online booking," Nellie said after she'd finished making her calls and noticed I was still responding to email inquiries.

"Then your job would be almost obsolete," I pointed out, sending her a smirk as I passed her a Post-It Note with an inquiry, a phone number, and a name.

"Scratch that, then," Nellie said, taking the Post-It Note from me. Our fingers brushed, and she smiled tentatively.

"At some point today, Damien is going to come in for that chat."

"Okay." Nellie drew in a breath, as if stabilizing herself.

"I'm going to sit in on the meeting, if that's okay, since we need to acknowledge we're dating. For unofficial official HR purposes. But as for the other situation..." I scratched at my chin thoughtfully.

"What about it?" Nellie asked. She was sounding more nervous now.

"I was thinking, if you were okay with it, that I'd tell Damien I'm the father of the baby?" My throat felt impossibly dry as I waited for Nellie to say something, anything. Maybe it was presumptuous of me to assume that'd be okay, which is why I'd asked her ahead of time. But in my head and in my heart, I already considered that baby mine, like I considered Nellie mine. "I mean, he already knows we hooked up at the Witches' Ball."

"I think everyone in town knows that. I'm beginning to think it went out in some town-wide newsletter.," Nellie sighed, resting her hand on her stomach absently. She chewed on her bottom lip, deliberating. "But you don't even know yet if—"

I interrupted her by tugging her chair closer to mine.

"I know that in all the ways that matter, I'll be a part of this baby's life, and yours," I cut her off. "People are going to assume anyway, since we're together. Might as well run with it."

"I feel like that locks you in."

I lifted my hand to cup her chin. "I want to be locked in," I assured her.

NELLIE

NOAH'S WORDS kept playing over in my mind for the rest of the day. After lunch, he went down to his office to do some paperwork and when he left me alone, I texted Sage in a half panic, letting her know about how at any time, I'd be meeting with Damien and Noah intended on telling him he was the father of my baby.

Sage told me to roll with it, that if Noah wanted to be involved—and it really sounded like he did—to let him.

Noah's reassurance and Sage's encouragement settled my racing heart and thoughts a little, and I toyed with the moon-shaped pendant on my neck.

I wasn't used to letting people in. Especially men. I'd guarded my heart up so tight, protecting myself from everyone who I felt could cause me harm. It was different with Sage. I knew I'd found a friend for life in her, my kindred spirit. It wasn't easy to tear down the wall I'd hidden behind for years, if not decades, for a smooth-talking man with a reputation as a playboy.

The dryer chimed, and I automatically stood up to go switch the load. I was in the middle of folding a load of towels when the back door opened, and Damien walked in. His hat and winter jacket were covered in snow. He stomped the snow off his boots outside, sending me a tight smile.

"Ready for that meeting?" he asked, taking off his jacket and hanging it on the hook. His voice was gruff, but his expression was neutral—no scowl present.

"Yeah, sure," I said, fumbling with the last towel in my hand. I refolded it and added it to the pile, trying to disguise my shaking hands. Thankfully, Damien was too busy taking off his snow-covered work boots and putting on a pair of indoor shoes to notice.

"Great. I'll go get Noah. Meet us in the dining room." He took off toward the door that led into the back hallway.

I paused at the desk to grab my water bottle, then walked into the dining room. A few minutes later, Noah and Damien walked in. Damien had a folder in his hand, and I inwardly panicked, fearing it was my resignation packet. Noah's relaxed smile eased some of my anxieties, but I shifted in my seat anyway, antsy and uncomfortable.

Damien sat across from me while Noah walked around the table. His blue eyes locked on mine as he pulled out a chair and sat down beside me, and I felt a gentle swirling unlike anything I'd felt before. With the table blocking Damien's view of my lower half, I held my palm to my lower abdomen, expecting the sensation to go away. It increased, and my breath caught.

"So, we're calling this meeting because it seems like you and Noah have decided to see each other. While we don't have any official rules or regulations about employee relationships, I still wanted to touch base with you and make sure this was something you wanted."

"I...what?" I was confused.

"Noah is in a position of authority, and I want to make sure you're not agreeing to see him because he's your boss," Damien clarified, his voice as gruff as ever.

Noah sent his brother a dark look, as if offended at the insinuation.

"No, I want to see him," I said hastily. "I wasn't sure if that was allowed or not."

Damien nodded slowly. "Like I said, we have no rules against it. But Charlotte did draw up some paperwork in case things turn south for you guys. Obviously, we hope that's not the case, but we can't be too careful," he said, opening the folder and organizing the papers inside. He handed a stack to Noah, and one to me.

"A contract?" I said, my eyes widening. Sensing my alarm, Noah put his hand on my knee and gently squeezed.

"It's basically a voluntary agreement between the two of you that acknowledges your relationship is consensual, and a guideline that outlines expectations for employees in romantic relationships, as well as an agreement to follow the resort's policy on public displays of affection. It looks like a lot of paperwork, but it's not. There are three copies. One for you to have, one for Noah to have, and one for us to have on file," Damien explained.

"Okay," I tried not to let the panic overtake me. We went over the paperwork and signed where we were supposed to and handing one of the copies back to Damien, who put it back in the folder.

"If that's everything?" Damien asked, looking between Noah and me.

"Well, there's something else." Noah glanced at me, as if silently asking me if I wanted to take the lead.

"I'm going to need a half day off once a week for the foreseeable future."

Damien's brow furrowed, like this news irritated him immediately.

"I'm...I'm pregnant, so it's to go to my obstetrician appointments."

Whatever Damien had been expecting me to say, it clearly wasn't that.

"You're pregnant?" he repeated, glancing at Noah for an explanation. Seeing that Noah wasn't surprised by the news, he sat back in his chair and ran his hand over his jaw. "Congratulations. That's great news. When are you due?" Damien's tone was a lot more gentle and less gruff.

"Thank you. I'm due July nineteenth. It's uh, a rather unexpected situation." I could see the wheels spinning as Damien took in that information. "I know that kind of leaves you guys in a lurch for the summer."

"We'll figure all that out later," Noah assured me, squeezing my knee again discreetly under the table.

"Yeah, don't worry about that." Damien nodded in agreement. "That's a ways off still. Let me know in advance when your appointments are so we can make sure someone is covering the phones."

"I am trying to make sure they don't book them for Fridays, since that's one of our busier days. But I'll make sure I keep all my appointments as consistent as I can. My next appointment is Thursday afternoon."

"I'm going to need that afternoon off too," Noah said.

"Okay." Damien nodded, his eyes flitting back to Noah for a beat. "I'm sure Charlotte can handle the office. I'll put her on the schedule."

CHAPTER TWENTY-FIVE

Nellie

I FELT unmeasurable relief after finally coming clean to Damien about my little situation. It'd been nerve-wracking, sitting in that meeting and laying out all my cards.

While I know he assumed, I was thankful Damien hadn't point-blank asked Noah if he was the father. That would have made for a more awkward conversation.

He also assured me that my pregnancy would remain a secret until I felt I wanted to share it with other employees.

"Does that mean you won't tell Charlotte?" Noah had jokingly asked, and Damien sent him a glacier look.

"Yeah, that means I won't tell my fiancée. It's not my news to share. I respect all employees' right to privacy."

Damien's answer made me smile a little. "Thank you. I'm not sure when I'll be ready to share the news with everyone," I said. I was having a hard enough time wrapping my head around the fact that I'd basically signed a love contract with Noah, and I couldn't help but worry about the other employees' reactions. Maybe not Noah's family, per say, but the housekeepers.

Rhonda and Denise were tight, and while they didn't really seem like the type to gossip, they weren't exactly rolling out the red carpet for me. I mean, they were nice, but removed. Our interactions were limited to lunchtime, when they mainly spoke to each other, and the occasional run-in in the laundry room.

They didn't seem put out by me. Rhonda had complimented my bed linen folding skills a few times now, and Denise smiled every time she came into the laundry room and everything was washed and put away.

I was winning points with them both for that, but I worried that by dating Noah, I'd go down a few levels in their books. I didn't even want to think about what they'd think when they found out I was pregnant.

After the meeting, there were only a couple of hours left in the day. Noah had to finish up whatever work he'd been doing in his office, so I was left alone in the main office to answer calls and emails.

I didn't have a whole lot of time to sit and think. The phones were ringing off the hook with reservation requests. Lots of calls were for the May long weekend, but that was basically already booked up. I had to redirect a few guests and urge them to book at a different time, which I was able to do easily enough.

By three thirty, I was drained. I was in the backroom putting my winter boots on when Noah came in.

"Heading out?" he asked.

"Yup, I'm officially off the clock as of five minutes ago," I replied, slipping my coat on. "Unless you wanted me to stay later?" I added, glancing up to see that he'd moved closer to me.

"Nope, you're good to go. Drive safe," he said as he zipped my coat up for me. His eyes locked on mine, and he flashed me that smile—the one that made the butterflies swoop in my stomach and my head feel all light and dizzy.

Only this time, the butterflies in my stomach was the swirling sensation that I'd felt earlier at our meeting, and it was stronger than it had been earlier.

"Woah," I breathed, putting a hand over my stomach. I couldn't feel anything through my coat, but the warmth made the swirling increase.

"What's wrong?" The easy smile was replaced with a look of concern.

"I think..." I paused, focusing on the sensation again. "I think I'm feeling the baby move."

Noah's expression transformed again from concerned to elated. "Really? That's awesome."

I unzipped my coat and reached for his hand, putting it over my womb where the swirling was. "I don't know if you'll be able to feel it."

Noah's hand felt warm against my belly, and the swirling and fluttering grew even more apparent. His brow furrowed in concentration as I pressed his palm firmer against me.

"I think I feel it, too," he said a moment later, lifting his gaze to meet mine. He looked bewildered and mystified.

Before either of us could say anything, the back door to the laundry room beeped and opened, and we broke away.

"Don't tell me you already need a reminder on appropriate workplace behaviour," Easton said when he caught us breaking away and looking guilty.

"Nope, we're good, thanks." Noah said, shooting me a smile. "Drive safe, and text me when you get home?"

"Okay, sure. I'll see you guys later," I said, returning to the front office long enough to grab my things and make a hasty getaway.

IT WAS A LITTLE STRANGE, having Noah accompany me to my obstetrician appointment. I was so used to doing everything by myself. Heck, I hadn't even had my mom attend a doctor's appointment with me since I was thirteen years old.

The only thing Noah insisted on was driving me. We were supposed to get a snowstorm later, and Noah said his truck handled snowy conditions better than my little car. That was probably true, but it still felt odd having him drive there.

Noah didn't speak much during the initial appointment, aside from introducing himself to the obstetrician. I kind of took the lead, awkwardly explaining that we were pretty sure he was the father, but that we'd like a DNA test to confirm.

Dr. Kramer didn't seem surprised at all, as if expectant mothers regularly brought in their potential baby daddies for DNA tests. I mean, I suppose it was more common now for people to be a little freer with their love, but it was still an awkward experience. One I had to remind myself that I'd wanted.

I'd been the one to insist that knowing one way or the other was important to me. Noah was going along with whatever I wanted.

Dr. Kramer did a quick exam while Noah waited in the other room. I wasn't there yet, and he didn't seem slighted in the least. Once my exam and appointment were over, Dr. Kramer told me an ultrasound would be booked for when I was between eighteen and twenty weeks.

"We're mostly checking for growth markers and development, and during this ultrasound, we'll be able to determine the sex of the baby, and we can either tell you, or you can keep it a secret until the delivery."

Then Noah came in, and we did the DNA test. A nurse took a sample of my blood and then swabbed his cheek, and we were told we'd get the results in a week or two. We'd probably get the results the day of my ultrasound.

After the appointment, we walked to Noah's truck in a heavy silence. My thoughts were wrapped up in the DNA test and the upcoming ultrasound. I barely noticed the darkening sky with the impending storm until Noah pointed it out.

"I was hoping to take you out for dinner, but I think we should try to get back to Hartwood Creek before the storm hits."

"I agree," I said, glancing up at the ominous sky. The baby moved about in my stomach, as if dancing with anticipation. I'd been feeling movements more and more lately, usually when Noah was around, or when I was thinking about him.

He held his truck door open for me and I climbed up, with him assisting by placing his hand on the small of my back. I could barely feel it through my winter jacket, but I was aware of his presence.

It was as if I was completely tuned in to his every move-ment. He could be about to enter the room, and the awareness would hit. I'd know that he was close. The baby seemed to know, too, which was disconcerting.

I'd been so perplexed by it that I'd started to feel a little crazy, and had texted to ask Sage and Tabitha if they'd ever experienced the same thing. To my surprise, they both had. Tabitha said all her babies had danced in utero for Parker.

Sage told me she was experiencing it with Nix, but admitted she didn't have that awareness or that reaction to Daphne's sperm donor. Not that he'd been around enough to test the theory, nor had she paid attention the way she was now.

Sage had expressed how much she regretted blocking out a lot of her pregnancy with Daphne. She'd been scared and uncertain and had never felt so alone. This time, with Nix, was an entirely different experience for her, and she wanted to soak up every minute of it.

It was an indescribable relief to have both Sage and Tabitha to talk to about the pregnancy stuff, and the feelings stuff. I'd recounted the meeting with Noah and his brother, and the interaction in the laundry room after, when Noah had put his hand on my stomach and felt the baby moving. They both seemed to be cheering hard for Noah.

I expected to self-sabotage, because that's what I'd done in the past every time I felt myself catching feelings, but there was something about Noah that kept me from blowing everything between us up. Or maybe it was the baby.

Maybe I didn't want to do everything alone, not if I had Noah by my side—not when he seemed to want to be there as much as I wanted him there.

Noah

IT STARTED SNOWING the moment we left Springwood, but the flurries got heavier and thicker the closer we got to Hartwood Creek. The roads were getting slick, and I gripped the steering wheel tightly, trying to keep control of the truck through each snowdrift on the highway back to town.

"It's a good thing you insisted on taking your truck," Nellie said. "You were right. I don't think my car would have made it through these drifts."

"I don't think it would have, either," I replied, keeping my eyes on the road despite the urge to look at her. My truck could handle the drifts easily, but her car was so low to the ground, it'd likely get stuck.

"It's really coming down."

I could sense the uncertainty in Nellie's voice, like she was scared. It wasn't just the amount of snow we were getting, it was the winds, too. A hundred and sixty kilometres per hour winds were no joke, especially when coupled with heavy snowflakes. I grew up in the north, I was used to driving in snowy conditions, but this was quickly turning into an all-out blizzard.

"Yeah, it's not great to be out in. My place is closer, how about we head there?"

We were about fifteen minutes out from my road, and another twenty-five from town.

"But it's going to keep snowing, we could end up snowed in."

"That's true." I didn't mind the prospect of being snowed in with Nellie. I welcomed it over being out in this. "But Damien could make sure the road and my driveway are clear enough for us to get in safely. I don't know how quickly the township will be able to clear the roads."

"Okay, yeah. You're right," Nellie said, as another gust of wind rattled the windows of my truck. I called Damien, thankful for Bluetooth.

"Hey, you guys get back to town yet?" Damien asked as soon as he picked up, the concern evident in his tone. "It's getting hairy out there."

"We're about fifteen minutes out from the road. Any chance you could jump in the plow truck and clear my driveway?"

"Sure, I'll do it now." I could hear rustling, like Damien was putting on his jacket. "Char, I'll be back in a bit. I'm going to clear Noah's driveway."

"Okay!" Charlotte's voice called out faintly as a door clicked shut.

"I'll see ya there. Drive safe," Damien said, cutting the connection.

The road to the resort, and all our individual properties at what Charlotte jokingly referred to as the Wood family compound, was barely visible at all. Anyone else wouldn't have known where it was, but I'd grown up in the area. I drove that road so frequently, I could drive it in my sleep. Still, I took extra caution, driving slower than I would have if Nellie wasn't in the passenger seat.

I could see Damien's headlights as he drove down my freshly plowed driveway. He honked, rolling down his window and slowing. I rolled mine down, too, to talk to him.

"Thanks, Damien," I said, dipping my head in a nod.

"No problem. I think tomorrow will be a snow day for everyone. We're supposed to get twenty-five centimetres tonight, and another fifteen throughout the day tomorrow. It's not letting up until tomorrow night."

"Jesus, that's a lot of snow."

"Yup. We have no guests staying right now. I'll call Rhonda and Denise and tell them to stay home tomorrow, too." Damien said.

"Probably a good call," I agreed. It was rare we shut down the whole resort, but we would if we had no guests. With no guests, there was no pressing need to clean the cottages. Calls could be returned, and reservations could be booked later, there was no sense in endangering any of our employees.

I drove the rest of the way up my driveway, parking in my usual spot in front of the detached garage. Although Damien had just plowed, the snow was already quickly accumulating. I walked around the side of my truck, opening the door for Nellie.

"Careful, it's slippery," I warned her, helping her out of the cab of my truck. As soon as I had finished warning her, she slipped. I was holding her arm and able to prevent her from falling.

"Woah! You weren't kidding," she said. She held on tight to my arm as we walked toward the front of my cabin. The wind was blowing snow in our eyes, and neither of us could keep our eyes open. "Okay, I'm glad you suggested this. It's gotten worse."

"Yup. We're in for an intense blizzard," I said, unlocking the front door to my cabin, and holding it open for her. Nellie knocked her boots on the doorstep then stepped inside.

"What if the power goes out?" she asked.

"I've got a generator, and I've also got the woodstove for heat," I replied, toeing my work boots off. I set them over the vent to dry out and put Nellie's boots beside mine. I took her coat from her, hanging it in the small front closet with my own, trying to ignore how much I liked the sight of her things with mine. "Make yourself at home," I urged her.

Nellie walked deeper into my cabin, taking it all in like it was the first time she'd been there. Of course, she'd been really drunk the first time, and we'd only had eyes for each other that night.

"This place is gorgeous, Noah," she said, running her hand along the pine paneled walls.

"Guess you don't remember it from the last time you were here." I leaned against the wall as I watched her explore the kitchen.

"Not really," she smirked. "That night's still a blur."

"I thought it was an unforgettable night," I told her. There wasn't a hint of teasing in my voice, and Nellie's head snapped up to look at me.

"Parts of it were unforgettable," she allowed. "But I wasn't really paying attention to my surroundings."

"That's kind of alarming. You should always pay attention to your surroundings." I cocked a brow, smirking.

Nellie hadn't seemed that drunk the night we hooked up, but I was pretty much three sheets to the wind. I might have remembered more than she did, but I was missing details, too. Like whether we'd used a condom—which was kind of an important detail to know.

I suppose we'd find out soon. The prenatal paternity test results would be available within a week or two. They'd swabbed my cheek for a sample from me and took a sample of Nellie's blood. Truthfully, I'd almost fainted when they took the blood sample from her. I was thankful they didn't opt for the other DNA testing.

Neither one of us had wanted to risk the more invasive amniocentesis sampling, which is when they drew amniotic fluid from the abdomen. Frankly, I stood by what I'd told Nellie. It didn't matter to me one way or the other, but it was important to her to know. I could respect that.

Hell, maybe she had every intention of dumping my ass if it came back that I wasn't the father. Maybe she'd rather go at parenting alone then continue to date me.

"What's the frown for?" Nellie asked, catching the expression on my face.

"Nothing," I said, trying to school my features.

She waved her finger at me. "Nuh-uh, we're not doing that. If we're doing this whole relationship-thing, we're going to communicate. It's the only way this is going to work—or so I'm told."

"Fine, remember you asked for honesty," I warned her. "I

was thinking about the DNA test and wondering why it was so important to you to find out if I was the father. Do you plan on breaking up with me if I'm not biologically the father?"

Nellie's jaw dropped, and she blinked away her surprise. "No, I just, I wanted to make sure you had all the information before you made a lifelong commitment to raising a child with me."

I nodded, accepting that answer, and walked over to her. I tucked a strand of her hair behind her ear, running my fingers along her jawline. "I'm telling you, I've already committed to raising a child with you. To being with you. Heck, I signed the paperwork, didn't I?"

"You did." Nellie's lips twitched as she nodded. "And now, I guess we're having our first sleepover. Alone." She sounded nervous about it.

"Have you never slept over at a guy's house before?" I asked, cocking a brow.

"Not sober, and I usually dip out before morning."

"Why?" even in my playboy days—which granted, weren't that far behind me—I'd let my conquests spend the night. I didn't expect them to get dressed and leave the minute we'd finished.

Nellie shrugged. "There's something intimate about someone seeing you in the morning."

"Ah, I see. Well. I'd prefer to get super intimate with you as soon as possible, but I promise I'll go at your speed. Whenever you're ready, Nell. In the meantime, I have two guest bedrooms you could choose from if you'd rather not spend the night with me in my bed."

Nellie seemed surprised by my answer. "Okay, thank you."

"Are you hungry?"

"I'm always hungry these days," she said, her hand going to her stomach.

My heart seemed to skip a beat in my chest when I remembered how she'd held my palm to her womb the other day, and I'd felt the baby moving.

"I've got some steak in the refrigerator I could toss on the barbeque, and some potatoes. There's probably enough stuff to make a salad, too."

"That sounds good," Nellie whispered.

"Gotta keep my girls fed," I said, pressing a kiss to her forehead. I moved around her and headed to the kitchen.

"Girls? You think the baby's a girl?"

"Yeah, I do."

"What makes you say that?" Nellie asked, following me into the kitchen.

"It's just a feeling I have. I have no clue if I'm right. Guess we'll find out in time."

CHAPTER TWENTY-SIX

Noah

I APPLIED a dry rub to the steaks, tossing them and some potatoes on the barbeque while Nellie insisted on making the salad. I had a dining room table, but I rarely used it. Instead, we sat at the island and ate our dinner while the woodstove warmed the cabin and the snow fell outside, blanketing the world around us.

"Gosh, it's so gorgeous," Nellie said, her gaze yet again going to the sliding door off the dining room that led to the back deck. "It must feel like a vacation living here."

"Sometimes," I replied, setting my fork down and wiping my mouth on a napkin. "But since I work at a cottage resort, it usually doesn't feel like I'm ever in vacation mode. There's always something to think about or do to make sure other people's vacations are perfect."

"Good thing we have no guests right now at the resort."

Nellie shook her head, looking back at me. "How long do you think it'll take you guys to dig us out tomorrow?"

"Probably a couple of hours, at least. I've got a snowblower here to dig us out. There's also Damien's truck with the plow, and at the resort, we've got the ATV with a plow, and another two push snowblowers. Usually for heavy storms like this, we contract Jim at S'no Problem Snow Removal. He comes out and clears all our roads and driveways, then we can handle the rest."

"S'no Problem?! Seriously?"

I nodded.

"Every business in this town has a ridiculously adorable name." She giggled from behind her own napkin.

I smiled, finding her amusement adorable. "I never really noticed before."

"I wonder if it's a prerequisite to opening a business here. Like your permits will be denied if your name isn't adorable or quirky enough." Nellie smiled, pausing to take a sip of her water.

"I don't think it's a prerequisite, but you're right; a lot of businesses have quirky, cutesy names in town." I chuckled, standing up to clear our plates. Nellie stood to help. "No, you sit, I've got this."

I took her plate and carried it over to the sink, rinsing it and putting it in the dishwasher. I might live in a cabin in the woods, but I didn't skimp out on things that'd make my life easier. I had a dishwasher and a washer and dryer—high efficiency, like my furnace.

"Thanks, for dinner. And everything," Nellie said from the counter, watching as I moved about in my kitchen. "I'm sorry to be crashing your evening."

I moved to the island, putting my palms on the countertop across from her.

"It's my pleasure," I told her sincerely. "In case you haven't realized it yet, I enjoy being with you, Nell. I'm happy you're here."

I couldn't ignore the little spark of happiness that brightened her eyes. "Well, I'm happy to be here. It beats being stuck on the highway in the snowstorm. Or trying to climb up the stairs to my apartment after all that snow." Nellie wrinkled her nose.

"You're welcome to stay here whenever you want," I told her. I didn't care if it was 'too soon' to make such an offer, the idea of her climbing up the slippery stairs to her apartment in this weather made me feel like locking her in my cabin until winter was over.

"Thanks for the offer, but I like my apartment." Nellie smiled. "It's the first thing that's truly been mine. I mean, I moved out of my parents' house young, but I always lived with roommates, and the space never really felt like it was mine, you know?"

My possessiveness melted away like ice in the sun.

"I can respect that." I nodded. "There's something to be said about having a space that's all yours." I hoped that one day Nellie would feel at home here.

"So, your brothers live around here, too, right? And your parents?" she asked.

"Yeah. Everyone's about a five-minute drive away from each other by ATV or snowmobile. It's comforting to know that although I can't see them, they're nearby," I explained. "Charlotte jokingly referred to it as the family compound when she started dating Damien. My dad loved the term and it ended up sticking, unofficially, anyway."

"That's pretty neat, that you guys have that kind of relationship with one another."

"You're an only child, right?" I asked. Nellie nodded,

smiling almost sadly. "Whenever I'd fight with my brothers, I'd wonder what that'd be like."

"It's lonely," Nellie admitted, lifting her shoulder in a shrug. "I've never been able to call a sibling for help or know that my parents are around the corner. Even when I lived with them, they were never really around."

"I'm sorry, that's rough." I leaned forward, taking Nellie's hands in mine.

"I'm pretty much used to it," she said, looking down at our hands. "It got a little less lonely when I met Sage. She's like the sister I never had."

"Sometimes, family isn't forged by blood, but circumstance and chance," I said. "But you can consider yourself an honorary member of the Wood family. Heck, you already were once you became an employee, but now that we're dating and you're carrying my baby—"

"*Might* be carrying your baby," Nellie interrupted, her lips twitching with a smile that she struggled to hold back.

"Regardless of what that test says, I consider that baby mine, as much as I consider you mine," I told her, holding her gaze.

Nellie's mouth opened and closed, like she was searching for something to say. I stroked the back of her hand with my thumb, slowly rubbing it.

"The sooner you accept both those facts, the sooner we can get to the fun part."

"What's the fun part?"

"Getting reacquainted with each other physically." I waggled my eyebrows at her playfully, but I was serious. Holding Nellie's hands in mine made me think about how those hands had felt on my body, and it made me crave that again. Touching her in all the ways I'd thought about over the last few weeks, without the muddled haze of alcohol to dull my senses.

"You're such a guy." Nellie rolled her eyes dramatically, pulling her hands away from mine. I let her retreat, knowing she wasn't going far.

Nellie was skittish, and it was easy to see why. Aside from Sage, she didn't have people in her life that fought for her, and as a result she didn't let many people get close. We'd talked a few times about her parents, and although I wanted to peel back the layers there, I could tell it was a sore subject.

But I had patience; I could wait as long as it took for her to realize I meant every word of what I said. I could wait for her to realize that I was here to stay, regardless of the results of that DNA test.

I moved around the island with intent, stopping in front of Nellie. Peering down at her, I cupped her chin with my hand, tilting her face up to meet my gaze.

"There's nothing wrong with admitting your feelings and desires. I have feelings for you—so many feelings—and I desire you."

Nellie's eyes widened, and she swallowed. I lowered my face to hers, capturing her lips in a slow kiss, making those intentions known. She kissed me back, her own need sparking with mine.

She stood, never breaking the kiss, her hands going to the back of my neck and embracing me. My hand dropped from her face and I gripped her hips, tugging her against me. She let out a gasp that I swallowed when she felt my erection against her, hot and heavy and hard.

"I want you, too," Nellie whispered against my lips, her eyes searching mine.

"You have me, however you want me," I assured her, unable to resist pushing my erection against her to punctuate that point. I wasn't about to talk her out of anything, but I wanted her to be certain the next move was completely hers.

She went back to kissing me, her hands exploring my trapezius muscles and slowly moving down the back of my arms. She squeezed and tested every hard ridge of me through my clothes, all while she kissed me like she was starving for my taste—like how I kissed her.

I grunted when she slipped her hands under my shirt, her fingers grazing against my Adonis belt. I broke the kiss long enough to pick her up and set her on the island, then slanted my mouth over hers again. I kissed her so deeply, I felt her desire turn molten as her thighs spread, making room for me to step between them.

"Tell me what you want, Nell," I urged her, as I moved to kiss along the side of her neck. The little gasps she made had me jutting toward her, pressing my erection into her centre.

"You, Noah. I want you, now."

"I've got condoms in my room," I told her, about to lift her and carry her.

"Are you worried I'm going to get pregnant?" she said, a teasing lilt to her voice.

"Uh, no." She had my brain completely frazzled.

"Well, I've been tested recently, and I'm good to go if you are?"

Her questioning gaze and the note of vulnerability had my heart stuttering.

"I am," I said, my voice gravel and grit. I might have enjoyed my bachelorhood, but I'd always used protection. Or at least, I had until Nellie. But still, despite using protection, I regularly got check-ups. My last one was a few weeks after Nellie, and I'd been given the all-clear.

Nellie nodded, her hands going to tug the hem of my shirt. I allowed her to pull it off me, enjoying the way her eyes heated as she took in my naked torso. I couldn't help but flex under her gaze.

With the preamble over, we went back to our heated makeout session and desperate touches. Nellie's fingers felt like fire against my skin—the best kind of burn. I continued kissing her as I unbuttoned her blouse, aware of her panting breaths.

When her blouse fell open revealing the white lace of her bra, I let out a tortured groan, my cock pulsing in response. I could feel the moisture beading at my tip and knew I wouldn't be able to last long.

I pushed the blouse off her shoulders, and she let it fall to the countertop in a pool of material. I palmed her breast, my thumb circling her nipple over the lace, and Nellie arched her back in response, letting out a delicious moan that made my cock press painfully against the zipper of my jeans.

I lowered my mouth to her breast, kissing the cleavage that spilled out over top of the lace, pulling back and tugging the material down, revealing her pretty pink nipple. I blew air on it, watching it tighten as if transfixed, then brought my mouth to her nipple, sucking it into my mouth.

Nellie whimpered as my teeth gently scraped against the sensitive bud, her hands going to my head, her fingers tangling in my hair and tugging me tighter to her. I didn't mind the pull against the strands of my hair. I invited it, relishing in her subtle cues for more.

As my tongue toyed with her nipple, my hand slipped around her waist, moving up against her spine to find the clasp of her bra and releasing it. The straps fell down her shoulder, and I pulled away long enough to toss it over my shoulder. I moved to her other breast, giving that nipple the attention it deserved while I went back to gently squeezing the first.

My cock was so hard, I could feel my tip weeping with the need to bury myself in her. Nellie let out a choked sound, her hands going to the button of my jeans and struggling to pop it open.

I smiled around her nipple, helping her out. I unzipped my pants, letting them fall around my ankles, and barely had a moment to breathe before Nellie's soft hand was sliding down my abdomen into my boxer briefs and wrapping around my cock. She squeezed it, pumping me.

"I need you. Now, Noah." Nellie's voice was breathless, but there was an underlying determination.

"I need…" I paused, my muscles all straining when she pumped me again. "I need to get you out of those pants, first."

Nellie was still dressed from the waist down. She released me long enough to unbutton her own pants and lift her hips. I helped her, grabbing hold of the material and pulling them over her thighs and down her legs. Then I ran my hands back up her legs, slowly touching her inner thighs. She parted them for me, revealing a matching pair of lacy underwear that I could see were damp with her need.

I let out a groan, running my thumb over the seam of her, feeling how drenched she was through the lace.

"I want a taste," I said, my voice rumbling. Before she could argue, I was moving aside the material and bringing my mouth to her heated core.

My tongue swept along her entrance, lapping up the desire leaking from her. She tasted like the sweetest nectar, and I knew I could get drunk off the taste of her. Another pass of my tongue had Nellie arching her hips to meet me.

"Please, Noah!"

Not wanting to make her wait a moment longer, I forced myself to rise, pushing my boxers down as I did so. My cock jutted out, and Nellie's eyes darkened as she took it in. She bit her lower lip, then shimmied out of her underwear.

Having her bare and spread out before me was the most

captivating of visions. I fisted my cock, pumping it slowly while I took her in. "You sure you want this, Nell?"

"Yes," she nodded eagerly, letting her thighs fall open in welcome. I stepped toward her, rubbing my thick tip against her soaked entrance, coating myself in her juices. "Hurry!" she pleaded, sliding closer to the edge of the counter.

I pushed in slowly, feeling her stretch over every inch of me. Nellie's fingers gripped the edge of the counter for dear life, and she let out a deep moan I felt in my bones.

"God, you feel amazing, Nellie," I murmured when I was fully in her.

"So do you. Now fuck me, Noah." she panted.

I smiled, then I delivered exactly what she asked for.

I pounded into her like I'd been thinking about doing since seeing her again at the grocery store. With each thrust, I claimed her. It wasn't long until her thighs were trembling against me. I held them for her, not slowing even when I felt my own orgasm building. I fucked her through her release, feeling her walls clench around me and her orgasm seeping out against my balls.

"Holy shit, Nell." I grunted, feeling her cum again. I rotated my hips, drawing it out, and then lost control, pumping into her with shaky thrusts as my own orgasm blew through me like a freight train.

CHAPTER TWENTY-SEVEN

Nellie

I'D REALLY WANTED to sleep with Noah in his bed, so naturally I decided the best place to be was anywhere but in his bed. I chose the guestroom furthest away from his, hoping the distance would provide me with some clarity after our intense coupling.

It did not. I tossed and turned all night, thinking about how close he was. Just down the hall. Zero clarity was achieved.

My body ached in the best way. I felt deeply satisfied and yet, I craved more.

Noah had done everything right; he had made his interest in me apparent, but he respected that I was teetering still, and hadn't pressured me once. He'd let me call the shots, and even when I begged him, he'd made sure it was what I truly wanted.

Afterwards, he'd drawn a warm bath and climbed in with me, then washed my hair and my aching body with such tenderness, I'd almost wept. The intimacy of it was staggering, and I didn't exactly know what to do with all of it.

But Noah hadn't so much as pouted with disappointment when I'd told him I thought it'd be better if I slept in one of the guestrooms. He'd given me a cozy pair of plaid pajama bottoms and a T-shirt of his to sleep in, and made sure I had everything I needed to be comfortable.

And I was comfortable. The bed I was in felt like a cloud, and the woodstove kept the entire cabin cozy and warm. But I knew, even though I'd never spent the full night in Noah's arms, that sleeping beside him would have been a thousand times more comfortable. There was something about him that put me at ease, and I couldn't figure out why.

On paper, Noah was a player who hadn't had a serious relationship in almost a decade, much like me. I shouldn't have found that as reassuring as I did, but I somehow knew he was safe.

I knew he was home.

And those were dangerous thoughts to have this early on. Sure, I might be pregnant with his baby—maybe—but that didn't mean I could trust that everything would all work out like magic. Even if our chemistry was off-the-charts hot.

I didn't fall asleep until nearly two o'clock in the morning, and I awoke around ten to the scent of bacon and coffee. My stomach growled as if it'd been weeks since my last meal.

My phone buzzed on the nightstand beside me, and I reached for it noticing I had several missed text messages from Sage as I unplugged it from the charger.

Sage: The blizzard is getting out of hand. Text me when you get back to Hartwood Creek!

Sage: Tabitha said you didn't come home last night! Are you okay?! You're not in a ditch somewhere, right?

Sage: Okay, now I'm really getting worried. TEXT ME BACK!

Sage: ...HELLO?!

I'D BEEN SO DISTRACTED by being in Noah's space and spending time with him, that I'd completely forgotten to text or call Sage last night. My phone had died at some point after my appointment and before I'd gone to bed, and I'd plugged it in to charge overnight.

Before I could finish texting out a reply, my phone rang with an incoming FaceTime—Sage's name and photo popping up.

I answered it, and Sage's worried face filled the screen. "Oh good, you're alive." She eyed me with suspicion.

"Hey, sorry. My phone died and I'm waking up now," I answered, feeling guilty for making her worry.

"Where are you? That's not your room." Sage leaned in closer, as if she could figure out where I was by taking in all the details.

"Yeah, I crashed at Noah's last night. The blizzard hit when we were driving home, and we decided it'd be better to get to his place instead of trying to make it all the way to town."

"Makes sense." Sage leaned back, appeased by my answer. Her eyes sparked with delight, and she smiled. "So, you spent the night with Noah, huh?"

"In his guestroom," I corrected, frowning.

"Foolish girl. Should have jumped his bones. You're delaying the inevitable," Sage predicted, and I rolled my eyes at her dramatics.

I mean—she was right, I had been delaying the inevitable by trying to resist my attraction to Noah, but I wasn't about to admit that.

"The inevitable already happened."

"What do you mean?" Sage asked.

"I mean, I did jump his bones last night. I slept in the guestroom after."

Sage shook her head. "It's both amusing and concerning that you think sleeping with someone is more intimate than having sex."

"Because it is," I insisted. I'd been the queen of casual for so long, and spending the night sleeping beside someone—having their arms around you—that was the opposite of casual.

Then again, so was having a baby with someone. This entire situation with Noah was as far from casual as it could get, and I don't know why I was even bothering to try to cling to the semblance of casual.

"Whatever," I said, fighting a yawn. I was too tired to analyze my behaviour. "Is it still snowing?"

"Yup, and it's supposed to snow all day," Sage answered. She smiled, as if pleased. "Looks like you're snowed in with Noah for at least the rest of the day."

"And?"

"And that means you'll probably have to have an actual conversation—"

"We have been having conversations," I interrupted, whispering so that Noah wouldn't overhear me. "Lots of conversations, actually. He's great, really understanding of everything. I don't know why I'm still trying to fight it; I already know I'm screwed."

"Well, you will be." Sage giggled.

I sent her an unimpressed look. "I mean I'm dangerously close to feelings, if not already there."

"That's not a bad thing, Nell," Sage said gently. "Anyway, how did the appointment go?"

She must have been able to read the expression on my face, and how I wanted—no, needed—to change the subject.

"It went well. Everything looks okay. Booked the anatomy ultrasound for a couple weeks from now, and we did the DNA test. We should get the results for that in a couple weeks, too."

"That's exciting." Sage's eyes were shining with elation. "Are you going to find out the gender?"

"Haven't decided yet." I shrugged.

"We'll probably find out if the baby cooperates. Nix wants to know, and it's his first baby and all," Sage said.

"I can't remember, did you find out for Daphne?"

"Yeah, I did. Everything was so uncertain, I needed to find out as much as I could about everything I could to feel a little more prepared." Sage smiled wistfully. "This time, I could wait until the baby is born before finding out, but I want to do whatever Nix wants."

"Makes sense." I got the impression Noah would do whatever I wanted.

"So," Sage started, biting her lower lip as if she was holding in an awkward question.

"Spit it out." I sighed.

"Is it going to matter what the DNA results say?" she asked softly.

"I don't know." I shrugged. "He says it doesn't matter, but I want to make sure he has the answer before he commits to that decision."

"Will it matter to you, though?" Sage clarified her question.

I was taken back to last night, and the look in Noah's eyes when he said: *Regardless of what that test says, I consider that baby mine, as much as I consider you mine.*

"No, it wouldn't matter," I said lowly, keeping my voice at a near-whisper.

If Noah wasn't biologically the father, but still wanted to be a part of our lives, I would let him. I was scared that if the DNA results proved he wasn't the biological father, that it would change his desire to be a part of this. I knew I was clinging to that fear, but I didn't know how not to.

"Well, if it doesn't matter, I think you have to let go of that fear that's holding you back," Sage said wisely. "I know, it's easier said than done, but stop hiding behind walls and let him in. He wants to be there, Nell. It's obvious."

"I know, you're right," I whispered, thinking about all the ways Noah had proved that over the last few weeks.

After getting off the phone with Sage, I put on my bra and followed my nose to the kitchen. Noah was setting two plates down on the island. They were overflowing with eggs, bacon, and toast.

"Morning, I was just about to wake you. I hope you're hungry," he said, smiling as he took me in. I 'd washed my makeup off the night before and had done my best to run my fingers through my hair to comb some of the tangles out. I by no means felt beautiful, but Noah looked at me like I was.

"I could eat," I said, trying to ignore everything I was feeling. It was confusing, conflicting. I expected to feel vulnerable, that the intimacy level of being with him without my mask in place—my makeup, my clothes—would send me wanting to run.

But I didn't feel all that vulnerable. Somehow, I felt almost at ease. I was aware of his eyes on me, aware of his every move, aware of the sexual tension sparking between us, but I didn't want to run.

"God, you're a fucking vision, Nell." Noah shook his head, as if trying to clear it. "Seeing you in my clothes; it does something to me." His voice had deepened, his gaze smouldering, making his need apparent.

"Oh stop," I flushed, pulling out a chair at the island and sitting in front of one of the plates.

"Coffee? I, uh, unfortunately don't have any tea." He scratched at the back of his neck, looking sheepish.

"It's okay, I'm still trying to limit my caffeine intake," I answered.

"Orange juice it is," Noah said with a nod, turning around to grab a glass from the cupboard. He filled it with juice from the refrigerator and set it beside my plate, then grabbed his cup of coffee and walked over to sit beside me. "How'd you sleep last night?"

"Good," I lied, not wanting to admit I tossed and turned all night thinking about him. About how he'd felt moving inside me. It was very difficult not to think about that, especially when I was staring right at the place it happened.

"I'm glad to hear that. I slept like shit. Kept thinking about how close you were, yet how far away." He winked, picking up his fork and scooping some eggs up.

I hid my smile behind a glass of juice. I glanced out the sliding door and nearly choked on the juice. I coughed, and Noah patted my back to help.

"Looks like we got even more snow than they called for," I said when I could finally speak again. The snow was piled almost halfway up the glass of the sliding door, and heavy, fat snowflakes were still coming down. Sage was right, I was snowed in with Noah still.

"Yeah, we got about twenty-five centimetres last night. I'll need to head out and do some shoveling after breakfast."

"I can help," I offered. Noah shot me a look. "What, I'm pregnant, not incapable."

"You're definitely not incapable, but you are pregnant, Nell. And I don't want you overexerting yourself when I can handle it."

"I don't mind helping," I tried again. "Besides, you didn't mind me 'overexerting' myself last night," I reminded him, using air quotes to accentuate my point.

Noah's eyes sparkled. "That's a totally different type of exerting yourself, and since I plan on a repeat, I'd rather you rest inside and stay all warm and cozy. Plenty of time to exert yourself later." He winked.

I tried to argue a little, but Noah wasn't having it. We ate our breakfast, me in a reflective silence and Noah stealing glances at me, trying to hide his smiles.

After breakfast, I tidied up the kitchen while Noah geared up and went outside to shovel and snowblow his driveway.

I hadn't been a fan of him ordering me to stay inside and rest, even if I was secretly thrilled that he cared enough to, well, care for me, so I had to even the score by cleaning the kitchen.

Not that there was much to clean. Noah was an unusually tidy person. Within five minutes, the dishwasher was running, and the frying pans he'd used were air drying in the dish rack on the counter by his sink.

I'd wiped down the countertop until it sparkled, and with nothing else to do, I wandered around Noah's cabin, taking it all in. It was beautiful, if not a little sterile. He didn't seem to have many knickknacks on the shelves or artwork on the walls. It was almost as if he'd recently moved in and hadn't truly had time to decorate, or perhaps it hadn't occurred to him to do so.

I wandered up the stairs to the loft. Noah had a huge TV on the one wall, and a sectional couch across from it. Underneath the TV was a shelving unit full of DVDs. Noah had a major DVD collection, mostly thriller and action movies, of course. I took my time perusing titles, but none really called to me.

What did call to me was the feeling of being at home at last.

CHAPTER TWENTY-EIGHT

Noah

THE SNOW WAS HEAVY. It had taken me a good two hours to snowblow the driveway, clear the front porch, and make sure the back deck was cleared, too. All the while snow was still coming down with no signs of stopping. By the time I headed inside, it almost looked like I needed to go back out and start again.

I kicked as much snow off my boots as I could, then walked into the house, where the warmth of the woodstove greeted me, along with the scent of hot chocolate.

I found Nellie in the kitchen, gently stirring a pot on the stove. She was still dressed in my pajama bottoms and T-shirt, her dark hair piled in a messy bun on top of her head. The sight of her standing in my kitchen made a visceral longing ache in my chest.

I wanted this. I wanted her here, in my space, comfortable and at ease, all the time. It was so strange, this want to have forever with her, this ability to envision it so easily. She fit in all the ways I'd stopped looking for someone to fit, like a puzzle piece I'd never realized was missing until I took a step back and looked at the greater picture.

"Oh, hey," she said when she noticed me standing there staring at her. "I found some hot chocolate mix in your cupboard and figured I'd make us some. I hope that's okay?"

"It's more than okay," I assured her, coming up behind her and wrapping my arms around her, letting my hands rest on the swell of her belly.

Nellie was beginning to show, although she avoided wearing snug-fitting clothes while at work. I hadn't realized how much she was showing until that day in the laundry room, when she put my palm against the swell of her stomach so I could feel the baby move.

I could feel the subtle fluttering sensation beneath my hand, as if the baby was reacting to the feel of my palm. It made me smile against Nellie's neck. I expected her to tense in my arms, but to my surprise she relaxed, leaning back against me as she continued to gently stir the hot chocolate.

Last night's sexcapades seemed to chisel away some of her walls, and for that I was thankful. I wasn't kidding when I'd told her I'd be as patient as she needed, but I was thankful she hadn't made me wait to have her again.

"It's still snowing, isn't it?" she asked, trying to turn her head to see around me.

"Sure is. I'll probably have to go back out and shovel again. It's supposed to stop later this evening."

"Hmm." Nellie frowned. "Will I be able to get home tonight?"

"It'll depend on how fast the township can clear the roads, but I could try to get you home, or..."

"Or what?"

"You're welcome to stay another night." I couldn't help that holding her had my cock thickening against her, but sex wasn't the only reason I wanted her to stay. I liked having her in my cabin. It felt more like a home with her.

"I don't have clothes here," Nellie pointed out. She went to remove the pot of hot chocolate from the burner, and I released her to grab a couple mugs from the dishwasher.

"We could wash your clothes, I have a washer and dryer," I pointed out with a wink.

"I can't wear the same clothes I wore the other day. What would everyone at work think?"

"That you were snowed in like the rest of us for a couple of days?" I smirked. "I doubt most of them would even notice. Rhonda and Denise don't exactly pay attention to that sort of thing, and my brothers already know you're here."

"If it's alright with you, I'd like to go home tonight," Nellie said softly.

"Of course, it's alright with me, Nell. I'll admit, I'm greedy and I'd keep you here forever if I could, but I understand you're not there yet."

Nellie's lips twitched with amusement. "It's just, all my things are at my apartment. My clothes. My makeup. My hairbrush. And yeah, I don't really know where I'm at with all of this." She gestured between us with the whisk.

"I understand," I nodded.

And I did, even if I couldn't help the disappointment that swelled at her words. I wanted to rush full speed ahead, but Nellie was still holding back. It was like she didn't trust what I was saying, but I knew I couldn't force that trust. It had to happen on its own.

"Thanks, Noah." Nellie smiled softly and tucked a strand of hair behind her ear. "You've been amazing, throughout everything. I'm sorry I'm so messed up and can't seem to—I don't know."

Nellie seemed to be struggling with how to word what she was feeling. I might have been relationship-wary for the past decade, but I'd never struggled with communication the way Nellie seemed to.

I had a feeling it was our upbringing. I'd been raised by loving, involved parents, and had siblings. My entire family wouldn't stand for me shutting down and retreating. Someone would hammer their fist on my door until I answered.

I didn't know Nellie's parents, but she'd mentioned on more than one occasion that their involvement in her life was limited. I could only imagine how that would affect her ability to communicate and let people in.

WE DRANK our hot chocolates in the great room and played a game of chess on the old wooden set my grandpa left for me. Nellie was surprisingly cutthroat at chess. She kicked my ass three times until I finally surrendered.

"How are you so good at this?" I exclaimed after the third time she declared checkmate.

"Chess was the only game my parents were ever interested in playing." Nellie shrugged, her smile slipping a little. "I could never get them to play Candyland or Trouble with me, but they'd play chess. Chess is a game of strategic thinking, and strategic thinking equals silence."

The look on her face had made something clench in my heart. "Damn, that sucks. Family boardgame nights were a regular occurrence for us growing up. Our kid will be playing all the boardgames. Candyland, Trouble, Monopoly, Guess Who, The Game of Life, Mouse Trap, Snakes and Ladders. Chess too, because it's awesome, but we'll be rowdy about it." I'd assured her with a wink, bringing that smile back to her eyes.

For dinner, Nellie insisted on cooking. She was somehow able to scrounge up the ingredients in my kitchen to make a pasta meal from canned tomatoes, jarred pesto, and cheese. We ate the rest of the salad with it.

The snow finally stopped around six o'clock, and after an hour and half of snowblowing my driveway, I was able to get Nellie home around eight.

Someone, likely Parker, had cleared the snow off the stairs leading up to her apartment and tossed down salt, but I still walked her up, hating that there were so many stairs leading to her front door.

"Thanks, Noah," Nellie said as she unlocked her door. "For coming to the appointment, and letting me crash at your place."

"It was my pleasure," I assured her, leaning against the door frame and tossing her a self-assured grin.

"See you at work tomorrow?" she asked, and I nodded.

GETTING Nellie out of my head after our snow day was an impossible feat. Even though work provided us both with a busy distraction, any moment I could, I was thinking about her, about how perfect she'd felt and how delicious she'd tasted.

But I wasn't just consumed with my sexual attraction and compatibility to her. I kept thinking about the little things she'd revealed to me, the small truths she'd shared, and wanting to discover more about what made Nellie Banks tick.

We had two weeks until we could find out the results for

the DNA test, but I wasn't about to let the days pass without me proving to Nellie those results were more for her than me.

On Tuesday night the following week, I picked Nellie up at five o'clock for our date to the author signing event at Beyond The Pages for Atticus Connelly.

"This is so cool, I've never been to an author signing before," Nellie said. She hadn't read the book but that didn't seem to lessen her excitement. I'd only gotten halfway through it myself, what with my thoughts so consumed by a certain brown-eyed girl. What I had read so far had been intriguing. Atticus was a good storyteller, and I was interested in hearing his process and what had inspired his writing.

There seemed to be a lot of similarities between Hartwood Creek and Coldwater Bay, especially with the witchy paranormal elements. Only in Atticus's story, the witches hadn't crafted a love spell, but a spell to ensnare the townsfolk of Coldwater Bay to do their evil bidding.

The signing event was on the second floor of the bookstore. The bookstore had an old birdcage elevator to the second level, but most people took the spiral iron staircase up because it took time to operate the elevator manually.

There were a lot of people at the event already, almost every folding chair was occupied. The Hartley triplets were in attendance, and their faces lit up at the sight of me and Nellie walking in together. They waved at us, then started whispering their conspiracies.

We managed to find two vacant chairs near the back of the room, and I helped Nellie out of her jacket, setting it on the back of one chair.

I glanced around as I took my own jacket off and draped it over the back of my chair, spotting Arwen Love standing with her mother, Agatha, and another woman I didn't recognize at the side of the room.

I'd gone to school with Arwen, although she'd always been super shy and reserved. I dipped my chin in greeting, and she smiled shyly back and turning her attention back to her mother and the other woman, who was saying something to Agatha.

"Who's that?" Nellie asked curiously, catching the exchange.

"That's Arwen Love, she's the daughter of the bookstore owners, Corin and Agatha. She's also the CEO and head librarian of the Hartwood Creek Public Library," I replied.

"Oh, that reminds me, I need to get a library card," Nellie said.

"That will be our next date then." I smiled at her.

"Good evening, everyone!" Agatha's voice pulled our attention to the front of the room. "Thank you all for coming out tonight! We are so excited to host Atticus Connelly. Please, help yourself to refreshments along the back wall! We have lemonade, coffee, tea, and baked goods donated by Tout de Sweets. Atticus is running a little late, but he'll be here within the next fifteen minutes." She gave a warm and welcoming smile, gesturing to the refreshment tables at the back of the room.

"Hungry? Or thirsty?" I asked, gesturing with a tilt of my chin to the refreshment table. Nellie glanced in the direction of the food.

"Mmm, I could probably eat. Let's be real, I could always probably eat," she said, letting out a small laugh as she put her hand on the swell of her belly. I covered her hand with my palm.

"Well, you are eating for two right now," I reminded her lowly, winking at her. "I probably should have taken you out for real food, first."

Nellie's cheeks heated, and she smiled. "It's okay, I did eat dinner, I promise. I'm feeling snacky. That's nothing new." I let my hand fall away as we stood up, moving it to the small of her back as we made our way over to the refreshment table.

We both grabbed glasses of lemonade and a small plate of brownie bites to share. I said hello to a few familiar faces, making introductions to Nellie.

Before we could make it back to our seats, Betty, Alice, and Dorothy intercepted us. "Look at the two of you! You make a lovely couple," Alice cooed.

"The gene pool is going to result in some adorable little ones," Dorothy giggled in agreement.

Nellie froze, and I could sense her discomfort.

"I thought you three preferred romance books to thrillers?" I asked, changing the subject as abruptly as I could.

"Oh, we do. But we had fun reading this one." Betty grinned. "Atticus has such an interesting mind, don't you think?" She directed this question at Nellie.

"I haven't read it yet," Nellie admitted. "My genre of choice is romance, too. But I've never been to an author signing though, so I thought I'd check it out with Noah."

"They are fun!" Alice said. "The Loves know how to host a good event. It's a shame Atticus is running behind, although I'm surprised he agreed to this at all."

"Yes," Dorothy nodded. "He's usually not one for public appearances. We should feel honoured that he chose Hartwood Creek as his first bookstore event."

"He probably did it to rub it in." Alice chuckled, not seeming the least bit deterred by that possibility. "When you do read it, I'm sure you'll be able to spot all of the similarities between Hartwood Creek and Coldwater Bay."

"Although he's taken a lot of creative liberties," Betty said with an arch of her penciled-in brow. "If he weren't such a captivating storyteller, I might be offended."

"Writers take creative liberties all the time," Alice reminded her sister with a wry smile.

Before anyone else could get another word in edgewise, Agatha Love was speaking into the microphone again. "Could I have your attention, please! The event is about to start, please find your seats."

Atticus Connelly was exactly how Corin described him: a recluse. He appeared put-out by the amount of people in attendance. The woman I'd seen earlier—his assistant—seemed to run the show, directing questions to an unwilling and reserved Atticus.

But after a few moments, he seemed to relax and started to engage a little more willingly with the audience as he explained his writing process and where he drew inspiration from.

Betty raised her hand during the question segment, and when Julie called upon her, she stood up. "Your writing is very descriptive, Atticus. My sisters and I were deeply impressed with your prose. However, there seems to be a lack of, shall we say, human connection?" Betty's lips twitched with a smile as Atticus's expression darkened.

"I'm not sure what you're asking," he grumbled into the microphone.

"Well, everyone is either evil or trying to defeat the evil, but there seems to be a lack of deeper relationships and connections between the characters. Was that," Betty paused here, inserting her flair for dramatics, "intentional?"

"Not every story needs to have a romantic element to it. If you were looking for that, you shouldn't have picked up a dark paranormal thriller," Atticus responded gruffly.

Betty didn't seem put out by his tone or his answer at all. She waved her hand, as if batting away his grumpiness. "Ah, but you see, how can the town truly fight the evil embedded in it without those connections and that drive to fight for their relationships?"

Atticus blinked, as if he'd never truly considered that, then cleared his throat and leaned forward. "The townsfolk want to defeat the evil witches to be free of their control, and that is their motivation to keep fighting. It's dangerously distracting for them to form authentic relationships whilst being controlled by evil. As I said, I don't write whimsy or romance. I write about the darker side of humanity—greed, control, possession."

"And you do it very well." Betty nodded in agreement, a mischievous smile on her lips as her gaze darted to the side of the room—seemingly to Arwen Love—and returning her focus to Atticus. "I just think you'll find, in time, that love can be the motivation, too. Often, a stronger motivation to defeat the evils of the world."

Atticus smiled, but it wasn't a warm, inviting one. It was a challenging, defiant one. "We'll see what happens as the series progresses."

Another person raised a hand.

"Yes?"

"So, there will be more books in The Witches of Coldwater Bay series?"

"Of course, they may have won the battle, but the war is far from over. The witches of Coldwater Bay will be back," Atticus answered with a terse nod.

I waited long enough for Atticus to sign my copy of the book, then Nellie and I snuck out when the Hartley triplets seemed intent on cornering Arwen Love at the refreshment table.

"So, it appears the Hartley sisters have a new target," I murmured once we'd made it to the street. Nellie zipped up her jacket, sending me a questioning look. "Their focus was very much on Atticus tonight."

"Well, he was the reason for the event. Perhaps they're interested in his writing and future books?"

I thought back to how the triplets had cornered Arwen, who'd seemed completely off kilter from the moment Atticus walked in. There was no way the Hartley triplets hadn't picked up on Arwen's reaction if I'd picked up on it. Arwen had always been shy, but she'd seemed outright shaken to her core tonight and that difference hadn't appeared until Atticus had.

Something was brewing there, and the Hartley triplets had their hands in it. That meant that their focus might veer from us a little, and I wasn't mad about that.

"We'll see," I grinned. "Are you still hungry? We could go to the diner for some food if you'd like."

"I should probably get home," Nellie said. "I work tomorrow, and I apparently need a good nine hours of sleep or I'm a walking zombie the next day."

"Okay." I nodded, taking her hand as we walked. "Well, thank you for coming out with me tonight."

"I had a lot of fun," Nellie admitted.

CHAPTER TWENTY-NINE

Nellie

WAITING for the results of the DNA test and the date of my ultrasound seemed to take forever. Work kept me busy, especially after the snowstorm. We had so many calls and emails to return after the snow day.

Then there was Noah. He'd insisted on taking me out on a few dates. We went to the author signing with Atticus Connelly—which had been one of the most interesting town events I'd witnessed yet, especially with the stand-off between Betty and Atticus. I'd started to feel a little hopeful that the Hartley sisters had lost interest in my and Noah's relationship, but that proved to be false when I ran into them at the grocery store.

They had all kinds of questions for me about Noah, although they didn't drop any more comments about babies or gene pools, so I considered that a win. I was showing more and more every day, and thankful for the layers winter required I wear to stay warm.

I'd managed to avoid attention so far, but I could tell Charlotte was growing suspicious of me. She hadn't outright asked me any intrusive questions, but she seemed to study me closely when she thought I wasn't paying attention, as if looking for answers in my behaviour or movements.

But finally, the day for my appointments arrived. I'd given Damien plenty of notice that I'd be out for the entire day, so Charlotte was covering for me. I had the ultrasound appointment in the morning, followed by my afternoon appointment with Dr. Kramer.

At first, I hadn't been sure if I should invite Noah or not, but Sage and Tabitha worked their magic and convinced me that I should ask him. So, I'd told Noah that he was welcome to join if he could get away for the day, and he'd assured me he could.

I was finishing putting on my mascara when a knock sounded at my door, alerting me to his arrival.

"You're a little early," I told him when I opened the door for him and stepped aside.

"Sorry, I'm excited to see you," he said as he stepped inside, not looking very sorry at all. He pressed a kiss to my temple. "I can wait, if you're not finished getting ready?"

"I need to brush my teeth, then we can go," I said, trying to ignore the way my heart raced in my chest at the sight of him.

Noah nodded, shoving his hands into his coat pocket, and waiting by the front door while I went back to the bathroom to finish getting ready. Once my teeth were brushed and lip balm applied, because winter sucked all the moisture out of my lips the moment I set foot outside, I was ready to go.

I tried not to be silent on the drive to Springwood, but I couldn't help the way my mind was whirling.

I'd had an ultrasound during my first trimester, but the baby was the size of a bean then. This time, the baby would be more baby-like, and they'd be able to determine what gender it was.

I'd decided I wanted to know. I figured it'd make telling my parents about the baby easier. Telling them they'd be having a grandson or a granddaughter in a few months' time might warm them to the idea. I knew, regardless, they'd likely start questioning all my life choices.

I wanted to know for me, too, and a large part of me was curious to see if Noah was right.

"So, did you want to come in during the ultrasound?" I asked him when we'd almost arrived at the hospital. He glanced at me, his eyes widening with surprise. "I mean, you don't have to if you don't want to."

"No, I want to. I do, I figured you'd want me to keep my distance 'til after you got the results." Noah seemed hesitant, as if he was afraid to trust that I wanted him there.

"I want you there if you want to be there," I said. "I mean, I want to see your face when you're told you're wrong and it's a boy," I added with a teasing smile, trying to lighten the mood with him.

"Wanna bet?"

"What kind of bet?" I asked, intrigued.

Noah paused for a moment, as if thinking.

"If the baby's a girl, you crash at my house this weekend, in my bed," he finally said.

"And if it's a boy?" I asked.

"I crash at your place tonight, in your bed."

"Seems like you win in either scenario."

"Well, that's because I do win in either scenario." Noah's declaration and the look he sent me made me swoon, and the baby started wiggling about as if dancing in agreement.

"Fine," I said, fighting the urge to melt into a puddle at his feet.

After we found parking in the hospital lot closest to the ultrasound department, we went up. We'd arrived twenty minutes before my appointment time, and things seemed to be moving on schedule.

"Ellen Banks?" The ultrasound technician called my name, and I stood up.

"It's Nellie," I corrected her automatically, and she gave me a warm smile.

"My apologies, Nellie. I'm Allison, and I'll be your ultrasound technician today. If Dad wants to come in, he's welcome to," she added, spotting Noah beside me.

I didn't bother to correct her on Noah's status as the maybe-father, especially not when I noticed the spark in Noah's eyes and the soft tilt of his lips as he smiled, as if he liked being referred to as Dad. It warmed my heart. His words resurfacing again, that it didn't matter to him either way—that he already considered this baby his. The look in his eyes made me realize that he wasn't telling me lines he thought I wanted to hear, he meant those words wholeheartedly.

Noah stood, and we followed the ultrasound technician into a room. There was a chair at the end of the bed, which he sat in, his eyes taking in the ultrasound equipment with a nervous interest.

"Please get comfortable, this scan is a little longer than the first ultrasound you had," Allison smiled, waiting while I climbed up on the table and rolled down my sweats. "This might be a little cold," she added, smearing the cold ultrasound gel against my stomach. I tried not to flinch, but it really was cold.

Noah's fingers tapped restlessly against the chair's armrest as Allison got everything prepared for the ultrasound. Once she was ready, she brought the ultrasound wand to my belly, pressing it in.

The wand moved against my womb for a moment, then Allison found the baby, and the sound of the heartbeat filled the room. "That's the baby's heartbeat we're hearing, very healthy and strong. And look, baby's waving!"

Noah leaned forward, looking at the screen, and I glanced, too. The baby's hand was moving back and forth, and although I wouldn't quite call it a full-on wave, it was adorable.

"Aww," I cooed, my eyes welling with tears. If asked, I wouldn't have been able to articulate the feeling I had upon seeing my baby.

"Woah," Noah said, his eyes widening as he looked at the screen. I could hear the awe in his voice and see the visceral reaction happening within him. His eyes misted, too.

"I'm going to take some measurements, then we'll get to the fun stuff. Will you be wanting to find out the baby's gender today?" Allison asked, glancing at me.

I looked at Noah. "Yeah, we'd like to find out if we could," I answered, looking back at the screen. She nodded, turning the screen a little so she could see it better to take her measurements.

That process took about fifteen minutes, and once she was done, she turned the screen toward me more and called Noah over. "Are you ready?"

"Sure are." Noah sent me a wink, taking my hand and giving it a firm squeeze.

"It's a girl," Allison said, her smile wide. I expected Noah to gloat, to shoot me a *see, told you so* look, but he was captivated by the screen. She clicked a few buttons, zooming in to show us the evidence.

Allison printed off a few photos of the ultrasound for us, then the appointment was over. I wiped the ultrasound goop off my stomach with a paper towel, tossing it in the trash and standing.

Noah stepped toward me, putting his arms around me and pulling me against him. "Thank you for letting me be a part of this. That was probably the coolest thing I've ever experienced."

Noah was an excellent hugger. His tender embrace made me feel safe, and his earnest words had me overcome with emotion. "Well, it looks like you were right about the baby being a girl."

"I would have been happy either way," Noah assured me, pressing a kiss to my temple. "But I do love hearing you say that I was right. Say it again?"

"Don't get used to it," I said, narrowing my eyes playfully.

Noah helped me into my coat, and we left, walking to his truck. "I think we have time to get something to eat before the next appointment. What are you craving?"

"I could actually go for pizza, or maybe pasta," I replied, mulling over between the two.

"You're in luck. There's a decent Italian place around the corner that has both pizza and pasta," Noah grinned.

We went to an Italian restaurant in Springwood, halfway between the hospital and my OB's office. They had an overwhelming menu to choose from. Since I was craving pizza and pasta, we decided to order both and split them, as well as an order of bruschetta bread for an appetizer.

We ordered our drinks and an appetizer first. For the main course, I ordered the creamy cappelletti with bacon, and then Noah made me pick the pizza, too. I went with the Honey pizza. It had a garlic base with pineapple, caramelized onion, bacon, and feta.

After relaying our order to the server, and watching her

walk away, Noah had the audacity to admit he didn't like pineapple on pizza.

"Why did you let me pick that, then!" I exclaimed, flabbergasted.

"Because you got so excited about it. I don't mind, maybe it'll sway me." Noah leaned back in his chair. "And if I hate it, there's always the cappelletti."

I shook my head. "I bet you'll love it," I declared, eyeing him with confidence.

"Oh really? What do you want to bet?"

"I guess my cappelletti." I pouted, not liking the idea of giving it up even if I was certain he'd like the pizza.

When the server arrived with our main course, I made Noah take the first slice of pizza, eyeing him the entire time he chewed. His face belayed nothing, and I fidgeted impatiently while he considered it.

"You were right—I like it. The pineapple is oddly complimentary," he finally said.

I ended up giving him half of my cappelletti anyway.

Noah

NELLIE'S OB, Dr. Kramer, walked into the exam room with a friendly smile. "So, I was checking out the results from your ultrasound this morning! Everything looks great with the baby."

"That's a relief," Nellie relaxed, the tension leaving her shoulders.

"And we also got the results from the DNA test. Do you want me to go over them now?" she asked, glancing at me, then returning her gaze to Nellie.

"Sure." Nellie reached for my hand, taking it in hers.

Normally, I was the one reaching for her hand, but this was a welcome change.

"The probability of paternity is ninety-nine point nine nine percent," Dr. Kramer announced, passing a copy of the results to me so I could read it for myself. "Congratulations!"

I glanced up at Nellie, unable to hide my grin of elation. It really wouldn't have mattered to me either way, but her look of relief was palpable.

"Well, that is good news." Nellie nodded.

Dr. Kramer proceeded with the exam, feeling Nellie's growing belly, listening to the heartbeat, and questioning Nellie on how her symptoms were.

"I'm surprised at how good I feel. I still get nauseated on occasion, but only if I forget to eat. And the pain has been very limited."

"That's good to hear. We'll need to book a glucose test for when you're between twenty-four and twenty-eight weeks."

"Oh, okay."

"It's standard for pregnant women, but endometriosis can increase the risk of gestational diabetes, so we'll want to keep an eye on that. Symptoms of gestational diabetes can include increased thirst, frequent urination, especially at night, dry mouth, fatigue, blurred vision, genital itching or thrush, nausea and vomiting, unintentional weight loss, frequent skin, vaginal, and bladder infections," Dr. Kramer said, relaying a long list of symptoms that made my head spin. "But oftentimes, gestational diabetes doesn't cause any symptoms, or they're mild, so that's why we do the glucose test."

Nellie nodded, as if she understood completely. My head was still trying to wrap around medical terms and symptoms, but I figured I had plenty of time to ask her later.

Dr. Kramer stood up. "Take care, I'll see you at your

appointment in a week, and Jenny will book your glucose test with the hospital. They'll have to call you to confirm."

"Okay, thanks, Dr. Kramer."

Once we were in the truck, I turned to look at Nellie. "So, what's endometriosis?"

Nellie drew in a breath as if preparing herself as she buckled her seatbelt. "It's a condition I've had for a while now. It's a disease where tissue similar to the lining of the uterus grows outside the uterus. It leads to inflammation and scar tissue forming in the pelvic region and sometimes, elsewhere in the body, although that's rare. It can cause severe pain in the pelvis and makes it harder to get pregnant," she explained.

"Oh. That sounds unpleasant."

"It usually is." Nellie smiled ruefully. "I was always told I'd probably have a lot of difficulties conceiving without fertility treatment, so this pregnancy...well. It was surprising in more ways than one. I know this entire situation is a little unorthodox, but I didn't want to risk losing out on my chance to be a mom, especially if it's my only chance," she said softly.

I reached across the cab of the truck, putting my hand on her knee. "I get it," I said gently. "I'm glad it happened, seriously. It brought you back to Hartwood Creek, and to me."

"So, you're ready to be a dad?" Nellie joked, trying to hide how affected she was by my words.

"I've got about five months to get ready," I replied with a wink.

"I guess that's true." Nellie laughed lightly.

"The idea of it doesn't scare me as much as I thought it would," I admitted, removing my hand from her knee so I could pull out of the parking lot.

"You were scared of knocking up some one-night stand and being saddled with them for eighteen-plus years, huh?"

"I used to fear knocking someone up, yeah, but not just

because of having to be committed to them without really knowing them. I watched Damien struggle with single parenthood. The girls' biological mother didn't want anything to do with them, and she took off after they were born, leaving Damien alone with two newborn babies. It was a lot for him. He's always loved those girls, but taking care of babies and raising kids, that's not for the weak," I explained, glancing at her to find her watching me with a reflective look in her eyes.

"No, it's not," Nellie said quietly. "I was prepared to do it alone, because I've been on my own for so long anyway."

"Well, you're not alone anymore."

"I know," Nellie replied.

"So, about that bet." I said, lifting a brow at her.

"Yeah, yeah," she rolled her eyes, fighting a smile. "I'll crash at your place this weekend."

"Good. And I'm hoping you'll feel up to meeting my parents."

"What?" The shock of my suggestion was palpable.

"I want them to meet you, and I kind of want to tell them, you know?" I cast her a worried look, wondering if I'd over stepped. Nellie swallowed, trying to disguise her discomfort. "Have you told your parents yet?"

"No, I haven't. Not yet, anyway," she admitted. "I keep finding reasons to put it off. At first, I wanted to wait until I was sure the pregnancy would stick. Then I wanted to wait until I knew the gender, because I was hoping that would soften them to the news."

"You think they're going to take it hard?" I asked.

"I don't know," Nellie lifted her shoulder in a shrug. "I think I'm afraid of their indifference."

I drew in a breath. I could acknowledge how indifference would sting, even over anger and disappointment. With anger and disappointment, you knew it came from a place of caring. With indifference, though...

"We can wait until you're ready to tell them about the baby, but I do want them to meet you."

"Okay, yeah, I can meet them," Nellie nodded, as if convincing herself. "But I'd like to hold off a little on telling them about the baby. At least until I work up the courage to tell my parents."

"That makes sense."

CHAPTER THIRTY

Nellie

"OH MY GOSH, look at her sweet little face!" Sage cooed, peering at the ultrasound picture I brought out for her and Tabitha to see later that afternoon.

Tabitha looked over Sage's shoulder, her smile wide. "Aww! This is giving me serious baby fever."

"No! Absolutely not! Not happening!" Parker's frantic voice called from the living room, where he was currently undergoing an intense makeover session with Bella, Brielle, and Daphne. When I'd walked in, Bella was applying so much blue eyeshadow, Mimi from the Drew Carey Show would be proud.

"How did he hear that?" Tabitha whispered, covering her mouth to hide her giggle.

"He must have supersonic hearing." Sage smiled.

"Supersonic selective hearing," Tabitha muttered, rolling her eyes with a smile. "Anyway, when's your ultrasound, Sage?"

"Monday!" Sage replied. "Nix and I are going to pull Daphne out of school so she can come, too."

"Oooh, yay! Then we need to get planning some baby showers," Tabitha said gleefully, clapping her hands and giving her hips a little wiggle.

"I still need to tell my parents. And Noah wants to tell his soon, too." I groaned, putting my head down on the countertop.

"You haven't told your parents yet?" Tabitha sounded surprised.

"I know I need to, and I will. But. Ugh." I sighed, and Sage put her arm around my shoulders. "I haven't talked to them since their brief call on Christmas morning."

"Rip it off, like a Band-Aid," Sage suggested.

"Did you tell your mom?"

"Yeah, last night, over text message. She replied with a thumbs up, so..." She shrugged. If her mother's reaction wounded her, she didn't let on.

"Ouch." Tabitha frowned, looking hurt on behalf of Sage.

"It's fine, I expected it. My mother hasn't been out to visit once since we moved to Hartwood Creek, and she knows where we live. She's never even met Nix." Sage pursed her lips. "It's her loss. Nix's parents and Auntie Em and Uncle Ed are excited enough."

"Laurel and Keith are amazing grandparents, and Em and Ed will be, too. They were made for it." Tabitha smiled, then turned her attention to me, fixing her warm blue eyes on my face. "And no matter what your parents' reaction is, your baby is going to be so loved and spoiled by Noah's parents. Aunt Gloria and Uncle Will are very involved with Damien's daughters."

I smiled, feeling bolstered by both Sage and Tabitha's reassurance. I knew from what Noah had shared about his family that the reception would probably be a lot warmer than whatever I'd get from my parents.

An hour later, I trudged back up to my apartment feeling motivated enough to call my parents. It was time to tell them, if only to get the painful process out of the way so I could focus on the things that were good with my life.

After a day of being with Noah and an afternoon of hanging out with Sage and Tabitha, I could admit there was a lot of good in my life—a lot of supportive people who were excited for this baby.

I curled up on my couch with a warm blanket over my lap and dialed my mom's phone number. It rang a few times, and I was convinced I'd end up getting her voicemail.

After the sixth ring, she answered. "Ellen? Is everything alright?"

To her credit, Mom sounded a little concerned. I suppose it wasn't common for me to call out of the blue anymore. On holidays and special occasions, absolutely, but I'd long since stopped calling them to chat casually. I always felt like I was pulling them away from some important engagement.

"Hi, Mom. Yeah, everything's fine. I'm calling with some news." I didn't want to beat around the bush, but it was harder than I anticipated to blurt it out.

"What news? What's going on? Are you okay?" Instantly, she was on edge. I could hear it in her voice.

"Is that Ellen? What's happening?" I could hear Dad's voice in the background.

"I'm fine, Mom. Better than fine, really. I've got some exciting news to share."

"What?" Mom sounded suspicious, and I couldn't blame her.

Drawing in a deep breath, I repeated Sage's words in my mind: Rip it off, like a Band-Aid.

"I'm pregnant. I'll be having a baby in July," I said, hating how my voice wobbled.

"What? How can that be! You aren't even seeing anyone!" Mom exclaimed, sounding scandalized.

"Actually, I have been seeing someone. His name is Noah, and he's from Hartwood Creek."

"And he's the father?"

"The what?!" I could hear the outrage in my dad's voice.

"Hush, Herb, I'm trying to get to the bottom of this," my mom scolded him. It sounded like she'd covered the receiver, as her voice was a little muffled.

"Yes, he's the father. He's excited about the baby, and so am I," I said, thankful that my voice was sure and stable.

"I thought your endometriosis made you infertile?" Mom asked, sounding as if she couldn't wrap her head around the news.

"I thought so too, but evidently not," I answered. "I'm having a girl."

My mother was silent for several beats. "Oh. Well. Congratulations, I suppose. You are in your thirties."

"Yes, I am."

"I'd hoped you would be married before bringing children into the world. How does this...Owen...feel about marriage?"

"It's Noah, Mom." I sighed deeply. "And marriage isn't a requirement to parenthood," I added. I wasn't about to get into the circumstances of the situation for her. I knew she wouldn't understand. My parents were very traditional and rigid with their beliefs.

"Raising a child is a serious job, Ellen. Knowing that you have a stable partner is crucial. What if this...Noah...takes off? Or isn't up for the task?"

"Marriage wouldn't prevent him from leaving if that's what he wanted to do." I massaged my temple, trying to ease the headache this conversation brought on. "Anyway, I'm pregnant, and I'm happy about it. I wanted to let you guys know."

"Oh, well. Thank you for informing us." My mother's voice was formal and lacked warmth. It shouldn't have surprised me or stung, but it did.

I felt both defeated and relieved when I finally hung up the phone after a terse goodbye. I suppose I should be happy that my parents' reaction wasn't the indifference I feared, but I could have gone without the blatant judgment.

Noah

NELLIE LEFT work on Friday at her usual time, heading home to pack a bag for the weekend with plans to meet me at my place around five thirty, then we'd drive over to my parents' house for dinner.

I'd told my mom she was coming, and Mom was ecstatic to meet her. I hadn't yet mentioned the pregnancy, but Nellie was showing more. Charlotte was getting suspicious, although Damien had kept it a secret from his fiancée, since his stance on the whole thing was 'it's not my place'.

I was hoping to tell them soon, but I could understand Nellie wanting to meet them first as my girlfriend.

Once Nellie dropped off her overnight bag, we walked out to my truck to make the short drive over. I could tell she was nervous. She kept fiddling with her zipper, zipping it up to her chin and back down again.

"Are you nervous?" I asked.

"A little. I've never done this before; met the family of a guy I was seeing," Nellie admitted.

"I promise, my family's pretty cool. You already know

Easton, Damien, and Charlotte," I reminded her. "Besides, technically, you've met them briefly already. Before Christmas, at the park."

"Yeah, that's true." She let out a breath. "I didn't meet them as your girlfriend. Your pregnant girlfriend."

"We don't have to tell them that second part yet," I replied, turning onto my parents' driveway.

"I was thinking maybe we should. It's getting harder and harder to conceal this baby bump, and frankly, I'm tired of keeping it a secret from everyone. Word is going to get out soon, and I would hate for your family to find out from someone else."

"It's totally up to you," I assured her. "If you want to wait, we can wait. If you want to tell them tonight, we can tell them. No pressure at all."

"Except some pressure, because I'm meeting your family, and what if they hate me?"

"They could never hate you."

"My own parents barely tolerate me," Nellie muttered, looking out the window to hide her face. I could hear the heartache in her voice.

"Nell." My heart broke for her, and I put my hand on her knee as I slowed down and put my truck in park. We only had a few minutes until we arrived at my parents' house, and I knew they'd be watching from the front window. "I'm sure that's not true," I added, turning to her.

"I told them about the baby. My mom lectured me, and we ended the conversation on the 'well it's your life and you're a grown woman' note, but I could tell they weren't thrilled with me," Nellie admitted, blinking away the tears that had formed. "My dad didn't say anything to me directly, but I could hear him ranting in the background."

"They'll come around," I said, putting my arms around her.

"And even if they don't, well, that's their loss. This baby of ours is already so loved and wanted, she will never feel their absence." I could promise her that much.

"But I will," Nellie whispered, looking at me. The hurt in her eyes gutted me. I couldn't think of a single thing to say in response. I held her close.

"We don't have to do this right now; I can tell my parents something came up. We can order a pizza and stay in."

"No, I'm fine. It's pregnancy hormones, I swear." Nellie pulled away, drying her eyes, and giving me a brave smile. "It's probably better I let them out now than at your parents place."

I opened my mouth, about to argue with her, when honking sounded behind me. Glancing over my shoulder, I saw Easton pulling up behind me in his beat-up pick-up truck.

"I'm fine, I swear," Nellie repeated. "Let's get this over with."

"Gee, don't sound so excited," I said, trying to lighten the mood.

We finished driving up the driveway. I hopped out, going to open Nellie's door while Easton parked beside me.

"Hope I didn't interrupt anything," Easton said, walking over to us as I helped Nellie out of the truck.

"Nope," Nellie responded. "Just a bit of pre-meet-the-parents nerves."

"Ah, those are the worst." Easton nodded with understanding, his eyes sympathetic.

"Whose parents have you met?" I retorted, and my younger brother laughed and shook his head.

"None, actually. I haven't found a girl I'd be willing to meet her parents for," Easton answered, walking ahead of us up the front steps. Before we reached the door, it swung open, revealing my mom.

"Hey, Mom!" Easton said, slipping inside and giving her a kiss. Nellie and I stepped in after him.

"Hello boys, hello Nellie! So nice to officially meet you!" Mom said, pulling Nellie in for a hug immediately.

"Oh, hi!" Nellie's eyes found mine, and she looked a little panicked.

"Noah has told us so much about you. How are you liking Hartwood Creek?" Mom asked, pulling away but keeping her hands on Nellie's upper arms.

"It's very welcoming," Nellie answered, smiling politely. I could tell she was a little uncomfortable, so I came to her rescue.

"Let me get your coat, Nell," I said.

My mom stepped back so I could help Nellie out of her coat, watching us with a knowing smile.

"Thanks," she replied as I took it from her and hung it in the hall closet with mine. Nellie was still trying to hide her belly. She was dressed in layers, wearing a loose-fitting navy-blue T-shirt under a white and blue striped button up.

"I hope you're hungry! I made my famous creamy chicken lasagna tonight," Mom exclaimed, leading us deeper into the house. We followed, my hand on the small of Nellie's back as we walked. "There's also garlic bread, and Caesar salad."

"Sounds delicious, Mom," I told her, and she beamed in response.

"It should be ready in a few minutes. Could I get you anything to drink, Nellie?"

"I'm okay, Mrs. Wood."

"Please, call me Gloria," Mom insisted, her smile warm and inviting.

"Gloria," Nellie corrected softly, smiling back.

We walked into the living room where my dad, Easton, Damien, and the twins were hanging out. A PWHL hockey game was on the television, the volume turned up enough that Dad would be able to hear the announcers should anything exciting happen, but low enough that conversations could still happen.

Easton and Damien seemed to be in a heated debate about one of the players. Dad was talking to Aria and Ronan about their most recent game. Everyone looked over to us when we walked in.

"Ah, Noah. You're on time for a change," Dad joked as he stood up from his armchair, his eyes twinkling. "And you must be Nellie," he added.

"Yes, hi. It's nice to meet you, Mr. Wood." Nellie smiled, holding out her hand to shake his.

"Call me Will," Dad said, his grin widening as he shook her hand. "Mr. Wood makes me feel old."

"Feel old? You are old, old man!" Easton said.

"Well, that may be true, but, just because you are old, it doesn't mean you need to feel old," Dad said, winking at Nellie.

"Hey, Nell," Charlotte greeted with a smile as she joined us in the living room.

"Hey." Nellie smiled.

"Go wash up girls!" Charlotte said. Aria and Ronan took off running, shoving each other to get to the bathroom first. Almost everything was a competition with them; who could wash their hands first, who could get to the table first, who could finish eating first.

They got their competitive nature from the Wood side. My brothers and I were the same growing up. I glanced at Nellie and smiled, wondering with reverence if our baby would be as competitive.

We headed to the dining room, where the table was set for everyone. It didn't matter if it was a casual get together or a formal function, Mom always had a beautifully set table. She believed meals deserved a certain level of ambience and effort.

Mom had decorations for every season, and her casual table set up was a long cream coloured runner with candles and greenery and matching round table mats. Each place was set with plates, salad bowls, cutlery, and napkins.

Dad carried the tray of lasagna to the table, placing it down on the trivet. I pulled a chair out for Nellie while Dad started serving the lasagna.

Mom carried out a basket of garlic bread, lifting it so the girls wouldn't knock into it when they ran into the dining room.

"Beat you!" Aria declared, sitting down half a second before Ronan.

"Barely! And you cheated, so it doesn't count!" Ronan insisted with a scowl.

"Girls, no bickering," Damien scolded them, his tone somehow gentle and firm at the same time.

"Yeah, no bickering! Besides, you both win on lasagna night!" Easton winked, holding his plate out for Dad to serve him a heaping helping.

"That's true." Charlotte made sure the girls had some salad, then she passed the bowl along. "Gloria makes the best lasagna."

"It's a family recipe," Gloria replied, her cheeks pink as if the attention made her blush. "It's been in my family for generations."

"I've been trying to get her to give me the recipe since the first night she made it for me," Charlotte whispered to Nellie. "She won't give it up."

"You'll get it one day," Gloria promised, her eyes sparkling. "For now, it ensures you'll all come over for dinner every once in a while."

"You don't have to bribe us with your homemade lasagna, Mom. But it does help," Easton smirked.

Conversation slowed for a few moments while food was passed out and around the table. When everyone's plates were loaded, we dug in.

CHAPTER THIRTY-ONE

Nellie

DINNER with the Wood family was a lot like having dinner with the Alcotts. Everyone seemed to talk over each other, and laughter was abundant. Mrs. Wood—Gloria—was an exceptional cook.

Noah's entire family was warm, inviting, and happy. There was a familial comfort between them all, and I could tell that they genuinely enjoyed each other's company. Even Damien was smiling, something I'd rarely seen him do unless around Charlotte.

After everyone had finished their meal, they remained around the table for coffee and dessert. Someone—either Noah or Charlotte—must have told Gloria I preferred tea to coffee, because she brought me out a cup of herbal tea.

"You let me know if you want more hot water," she told me when she set the teacup down in front of me.

The twins, Aria and Ronan, ate their slices of cake quickly

and asking to be excused so they could go play, but the adults remained around the table.

"So, Nellie, how are you liking working at the resort?" Mr. Wood—Will—asked, sending me a considering look.

I'd taken a sip of my tea and had to swallow before answering. "I'm really enjoying it. There's always something interesting happening."

"That's resort management for you." Will chuckled, shaking his head. "Never a dull moment! The stories I could tell you. Wait until the summer! You'll be meeting some interesting regulars."

"Ooh, like the Burns!" Easton said gleefully. "They really know how to keep things entertaining."

"Summers are my favourite time of year at the resort," Gloria said, her smile wistful. "Fall is beautiful, and winter can be fun, but summers have a special place in my heart." Gloria smiled at Will, her eyes aglow with love.

I exchanged a look with Noah, my thoughts on how my due date was mid-summer. Noah put his hand on my knee and gave it a gentle squeeze, as if he knew where my mind had gone.

He tilted his head in the direction of his family as if asking if I still wanted to tell them. I nodded, worrying my bottom lip. Dinner had gone so well, and I was afraid to shift the jovial mood, but I hadn't changed my mind. I wanted to tell them.

I had grown tired of hiding it from everyone. I wanted to be able to walk around town without worrying someone would discover my secret, and that it'd get back to Noah's family before we had a chance to tell them.

"Speaking of the summer, we actually have some news to share," Noah said, still looking at me. I gave him a small smile, and Noah's hand found mine.

"Oh? What news is that?" Gloria asked, drawing Noah's

attention away. He glanced around the table at his family members, all of them waiting expectantly for him to speak.

Damien surprised me by giving me a small, reassuring smile and subtle nod.

"Nellie and I are going to have a baby," Noah finally said.

For a moment, nobody said anything. The silence seemed to stretch on and on, my heart pounding in frantic beats with each millisecond that passed.

I envisioned Noah's parents flying off the handle, demanding that I leave their home immediately. I imagined them accusing me of trapping their son and defiling their good name. I could scarcely breathe, even with Noah reassuringly squeezing my hand.

Gloria blinked as if coming out of a stupor. "Really?" she asked, her hand going to her mouth and her eyes welling with tears when Noah nodded in response. "That's amazing news! Congratulations!" she added, practically flying out of her seat to rush around the table and wrap her arms around both Noah and me.

Charlotte and Will congratulated us too, and to my utter surprise nobody looked angry or upset at the news. Easton appeared shocked at first, but that shock faded away at the sight of his mother's notable excitement, and he was grinning.

"Well, damn. Congratulations!" Easton said, lifting his coffee mug in a cheers. "That will certainly keep attention off me for the foreseeable future. Thank you!"

Noah rolled his eyes and shook his head, but he was still smiling.

"When's the due date?" Gloria asked as went back to her seat and picked up a napkin to wipe the tears from her eyes.

"July nineteenth," I replied.

Gloria's lips parted with surprise, as if she'd done the math and concluded that it didn't exactly add up to when Noah and

I started dating. But she didn't say anything, and I had a feeling she wouldn't have, if Noah's younger brother hadn't pointed out the obvious first.

"Wait a minute. So, this baby-making night happened back in October, after the Witches' Ball?" Easton blurted, his eyes wide with scandalized surprise.

"Easton!" Gloria scolded, shooting her youngest son a chastising look.

"What! I'm just saying." Easton raised his hands in surrender, a cocky smirk on his face. "Did you guys have the shots?"

"There were a lot of shots had that night," I muttered, my face heating with embarrassment.

Easton let out a cackle. "The Hartley triplets did it again!"

"Did what again?" I frowned.

"They always have a hand in planning the Witches' Ball. Yeah, the Hastingses put it on. But the Hartley triplets are behind the drink menu. They've been known to make certain cocktails and shots with the love elixir," Easton explained, his eyes bright with amusement.

I'm glad somebody was entertained.

"How do you know that?" Noah asked, his brows furrowing.

"Aliza Hastings told me a few years ago. After I almost did a few shots with Leah Michaels." Easton shivered, as if the memory gave him the heebie-jeebies. "Leah went on to do shots with Beckett Brown, and nine months later..." he gestured, rocking an invisible baby.

"Uh..." I glanced at Noah for help. "There isn't any merit in the whole love elixir folklore, right?"

Noah's parents, brothers, and Charlotte all exchanged looks with one another, as if they were nonverbally conversing about how to break it to me.

"I mean, it's not like it's been scientifically proven or

anything," Charlotte tried.

"I'm sure it's just a coincidence." Gloria smiled.

"Or fate," Will added helpfully, giving me a comforting smile. "Either way, we're going to be grandparents again! That's exciting news, right, Glo?"

"Sure is!" Gloria's smile brightened.

Was nobody else concerned that a trio of elderly ladies was supposedly spiking the drinks of unsuspecting townsfolk with a love potion? I'd laughed when Sage had been so worried about unwittingly drinking the love elixir with Nix by way of the chocolate stout Nix had purchased for their first-ever date, but now I saw her point.

"That feels very dub-con-y," I said, glancing at Noah with alarm.

"Dub-con-y?" Easton raised a brow, confused.

"It means dubious consent, and it refers to a situation where consent is unclear or dubious." I explained, shaking my head. "The Hartley triplets tricking unsuspecting couples into taking the love elixir would fall under the dub-con category."

"I really don't think the Hartley triplets are in the habit of forcing people to unwittingly take the love elixir," Gloria explained with a patient smile. "Anything in the café that contains the love elixir is labeled with a little heart."

"Yeah, but they've expanded to include the love elixir in other items around town," Damien pointed out. "The Choco Temptation chocolate stout from the brewery for example—which we include in our Couples Retreat baskets."

"The Choco Temptation is labeled appropriately," Charlotte countered. "It's why you and Noah refuse to drink it."

"What about that new wine that came out from the winery? Amour Au Chocolat?" Damien argued. "I don't recall seeing a label on it."

"It's small, but it is there," Charlotte insisted.

"See!" Easton exclaimed, pursing his lips.

"Maybe Eliza only said that because she was jealous and wanted to keep you from going home with Leah?" Charlotte ventured.

"I mean, maybe." Easton shrugged. He seemed delighted that he'd caused such mayhem.

I, however, was still reeling.

We stayed for another half hour while Noah, Damien, and Easton cleaned the kitchen. Will was in the living room with Aria and Ronan, watching The Mighty Ducks while Charlotte, Gloria, and I sat at the table and talked more about the pregnancy and other, safer topics. I could tell they both felt a little guilty for all the love elixir talk.

Once the kitchen was cleaned, Damien and Charlotte got the girls ready to head home, and Easton skipped out shortly after, claiming he had a hot date. Noah and I were the last to leave, and as he was getting my coat, Gloria put her arms around me in a hug.

"Thanks for dinner, Gloria. It was delicious," I told her, hugging her back. I thought I'd feel more awkward about it, but Gloria was the kind of person who was just good at hugs. I could see where Noah got it from.

"Thank you," she said sincerely, her voice ladened with emotion. She pulled back and smiled at me. "I was beginning to worry my son would never let love in."

"We've only started dating recently," I murmured, feeling my face heat with embarrassment.

Gloria smiled kindly. "I can tell that this is the real deal between you two. Pregnancy is going to fast track everything, because you only have so much time before the baby arrives."

"Don't scare her, Ma." Noah frowned, overhearing the last bit.

"Oh! I hope I didn't," Gloria fretted.

"It's okay. I mean, this whole pregnancy thing is scary in itself," I joked, shrugging my shoulders.

"Everyone feels that way, even when they're super prepared for the idea of it. Pregnancy, and parenting in general, can be scary. You're responsible for a whole other being, but you'll be okay," Gloria assured me. "You've got us!"

Her words were a calm balm to my anxieties, something I'd wished my own mother would have said to me, instead of chastising me for not being married.

Noah

IT WAS NEARLY nine thirty when we finally got back to my place after dinner with my parents. Nellie seemed quiet on the drive, and I could tell she was stuck in her head about things. I parked the truck beside her car and turned it off, letting the silence sit between us for a moment.

"That went well," I said as I glanced at her, needing to see where her thoughts were.

"It did," she agreed, looking at me. She gave a hesitant smile when she caught my eye.

"Do you feel better about things?"

"Sort of?" Nellie shrugged. "I mean, I still can't believe this is all happening. The pregnancy. Us. It's just—it's a lot."

"A lot in a bad way?" I asked, trying to keep the worry out of my voice.

"No! Not at all!" Nellie exclaimed. "I never let myself imagine life like this. That I'd be in a relationship and expecting a baby," she added.

"Yeah. I mean, I get that. I do. If someone had told me this time last year that I'd meet someone I wanted those things with, I would have laughed in their face," I said, sending her a rueful grin. "I didn't think I was even capable of monogamy."

"How do you know you are now?" Nellie asked.

"I've been monogamous since the night I spent with you. Drunk as we both were, something told me this is what I've been waiting for," I told her, reaching across the cab of the truck to take her hand in mine. "Of course, I didn't know that's what was going on at first. I attributed my dry spell to being busy with the resort, not a lack of interest because no one was you."

"Something changed that night," Nellie admitted. "I tried to fight it. Which, you know, led to a bad decision. But that bad decision only made the fact that I felt something different with you even more pronounced."

I nodded, understanding what she was saying. "I get it."

"Do you think—" Nellie shook her head as if she was talking herself out of voicing whatever thought she had. "Never mind, it's stupid."

"No, say it. I bet it's not."

Nellie hesitated for a moment, then sighed. "Do you think Easton was right about the night of the Witches' Ball?"

"I wouldn't put it past the Hartley triplets to tinker like that." I shrugged, rubbing circles on the back of Nellie's hand with my thumb.

"So, we could have potentially had the love elixir?"

"Maybe," I replied. "But being sneaky like that is not really their style. They prefer a more in-your-face approach. And like Charlotte said, there's no science behind it even working. I think it's a cute and fun notion, but relationships still take effort, regardless of a love elixir."

"That's true, I guess." Nellie sighed, worrying her bottom lip.

"I think we had a lot to drink that night, and let our walls come down enough for something to take root and bloom," I said, reaching to tuck a strand of her hair behind her ear.

"So, what now?" she asked, her lips pulling up in a small smile.

"We keep doing what we're doing. Getting to know each other better, taking it one day at a time and preparing for the arrival of this baby," I answered.

Nellie nodded slowly in agreement and leaned toward me, her eyes locking with mine. "I can do that."

"Good," I murmured, my hand framing the side of her face as I moved closer. I kissed her, slow and deep, telling her without words how much I needed her.

Nellie kissed me back, moving closer to me. I could feel her hands on my jacket, pulling me against her. I went willingly, without hesitating. This woman could lead me into a fire, and I'd eagerly follow.

The kiss turned frantic, and when the windows started to fog up, I pulled back enough to look at her. "Shall we go inside, get warmed up by the fire, maybe get naked?" I said, wriggling my eyebrows at her suggestively.

That earned a laugh. "Okay, let's go. I'm getting cold anyway."

We walked into my house, and I tossed a few logs on the woodstove while Nellie disappeared in the bathroom. When she reappeared, she'd changed into her pajamas and was looking much more comfortable.

"I hope it's okay that I changed, my pants were feeling way too tight," Nellie explained, looking shy.

She tried to walk past me to the couch, but I caught her by the hand and gently tugged her toward me. I wrapped my arms around her, rubbing my hands along her hips, massaging them with my fingertips.

"You're gorgeous," I murmured in her ear. I'd been rocking a chub since our heavy makeout session in my truck, but now that I had her beneath my fingertips, that chub thickened into a full-on erection that I knew she could feel against her.

Pushing my hips forward, I heard the sharp intake of her breath, a sign that my words and my touch were getting her going, and I fed off that passion.

I trailed kisses along her neck and jaw, tasting my way to her pillowy lips.

She kissed me back, her hands sliding down my torso and cupping me over my jeans. Feeling how hard I was, she broke the kiss and let out a guilt-ridden sigh. "I'm sorry, I want to, but I'm also super bloated." Her voice was full of apology.

I shook my head. "Don't feel bad. I'm not expecting anything right now." Nellie sent a pointed look to my throbbing erection, and I chuckled. "Yeah, you make me incredibly hard. But that doesn't mean I expect us to do something about it. If you're not feeling up to it, that's perfectly alright with me. Having you here is enough."

My words made Nellie take pause, her brow furrowing as she processed them. "You really mean that?" she asked, studying me as if looking for any sign of dishonesty.

"Of course, I do," I assured her, pressing another kiss to her lips. "Want a hot chocolate? Or a tea?"

"You have tea?"

"I stocked up on some of the ones you have at the resort," I admitted sheepishly. Nellie's beaming smile made me feel like that had been the best decision I could have made.

"A tea would be great," she murmured, wrapping her arms around my lower back and hugging me.

A little while later, we curled up in a thick blanket on the couch in the great room, the woodstove throwing off the perfect amount of heat. My arm was wrapped around her, and she rested with her head against my shoulder. She yawned, nestling in closer to me.

"Are you tired? We could go to bed; it's been a long day."

"I probably should," Nellie admitted, sounding exhausted. "I'm usually asleep by nine o'clock every night. This is late for me."

"Well, let's get you to bed then." I stood, offering Nellie my hand to help her up. "Did you want one of the guestrooms, or did you want to sleep in my bed with me? I promise, I won't try any funny business."

Nellie tilted her head, considering my offer while she studied me. "Do you snore? Because if you keep me up snoring all night, I won't be responsible for shoving a sock in your mouth."

"I don't actually know if I snore," I answered. "Nobody's ever complained, but it's not like I've had regular sleepovers while sober."

Nellie paused, as if thinking. "I don't think I'm there yet, Noah. I want to be...."

"I understand," I told her, and I meant it. While I was a little disappointed, I knew Nellie had her reasons for keeping her distance. I could tell she was falling for me; I could tell that some of her walls were weakening, but I knew it wouldn't be an overnight thing.

Nellie squeezed my hand and stood on her tiptoes, pressing a kiss to my lips. "Thank you, Noah. I know I'm not easy to deal with, but I appreciate you trying."

"Who said you weren't easy to deal with?" I countered. "I find you very easy to deal with. It's okay if you're not there yet, I told you we'll go as slow as you need."

Nellie smiled, then went to get ready for bed.

CHAPTER THIRTY-TWO

Nellie

I AWOKE the next morning to the scent of breakfast and coffee, much like the last weekend I spent at Noah's. Also like the last time, I awoke to a slew of text messages from Sage, wondering how dinner at Noah's parents' had gone.

I answered her before even getting out of bed, letting her know that it went okay. She texted back almost immediately.

Sage: and how did the rest of the night go? ;)

Me: Fine. Came back to Noah's, hung out for a bit, then crashed.

Sage: With him or in the guestroom?

Me: Why does that matter?

Sage: So, in the guestroom. Sigh. I know you've always been weird about how intimate it is to sleep next to someone, but I think having a baby with them is more intimate.

Me: Shush.

I decided to stop replying because Sage was right, and that irked me.

I'd almost said yes when he asked me last night, but then I panicked. At least I wasn't running too far. Just down the hall, to a guestroom. Old me would have grabbed my shit and left the premises.

Rooting through my overnight bag, I found my hairbrush and brushed the tangles out of my hair then getting dressed in a pair of my comfortable weekend clothes. Standing naked in Noah's guest bedroom, I noted with surprise that my belly seemed to have grown overnight.

Once dressed, I walked down the hall toward the dining room and kitchen. Before I slipped into the bathroom, I saw Noah at the stove, flipping pancakes with his back to me. I did my business and brushed my teeth as quickly as I could, not wanting to keep Noah waiting too long.

I longed for a shower but felt weird about taking one without asking first.

When I came out of the bathroom, Noah was setting two heaping plates down on the island beside the tray of butter and a glass bottle of maple syrup. He glanced up at me, a radiant smile gracing his lips.

"Morning, gorgeous. Hope you slept well."

"I did," I answered, pulling a stool out and climbing up on it. The baby was awake and started doing somersaults in my belly, as if excited to hear Noah's voice. That made two of us.

Noah's grin widened, and he turned around long enough to grab me a glass of juice and flick on the kettle for a tea. He grabbed his coffee and then joined me at the island.

"I hope you like pancakes," he said, settling in. "I probably should have asked, but I didn't realize I was out of eggs until I started making breakfast."

"Pancakes are great," I assured him. Noah nodded, the relief evident.

We didn't talk much as we dug in. I put a generous amount of butter and maple syrup on my pancakes, then moaned when the flavour hit my tongue. "Oh my gosh, this is the best maple syrup I've ever tasted."

"Thanks," he said.

I glanced at the bottle, seeing the Whimsical Woods Maple Syrup label.

"Shut up. You didn't make it?"

"Well, it's a family effort. Been a tradition for over a hundred years! It's from the sugar bush north of my parents' place," Noah explained. "We've got a sugar shack and everything. My dad and my brothers and I tap the trees and Dad handles the boiling part, since we're busy with the resort. We also started offering maple tapping packages in March, so that resort guests can experience what it's like and make their own bottles."

"That's so neat!" I said, the awe apparent in my voice. There was so much heritage here. I didn't know much about my ancestors, aside from the general area they immigrated from, but Noah seemed to have centuries of known history.

"Yeah, it's pretty neat." Noah smiled, finishing up the rest of his pancakes. I still had half of my tower to get through, but I was already stuffed. The baby took up a lot of real estate, and although I was usually famished every few hours, it didn't take much to make me feel full again.

"So, what do you want to do today?" I asked, wondering what the plan was—or if there even was a plan.

"Well, I was going to take you sledding on the trails, but I stayed up too late reading about how it's not recommended while pregnant due to the high risk of falls and sudden movements that could harm the baby. Plus, the jarring motions of the snowmobile can potentially stress the placenta, and I don't want to stress your placenta."

"Thank you for considering my placenta," I said, arching a brow and trying to keep a straight face.

"So instead, I figured we could hang out, watch some movies. Maybe talk," he suggested.

"Talk about what?" I could sense Noah had a few topics in mind, from the way he tried to slip that in casually.

"Anything, everything. You, me, the baby, that sort of thing," Noah stood, carrying his empty plate to the kitchen sink. He set to preparing me a tea.

"Can you elaborate a little more?" I asked, suddenly feeling anxious.

"I was kind of wondering what things would look like when the baby arrives." Noah scratched at the back of his neck, avoiding my gaze. "Parker and Tabitha's apartment isn't very big. It only has the one bedroom. I was thinking, maybe you should move in."

"I should move in?" I repeated slowly, frowning. I was stunned.

"I know we only technically just started dating, and while I can promise you until I'm blue in the face that I'm here to stay, I understand that you still have some hesitations," Noah explained, bringing me the cup of hot tea. "But I've got three bedrooms here. Even if you weren't ready to spend every night in my arms, there's enough room here for you to have your own space and the baby to have her own room. And I could be here every step of the way to help."

My jaw dropped, and I felt like I was careering off the edge of a cliff. "Noah, I only just met your family, and—"

"I know, it probably feels like it's all too fast for you." Noah sighed, scratching at his jaw.

"It's—well, it is. But..." I paused, searching for the right words. "I don't want to fast-track everything. I want you to be sure about your decision to be with me, and I want to be sure about mine. I don't want our relationship to be a last resort just because I'm pregnant with your baby."

"I promise you, it's not a last resort. Not for me. It's my first choice," Noah said, sounding sure. The look in his eyes was sincere and determined. "I can understand if I'm not your first choice..."

"That's really not it." I shook my head, struggling to find a way to explain it. But I couldn't even explain it to myself.

"Think about it. We still have five months to figure out what everything's going to look like, but I want you to know it's an option for us." Noah took my hands in his.

AFTER OUR HEAVY conversation that morning at breakfast, Noah had to go out and shovel and snowblow the driveway from the ten centimetres of snow we'd gotten in the early hours of the morning. While he did that, I took advantage of the empty house and grabbed a shower, then called Sage.

I filled her in more on what happened during the Wood family dinner, including Easton's declaration that the Hartley triplets tended to spike the drink menu.

"The Hartley triplets wouldn't do something that chaotic," she insisted. "They might love playing matchmaker, but they couldn't control the results over who drank it, and they love their control."

"Well, you can't blame me for wondering. I thought Noah was a playboy, but from the moment I've moved back, it's like he only has eyes for me."

"Noah was a playboy, and he does only have eyes for you. It's evident every time you guys are around each other."

"So, it's not unreasonable to worry that we unwittingly drank the love elixir. Why would a former playboy suddenly change his tune?"

"Because he found someone worth changing for?" Sage countered.

"Yeah but, this much? I mean, he asked me to move in with him this morning over pancakes!"

"He asked you to move in with him?" she repeated, sounding surprised.

"When the baby's born, yes. He pointed out that he has three bedrooms and plenty of room for me to have my own space if I still had hesitations about us," I explained, peeking out the window to see that he was still working on the driveway. "He said he wanted to be there every step of the way to help when the baby arrives."

"And what did you say?" Sage asked.

"I told him I didn't want our relationship to be a last resort just because I'm pregnant. I don't want him thinking he needs to be with me because I'm having his kid, you know? Plenty of people co-parent without forcing a relationship."

"Do you truly think he's trying to force a relationship?" Sage demanded.

"Well, no. I don't think that. I think he is interested in me, but what if that interest is only because I'm pregnant?"

"And what if Nix's interest in me is only because we accidentally drank the love elixir on our first date?" Sage countered.

"You know that's not true." I rolled my eyes.

"Well, you seem to think that Noah's changed his tune because you two may have drunk the love elixir at the Witches'

Ball, so how is that any different from Nix and I actually drinking Choco Temptation?"

"I mean...true."

"Both of those notions are ridiculous, and I think you're looking for reasons to doubt that what you guys have between you is the real deal because you're scared," Sage continued.

"Well, probably." I rolled my eyes again.

"Stop being such a scaredy-cat, Nell. You're made of tougher stuff than this," Sage told me. "Even if things don't work out between you guys, you will survive it. But you owe it to yourself and that baby you're carrying to give him a fair chance. Which means, stop hiding."

"I'm trying," I murmured, closing my eyes. I was, I really was.

"Well, try harder. I challenge you to actually sleep in his bed with him tonight." Sage sounded pleased with herself. She knew I loved a good challenge.

Before I could respond, I heard the front door opening and closing.

"We'll see, I've got to go. I'll talk to you later."

I walked toward the hallway, watching Noah as he pulled off his boots.

"I'm about ready for spring." He sighed, sending me a tired smile. "Between the resort, here, and my parents place, I'm getting tired of shoveling snow."

"I don't blame you, I'm ready for spring too. But I would have helped, if you'd let me," I reminded him, folding my arms across my chest.

He sent a pointed look at my rounding belly. "You're doing enough."

"Are you really going to bubble wrap me for the rest of this pregnancy?"

"If I can get away with it, yes," he answered sincerely,

straightening. He crossed over to where I was standing and put his arms around me, pulling me to him for a kiss. His lips and his hands were freezing, and I squealed, trying to push him away.

"You're freezing!"

"Warm me up, then," he dared, nuzzling his cold chin against my neck. I shivered, nestling in closer despite the cold.

We put on a movie and cozied up in his loft under a warm blanket. I tried to shut off my mind from whirling and buzzing. About our conversation in the kitchen that morning, about the pregnancy, about meeting his family, and Sage's words, but it was challenging.

"I can practically hear you thinking," Noah murmured halfway through the movie, his lips against my temple.

"Yeah, well. I've got a lot to think about," I retorted, huffing with exasperation. Maybe I wouldn't be so caught up in my thoughts if he hadn't broached the topic of moving in with him so soon.

"Well, let me help you work through it." Noah paused the movie and shifted to face me, his blue eyes sweeping over my features.

"I think it's something I have to work through myself," I finally said. He nodded slowly, as if processing that.

"Okay, well. Allow me to distract you, then," he offered, moving closer. His hands tangled in my hair, still damp from the shower. His lips captured mine in a slow, reverent kiss.

It was every bit as distracting as he promised it would be. From the moment his lips pressed against mine, I was distracted. The thoughts and worries that had been buzzing about my head like angry bees scurried away, and all I could think about was more.

I wanted more of Noah's touch, more of his kiss, more of this.

I kissed him back, meeting each swipe of his tongue with a hunger I couldn't deny. My physical reaction to Noah was instantaneous, and it had been since the moment I laid eyes upon him.

Pausing the kiss long enough to rip his shirt over his head, I ran my hands along the firm ridges of muscle along his chest, feeling his heartbeat pounding beneath my palm.

The primal urge to have him claim me washed away every hesitation and fear. Noah read each cue from my body like an expert, like he was fluent in the language of what I wanted.

His hands made their way to my hips, and he hoisted me up on his lap, never breaking the intensity of the kiss. Once I was positioned exactly where he wanted me, his hands started moving up, slipping beneath my loose T-shirt and along my heated skin.

They admiringly moved over my rounded belly, pausing long enough to feel the baby kick against his palm. I froze for a minute, displaced by that, but Noah's smile against my lips had me relaxing again into his touch. He massaged my skin with the gentlest of touches, and it almost contradicted the hunger behind his kisses.

His fingers brushed against the underside of my aching breasts, running along the lace bralette. He stopped kissing me long enough to pull my T-shirt over my head and tossed it behind me, his eyes drinking me in. The way he was looking at me didn't give me a chance to feel insecure about my changing body.

"Your body is incredible, Nell," he murmured with piety. Noah's attention made me feel like I was a divine being, each touch felt as if he was worshipping at my altar.

I couldn't think of a single thing to say, especially when he lowered his mouth to my nipple and started sucking and nibbling on it over the lace. The sensation of his hot mouth and the lace rubbing against my sensitive peaks was enough to send me straight over the edge into an orgasm.

I ground against his erection through both of our pants, feeling him hard and unyielding. It did nothing to satiate me; it only made me more frantic.

"Noah." I tugged his head back, the sensations too much and not enough all at once. "I need you in me."

"Don't have to tell me twice." He grinned. He helped me off of his lap and shoved his pants and boxers off. I stripped slowly, feeding off the way he was watching me, the arousal evident in his eyes and in the rigid erection he sported.

Once my panties and sweatpants were in a pile at my feet, I reached up and took my bralette off. Noah gripped his cock and stroked it while he watched. My eyes dropped down, tracking every movement of his hand, licking my lips when his tip beaded with pre-cum.

"Come here," he demanded, reaching for me.

He tugged me towards him, guiding my legs apart enough and bending so that he could slip his thick digit into my pussy. Each stroke of his finger made my knees tremble, and when he added a second finger, curling them just so, my legs almost gave out.

He removed his hand, bringing his fingers to his mouth to suck the taste of me from them. His eyelids fluttered and he let out a groan.

I climbed into his lap again, and raised my hips so that I was hovering over his weeping erection. Noah rubbed the tip of his hard cock against my soaked core, swirling around my juices until I was trembling, my nails digging into his shoulders and my eyes pleading with him.

"Take it," he instructed, his deep voice and command sending sparks of arousal up my spine. I did as he told me, slowly sliding down on him, taking every thick inch until he filled me to the hilt.

I paused for a moment, adjusting to the sensation of him stretching me. My head dropped against his shoulder. "You feel so good," I murmured.

Noah's hand came up to hold the back of my head, his fingers tangling in my hair. "So do you," he said, the desire apparent in his voice. "Now ride me, gorgeous."

I did as he instructed, my hips rolling forward slowly and deliberately. My slow torturous dance on his lap had moans spilling from both our lips.

Noah's hips rose to meet mine, his cock driving deeper into me than before. Each pounding thrust had me climbing higher and higher towards climax, but still wasn't quite enough to send me over the edge.

As if he could sense that I was close but needed a little more, Noah's thumb pressed against my clit while his hips pistoned up, driving into me so hard that he sent me careening off the edge into an intense orgasm. I could feel my inner walls clamping around him, squeezing him.

Noah swore and pumped inside me a few more times until he found his own release.

Both of us were breathless by the time we finished. I couldn't even hold my head up. Noah supported me, even though he seemed to be just as affected.

"Can I say: I love doing that with you. It's like your body was made for me. It's like you were made for me."

Noah's words made my heart flutter. I'd had guys feed me lines over the years, but I could tell the difference. Noah meant every word he said.

Maybe, at first that's what he'd done; during our one-night stand and later when we ran into each other at the grocery store. But now, his words were filled with honesty, vulnerability, and intention.

"Yeah, it does kind of feel that way, doesn't it?" I stood up, my legs still trembling with the aftershocks of pleasure.

"Where are you going?"

"I need to get cleaned up. And I worked up a bit of an appetite." I said, pulling my shirt over my head. I didn't bother picking up my bralette. I had a feeling Noah would be removing my clothes again before the day ended.

"Let's find you some food." He stood up to grab his boxers.

We had a light lunch of grilled cheese sandwiches and soup, and put the movie we'd abandoned back on. I fell asleep on the couch, nestled cozily in Noah's arms.

WHEN I AWOKE, the TV was off, and Noah was reading Atticus's book.

"Hey, sleepyhead." He smiled down at me while I rubbed the sleep out of my eyes.

"What time is it?"

"After six, I think," Noah answered. "You looked so comfortable; I didn't want to wake you. Figured you needed the sleep."

I'd slept for over four hours. "Yeah, I guess I did." I yawned, sitting up. My stomach grumbled and the baby kicked, both letting me know that I was due for another meal.

"Good thing I put an order in for pizza," Noah said, hearing the hungry complaints my stomach had to make. I blushed with embarrassment. "Hey, don't be embarrassed. We burned a lot of calories, and you're eating for two."

Half an hour later, a driver dropped off two medium pizzas

from Pizza Picasso, which we ate in the great room with the woodstove throwing off a comforting heat.

He'd also stocked up on chips, including a couple bags of dill pickle chips for me.

"I noticed you liked them," he told me, smiling that secret smile that always made me feel like he was paying more attention than he let on.

"You did catch me red-handed trying to fill my cart with them." My lips twitched with amusement, and Noah laughed.

CHAPTER THIRTY-THREE

Noah

WE HAD A QUIET SATURDAY, our loft romp aside, and I loved every minute of it. We stayed up late snacking, talking, and playing a trivia card game, which Nellie kicked my ass in. The girl had a fount of trivia facts in her arsenal, and she wiped the floor with me.

"Damn, you'll be a great addition at family boardgame night," I said as I packed away the cards.

"Do you guys still do family boardgame nights?" Nellie asked, surprised.

"On occasion, yes. Not as regularly as when we kids, but we usually break out a boardgame during special occasions like Thanksgiving, Christmas, or Easter."

"You guys do something for Easter?" Nellie's eyebrows rose, like she was shocked by that admission more so than the fact that my family still played boardgames together.

"Yeah, we do," I chuckled. "We're not a religious family,

but my mom loves any excuse to cook a big meal. And my dad loves setting up an insane Easter egg hunt for the twins."

"Ah, yeah. I could see that." She smiled softly.

"Well, what do you want to do now?" I asked, stretching beside her.

"After all the eating we did, I kind of feel like I need to go for a walk," Nellie said, rubbing her stomach.

"We could do that," I told her. "Or we could exercise a different way," I suggested, wriggling my eyebrows playfully.

"Ah, well. I'll need to recover a little longer," Nellie said, a note of apology in her voice. "I get sore post-sex. It's a not so fun side effect of endometriosis. Sex can cause inflammation to endometriosis tissues around the pelvic organs. I usually take an over-the-counter pain medication beforehand, but that doesn't always work, anyway."

"Shit, I'm so sorry, Nell, I had no idea." I felt like a jackass. I'd done some research on Nellie's condition, but I was mostly focused on reading up on the pregnancy related information, so that I'd know what to look for. "Let me run you a warm bath," I added, standing up.

Nellie seemed surprised by my reaction. "It's okay, Noah. It's not your fault. It's something that I've learned to live with over the years."

"I'm running you that bath," I told her, holding my hand out for her. The ensuite in the primary bedroom had a deep soaker tub that I barely used for baths. I was more of a shower guy, but in this moment, I was glad I'd had the foresight to add it into the build.

I led the way to my bedroom, holding Nellie's hand. She sat on the closed toilet while I ran the bath. I dumped a few scoops of Epsom salt into the tub from the bag my mom got me when I'd injured my knee a couple years ago.

"Thanks, Noah," Nellie said, her expression soft and full of wonder.

"It's the least I can do, Nell," I told her, swirling the water around so the Epsom salt would dissolve.

Nellie bit her lip and nodded, watching me. Once the tub was full, I offered to help her in. "I can manage, but thanks," she replied.

While Nellie took her bath, I tidied up the great room to give myself something to do with my restless hands.

I hated that I'd invertedly caused her pain, even if she said it was a common side effect of endometriosis. I would have forced her into the bath sooner had I known how much discomfort she was in, but Nellie hid her pain behind the same walls she hid her heart.

I fully planned on dismantling those walls, taking them down brick by brick, but I knew it was going to take time.

When I heard the tub draining, I went back into my room and got Nellie one of my T-shirts and a pair of boxers for her to sleep in. I knocked on the bathroom door gently, and she opened it. Her hair was piled up in a messy bun, and she had a bath towel wrapped around her.

"Feel better?" I asked.

"Much," she answered, smiling. I passed her the clothes, and she took them. "Thank you."

"You're welcome," I told her.

I let her get dressed and turned down my bed while I waited for her. She opened the bathroom door and leaned against the doorframe, looking relaxed in my clothes and extremely sleepy.

"Tired?" I asked, chuckling.

"I don't understand why, when I slept half the afternoon away," Nellie said, fighting a yawn.

"Well, it's almost midnight and you are growing a human.

That's got to be tiring work," I reminded her.

"Yeah. I think I'm going to go to sleep now," Nellie said, her eyes drifting to my turned down bed.

"Did you want to sleep with me?" I asked, hoping like hell the answer would be yes. "Because you're more than welcome to."

"Maybe we could try it?"

"We absolutely could try it."

I brushed my teeth and went to the bathroom then joined her. She'd cozied up on the left side of my bed, closest to the window, looking like she belonged there. I crawled in beside her.

THE NEXT MORNING, I awoke with my arms around Nellie and her ass pressed against my throbbing erection. This is how mornings were supposed to start, I had no doubt about that. I'd die a happy man if I could wake up like this every day, with this woman in my arms, softly snoring.

I tried to stay still as long as I could, basking in the feel of her in my arms, but Nellie stirred and stretched, her ass pushing even more against my erection.

"Mmm," she murmured, intentionally swiveling her hips. "Okay, I could get used to that."

"Could you?" I asked, amusement dancing in my tone as I playfully rutted against her.

She shifted in my arms, turning so that she could look at me. "I think so, yes. It's not as scary as I thought it'd be. Waking up in your arms feels kind of nice."

"Gee, thanks. I'm glad I wasn't a scary sight to wake up to."

Nellie smirked and gently slapped my chest. "That's not

what I meant, and you know it."

"I know," I told her, nuzzling into the side of her neck. She'd already explained her intimacy issues, and I was expecting this to take a lot longer than it had. I was happy it hadn't, because holding her felt right. "How do you feel about going out for breakfast?"

I felt guilty for locking Nellie up all weekend, keeping her to myself, and wanted to take her out for a few hours.

"Oh, that would be good! I've been craving eggs benedict," Nellie exclaimed.

Once we were dressed and ready for the day, we went for breakfast at The Hungry Hub. It was always busy on Sunday mornings, but we were able to walk in and find a recently vacated table.

The server, Emily, brought over menus and took our drink order. I ordered a coffee and Nellie, a tea. Emily returned a few moments later with a silver pot of tea and a coffee pot, and she filled up our mugs while she took our breakfast orders.

I ordered a Hungry Man breakfast while Nellie ordered the eggs benedict with sausage and a side of asparagus. We chatted for a few minutes, and then we were interrupted by a familiar voice.

"Ah! You guys had the same idea!" I turned my head, catching sight of Sage as she slid into the booth beside Nellie. "Mind if we joined you? There are no other tables available and I'm starving!" she added, looking at me hopefully.

Nix was with her, shooting me an apologetic look.

"Yeah, that's no problem," I said, moving closer to the wall to make room for Nix.

"I told her we could order and head home, but—"

"We rarely get a kid-free morning. Auntie Em and Uncle Ed have Daphne until this afternoon, and I wanted to go out for breakfast, not stay in," Sage explained, pouting a little.

"It's not a bother." Nellie smiled at her friend. Catching sight of the new arrivals to our table, Emily came back to grab their orders and pour more coffee.

"So, how's your weekend been?" Sage asked, turning her attention back to Nellie and me. "Get up to anything interesting?"

"We mostly hung out at Noah's," Nellie replied, glancing at me.

"Sounds like a good time," Nix grinned. "Did you go hot tubbing?"

"Actually, no," I replied. "I need to replace the motor in mine, it burnt out last fall."

"You have a hot tub, too?" Nellie asked, bewildered. "Where?"

"Off the back deck. It's currently empty of water, and buried under snow," I answered. "It's been on my to-do list to fix, but I didn't get around to it before winter hit." I chuckled, shaking my head.

"Well, that's neat," Nellie said thoughtfully. "Can you even go in a hot tub while pregnant?"

"You can, but you have to keep the temperature below a hundred and one degrees and you can't stay in longer than ten minutes," Sage replied. "What! I looked into it, this winter has been brutally cold, and my body aches. This pregnancy has been kicking my ass."

I furrowed my brow, confused.

"Oh! Right, I forgot to tell you. Sage and Nix are expecting, too," Nellie explained. "We're actually due around the same time."

"No kidding!" I exclaimed. "Congratulations."

"Thanks, we're pretty stoked," Nix said, his gaze going to Sage.

"Our babies are going to be built-in best friends," Sage

declared, squeezing Nellie's hand. "We're finding out Monday if we're having a boy or a girl."

"We don't care which, but Daphne really wants to know. She's helping design the baby's room at the new house."

"That's awesome."

"And congratulations to you, too," Sage said to me, smiling warmly. "I heard the official news."

Nellie was glancing around, looking a little uncomfortable. I followed her gaze, noticing a few of the patrons were watching us and listening in with a little too much eagerness. She averted her gaze, her smile frozen in place.

"Yeah, it's an exciting time," I replied, and changed the subject. "When do you think you'll be able to move into the new house?"

"Oh, probably by the end of May, if everything goes according to plan," Nix said.

While we ate, Nix and I continued to talk about what was left to do with the new house he was building, while Sage and Nellie whispered quietly across from us. I couldn't make out what they were saying, but I got the impression Sage was reassuring Nellie.

After we finished breakfast and paid our tabs, we headed out. "What's the plan for this afternoon?"

"I'm not actually sure," Nellie said, glancing at me. "I left my car at Noah's, so I guess we'll have to go back so I can get it."

"We were going to pick up Daphne and then catch the Sunday matinee at the Hartwood Creek Theatre, if you wanted to tag along? They're showing Pinocchio."

"Maybe another time? I don't think I'd stay awake through a movie today. I'm tired," Nellie said, fighting a yawn.

Sage and Nellie hugged outside of the diner, then Nix and Sage started walking back toward Sage's apartment over the hardware store.

I was secretly relieved that Nellie had turned down Sage's invitation to join them, not because I didn't like hanging out with Sage and Nix, but because I had plans for the afternoon.

We walked to my truck and climbed in, but before I started it, I turned to face her.

"Mind if we make a quick stop? I need to pick something up before we leave town."

"Yeah, sure," Nellie nodded, yawning again. She buckled up and we drove down Main Street. I parked in front of the art gallery, and Nellie looked at me expectantly. "Why are we here?"

"I got you something. Consider it a belated welcome to Hartwood Creek gift," I told her. "Wait here."

I disappeared into the art gallery long enough to buy the painting Nellie had been eyeing the first time I'd brought her in. "Thanks, Freyja!" I called over my shoulder as I left.

Nellie was watching the family across the road with a reflective look in her eyes, and didn't see me approaching with the painting, but she turned when I opened the back door and slid the painting in, leaning it against the floor.

"What's that?" Nellie asked after turning around to look at it, her eyes widening when she saw the painting.

"Your gift," I told her, grinning.

"Noah, I can't accept this! It's way too much!" she exclaimed.

"Of course, you can accept it." I chuckled, putting the truck in drive. I headed to Nellie's place, intent on carrying it up and hanging the damn thing for her. "I saw how much you admired it. It'll look great in your apartment. And when you're ready to move in with me, it'll look beautiful at my place, too."

"Wow, cocky much?"

"I prefer the term 'self-assured'," I corrected. Nellie fought a smile and rolled her eyes.

"How can you be so sure I'm going to move in?" she asked as I pulled up to her apartment and parked the truck.

"I saw the look in your eye when you found out I had a hot tub. If that's all it takes, I'll order the parts to fix it tonight and have it up and running by next weekend."

"Noah," she frowned, giving me a serious look. "You can't drop nearly a grand on me and call it a gift, that's insane."

"Better get used to it. I'll spoil you all I want, and I want to spoil you a lot," I warned her. "Besides, you're worth more than a grand, easily. Maybe even more than five grand," I added, reaching across the cab to take her hand.

Nellie laughed, shaking her head at my antics. "Ugh. You're impossible."

"I've been told that a time or two before," I said agreeably. "Shall we hang this up now?"

Nellie glanced back at the painting, worrying her lip. "I don't know. Why don't we bring it back to your place, if you're so sure I'll be moving in?"

"Because I want you to be able to see it every day, and until you do move in with me, it'll be at your place," I told her. "I don't mind hanging it twice."

I'd purchased a hook and wire from Freyja to properly hang the painting and grabbed the necessary tools from the back of my truck, then I carried the painting up and instructed Nellie to pick a place for it.

She chose to put it above the dresser in her bedroom, so she'd see it first thing in the morning and before she went to bed each night. While I hung it, I assessed the room. My memory had served me well; it would fit a crib, but it'd feel cramped.

I kept that thought to myself, though. There was no point in badgering her into saying yes. She'd get there on her own time, and I'd be waiting patiently for her.

CHAPTER THIRTY-FOUR

Nellie

IT FELT like time was passing by faster than it ever had before, but maybe it only felt that way because I was paying more attention to the passage of time than ever before. I was counting each week, marking each day off on my calendar. There was so much to do before the baby arrived in July.

My pregnancy went from being a well-concealed secret to the entire town knowing practically overnight, and I found that to be disconcerting. I wasn't used to all the attention suddenly thrusted upon me. Any time the Hartley triplets caught me around town, they fussed and cooed over how much my belly was growing.

Noah kept taking me out on dates. We'd go out for dinner once a week, and we'd spend every weekend together, alternating between hanging out at his place or mine, depending on what we wanted to do.

If there was something happening around town—an art

show at the gallery, or a special feature movie at the Hartwood Creek Theatre—Noah took me to it. I'd even joined him for a few more family dinners at his parents' house.

Despite all the time we spent together, Noah hadn't brought up the idea of me moving in with him again since that first weekend. But I found myself thinking about it a lot, especially when I was spending time with him at his place.

I had to admit, it did make sense. There was more space at Noah's, and the baby would have her own room. Plus, Noah's parents were conveniently a short drive away, so they'd be able to help if needed. Not that I'd feel comfortable asking them for help, but it was nice knowing they'd be close, and not a twenty-four-hour drive away, like my parents.

Since breaking the news to my parents, I hadn't heard from them. Of course, I didn't initiate any of the phone calls either, but a part of me thought that my mom would at least try more, knowing that I was expecting a baby, but that hadn't happened. They were still very much preoccupied with their own life in Florida.

I tried not to let myself think about it, because when I did, I couldn't seem to help the tears that spilled over, and the anger I'd feel not only at them, but at myself.

I shouldn't have expected anything different from them. But I guess feeling my own baby kicking and growing within me had me wondering how my parents could be so indifferent towards me. My daughter wasn't even born yet, and I was already obsessed with her; I couldn't imagine not showing an interest in her life or wanting to be a daily fixture in it.

Spring came with a major melt that had the creek and the lake flooding the surrounding areas. The resort was well-equipped to handle the melt, and we didn't suffer too many cancellations, despite all the mud.

My pregnancy continued to progress normally, and

although I still attended weekly appointments with Dr. Kramer, she had no concerns. My placenta looked good, and I was careful about my sugar intake, so my glucose tests came back showing nothing outside of the ordinary.

By mid-May, Nix finally finished the last touches on the house, and they moved in at the beginning of June. Their new house was close to Noah's, which was another positive for the pro and con mental list I had about moving in with Noah.

I'd be closer to my friend, and we'd both be raising our kiddos in a rural area, about a ten-minute drive to Hartwood Lake. I could already envision day trips to the beach with our little ones.

"Are you ready?" Noah asked, leaning against the bathroom doorway and peering in. I was putting the finishing touches on my makeup. We were getting ready to go to Nix and Sage's housewarming party.

"Just about," I said, putting my lip gloss on. I studied my reflection in the mirror. I was wearing a sunflower patterned sundress—officially one of the only things I could comfortably wear. Even Noah's sweatpants were getting too tight.

I'd gained a lot of weight with this pregnancy. My cheeks were full, and my breasts were huge, but Noah still looked at me like he couldn't get enough of me. Better still was how attuned he was to my needs. He knew how to give me exactly what I needed to satiate the insane horniness hormones brought on, and then provided aftercare that made me weep with how considerate he was.

"You look gorgeous, Nell," Noah said, coming up behind me and putting his arms around me. His hands went to my rounded belly, and the baby kicked in response. He smiled, nuzzling against the side of my neck. "And you smell incredible. Let's skip this thing and go to bed," he added, pushing his erection against my backside.

"Oh no, we're not skipping the housewarming. I promised Sage we'd be there."

"Alright, fine, but as soon as we get back..." he met my gaze in the mirror, his expression revealing his intentions.

Noah was so steadfast and consistent. He had managed to tear down every brick of my walls. He never wavered, even if I was being ridiculous because my insecurities had gotten the best of me. He knew exactly what to say and what to do to get me out of my head and back on solid ground.

I'd fallen so hard and so completely for him, and I was thankful every single day that I'd said yes to going home with him and letting myself float down this path with him. Even if it had been an unexpected ride.

Ready at last, we headed out to Noah's truck, the gift we'd purchased for Nix and Sage's housewarming tucked under Noah's arm. He set it on the back seat, then opened my door and helped me up.

My belly was so round I now struggled to climb in and out of the truck on my own, but Noah didn't mind helping. It meant he got to palm my ass while he helped push me up.

Every single time, he walked around the front of his truck like he'd scored the winning goal in a football game.

"You're ridiculous." I said when he climbed in beside me, rolling my eyes at the cheesy grin on his face.

It didn't take us long at all to get to Nix and Sage's new house. The beautiful sage green bungalow was set back on the two acres. We were some of the first to arrive, and we immediately were given a tour by a super excited Daphne, who showed us every nook and cranny while Sage and Nix trailed after her, smiling.

It had a stunning family room with soaring vaulted ceilings, expansive windows, and a cozy fireplace. They'd chosen luxury vinyl flooring throughout, providing style and durability. The kitchen was open concept with quartz countertops, a tile back-splash, and a stunning waterfall island, where a delicious spread of food was laid out for guests.

There were three spacious bedrooms on the main floor. The primary bedroom had a beautiful ensuite bathroom and a large walk-in closet, while the other two bedrooms shared a Jack and Jill bathroom. The laundry was on the main floor beside the mud room.

Nix had even finished the basement; it had eight-foot ceilings and two more bedrooms, as well as a recreational room and sliding doors that led to the backyard. It was the perfect home to entertain.

There was also an attached garage that was big enough for Nix's tools and two parked cars, with space to move around. My favourite feature was the small cupboard that opened to the pantry in the kitchen, so groceries could be unloaded from the garage directly into the pantry, saving you from making multiple trips carrying in heavy grocery bags.

"Okay, this is amazing," I declared, opening the small cupboard door, and poking my head inside the pantry. Sage joined me, peering in.

"I know, right?!" she grinned.

"Guys, this is stunning! Seriously, Nix. You ended up building Sage's dream house," I exclaimed, squeezing Sage's hand, and trying not to cry.

I was so happy for my friend; I knew how long she'd wished for a home of her own for herself and Daphne. Sage nodded, her own eyes misting with emotion. We were two pregnant, hormonal messes, standing in a newly built garage in near tears over a cupboard into a pantry.

"I know, it's crazy, right? He basically had the blueprints done when we met, and only made minor changes when

Daphne and I came into the picture." Sage moved to stand beside Nix, putting her hand over his heart.

"It's almost like I knew you were coming," Nix joked, putting his arms around her, and pressing a kiss to her forehead.

The distinct sound of gravel crunching beneath tires alerted us to another person arriving, and the five of us made our way out of the open garage in time to see Parker and Tabitha pull up in their minivan. They'd barely put the vehicle in park before Briella and Bella were opening the sliding door and jumping out, racing for Daphne.

"Aww, it's so cute! Love the colour you chose for the siding!" Tabitha exclaimed, peering up at the house while Parker got Bryson out of his car seat. Her eyes twinkled as she gave Nix and Sage hugs, then she moved to me and hugged me. "Doesn't it make you wanna move in with Noah even more? You'd be even closer to Sage!"

"I know," I murmured, my gaze darting to Noah to make sure he hadn't overheard his cousin. He was talking to Parker though and didn't seem to have heard. "It's definitely going on the pro list."

"Is there anything on the con list?" Sage asked.

"Er, it's getting shorter every day. Not that I don't love the apartment," I added for Tabitha's benefit, but she waved her hand as if dismissing that.

"I don't know how you're still willingly doing those stairs almost every day." She shook her head. "I'd have said yes to moving in just to avoid doing that many stairs in my last trimester."

Not long behind them were Nix's parents, Laurel and Keith. Paxton and Preston jumped out of the back seat of Laurel and Keith's truck, both carrying wrapped gifts and booze.

"You brought alcohol?" Nix asked.

"Well, duh! What's a housewarming without booze?" Preston asked, looking mystified by the idea.

"We know you can't drink any of this yet, Sage, but we figured we'd get you guys some Choco Temptation for after the baby arrives. You know, for old times' sake!" Paxton grinned.

"Thanks, guys." Sage said as her aunt and uncle pulled up.

Noah

THE DRIVE from Sage and Nix's house to mine was barely even six minutes, but Nellie managed to fall asleep anyway, exhausted from the day. So many people showed up to Nix and Sage's housewarming that the party had ended up spilling out onto the back deck.

My family members had also received an invite, so they'd all showed up too, giving my mother, Laurel, Tabitha, and Charlotte ample time to start plotting the next shindig: a combined baby shower for Sage and Nellie.

All of Sage's cousins came out, and it was cool to catch up with them. We'd grown up with Madeline, Livia, Cate, and Jo-Anna, although they'd all left Hartwood Creek after graduating college. They came back frequently enough, and Livia and her fiancé, Joseph, were booked to get married at the resort in the fall.

Madeline and her husband Patrick brought their adorable new baby, a little girl born in early May they had named Flora. Everyone couldn't help but fawn over baby Flora, myself included. Holding the new baby in my arms reminded me that we were a few short weeks out from welcoming our own little one.

Cate and Jo-Anna arrived together, but solo. Jo-Anna was almost as bad as Easton when it came to serious relationships, and Cate was consumed with her busy career as a film director, and often travelling.

Even the Hartley triplets made an appearance, bearing gifts congratulating Nix, Sage, and Daphne to their new home.

One person who was noticeably absent was Sage's mother, but Sage hadn't seemed upset about it, not with her Auntie Em there. I suppose Sage's aunt had long since stepped into the maternal role for Sage.

Nellie and Sage had originally bonded over their distant and estranged relationships with their mothers, quickly becoming each other's chosen family while living in Guelph. They understood each other's pain in that regard and, try as I might, I could only sympathize. Sage had an extended family that seemed very supportive and loving toward her. Nellie, however, didn't have that.

My family did their best to show up for Nellie, and she was definitely warming up to them all. I couldn't help but worry that it wouldn't be enough, that the sadness she felt over her own parents' lack of interest in our baby hurt her more than she let on.

A quiet sigh escaped as I pulled up in front of the garage, parking beside Nellie's car. She stirred when I put the truck in park and turned off the ignition, turning to blink sleepily at me.

"Sorry, I didn't mean to pass out." She laughed, rubbing her eyes.

"It's alright, it's been a long day." I reached across the cab and took her hand, holding it in mine.

"Yeah, but so fun. It was great seeing everyone again," Nellie said with a yawn, stretching while still holding my hand.

"Let's get you inside, sleepyhead." I said, bringing her hand up to my lips to kiss the back of it.

We made our way inside, and I helped Nellie pull off her strappy sandals. Her feet were swollen from being on them all day. I'd tried a hundred times to get her to sit, but she'd fluttered about the party like a butterfly.

"Alright, sit down on the couch. You're getting a foot massage."

"No, my feet are all sweaty and gross," she complained, trying to dodge me.

I picked her up in my arms. "Fine, then you're getting a cool bath before I give you a foot massage," I amended, carrying her into the bedroom.

"Noah!" she giggled, trying to squirm out of my arms. I wouldn't let her down until we got to the bathroom. "Alright, fine. But only because a cool bath sounds nice right about now. I don't know how I'm supposed to survive another month of this, and it's only going to get hotter." Nellie pouted, her hands rubbing her swollen belly.

"I'll call and get an air conditioner installed next week," I promised, turning my attention to the tub to start running her bath.

"Stop being ridiculous." Nellie huffed, rolling her eyes. "You're not going to have air conditioning installed just because I'm pregnant and overheating."

"Sure, I am," I said over my shoulder, tossing her a smirk as I tested the water with my hand. "I want you to be comfortable, and if air con will help get you to move in with me sooner, I'm all for it."

"People have made do without air conditioners for centuries, you don't need to put it in to get me to move in. I was already considering it."

"Oh, were you?" I asked, letting the tub fill up while I stood and walked over to her. I put my hands on either side of her hips, tugging her to me. "I didn't think you were interested. You haven't mentioned it since I brought it up all those weeks ago, and I didn't want to harass you about it."

"I know." Nellie worried her bottom lip. "It does make sense for us to live together. Then you can wake up with the baby at night."

"I'll happily wake up with the baby every night," I murmured, pressing kisses to the side of her neck. "I will gladly take the night shift. It's the least I can do, after you've been on the first shift for nine months without a break."

Nellie smiled, her eyes sparkling, and wrapped her arms around me, resting her head against my chest. "I'm actually getting excited. Seeing you hold Flora today did things to me."

"Oh yeah? What kind of things?"

"Things I'm much too tired to explain or do."

When the tub was full, Nellie peeled her sundress off and I did my best not to salivate over her while I helped her climb into the tub. She couldn't manage on her own anymore, not with her belly as round as it was and her hips constantly protesting.

I didn't mind helping her. She was doing all the work carrying this baby, the least I could do was help her whenever and however I could.

Nellie let out a contented hum as she got comfortable in the tub. Wasting no time, I started massaging her aching feet while she soaked in the cool water. Her eyes were closed, a serene smile on her face.

I found myself falling in love with her over and over again, deeper and deeper. In the quiet moments like this, when she submitted to allowing me to take care of her, and in the moments when she fought me tooth and nail.

Her vivacious spirit didn't deter me. If anything, it lured me in deeper. I loved everything about her, and I made sure I told her and showed her every chance I got.

Which is why I'd been working on the baby's room. After Sage sent me the Pinterest board where Nellie was quietly pinning her visions for the baby's room, I got to work, buying everything I could to make her visions a reality.

Last weekend, I'd coaxed my brothers into painting the baby's room while I hung out at Nellie's apartment for the weekend.

This week, I'd finished putting the baby's crib together. The matching dresser, change pad table, and the most comfortable rocking chair imaginable were all in place. Now all I had to do was show Nellie and hope like hell she was happy with the results.

Once Nellie started to shiver a little, I grabbed a warm towel and helped her out of the tub. I helped dry her off, ignoring her protests that she could do it herself.

I let her get dressed herself, waiting on the edge of my bed for her to exit the bathroom.

"Before we go to bed, I want to show you something."

"Okay." Nellie's eyes narrowed with instant suspicion.

I took her hand and led her to the bedroom closest to the primary bedroom. I paused by the door, glancing at her over my shoulder.

"Ready?" I asked.

She nodded, and I pushed open the door.

Her breath catching, Nellie stepped into the nursery, looking around at everything with wide, shining eyes.

"Noah, it's beautiful!" she exclaimed, turning to me. "When did you? How did you?"

"I found your Pinterest board," I admitted. "I wanted to create the nursery you've been dreaming of. I hope I did it justice."

"Yes, you really did," Nellie said, wiping the tears from her eyes. "It's way better than I could have ever imagined."

"Come check out the rocking chair. It's the most comfortable chair I've ever sat in," I urged her, watching as she did what I asked.

"Oh!" Her eyes widened with surprise. "That really is comfortable!"

"Isn't it? It's a rocker recliner. It reclines too," I told her. "We might as well be comfortable for all those late-night feedings."

"It's perfect," Nellie said, glancing around the room again, her eyes aglow with warmth. "So are you, Noah. I can't believe you did all of this. I must be the most unobservant person ever."

I'd stuck to her soft pink, white, and gold palate. The crib rested against the accent wall, where I'd put up a beautiful white and pink floral-patterned wallpaper with sparrows.

"I wouldn't say that. You're just easily distracted," I said. "I wanted it to be a surprise."

"Well, I'm surprised." Nellie said, wiping away more tears.

"Are you happy?" I asked, dropping to my knees in front of the recliner, my hands going to either side of the arm rests.

"So happy, Noah. So incredibly happy." She cupped my cheeks in her hands, tears were still pouring freely now, but I could tell they were the happy ones. "I love it, and I love you, Noah."

Her words were a shot of euphoria directly to my heart. "I love you too, Nell. So damn much. And I love our baby. I want you both to be happy and safe, to feel at home here."

"Well, we do," Nellie assured me, still smiling through her tears.

"Does that mean you'll officially move in?" I asked.

"Yes, I'll definitely move in."

"Tomorrow?" I waggled my eyebrows.

"I need to give Tabitha and Parker my official notice, but sure." Nellie smiled, her eyes sparkling.

I kissed her deeply.

EPILOGUE

Nellie

TABITHA, Charlotte, Gloria, and Laurel had planned a combined baby shower for Sage, Nix, me and Noah, and it was held at the resort a week into July. It had been a town-wide affair, with everyone showing up to support us all. Even some of the regular summer guests had made an appearance.

Somehow, Noah had even managed to get my parents out for the baby shower. I'd expected them to send us money; not show up a week in advance and declare that they'd be sticking around for a few weeks.

It had been awkward seeing them at first, after almost two years of not seeing them and barely hearing from them after I'd told them the news. I guess they'd needed some time to process the fact that I was having a baby.

Things between us were still awkward, to say the least, but they had remained in town. My parents told me they wanted to meet their grandchild before they left. They were staying in my apartment above Tabitha and Parker's garage, waiting for the call that their grandchild had decided to make an appearance.

For all intents and purposes, I'd basically moved in with Noah. It made the most sense. He had the space, and he'd spent the last several months convincing me that he was all in. I believed him irrevocably, and despite my initial reservations: I'd fallen hard for him.

The pivotal point of no return for me had been when he'd decorated the baby's room using the inspiration boards I'd made on Pinterest. He somehow managed to encompass all the vibes I'd had into a beautiful space, creating the most perfect nursery. With that action, he made me feel like his cabin was our cabin: our home.

Things weren't always copasetic and easy: sometimes, my pregnancy hormones and insecurities made me completely unreasonable, but Noah was able to weather those moments and remind me that I didn't have to do everything alone. He knew exactly what to say and what to do to get me out of my head.

We were about as prepared as we could be, but when my water broke at four o'clock in the morning on the twenty-third of July, four days after my expected due date, I quickly realized that you could never be fully prepared.

I shook Noah awake, and he jumped out of bed and into action before his eyes were even fully open. My hospital bag and the baby's duffle bag were already by the door, waiting for the baby to decide to make her appearance.

We'd spent months preparing for this, waiting for this very moment to happen. We took Lamaze class and toured the hospital in Springwood, but I felt all those months of preparation evaporate the second my water broke.

And I was more scared than I'd ever been in my entire life.

"I'm not ready!" I moaned through another contraction on the drive to Springwood.

"Sorry love, you're going to have to be." Noah grimaced. I knew he hated that I was in pain and that he couldn't do anything to alleviate that pain. "Did you text Sage?"

"I did, but she hasn't answered yet," I said through clenched teeth. Sage had wanted to be there if possible, but her baby was being stubborn too, and had yet to make his appearance.

Everyone had bets on who would give birth first. They called it the Baby Lottery, and pretty much the entire town had placed bets. Frankly, I'd been far too pregnant to find it amusing, but whatever entertained the masses, I guess.

We made it to the hospital with no time to spare. By the time I was being wheeled into labour and delivery, I was already nine centimetres dilated.

"Past the point of getting an epidural, I'm afraid," the delivery nurse apologized when another contraction nearly took me out. Her name tag read *Marcie* and she was in her mid-to-late fifties. She carried herself with an assured confidence that instantly put me at ease, despite her distressing news about the epidural.

They got us into a delivery room and the second nurse, Carla, helped me climb out of the wheelchair and into the bed.

Marcie checked my progress, then looked up and met my gaze with a resolute one of her own.

"The baby is crowning, it's time to start pushing, Nellie," she said.

"But, what about the doctor?" Noah asked, confusion and concern evident in his voice.

"The only obstetrician on the floor is in the middle of a caesarean," she replied. Noticing the panicked look on my face, she put her hand on my leg. "I've delivered thousands of babies over my career; I assure you that you're in good hands. You're progressing really quickly, but you're also progressing well. This will be an easy delivery, mark my words. But you need to push through the next contraction, Nellie. This baby is ready to be born."

Things were moving so fast I could barely grasp onto a single thought. The pain was intense, but my determination was strong enough to push through it.

Time seemed to warp; it felt like it was both hours and mere minutes of pushing. It felt like I was both in and out of my body. It was the strangest sensation. Noah was at my head, holding onto my hand and trying to help me push through each contraction.

Finally, after what seemed like a whole day and only a minute later simultaneously, I bared down and pushed hard, pushing the baby out. Marcie caught the baby and lifted her up, the umbilical cord still attached.

"Come cut the cord, Daddy." Carla passed him the scissors. Noah cut the cord with steady hands, and Marcie put the baby on my chest. She was still covered in blood and goo, but I didn't care. Carla wiped some of it off while I held her, crying.

I fell in love again for the second time when the nurse put the baby on my chest and I saw her big blue eyes, so much like Noah's.

"Congratulations, she's gorgeous!" Carla said, beaming. "You did a great job, Mama."

I was shaking so much, from the adrenaline and the pain that Noah wrapped his arms around me to stabilize me and help me hold our baby.

"She looks like you," he said, the awe and wonder in his voice apparent.

"She has your eyes," I murmured, my words coming out uneven.

Marcia administered some morphine to help with the pain, and another drug to help me calm down.

"Do you know what you're going to call her?" Marcie asked.

"Her name is Nova Grace Wood," I said, still unable to lift my gaze from the perfect little baby in my arms.

"That's really pretty," Marcie complimented. I didn't even have the energy to thank her, I smiled and nodded.

We'd chosen the name Nova because it meant "new star", and it was associated with new beginnings, hope, and optimism. We named her Grace after Noah's grandmother, and I'd wanted her to carry her father's last name because he and his family had given me the very thing I'd longed for my whole life: a sense of belonging.

"So sorry for missing the big show," the attending obstetrician said when he came into our room sometime later. "It's been an incredibly busy morning. We've had six labouring mothers come in, and your baby makes for the fifth birth today."

"That's a lot of babies," Noah said. He was holding Nova now; my arms had started trembling so much that I'd been unable to continue supporting her weight. The pain meds were finally kicking in though, and I was feeling pretty good, though exhausted.

"We call them the Halloween batch." Carla giggled as the obstetrician checked me out. "There's usually a huge wave of them around this time: nine months after the Witches' Ball in Hartwood Creek. I noticed on your chart that you guys are from there. Did you happen to attend?"

Noah and I exchanged a look.

"Er, yes," he answered sheepishly.

"Knew it! That makes three so far in the past twenty-four hours!" Carla exclaimed.

The obstetrician finished checking me over and gave me a clean bill of health. "Of course, we'll want you to stay for twenty-four hours, so we can make sure you and baby are healthy before we discharge you."

"Okay," I nodded, too exhausted to argue. The obstetrician went on his merry way, and the nurses went with him, leaving Noah and me alone with our beautiful baby girl.

Noah

I'D ALWAYS THOUGHT that Nellie was strong and brave but seeing her give birth to our beautiful daughter solidified that. She was the strongest, bravest woman in existence. She had delivered without an epidural, without hesitating, even when I baulked at the absence of an obstetrician.

She bore through the pain and the uncertainty and brought our beautiful Nova Grace into the world, and despite the pain she was in, her tears were of happiness and utter reverence.

A few hours later, Nellie was finally sleeping, and I was holding Nova in my arms and gazing down at her in wonder, at her tiny nose and lips and her little hand wrapped tight around my pinky finger.

A gentle knocking at the door alerted me to the arrival of company. I looked up, surprised to see Nix in the doorway with his own little bundle of blue blankets.

"Congratulations, man!" I said, smiling as I stood up and made my way over to him.

"Thanks, and congratulations to you guys, too!" Nix spoke quietly, to not wake up Nellie. "Sage begged me to pop over and check on Nellie. We're actually a few doors down, but Sage had a c-section, so she can't walk yet."

"Oh man! You guys must have been the c-section the nurses told us about. When was he born?"

"Around five o'clock this morning," Nix replied, grinning down at his son. "Introducing Reed Davis Hutchinson."

"This is Nova Grace Wood," I said, and we peered down at the little ones in our arms. "She was born about a half hour after Reed."

"That's crazy!" Nix chuckled lowly, but the sound of us talking woke up Nellie.

"Noah? Oh! Hi Nix." she tried to sit up more in bed, but then winced from the pain. "Oh my gosh! He's here!?" she added, catching sight of the bundle in Nix's arms.

"Hey, Nell. Sage is recovering from a c-section so she's not up and moving yet. She wanted us to pop over and see how you were doing."

"I'm fine, but how's Sage?" Nellie asked, concerned for her friend.

"She's not feeling any pain yet. They've got her on some good medication," Nix replied as he walked over to let Nellie meet the sleeping baby in his arms.

"Oh! He's so perfect! Congratulations. Are you sure Sage is okay? What happened?"

"Reed here was breech and wouldn't come out through the door, so they had to open a window," Nix joked.

I snorted. "Dad jokes, huh? Guess I better start practicing."

"Don't worry, they come naturally." Nix laughed. The baby in his arms started to whimper and root with his little fist. "Looks like someone's getting hungry. I better get back to Sage, but we'll see you guys soon. We'll probably be discharged tomorrow at some point."

"Us too," Nellie smiled. "Tell Sage I love her and to text me when she's up for a little visit."

"Will do. Congratulations again, guys."

WE WERE DISCHARGED the next day around ten o'clock. On our way out, we stopped off to see Sage and Nix, who were still waiting around for Sage's c-section incision to get checked before the nurses discharged her.

Nellie was still tender from giving birth, but she was able to walk and move around with relative ease. She hugged Sage gently, and then the girls shared their birth stories, comparing notes and laughing at the similarities.

"I'm so glad your first birth went so smoothly, it'll definitely trick you into having another," Sage said with a laugh, wincing when the movement caused her pain.

"I'm sorry, Sage. I couldn't imagine dealing with the pain of an abdominal incision right now and all the contractions. I can't believe they don't warn you more about that, about how contractions occur even after the baby's born. That's some bullshit."

"Yeah, I forgot about that part," Sage admitted. "But I'm so glad he's here. Nova, too!"

"Yeah, it was getting a little ridiculous being pregnant in this heat." Nellie said. "Text me when you're home, okay?"

The girls made plans to meet up as soon as possible, and then Nellie and I were on our way out. Due to hospital protocol, I had to wheel her out in a wheelchair as she held tight to Nova's car seat on her lap.

During the drive home, Nellie sat in the backseat with Nova and barely took her eyes off her. When we pulled into my driveway, Nellie didn't even look up to see all the cars already parked there.

I'd texted my family to let them know about Nova's arrival, and even sent a few pictures. I'd also texted Nellie's parents to tell them. My parents, Damien, Charlotte, my nieces, Easton, and Nellie's parents all were waiting for us to get home.

I helped Nellie out of the truck and then reached to unlatch the car seat. Nellie finally noticed the cars, and the sign in the front yard that read *Welcome Home, Baby Nova!* with a stork carrying a pink bundle.

"Oh!" she exclaimed, her eyes misting as she took in the sight of everyone waiting in the great room to welcome us home. My family all took turns hugging Nellie and me, and then peeking at the sleeping baby in her car seat.

The twins were obsessed upon first sight, and I knew from looking at them that they were going to be bugging their dad and Charlotte for a baby sibling of their own.

I think Damien knew it too, judging by the look on his face as he watched his daughters interacting with their cousin. Charlotte took his hand and leaned her head against his shoulder, smiling as she watched them, too.

The tears started flowing freely down Nellie's cheeks when she finally spotted her parents. They were more reserved than my over-exuberant family, letting them get in first to greet us, but they were there—and that was the important bit.

Nellie's mom came up to her and gently hugged her, saying something quietly to her, meant only for her ears. Nellie hugged her back and nodded. They parted, and her mom turned her attention to the baby, her eyes bright and shiny.

"She's so perfect," Nellie's mom exclaimed.

My mom stepped up to her and put her arm around her. "She sure is." Mom agreed, unable to take her eyes off the latest addition to the family.

While our moms were having a grandmother moment, Nellie's dad was hugging her. "I'm proud of you, Ellen," he said, pressing a kiss to her temple. "She looks like you did."

"Thanks, Dad." Nellie smiled through her tears.

Everyone wanted to let us get settled, so they didn't stay too long. Easton was the first to leave, then Nellie's parents left. Damien and Charlotte took the twins home not long after that.

My parents lingered the longest, so Mom could take the lasagna out of the oven that she'd brought over and steal a few baby cuddles.

"You let me know if you need anything, anything at all, okay?" she told us, making sure she made eye contact with Nellie. "We're around the corner and we are happy to help out."

"You will have trouble keeping her away." Dad predicted, putting his arms around Mom to try and steer her out of the house.

After they finally left, Nellie curled up on the couch to nurse Nova. She was watching our daughter with the sweetest smile on her face.

"What's going on in that pretty head of yours?" I asked, sitting down beside her, and passing her a glass of water.

"I'm thinking about how happy I am," Nellie admitted, looking up at me.

"That's funny, because I can't stop thinking about how happy I am too." I confessed. "I'm so thankful I was somehow able to get you to come home with me that night."

"Me too. And to think, I almost chose the VooDoo Man." she giggled.

My jaw dropped. "Don't lie," I said, trying to taper my jealousy.

She leaned forward as much as she could, meeting my lips in a tender kiss.

"I'm kidding. It wasn't even close. I've always had a thing for the Witcher."

PLAYLIST

1. Sin So Sweet – Warren Zeiders
2. You Didn't Hear It From Me – James Barker Band
3. Kismet – The Beaches
4. Risk It All – Chase McDaniel
5. High in the Clouds – Sam Donald
6. Ride – SoMo
7. Intoxicated – Warren Zeiders
8. Don't Wanna Say Goodnight – Wyatt Flores
9. Burning Down – Alex Warren
10. Wreckage – Cameron Whitcomb
11. With You – Dean Lewis
12. Someone To You – Matt Hansen
13. Mystical Magical – Benson Boone
14. Feels Like – Gracie Adams
15. Silver Spoon – Erin LeCount
16. Ordinary – Alex Warren
17. Give You Love – Alex Warren
18. Keep Me Honest – Michael Marcagi

19. Love Me Back – Max McNown
20. Fireflies – Sam Donald

OTHER BOOKS BY J.C. HANNIGAN

Collide Series

Collide

Consumed

Collateral

Damaged Series

Damaged Goods

Reckless Abandon

Rebel Series

Rebel Soul

Rebel Heart

Rebel Song

Rebel Christmas

Standalones

The Key to 19B

Coalescence: A Welder Romance

Riverside Reverie

Forgotten Flounders Series

Off Beat

Off Limit

Hartwood Creek Romance

Wood You Knot

Last Resort (Releasing Summer 2025)

ACKNOWLEDGMENTS

First and foremost, I feel like I need to thank this book and its predecessor (Wood You Knot) for seeing me through one of the most heartbreaking seasons of my life.

The opportunity to create the Hartwood Creek world came just after my beloved Granny slipped and fell, breaking her neck in the autumn of 2023. In the months that followed, we thought we were going to lose her, so I created a fictional world I could always find her in, where bits and pieces of her magical light would illuminate even the darkest of days. She was so excited to have the Hartwood Creek series dedicated to her, she told all her nurses about it. Granny, true to her nature, proved us all wrong and hung on for another year. I will cherish each additional moment I got with her.

We lost her at the end of January of 2025, and if I didn't have *this book* to write, this book to drop little pieces of her in...I don't know how I would have survived that loss.

So, thank you to this series, to this book in particular, for helping me through that loss. For giving me a purpose to keep going and keep creating.

I'd also like to thank my incredible author friends for allowing me the space to grieve and create, as messy as it was— as I was. Thank you especially to Erin; you really shouldered a lot of that behind-the-scenes grief, and you were encouraging and supportive every step of the way.

Thank you to the wonderful beings in the accountability

chat, for holding me accountable and motivating me to keep going, even when I felt like sinking.

To Catherine, my fantastic editor, thank you for helping turn my messy ideas into gold. I'm so proud of this book, of this series, and a lot of it has to do with you. You really know how to shine a turd.

To Jess M, Holly, and Kristen, thank you for being the best alpha team ever. Your honesty and feedback helped me create the best story and characters.

And thank you to my non-book industry friends, Candice and Jessica F, for listening to me talk about my characters like they were real people. Thank you for allowing me to bounce ideas off you and work through plot issues.

To my husband, the love of my life, thank you for always providing the inspiration needed to create such incredible chemistry with my characters. Thank you for letting me record thirst traps of your forearms for the Internet. And most of all, thank you for your endless encouragement, for always cheering me on and reminding me that *I'm doing it; I'm writing the stories I want to write and I'm publishing them.* Thank you for reminding me that I don't need to be hit by lightning luck and go viral to feel successful and proud about what I'm doing here.

To my boys, thank you for being so chill with your mom's weird habit of turning everything into a story, and thank you for supporting me and being proud of me. I love you both so much.

To the rest of my family, especially Dad, thank you for your endless support and encouragement.

And to my readers, THANK YOU FOR READING! Whether you've just stumbled across my books, or whether you've been a long-time supporter...THANK YOU. It means so much to me that you read my stories.

ABOUT THE AUTHOR

J.C. Hannigan lives in Ontario, Canada with her husband,
their two sons, and their dogs.
She writes contemporary new adult romance and suspense.
Her novels focus on relationships, mental health, social issues,
and other life challenges.

Facebook: www.facebook.com/authorjchannigan
Threads: www.threads.com/@authorjchannigan
Instagram: www.instagram.com/authorjchannigan
Website: www.jchannigan.com
Goodreads: http://bit.ly/jchannigangr

If you enjoyed this story (or if you didn't), please take a moment
to **post a review** on Goodreads, your blog, or whichever
platform you use. Reviews help other readers find books, and I
appreciate any and all reviews!

Sign up for my newsletter to receive exclusive stories, sneak
peeks, and updates:
https://jchannigan.myflodesk.com/g343nxhzay

And if you like shenanigans, join my readers group FANnigans! There are exclusive giveaways, monthly live video events, and tons of other perks of becoming a FANnigan! https://www.facebook.com/groups/FANnigans/

www.ingramcontent.com/pod-product-compliance
Lightning Source LLC
Chambersburg PA
CBHW030745310726

48969CB00005B/1324